JUST DO IT

"Are you coming?" Will called from the foyer.

With a sigh, Patsy followed his voice. She could handle this. So she found him attractive. She was a red-blooded woman of the new millennium. She was supposed to find well-toned, good-looking men attractive, but she wasn't ruled by her hormones. She wasn't. She could do this.

Will was standing on the landing halfway up the stairs when she arrived. Her gaze drifted to the tips of his bare toes.

"You've already seen the downstairs, so I thought I'd show you the second floor." He motioned toward the landing above them.

Sure, why not? She'd like to see the second floor.

"There's a library . . ."

See, a library, how bad could that be?

". . . and four bedrooms."

Uh-oh.

BOOK YOUR PLACE ON OUR WEBSITE AND MAKE THE READING CONNECTION!

We've created a customized website just for our very special readers, where you can get the inside scoop on everything that's going on with Zebra, Pinnacle and Kensington books.

When you come online, you'll have the exciting opportunity to:

- View covers of upcoming books
- Read sample chapters
- Learn about our future publishing schedule (listed by publication month *and author*)
- Find out when your favorite authors will be visiting a city near you
- Search for and order backlist books from our online catalog
- Check out author bios and background information
- Send e-mail to your favorite authors
- Meet the Kensington staff online
- Join us in weekly chats with authors, readers and other guests
- Get writing guidelines
- AND MUCH MORE!

**Visit our website at
http://www.kensingtonbooks.com**

LOVE IS ALL AROUND

Lori Devoti

ZEBRA BOOKS
Kensington Publishing Corp.
www.kensingtonbooks.com

ZEBRA BOOKS are published by

Kensington Publishing Corp.
850 Third Avenue
New York, NY 10022

All Kensington titles, imprints and distributed lines are
available at special quantity discounts for bulk purchases
for sales promotion, premiums, fund-raising, educa-
tional or institutional use.

Special book excerpts or customized printings can also
be created to fit specific needs. For details, write or
phone the office of the Kensington Special Sales Manager: Kensington Publishing Corp., 850 Third Avenue,
New York, NY 10022. Attn. Special Sales Department.
Phone: 1-800-221-2647.

First Printing: May 2005
10 9 8 7 6 5 4 3 2 1

Printed in the United States of America

My family is both unique and entertaining. Without them this book could not have been possible, and while I love each and every crazy one of them, I dedicate this book to my great-grandmother, Granny. At the age of eleven she left a bad home situation to marry a man twenty-one years her senior. A year later, she gave birth to her first child. By eighteen she'd had four children and by twenty-eight she was a grandmother. She spent the first half of her life in dirt-poor conditions in rural southern Missouri, but never seemed to resent any of the bumps life had dealt her; instead, she tied on her apron and faced the challenges head on.

If my great-grandmother had not been the woman she was, none of us (my family) would be the people we are. To me, she exemplifies what makes people of the Ozarks special—fortitude, fun, and faith.

Chapter One

Patsy Lee Clark twirled a daisy between two fingers. Life here was a lot like this flower—all simple and charming from a distance, but up close, it just stunk.

"So, you gonna apply at the BiggeeMart?" Her best friend, Ruthann Malone, interrupted her thoughts.

Patsy stared at her. Ruthann had known her since they were three. You'd think she'd understand Patsy better by now.

Tucking the daisy behind one ear, Patsy leaned against Ruthann's Cavalier and replied, "I'm not planning on being a career checker."

"You got another option I don't know about?"

Patsy bit her lower lip. "I have plans."

"You heard Bruce. The Bag & Basket's closing in two months." Ruthann tugged on her purple smock, hiding the smiley face that twinkled from her belly button. "BiggeeMart's hiring now, and they got good benefits. My cousin Earlene retired at thirty-eight. You can't ask for more than that."

Patsy thought you could ask for a lot more, even in po-dunk southern Missouri. "That's nice for Earlene."

Apparently missing Patsy's tone, Ruthann smiled in agreement.

Shaking her empty Pepsi can, Patsy asked, "What you have planned for after work?"

"Nothing." Ruthann sighed. "Not like I have a date."

Condensation from the can had dampened Patsy's

hands. She wiped them on her shorts. "You want to head out to Gordie's?"

"I guess. I don't have much money though." With her fist shoved into her smock's pocket, Ruthann continued, "The BiggeeMart pays nine dollars to start. They don't dress like overripe eggplants either."

"No, it's more like a rancid radish."

Ruthann straightened up. "I like the hats."

To each her own. "So, Gordie's?"

"Sure. Hey, you hear Will Barnes is back in town? You remember him?"

A soft, late summer breeze caused the daisy to flutter against Patsy's cheek, but did nothing to lessen the heat reflecting off the sizzling asphalt. Pulling her sticky T-shirt away from her skin, Patsy replied, "Lisa's brother? What's he doing here? They moved away when we were what, twelve? I didn't expect either of them to come back here."

"Yeah, last I heard Lisa was married to some executive in Chicago."

"And Will was what, in jail?"

Ruthann shook her head. "You shouldn't say that, even if he was kind of a . . ."

Remembering the gossip, Patsy finished the sentence, ". . . druggie?"

Ruthann looked uncomfortable with the term. "He ran with the Gormans."

That said it all. Everyone knew the Gormans were destined to orange jumpsuits and careers in license plate manufacture.

Patsy rescued Ruthann from saying the ugly obvious. "So, Lisa's in Chicago?"

With a look of relief, Ruthann answered, "Yeah, Will lived there too, before he made a bunch of money on the Internet. Bought the old Barnett place. Jessica Perry was his realtor. She told me all about him. To hear her tell it, he grew up real nice." Ruthann wiggled her eyebrows up and down.

"Jessica Perry thinks any man with more than fifteen teeth and less than four ex-wives is real nice." After yanking the daisy out of her hair, Patsy twisted toward her friend. "Still, I don't understand what he's doing back in Daisy Creek. His sister never liked it here, or us for that matter, they don't have any family around, and if he has a bunch of money, he could live anywhere he wants. Why pick Daisy Creek?"

"Maybe he just missed us. Stranger things have happened. Listen, I gotta go. My shift started five minutes ago." Ruthann pushed away from her car. "Give me a call later."

So Will Barnes was back. Just what Daisy Creek needed—another good-for-nothing layabout, and Ruthann said he had money, made it on the Internet. Plenty of opportunity there for the less than scrupulous. Will Barnes's type was hard enough to tolerate poor, but with money? That was more than Patsy could handle.

Not that he'd be crying on his pillow from loneliness. If he had money and was half as good-looking as Ruthann said, Jessica probably already had her hook set and was reeling him in.

Patsy didn't care. Jessica could have every man in Daisy Creek County. Patsy had bigger fish to fry.

Will Barnes sat on the bottom step of the once-grand staircase leading up to the second floor of his new home. The place was a mess. It was still structurally sound, but needed work. Gold sculpted carpet and green brocade wallpaper were everywhere. It was almost painful to look at, and the smell indicated a cat with litter box issues had been a recent resident.

His realtor had assured him that was all an easy fix. She could get him a "good deal" on some new Berber or a "nice" Saxony at her father's flooring store. Not that Will planned on covering up the oak floors he was certain were hidden under the fragrant monstrosity currently underfoot.

The cell phone in Will's pocket rang. Hell. Who could that be? The digital display flashed his sister's number. Great, she probably ran into Cindy at Pottery Barn or DKNY. This would be a treat. Might as well look at it as a practice run for when his parents found out what he'd done.

He punched the call button. "Lisa?"

"Where are you?" His sister had a terminal case of impatience.

"Nice to hear from you," he replied.

"Don't toy with me. Cindy called."

A planned attack.

"It took two lattes just to calm her down. What were you thinking?"

"Decaf, I hope?"

"She said you broke off the engagement."

Apparently Lisa had opted for fully leaded. "She made the choice," he replied.

"Right. Some choice. She worked herself silly getting things ready for the wedding, even researched neighborhoods. You were lucky to get a lot in Harbor Heights. The realtor was expecting a check today to hold it. You put Cindy in a horrible spot."

"I researched different neighborhoods."

"In Daisy Creek? Be serious. You can't expect Cindy to pack up and move to redneck central. For God's sake, the place probably doesn't even have a Starbucks." Lisa exhaled loudly. "Anyway, I got her calmed down. Just call her to let her know you've come to your senses. A few dozen roses and everything will be fine."

"Good-bye, Lisa."

"What? Are you calling her?"

"I'll call you in a month." Or twelve. He disconnected in the middle of his sister's outraged shriek.

"You think she'll track us down?" He asked Ralph, his

mop of a dog, who was busy sniffing the carpet. "It would mean coming to 'redneck central.' So, I don't think we need to pull out the guest towels just yet."

Ralph seemed to agree.

"Now, when Dad and Mom get back from Europe, it'll be a different story. Then all hell, and by hell I mean Dad, will break loose." He ruffled Ralph's curls. "Scared, aren't you?" Will grinned.

Not that Will was looking forward to the confrontation, but it was a lifetime overdue. He and his father didn't see things the same way, didn't value the same things. He'd first realized this here, in Daisy Creek. He'd rebelled, as only a sixteen-year-old with too much money, too much time, and too little loving attention can, then spent the next thirteen years trying to prove he wasn't a screw-up.

Will was done apologizing for who he was, done being something someone else wanted him to be. He was starting over and this time he was doing things his way.

Will looked at the dirty mess surrounding them. "We better get going, boy. We have a lot to do."

Patsy pulled into the overflowing parking lot. Gordie's was jumping. Dented pickups with gun racks and spotlights sat next to mid-sized American models. A few nicer "grown-up" cars were sprinkled around. Patsy doubted the teenagers who drove them told their parents of their destination. Not that it mattered. Brenda, Gordie's wife, would be on duty at the door. She didn't put up with underage drinking.

Country rock blared out as the door to the roadhouse was flung open and two high-school boys were pushed out. "Don't be showing me some fancy ID, Brad Stevens. I've known your daddy all his life. You're no more twenty-four than I'm a natural blonde. Now get your sorry butts out of here or I'll call your momma and the sheriff."

With her back pressed against the railing, Patsy let the

grumbling teens stomp past. "Hey, Brenda. Looks like a full house already."

"Yeah, we got a hot band tonight. They're bringing in the crowd. We got people here from all over." Brenda flipped a length of white-blond hair over her shoulder and pointed inside. "Your brother's playing pool with Randy Jensen. Ruthann's inside somewhere too."

Patsy squeezed past Brenda into the smoke-filled bar. It was one big rectangular room. To the left was the stage and dance floor. Behind her to the right was the bar and in front of it sat three pool tables, all surrounded by locals in feed hats and worn Levis. Her brother Dwayne leaned against the back wall, a cue stick in his left hand and a long-neck Busch in his right. Patsy turned away before he or his companion, Randy Jensen, could spot her.

Randy wasn't a bad sort: steady job as a mechanic at the Ford dealership over in Sylvester; a nice, if small, house off 32 Highway north of Daisy Creek; attractive with a lean build and ice-blue eyes; and he was interested in Patsy. She didn't need Dwayne's increasing hints to know that. The way Randy tracked her like a toddler did an ice cream cone when she entered a room said enough.

He could track all he liked. He wasn't her type. She wasn't a snob, but a man with grease under his fingernails, a garage full of four-wheelers, and yard full of coon dogs was not her idea of ideal dating material, never mind anything more permanent.

Where was Ruthann? Patsy searched the small tables where people sat drinking, finally spotting her friend only a few feet away from where Dwayne and Randy stood. Patsy weaved her way through the crowd and pulled out a chair, keeping her back to the pool area.

"Hey, new top?"

"Yeah, I got it last weekend when we went to St. Louis." Ruthann tugged the skin-hugging material of her halter. "You look good too. Where'd you get that?" She pointed to Patsy's paisley cotton tank.

"I bought it online. It was a bargain, because the 'romantic' look is out, but I liked it." Patsy's thin cotton and lace shirt wasn't flamboyant like Ruthann's red halter, but she felt good in it, flirty but comfortable. The purple-blue color made her eyes look even more green than normal and the short length made the most of her flat stomach. It might draw a little too much attention to her butt, which was rounder than she would have liked, but still the overall effect was good. She adjusted her denim shorts slightly so her legs didn't stick to the vinyl chair and waved her index finger at the waitress.

"Looky, looky who's here and what she's towing in behind her."

Patsy glanced up to see who Ruthann had spied. Jessica Perry had entered Gordie's in a skin-tight dress that was a walking advertisement for Wonderbra and thong underwear. She beamed up at the man attached to her arm before she spun toward the room, giving everyone a full view of her outfit and date.

"Who's the tall, dark, and handsome?" Ruthann openly stared at the couple.

"Your guess is better than mine. You're the one who was just talking with her." Patsy paid the waitress for her Bud Light and took a sip.

"Oh, my God. Is that Will Barnes? She said he grew up nice." Ruthann waved her hand in Jessica's direction.

"What are you doing? Oh, great, they're coming over." Rolling her eyes, Patsy put a hand over her face. "I hope she doesn't bust out of that dress while she's here. Nobody needs to see that."

The comment earned Patsy a keep-quiet look from Ruthann. "Shush, she'll hear you. Here they come."

"Hey, Ruthann," Jessica flashed the full force of her former Miss Daisy Creek smile. "Patsy." Her tone deepened slightly. "You all remember Will Barnes, don't you?" Jessica performed a little shimmy move up her companion's side, sending the tiny heart-shaped charms on her bracelet to tinkling.

So it was Will. Patsy watched as Ruthann made a fool of herself, stuttering out nonsense and twisting in her seat. You'd think the man was Clint Black, the way she and Jessica were carrying on. Sure, he was good-looking—probably six feet two or so, brown hair just long enough to curl at the ends and an even, white smile, but so what?

As Granny said, you could dip a cockroach in chocolate, but that wouldn't make it go down any easier. Not if you knew what was hiding under that tasty coating. Will Barnes showed his nature a long time ago. Just because he had money didn't make him any sweeter.

"You remember Patsy, don't you, Will?" Ruthann was sucking Patsy into the conversation. Patsy rolled her head to the side and looked up into warm gray eyes.

Make that eye.

She didn't remember that. His eyes were two different colors—one gray, one blue. Patsy wondered what Granny would say about that. In her world of hill-lore, there had to be some kind of warning about a man with mismatched eyes. A kick from Ruthann alerted Patsy she was staring.

Patsy sat up. "Excuse me? You say something?"

Both eyes, the blue and the gray, clouded with confusion.

"You remember Patsy, don't you, Will? She was always scrapping with somebody." Jessica smoothed her hands down her hips. "I believe Patsy was the one who filled Lisa's thermos with worms. Wasn't that you?" She pursed her lips and looked at Patsy, mascara-heavy eyes wide.

"Oh, I don't remember that at all. You must be thinking of somebody else." Ruthann twisted her head back and forth between the two women.

"Crickets. They were crickets, not worms," Will said. "It was on the bus. Lisa took the lid off her thermos. They jumped out and went flying all over the place. She wouldn't take a thermos for the rest of the year. Mother had to give her money for milk."

Jessica grinned at Ruthann. "See? I thought that was Patsy."

Patsy took a drink of her beer. She knew the polite thing would be to pretend remorse she didn't feel, but it wasn't going to happen. "It was her own fault. I told her they were there. Dwayne was going fishing that afternoon, and he said he'd pay me a penny for every cricket I caught. Lisa drank her milk at lunch. I just borrowed the thermos. She got all uptight because I had it and insisted on seeing what was inside. I told her what was in it, but she twisted off the top anyway." Patsy's bottle landed on the table with a clunk. "What'd she expect them to do, just chirp at her from the bottom?"

Taking a deep swig of her drink, Ruthann looked around the room. Patsy raised both eyebrows and stared at Will.

"One of them jumped down Lisa's shirt." His face was solemn, not revealing his thoughts. "I don't think I've ever laughed that hard. How've you been, Patsy Lee?" A small smile edged his mouth upward.

Patsy was taken a bit off guard by his good-natured response. "Uh, fine." She blinked up at him.

"You have certainly changed. I wouldn't have recognized you if Jessica hadn't brought up that old story." His voice was low and velvety and when he smiled, the skin around his eyes crinkled. Patsy felt something in the vicinity of her chest do a little skip at the sight. It wasn't attraction, not to the good-for-nothing rich boy. No, it was the beer, definitely the beer. She took another mouthful.

Jessica shifted her gaze between Will and Patsy. "Patsy was quite the little tomboy, even through high school. She spent so much time tromping around the woods with that Ozark history group, it's a wonder she even had time to date."

Patsy's fist tightened around the top half of her beer

bottle. "I don't think Will's interested in what I did in high school."

"No, probably not. But being a tomboy can make keeping a man a challenge."

Patsy ran her thumb around the circular ridge of the bottle neck. "You know much about keeping a man? I thought stealing was more your specialty."

"It isn't stealing if he's already lost." Jessica's voice had a slight tremor. Remorse, from the bimbo? Couldn't be.

Ruthann placed a cold hand on Patsy's free arm. "You need another beer?"

Seeing Ruthann's tense face, Patsy relaxed her grip on the beer bottle. "That's true, you can't steal what's already lost, and I guess every town needs a lost-and-found. Nice to know you're doing your civic duty."

"How about a drink, Jessica?" Ruthann leapt from her chair, almost knocking Will down.

As Ruthann tugged Jessica toward the bar, Will stayed next to the table, analyzing Patsy with an inscrutable light in his eyes. "Excuse me, Will. It was nice seeing you again, but I think I need to take a trip to the little Tomboys' room." She pushed herself away from the table and walked toward the restroom.

Will watched as Patsy Lee Clark sashayed away from the table. She was something. Little and cocky, that was the same. What was different was her looks. Her blond hair used to look like her mother cut it using a soup bowl as a guide, and he didn't think he'd ever seen her without a film of dirt covering most of her. Now green eyes competed with full lips. Her hair was still short, but it flipped out in a random manner that gave him the urge to run his fingers along her scalp to try and calm it. And the back view as she walked away—well, it gave him thoughts the earlier dirt-covered version of Patsy Lee never had.

He needed a beer. Free of Cindy less than twenty-four

hours and already scoping out replacements. Not this time.

Refocused, he scanned the crowd. Normally, he avoided scenes like this. Crowds, especially loud, jostling crowds, set his teeth on edge, but Jessica had assured him she could reintroduce him to a couple of men he'd known as beer-guzzling teenagers. Somehow they'd grown into big shots in the community. The profits from selling Consult.com weren't going to last forever, and if he wanted to stay in Daisy Creek, he needed all the contacts he could muster.

Patsy leaned against the pool table watching Randy Jensen line up a shot. Dwayne had caught her on her way back from the bathroom. There was no way to avoid him and Randy without being obviously rude. Plus, Patsy had nowhere to go. Ruthann was still standing at the bar with Jessica, and Will Barnes had taken over their table. He sat there now, laughing and talking with a couple of Gordie's regulars. One was the assistant DA, and the other owned the local paper.

They were both rednecks, rednecks with fancy jobs and impressive titles, but rednecks all the same. They were the types who got a little money and suddenly thought they were operating on a higher plane than everybody else in town. They were probably sucking up to Will though. He had everything they respected—pedigree, connections, and money. The little issue of his past would be nothing when weighed against that, especially the money.

Carrying a frothy pink concoction, Jessica returned to the table. She placed the drink in front of an empty seat and batted her eyes at Will as he pulled out her chair. The DA made a production of wiping the table before she set down her glass and a laughing Jessica slapped his arm. Patsy wondered where his wife was. Probably at home with their two kids. Annoyed with all of them, she turned her attention back to the pool game.

"Hell, Dwayne, that's two in a row. I don't need to lose any more money tonight." Randy placed his cue back in the rack that hung on the wall. "Besides, there's ladies here now."

After taking a swig of Busch, Dwayne replied, "I don't see nobody but Patsy. But if you two got plans, don't let me stand in your way." He gave Randy a wink.

Rolling her eyes at her brother, Patsy picked up the cue Randy had deserted. "I'll play you. What's the bet?"

"I'm not playing you. I have standards." Dwayne pushed his thumbs into the front pockets of his Levis and rolled up onto the toes of his Red Wing boots.

Appearing behind him, Ruthann drawled, "Yeah, and you don't like to lose either." Eyes lowered, she said, "Hey, Randy. How's Luke doing? He sure looked cute all dressed up for church last Sunday."

"He's doing good. He's staying with my mom tonight." Randy watched Patsy. "I told her I might be out late."

Ignoring him, Patsy addressed Ruthann, "How's the barracuda? Looks like she has a few fish lined up all ready for a snack."

"Yeah, well, she has better luck than I do. That's for sure." Ruthann flicked her gaze at Randy before looking back at Patsy.

"You girls just aren't packing the right bait. Ain't that right, Randy? A man likes to see a little bounce and twist." Dwayne cupped his hands over his chest and shook his skinny ass. Patsy resisted the impulse to whack him with the pool stick.

There's the girl I remember, Will thought as he watched Patsy Lee Clark lean on a pool cue, her green eyes snapping. He could see by the way Dwayne was laughing that he was taunting her. It would probably serve him right if she belted him. Will was sure Dwayne and Patsy Lee had survived more than one argument that ended in blows. Even with the seventy or so pounds Dwayne had on her, a smart man's money would always ride on Patsy Lee, and Will was a smart man.

Jessica leaned over the table, brushing her breasts against his bare forearm. Her musky perfume stomped past the smell of stale beer and cigarette smoke that filled the bar. Strangely, he missed the beer and smoke.

"So, what do you think, Will? You going to need some office space? There's a real nice building open next to David's." She motioned toward David Wood, the current assistant DA of Daisy Creek County.

Taking a sip of Budweiser to cover his need for a fragrance-free breath, Will carefully moved his arm away from spandex-compressed flesh. "I don't know yet. I'm still weighing my options. For right now, I can just work out of the house. I won't be doing anything that'll violate the zoning laws." He smiled at his companions.

Richard Parks, owner of the weekly *Daisy Creek News*, balanced his chair on its back legs and laughed. "You don't have to worry about zoning laws here, Will. You could just about start a hog farm in the courthouse, and as long as it brought in jobs, nobody'd complain."

Will raised an eyebrow. Just the kind of offer his father would seize. Striving for a light tone, he said, "Well, that's reassuring." Maybe Daisy Creek needed a bit more help than he'd thought. Switching his gaze back to the scene by the pool table, he continued. "I see someone I haven't talked to in years. How about I give you two a call after I'm more settled?" He stood to leave. Jessica uncrossed her legs as if to follow, but he motioned for her to stay.

"I appreciate you walking in with me, and reintroducing me to people, but I'm fine now. You enjoy yourself. And thanks again for helping me get the house." He stepped away from the table before she could object. She was attractive, but a little obvious and way too needy. Best to make it clear right out of the gate where his intentions lay, or didn't. He wasn't looking for a relationship, or even a fling. It was time for him to start over, alone. There was no space for anyone but his dog in his plans right now.

He strolled to the pool table. As Dwayne twisted around the table next to Patsy, she reached out with the cue and snagged a full beer mug through the handle. Flicking her wrist like she was flipping flapjacks, she poured the beer down the front of Dwayne's jeans.

Will smiled. Slick move.

"What the hell is wrong with you? You have no sense of humor at all." Dwayne jumped away from the dripping mug and slapped his hands against his wet crotch.

As Will passed a nearby table, he grabbed a white bar towel and threw it to Dwayne. "Long time, Dwayne, Randy. How's it going?"

"Well, Will Barnes. I heard you were back in town." Dwayne mopped at his wet jeans. "Excuse my mess, my little sister is still as prickly as a cocklebur."

Looking completely devoid of remorse, Patsy stood at the pool table pretending to line up a shot.

"You looking for a game?" Will nodded his head at the empty table.

Still bent over the pool cue, Patsy ignored him.

"You don't want to play her," Dwayne interrupted. "Let me buy you a beer."

"So, are you looking for a game?" Will repeated, adding just a hint of a challenge.

Her eyes flickered. Standing, she replied, "I guess I can handle just one." She sauntered to the middle of the table and shoved quarters into the coin slots.

She had a natural sway to her step, almost athletic. Her short hair bounced against her neck, leaving Will again with the urge to comb his fingers through the teasing locks.

The balls rolled down with a thud, bringing him back to the moment.

"You break," Patsy said. "I don't want to be accused of cheating when I beat your city ass."

Will grinned. "No ladies first?"

"No ladies here." Dwayne guffawed. "Let's get a beer." He waved Randy toward the bar. Ruthann watched them leave, but took a seat at a nearby table.

Will went to select a cue. When he turned back to the table, Patsy Lee was stretched across the top, rolling the rack into position. The view of her shorts pulled high on her thighs stopped his breath somewhere around his heart. Nothing like a nice round rear to put a man off his game. He wondered if he could call a handicap.

Patsy popped back onto the floor. "All ready."

Something was ready, but he was pretty sure it wasn't what Patsy Lee was referring to.

With a smile, he replied, "Glad to hear it."

She stepped back. "You gonna break, or what?"

Or what, Will's inner letch screamed. "Just getting a feel for the table," he replied.

Patsy Lee rolled her eyes. "It feels like a pool table. Break already." She cocked her hip and leaned against the table.

Placing the cue ball on the felt, Will lined up his shot. Patsy Lee leaned forward, resting one fine-boned hand on the green felt. Her nails were short and unpolished. His fiancée's had always been long and fake. Couldn't open a pop can for fear of messing up her manicure. Will bet Patsy Lee faced the dreaded pop top head on.

Patsy drummed her soda-can-defeating fingernails on the tabletop.

Subtle.

Not bothering to aim, Will took his shot. The balls zipped to the four corners, but came short of falling into the pockets.

"What a shame. Guess it's my choice."

Will could feel her sorrow.

Grinning, she pointed her stick at a solid. "Corner pocket."

"You don't have to call them," Will commented.

"Oh, but when you're winning, it's so much more fun that way." A snap, a thump, and the sound of the seven ball rolling under the table followed.

"You might want to sit down," Ruthann called from behind her wine cooler. "Once she gets going, it can be a long wait till your turn—if you get it."

"You planning on clearing the table?" Will asked.

"Not the whole table, just the solids—then the eight ball, of course. Excuse me." Patsy brushed against him on her way to the chalk, leaving a light floral scent in her wake.

Her perfume was alluring but unpretentious, like kite-flying, Easter egg hunts, and rolling down a grassy hillside. All things Will never did as a child. All things his father said were a waste of time.

Irritated with the direction of his thoughts, he crossed his arms and awaited his turn.

Three balls later, he got his first shot. "Hope you don't mind." Will gestured to where Patsy stood, blocking the easiest shot on the table.

"Oh, if you want to take the easy shot." She shrugged.

"And I do." He grinned. She was too good a player for him to cut her a break.

"Fine, you take that one. After that you'll have nothing left to shoot at anyway."

Will analyzed the game. She was right. She'd left him with one clean shot and the rest were bank shots. He hated to lose, and he didn't plan on doing it now. He had a feeling once the cue was back in Patsy's hands, it would be a short watch on his part till the eight ball went to join his solid brethren under the table. Will had to clear as many balls as he could this turn, preferably all of them.

"Don't have much choice now, do I?" he asked.

"Not a Fudgsicle's in hell." She flashed him a grin.

Will gritted his teeth. That arrogance could become pretty annoying. No wonder her brother drank.

He sank the nine and walked around the table to assess his options. They weren't pretty.

"Eleven ball, corner pocket." He motioned to the end of the table where Patsy Lee stood.

"You sure you want to try that?" she asked.

He ignored her. With a quick tap from Will, the cue ball snapped the eleven into the cushion. He held his breath as it rolled toward Patsy Lee.

Closer, closer, in. He bit back the grin that raced to his lips. Better to act confident.

"Maybe I'll try a hard shot this time," he said.

Busy applying chalk to her stick, Patsy Lee looked up. "You miss already? I thought you'd at least get a couple."

"Twelve, other side." He winged another stripe into a pocket. He was feeling good. All those months hanging out at the pool hall when he was supposed to be in school really paid off. He should have played Patsy Lee for money, or something more tantalizing.

After grinding another layer of chalk onto her stick, Patsy Lee dropped the blue cube onto the wooden edge of the table. It bounced once, then fell on the floor. Will tensed in anticipation. As he expected, Patsy Lee bent to retrieve it, giving him an unhindered view of sexy behind and a glimpse of lace.

He swallowed. Lace. That was nice. All women should wear lace underwear. The kind that cupped their behinds, like a lover's hands. Hiding and hinting all at the same time.

Patsy rapped the cube against the wood. "You taking a shot sometime soon?"

"Ten, down here," he called and promptly knocked her five into the pocket.

"For me? You didn't have to." Patsy Lee sauntered to

the center of the table and lined up a shot. "Three, over there."

Will knew when he was beat. He dropped onto a chair next to Ruthann.

It took Patsy less than five minutes to clear the table. It took her ten to quit gloating.

Where was Dwayne with his beer?

As if called, Dwayne wandered up, two beers in his hands. He handed one to Will. "She beat ya?"

"Looks that way." Will watched as Patsy slid her cue into the rack on the wall. He could look at this view all night. Didn't know that he wanted to play her in pool again, but the view—it couldn't be beat.

"Tough break," Dwayne replied.

Randy, who'd pulled up a chair from another table, snorted.

"So, Will, what brings you back to these parts?" Dwayne asked, ignoring his friend.

"Nothing special," Will replied.

Patsy pulled out the chair next to Ruthann.

"Heard tell you made it big on the Internet. You know my little sis here is learning that stuff." Dwayne flicked his hand toward his sister.

Will said, "Really. Pool shark and the Internet too, what other talents do you have?"

"I'm not a shark. I told you I was going to beat you." Her look challenged him to deny it.

"I guess you did." But she hadn't answered the whole question. What other talents did she have? Swallowing the thought, he continued, "There's still a lot of money to be made on the Internet."

"That so? Exactly what kind of business did you have?"

He wasn't sure he liked this coy smile any more than her victory grin. It made him feel like she knew some deep secret he'd rather keep quiet.

"Consulting," he replied.

"Hmm." She took a sip of beer. "Lot of money in that?"

"Enough."

She studied him a moment, then turned to her brother. "There's nothing wrong with trying to learn something new. If you had a brain bigger than a walnut, you'd be trying too."

"What, and leave all this behind?" Dwayne held his arms wide.

Will smiled. Even with the constant banter, it was obvious Patsy and Dwayne cared about each other. He didn't have that kind of rapport with his family. They were polite, but there never seemed to be a lot of underlying emotion.

"So, you want to come?" Dwayne interrupted Will's thoughts.

He looked at Dwayne blankly.

"Floatin'. A bunch of us are heading to the Current Sunday." Flicking a balled-up Bevnap toward Patsy, he continued, "After church. Probably get in the water 'round one."

Will didn't have time to be floating down the river drinking beer and soaking up skin cancer. He should be concentrating on repairing his house and finding a new source of funds to keep Ralph in Iams.

Patsy Lee caught the paper napkin and whacked it back at her brother. As Dwayne ducked to avoid the missile his hand brushed his beer bottle causing it to topple into his lap. At his responding curse, Patsy's eyes sparkled with humor. She turned a carefree smile on Will.

Ralph might have to switch to kibble. "Count me in."

Chapter Two

The next day after a mind-numbing shift counting out change at the Bag & Basket, Patsy pulled into the drive that ran along the side of her grandmother's fieldstone house. The bumpy rocks, outlined by wide stripes of white mortar, were a patchwork of pinks, grays, and reds. The sight was as comforting as the old crazy quilts Granny kept folded in the cedar trunk at the foot of her bed.

She hopped out onto the drive and climbed the wide steps to the front porch. The welcome mat with two bug-eyed pugs and the words "Take A Paws" imprinted on it gave her a smile. The empty mailbox didn't. Fifty resumes and no answers. Not even a generic "we received your application" postcard. She was going to be stuck in Daisy Creek forever. She let the box's metal door clatter shut and stepped inside the house. Resisting the urge to flip on the floor lamp that sat next to the door, she took a moment to let her eyes adjust to the dark house.

"Granny, I'm home."

A small, wriggly body shot at her from the back of the house. "Pugnacious, what have you been up to? Miss me?" She squatted down to pick up the squirming dog.

Patsy's grandmother appeared from the kitchen. "She's been baying at the squirrels again. I'm telling you what, that dog is about the most confused critter I ever laid eyes on. You ought to just turn her over to your brother and let him make a coon dog out of her."

Granny plunked her round figure onto an afghan-covered gold recliner.

"Any phone calls?"

"I told you, me and the dog were out back." Granny swiveled her chair around to face the TV. "Click on the cable and see if the WWE is on. Now you're home to watch that hound wannabe, I need to do a little relaxing."

Patsy walked over to switch on the TV. After handing the remote to her grandmother, she wandered into the kitchen to get a glass of tea and check the answering machine.

It was unplugged, again. What did Granny have against her? It wasn't like she asked her to take a message—just leave the machine plugged in. Was that too much to ask?

After returning to the living room, she said, "The machine's unplugged."

Granny didn't look away from the screen. "Fancy that."

Yeah, fancy that. Patsy found a spot between the crocheted afghans and embroidered pillows and plopped down.

"Come here, Pug Girl." Pugnacious popped up from where she lay and scrambled onto the couch next to Patsy.

"What you all do last night?" Granny's chair spun toward Patsy.

"Nothing much." Patsy sipped her tea. Granny didn't approve of the roadhouse, and Patsy wasn't in the mood for a fight. "You remember the Barneses?"

"Can't say I do."

"They were one of the mine families. Lived here about five years before moving on. They had a daughter my age and a son a year or so ahead of Dwayne."

Granny nodded her head in recollection. "They weren't Baptist, were they?"

They could have been devil-worshipping goatsacrificers for all Patsy knew. "I don't know. Anyway, the son, Will, moved back to town. Ruthann and I saw him last night."

"He a good-looking boy?"

What did that matter? "He's okay."

"He get a job round here?"

"I don't know. He wasn't real clear on what he's doing. But according to Jessica Perry, he had an Internet business he traded for a wad of cash. She sold him the Barnett place."

Granny's chair creaked as she sat up a little straighter. "I heard someone bought that old place. He's a youngun, you say?"

"Older than Dwayne."

"Must have money to buy that old house. They was askin' near $200,000, I hear tell."

Resting the icy glass on her leg, Patsy combed through the fringe of an afghan.

"He must be planning on staying then."

"Who?"

"That Barnes boy you was telling me about."

"I guess, at least till he gets bored with us."

"There ain't nothing boring about us. You say he was a friend of Dwayne's?"

"Not really, he was older."

Granny's hazel gaze bored into Patsy.

"But Dwayne did ask him to come floating with us tomorrow."

"That's fine. It don't hurt none to be neighborly."

The theme music for World Wrestling Entertainment blared out of the television, saving Patsy from further discussion. She wasn't sure what Granny's sudden fascination with Will Barnes was, but she didn't want to encourage it. The more time Patsy spent on the computer, the more Granny seemed to plot to keep her in Daisy Creek. Patsy'd never confessed her plans to leave, but Granny seemed to sense Patsy's motive for learning web design.

If she thought a new man would keep Patsy here, she was dead wrong. Patsy'd made that mistake once before. She wasn't doing it again. Maybe she should fill Granny in a little more on Will's past. If she knew he had spent too much time cutting class and hanging out with the Gormans, she might back off. Then again, she might not. When Granny got focused on a cause, there wasn't much could shake her.

After depositing her empty glass into the kitchen sink and grabbing a Hostess pie to tide her over, Patsy wandered back to her room. It was a tiny space nestled in under the eaves. There was enough room for a daybed, computer table, and not a whole lot more. Patsy hadn't even added too much in the way of personal décor—a couple of posters of Australia hung on the white walls and family pictures sat atop the computer.

It wasn't much, but Patsy'd called it home since Granny suffered her first stroke about four years ago. A week later, Patsy'd found herself in need of new housing and moving in with Granny seemed to make sense.

At the time it had been perfect. She and Granny helped rebuild each other, Granny physically and Patsy emotionally. Lately though, Patsy realized she needed something more, something she wasn't going to find in Daisy Creek. She'd put her life on hold long enough. It was time to take some risks and meet the world.

While she waited for Windows to come on the computer screen, she walked over to some raw basket materials piled in the corner. Picking up a coil of white oak splits, she ran it through her semi-closed hand. It was smooth and strong. Patsy loved the feel of it against her skin.

Granny taught Patsy basket weaving when she was twelve. It was a special time for just the two of them, and Patsy loved it. But, basket weaving wasn't going to get her anywhere, least ways nowhere outside of Daisy Creek.

No, basket weaving was as country as dirt roads and fried okra. Patsy needed to concentrate on learning a skill with big city market potential. She carefully lowered the coil of oak strips to the floor and walked back to the PC.

"You know how to run that thing, son?" The delivery-man from Perry Flooring looked at Will with unease.

Of course Will didn't know how to run a floor sander, but how hard could it be? You plugged it in and held on, simple.

"You best get all those tacks out before you start." Kenny, according to the patch on his shirt, pointed to the corners of Will's living room where carpet tacks still marred the wood.

"I will." Will used his most assured tone. Remove the tacks, that made sense.

"You're gonna need to putty them holes up after too."

"Of course." Did the man think he was an idiot? "What kind of putty do you recommend?"

Switching the wad of Redman tobacco from his left cheek to his right, Kenny studied him. "You mean like a brand?"

"Sure, a brand. What do you recommend?"

"I don't reckon it likely matters." The Redman trav-eled back to the left.

Enough of this. Will thanked Kenny for delivering the sander and showed him to the door.

"You planning on keeping it awhile?"

How long could it take to sand a few floors? "A couple of hours and I should be done." Will checked his watch. Almost seven. The store was closed now, and tomorrow was Sunday. "You open tomorrow?"

"Yep, we're open—after church." Leaning back inside the house, Kenny craned his neck to see past the living room into the parlor, then twisted to look into the turret on his left. "I'll tell Merle you'll have it till Monday for sure. You need it longer, just call."

Will closed the door on Kenny's heels. The deliveryman obviously underestimated Will. He'd have the sander polished and sitting by the front door ready to return before the choir sang their first hymn.

Time to power up the sander. As Will dragged the machine to the front room, Ralph poked his nose out of the kitchen, and then quickly disappeared back behind the swinging door.

Did no one have faith in him?

Even Jessica's father, when he learned Will had zero home-improvement experience, had tried to talk him into hiring somebody to do the floors, but Will wanted to do it himself. He'd never seen his dad so much as swing a hammer. Hell, the man didn't even own a hammer, but other men did their own repairs and so would Will.

He slipped the plug into the wall and flipped the switch on the handle. The sander lurched forward out of his hands. With a heart-stopping crash, it broke through the front window. Three seconds later, a spark flying from the outlet and a dull thud from deep in the house heralded an intense silence. The one lamp Will had unpacked went black, and the vibrating sander stilled. Something was very wrong.

Standing in the growing dimness of the room, he thought, *I hope the choir sings an extra chorus—or fifty.*

Patsy slipped a Mindy Smith CD into her player and sang along to "Jolene," as she and Ruthann drove down Oak Street.

"What time is it?" Ruthann asked.

"After ten, why?"

"There's somebody over there." Ruthann pointed to the Barnett place, Will's new home.

"It's probably Will."

"Outside? In the dark?" Ruthann's voice quavered.

Patsy slowed the Jeep down to a roll and turned down

the music. The sound of breaking glass ripped through the air.

"Did you hear that?" Ruthann squeezed Patsy's arm.

"Probably kids shooting bottles at the fairgrounds." Patsy tried to sound confident, but her voice sounded unsure even to her own ears.

"I didn't hear a gun."

Patsy wasn't sure if that was good news or bad. She flipped off her lights.

"What are you doing?" Ruthann squeaked.

"If we're quiet, we can pull up beside the house and see what's going on from in here."

"I don't want to see what's going on." Ruthann rolled up her window and locked her door.

"Shush." Keeping her window down, Patsy turned into the drive that ran along the Barnett place. The ragged sound of Ruthann heaving for breath sounded like she had a bullhorn stitched to her lips. "Shush."

"I can't breathe."

Damn it all. Patsy slammed the Jeep into park and dug onto the floorboard for a paper bag. "Breathe into this." She shoved it toward her friend. With the rattling of the bag moving in and out each time Ruthann exhaled, Patsy gave up on stealth and flipped her lights back on. Will's front porch seemed to leap into view.

"Hell." Will Barnes teetered on a ladder next to the picture window, seconds before crashing onto the porch.

Oops. Guess it was Will making the noise.

"You think he's okay?" Ruthann rasped out.

What was the man doing on his front porch, on a ladder, in the dark? Patsy strode up the steps to the porch, Ruthann scurrying behind her.

"What were you doing?" Patsy was pretty proud of herself for leaving out the "in hell" part.

"Catching fireflies." Will replied without a trace of humor.

"It's best to do that right when it turns dark. Most lightning bugs are gone by now," Ruthann said.

Patsy resisted the urge to pull the paper bag completely over her friend's head.

"Why don't you turn on a light?" she asked the still prone Will.

"Can't see them with a light on." Ruthann walked over to examine the metal handle protruding from Will's front window.

Patsy walked into the house and flipped the light switch—nothing. "Your electricity's out," she announced.

"Thanks for the bulletin." Will had pushed himself up. "Hell."

"What?"

"Nothing, I just cut myself."

"Don't move." Patsy hopped down the steps and jogged back to the Jeep. Returning with a penlight, she bounced the beam along the porch.

"Thanks, that makes all the difference."

Patsy pointed the light like a laser, right between Will's eyes. "You don't have to be a smart-ass. It's not like we have to help you."

"Blasting your high beams on me is helping?" Standing, he grabbed the penlight and flashed it onto his palm. A two-inch piece of glass dissected his love line.

"Let me. You hold the light." Patsy pulled his hand toward her, resting it against her chest as she attempted to dislodge the glass with her fingernail.

"Hell," he said as she poked the piece in deeper.

"You said that already." Patsy took a perverse joy in watching him wince as she pushed the sliver of glass out of his palm. "There. Good as new." She traced the wound with the pad of her index finger. "I think I got it all."

"Are you sure?" Instead of pulling his hand back, Will seemed to lean forward, inhaling as his face approached hers. The beam from the penlight wavered off his palm, spotlighting a patch of worn gray paint on the porch's floorboards.

She tilted her face up, inhaling too. He smelled clean

and woodsy. Like freshly raked leaves. His wounded hand closed around hers. She couldn't see him now, but she sensed his warmth, couldn't stop herself from leaning toward it.

"Thanks." He pressed a warm kiss to her forehead.

A flash of annoyance skittered through Patsy. A kiss on the forehead? That was it?

"Patsy?" A panicked Ruthann crashed toward them through the shattered glass. "I have something on my hand." Waving her hand in front of her, she pushed between them. "My hand. There's something on my hand."

"Calm down. It's fine." Patsy led her friend to the steps and forced her down. "I'll get a wipe." After sprinting back to her car, she returned with a packet of wet wipes.

As she wiped Ruthann's hand, she explained, "She has a thing about getting stuff on her skin, so I keep wipes in the car."

Will leaned against a pillar. In the dark, Patsy couldn't make out his expression. "Can I have the light?"

He slipped her the small light. Flashing it onto Ruthann's hand, she said, "I don't see anything. It was probably just dew or something."

"There isn't dew at night." Ruthann scrubbed with the wipe.

Patsy could feel Will's gaze on her back. "She's sensitive about getting stuff on her skin." There was no reason to be defensive. He hadn't criticized Ruthann, but defending her friend was an old habit. "A lot of people are."

"You had a good idea."

The change in subject startled her. "What?"

"The headlights. I can use my car's headlights to see what I'm doing."

"What are you doing?" Patsy handed Ruthann another wipe and snapped the case shut.

"I had a little accident with a floor sander."

"Is that what broke the window or blew the fuse?" Patsy asked.

"Both."

A giggle escaped Patsy's mouth.

Will widened his stance and crossed his arms over his chest.

"I'm sorry." Struggling to keep the words from coming out with a snicker, Patsy held her breath. "I could call someone to help you. Dwayne's probably still sober, or there's my dad."

"Thank you. I can take care of it myself."

The air between them seemed to drop ten degrees. Forgive her for trying to be neighborly. "Well, since you have everything under control, I guess Ruthann and I'll head on home." She tugged her friend off the step. "Don't let the lightning bugs bite," she called over her shoulder.

"I didn't know lightning bugs bit," Ruthann said.

Patsy ignored her and tossed the wipe container into the back of the car.

What an ass. He'd been an ass. He knew it, but there was nothing he could do about it now, not that he wanted to. He didn't owe Patsy Lee Clark an apology. Not after she laughed at him. He might have been rude, but he didn't ask for her help, didn't invite her onto his property. He had a right to clean up his mess any way he liked.

With his BMW's headlights illuminating the porch, Will swept the broken glass into a pile and dumped it into a metal trashcan. He didn't need help. He could fix this.

Leaning on the broom, he stared at the jagged hole. It had to be midnight, and, like his father, he didn't own a hammer. Time to admit the truth. There was no way he could board up this window tonight.

Hell, he should have taken Patsy's offer, but after she laughed at him, he couldn't. "Pride goeth before a fall," he quoted aloud, or a plunge in this case.

He rested his forehead on the end of the broom handle. Before that giggle, things had been going well. Promising. Maybe too promising. Patsy's floral scent had enveloped him, pulling him toward her. He'd come damn close to kissing her. At the last minute he'd pulled out enough restraint to keep it to an innocent buss on her brow, but he still wasn't sure what would have happened if Ruthann hadn't created her bizarre scene.

Only in Daisy Creek two days and his plans were already going awry. Tomorrow he was getting back on track. He'd fix the window, fix the electricity, and refinish his floors. Then, fully confident in his ability to get things done, he'd meet Patsy Lee and friends for the float trip.

Will trudged up the stairs for a pillow and some blankets. This might not be a crime-ridden city, but he couldn't sleep upstairs with a window missing in the front. Laying the blankets next to the floor sander, he called to Ralph. He had six hours until dawn. It was going to be a long, uncomfortable night.

Chapter Three

Grateful that Granny and her mother weren't there to see her, Patsy wiggled into denim cutoffs and yanked her favorite "Down Under" T-shirt over her green bikini. They would both bust a seam if they saw her leave the house in shorts with a hole in the crotch.

Like it mattered. She was going to the river, not a tea party, and there wouldn't be anybody there to impress—unless you counted Randy or Will Barnes. Which Patsy didn't.

Will Barnes. What was his deal? She was still annoyed that he rebuffed her offer for help last night. It certainly wasn't like he had the situation in hand. She'd be surprised if Bad Boy Barnes knew which end of a hammer to hit with. No way he got that window fixed; probably slept on the porch last night.

He did have a buff body though—at least what she'd seen of it. It was hard to tell for sure in his suburban uniform of khaki shorts and polo shirts.

What was up with that? Who was he trying to fool? Like James Dean imitating the mailman. Talk about a turn-off, or at least not a turn-on. Okay, even in khaki, he was pretty hot. Not that she was lusting, more just noticing.

Lusting was best left to Jessica. It was her area of expertise. This brought to mind another point of annoyance. Ruthann had invited her to go floating today.

Sometimes Patsy's best friend didn't think. She was

always trying to push Patsy and Jessica together, to get over past problems. The thing was, Ruthann didn't know how big some of those past problems were, at least to Patsy. It wasn't that Jessica did anything technically wrong, but she'd crossed a line in their past and she knew it. Worse though was how her simple action made Patsy realize how big a fool she was, how close she'd come to giving someone the power to make a complete idiot out of her. She should probably be grateful, but she wasn't, and she wasn't ever going to be.

Patsy glanced down at her shorts. Why did Jessica get the talent for making everything sexy? Even when they were in high school and Jessica filled in for the mascot, the boys had hooted and hollered. Who else could don ears, whiskers, and a tail and look good?

Jessica and a Playboy bunny, that was who, not Patsy.

She considered her outfit again. The denim would be hard to dry if it got wet. Something else would be a more practical choice. Patsy dug in her drawer, pulled out a pair of low-rise knit shorts and tugged them on. They looked particularly good with her swimsuit top, and it was warm.

She pulled her T-shirt off and shoved it in her bag. Grabbing her keys, she squatted down to give Pugnacious a good-bye kiss and headed to her Jeep.

Patsy swung by Ruthann's house to pick her up before heading to Akers. The Jeep's tires spit gravel as they pulled into the canoe rental's lot. The grinding sound was a pleasant break from Ruthann's yammering about Will Barnes and how cute he was and how nice he'd been and how much money he had.

"Looks like Randy's here." Patsy pointed at the dented Chevy truck with a spotlight and gun rack.

"Hmm. Yeah, well, he'll be glad to see you, I'm sure." Ruthann tugged on the elastic of her bikini top.

Patsy slid her eyes sideways, watching Ruthann. "I was hoping you'd ride with him today. Dwayne's been pushing him at me a lot lately, and I just don't feel like dealing with it." Or watching you drool over Will.

"You want me to ride with him? I mean, sure, I don't mind, but how you gonna work that?"

How was she going to work that? "Don't worry. We just need to play some male egos is all, and that's easier than finding a crow near a cornfield." Patsy slammed the door and trotted toward the river.

Will stood to the side watching as a tan sixteen-year-old flipped the silver canoe up and held it over his head. The boy walked the twenty yards to the river and settled the canoe onto a sandbar. He looked self-sufficient and confident. Maybe Will could start hauling canoers up and down the river. He'd have to be better at that than home repair.

"Where the hell are the women?" Dwayne dug into the cooler and pulled out a Busch can.

Will flicked his wrist around to glance at his watch; five past one.

Grabbing the cooler Dwayne had deserted, Randy wedged it into one of the aluminum canoes. "Give them time. They'll be here. Besides, you're the one that invited them."

"All for you, bud. Just trying to give romance a little nudge." Dwayne held his beer can out in a mock toast. "'Course, I can't say that I mind Ruthann asking Jessica along. She knows how to fill out a bikini." He lifted an eyebrow and turned to Will. "I'm not stepping on your toes now, am I?"

Before Will could reply, Randy said, "Here they come, least ways Patsy and Ruthann."

Patsy Lee strode toward them in nothing but a green bikini top and a pair of low-riding navy shorts. She hopped over a fallen log and the shorts shifted down a half inch or so, revealing the slight curve of her stomach muscles.

Sporty, but feminine. Suddenly, Dwayne's beer looked inviting. Will flipped open the cooler and grabbed an icy Busch, wondering if anyone would notice if he shoved it down his shorts.

"Getting an early start, aren't you?" Patsy Lee gave the cans in their hands a questioning look.

"Don't start with me. Just 'cause you been Bible beatin' this morning, don't mean the rest of us can't relax a little," Dwayne replied.

Will expected Patsy Lee to come back with a cutting remark, but she seemed to stop herself. Like she was holding back. Instead, she rolled her eyes and spoke to Ruthann. "You sure you're not too nervous about going out in a canoe after last time?"

Ruthann replied with a blank look, but Patsy Lee kept talking. "I know you were pretty shook up when you got caught in that undercurrent."

"What are you blabbering about?" Dwayne interrupted.

Patsy gave him a suspiciously sweet smile. "A few weeks ago we went floating. You remember right after that big rain? Well, we thought we could handle it, but the river was just too fast. Ruthann tipped over, and she was sure she was gonna drown. Like to scared us to death. She's been nervous as a pig in a sausage factory ever since."

"I don't remember you telling that before," Dwayne said.

Patsy Lee ignored him. "Anyway, I was thinking Ruthann would feel a whole lot better if she was floatin' with someone who could handle a paddle, and everyone knows Randy can outmaneuver a mink." Patsy Lee fluttered her eyes and gave Ruthann a little shove.

Will took another sip of beer, while Dwayne let out a snort. Randy, though, seemed taken in.

Had to respect someone that good at manipulating.

"Well, I don't know about that, but if you think Ruthann'd be more comfortable riding with me, I'd be happy to help out." Randy pulled the bill of his cap down a little on his forehead. "Would that make it easier for you, Ruthann?"

Patsy Lee nudged her again.

She didn't give up. She'd make a hell of a salesperson.

"Yeah, that'd be real nice," Ruthann stuttered.

"Well, I hope you don't think I'm spending three hours stuck in a canoe with you," Dwayne said.

Patsy Lee bit her lip and jerked on the tie of her shorts. It was obvious she hadn't thought that far ahead in her plan. A stab of what might have been disappointment knifed through Will. He knew he'd been a bit rough on her last night, but for a minute, he'd thought her goal was to get paired with him. Instead, she'd been scheming to get Randy and Ruthann together. He pushed unexpected frustration aside.

"I need a partner." Join me, he willed.

Patsy Lee gave him a surprised look. "What about Jessica?"

Will shrugged. "I'm sure she won't mind riding with Dwayne, in the interest of sibling civility." And who really cared anyway?

"Now there's a plan." Dwayne grinned and popped open another Busch. "I like the challenge of keeping a canoe upright, especially with a top-heavy passenger."

"Your lack of brains should even it out," Patsy replied, but her eyes were on Will.

Jessica arrived twenty minutes late. Patsy had voted to leave without her, but Dwayne and Ruthann wouldn't hear of it. When she bopped into view, Patsy gave her a cool nod and busied herself tying the cooler down with a bungee cord. Damn it all. She was wearing cutoffs with a worn-through seat. All three men seemed focused on catching a peek of her red bikini bottom through the frayed material. Patsy wanted to wrap her own hole-free shorts around Jessica's skinny neck.

Sliding her locket along its chain, Jessica twisted her way over to Will. "You save a spot for me?"

"Over here, sweetheart." Dwayne waved at her. With a suspicious look at Patsy, Jessica trudged over to the other canoe.

Grinning, Patsy picked up her paddle and headed to the back.

"Where are you going?" Will stopped her. "The other girls are sitting in front."

"You know how to handle a canoe or you just eager for a dunking?" Patsy answered. "The best canoer sits in the back."

"I think I can handle it." Will moved to stand next to her.

Arrogant. Patsy raised an eyebrow. "Like you thought you could handle a floor sander?"

"Get in the front."

Testy, wasn't he? Patsy stared at him for a minute. She thought about arguing, but she could tell by the set of his jaw she wasn't going to get anywhere.

Fine, she wasn't afraid of a little cold water. "Have it your way, but make sure your gear's tied down. I'm not chasing your crap down the river when you tip us over."

Will grabbed the canoe and pushed it into the current. Patsy hurried to hop in before it was out of reach.

It was a perfect day for floating. The sun reflected off the river and the aluminum canoe, but the cool water surrounding them kept it from being hot. Patsy leaned back and enjoyed the ride. It was easy going at first, just a quiet lapping current running next to dark, deep pools. A blue jay squawked at a squirrel in a gnarled oak that grew out over the river. Patsy grinned as the squirrel gave up his fight and scurried out of the jay's territory.

About a quarter-mile past Akers, the current began to

run faster. Patsy sat up, but kept her paddle across her lap.

Time for Mr. I-can-do-everything-myself to perform.

The canoe bobbed and jerked. Will jammed his paddle into the water, fighting to stay on track. His biceps cramped as he struggled against the current. He could handle this. Everything was under control.

"Which direction?" he yelled at Patsy.

Leaning forward, she calmly surveyed the river ahead. "Left," she called.

Will plunged the oar into the water on his left side. The canoe immediately surged to the right. What was up with that?

"I said left," Patsy yelled.

"I put it on the left." What was her problem?

"No, go left. We're going to hit that—" Patsy ducked as the canoe charged under a low-hanging branch. Popping back up, she yelled, "Not . . . same . . . you . . . go."

What was she shrieking about? Didn't she know cool heads would prevail? Determined to show he was in control, Will attempted to steer to the left. The canoe's back end began to swing forward until he and Patsy had reversed their positions. What the hell?

"We're going backward," Patsy yelled back.

Talk about stating the obvious. Did she think he was an idiot or did she just enjoy making him feel like one? Annoyed with both himself and his passenger, he felt his composure slip. He frantically switched the oar from the left to the right and back again.

"What are you doing?" Patsy was turning an unattractive shade of red. "Watch out, there's a . . ."

What now? Will turned to see a boulder a foot from the canoe. He lunged forward, ramming against it with his oar.

Patsy's cry of, "No" was the last thing he heard before the icy water of the Current enveloped him. Swirling water sucked him down. He didn't fight it, just let the mini-whirlpool pull him to the bottom. His ego was quickly dropping lower.

He'd screwed up again. How had that happened? Lately, simple things other men did as naturally as walking upright seemed to be evading him. Something slimy and thick clutched at his legs, reminding him where he was. As grim as life on land looked right now, he wasn't solving anything lurking down here. He kicked off the bottom and surged to the surface.

Slogging out of the water, Will caught the canoe and dragged it onto the sandy beach. Patsy was already perched on a toppled tree, watching him through dripping bangs. She looked like a siren sunning herself while she awaited her next victim, though he suspected in reality he was about to encounter a shrew. Either way, Will had left his wax at home.

"So, done much canoeing?" Water flew from her hair as she shook her head like Ralph after a rainstorm.

Will concentrated on securing the canoe, wishing it had a mast he could tie himself to. Here it came.

"Know your left from your right?" She peeled off her shorts and draped them over the log.

Will blinked away the sight. The same muscle tone he'd noticed on her stomach was apparent on her butt and thighs. Hell, that wasn't a butt. That was a booty. A vision of his hands gripping her firm backside as she pulsed up and down above him fogged his brain. And her thighs, he could almost feel the strength of them wrapped around his waist as he . . .

"You thinking about it?" Patsy brushed water off the thighs in question with an impatient flick of her wrist.

He blinked at her, then down at his shorts. Was he that obvious?

"Your left from your right? You trying to figure it out?" She held up first her left hand, then her right. "Maybe you could get a tattoo or something, you know, a little *l* and *r*."

Oh, that. He tried to focus on her smart-ass question, but the pressure in his shorts was a bit distracting. Maybe he should try another dip in the frigid river. He jerked his soaked T-shirt off and pretended to wring it out.

Never show attraction or fear—they feed on it. "Just felt like a swim," he replied.

"Really? You usually take the cooler with you?" She held out her leg, removing a stray piece of flotsam with two fingers.

Swallowing hard, he focused on the tiny piece of debris pinched between her fingers. Don't look at her legs. "Keeps the beer cold." Good, nice and casual. He was under control.

"Well, that's important." She dropped his lifeline into the river and combed through her hair with her now unoccupied fingers.

He couldn't help but think of other things to occupy those skillful digits.

Unaware of his ongoing battle with his libido, she continued, "Next time, warn me though, so I can pull a can out. You caught me empty-handed."

He couldn't help but smile at her joke. "You have to stay aware." He flipped open the cooler and tossed her a beer. "This one's on me."

"I think the next keg's on you." She picked up her shorts and climbed into the canoe. Her bikini rode up, revealing a pale V of untanned skin where her butt cheeks peeked out of her swimming suit.

He stood watching her, wondering if it was safer to stay behind on the deserted riverbank.

"What you waiting for? Let's go, but keep the trick steering to a minimum this time. Don't want to show up the natives."

What do you know, the siren-shrew had a sense of humor. And from this angle—okay, any angle—a very fine backside. "No, we can't have that. They might get restless." Grinning, he placed his cold beer can next to his groin and slipped his oar into the water.

With her eyes on the river, she replied, "You have no idea."

No, he thought, adjusting the can, *you have no idea*.

An hour later, a much drier Patsy jumped out on the bank. The other canoes were already beached. Randy and Dwayne were skipping rocks off the river, while Ruthann rubbed on sunscreen, and Jessica stretched like a cat after a satisfying nap.

Or before pouncing on a well-fed Internet mouse.

"Where you all been?" Dwayne yelled.

If Patsy told Dwayne the story of their dunking, he'd make Will's life living hell. Patsy peeked over at her canoeing companion. He fumbled with the bungee around their cooler.

"Communing with nature," she replied.

"You couldn't wait till we stopped?" Dwayne asked.

"Nature called."

Dwayne strode over to help Will with the cooler. "Glad you're stuck with her instead of me." He slapped Will on the back.

Will popped the tab on the beer Dwayne handed him. The scrutiny in his two-toned eyes made Patsy nervous. He'd been staring at her ever since their tip-over. She'd tried to keep the mood light, but the look in his eyes had been anything but. There had been something dangerous stirring around behind those eyes. Something that made her want to run away and creep closer at the same time.

This look was different but almost as disconcerting. She shifted her gaze away, letting it rest on his chest.

Bad move. He hadn't replaced his shirt after their jaunt into the river. It was a nice chest, but nothing special. Yeah, right. His pectoral muscles flexed as she stared.

As Will turned to secure the canoe between two rocks,

she glanced over at Randy. Not even close. First, Randy had a farmer's tan going—white chest, tan arms. Second, while Randy had a decent build, he had nothing on Will. No broad shoulders that tapered to a sinewy waist. No deep grooves to define the muscles in his back.

Bottom line, no contest. Why did the most tempting things in life also have to be the worst for you?

Her gaze shifted to Will's stomach. She could barely keep herself from reaching out and running her fingers over each smooth, hard ridge. Damn it all. This was bad. Think spoiled rich boy, arrogant rich boy. Not willing to ask for help. Stubborn, sexy, irresistible rich boy.

Damn it all. She couldn't see the cockroach, just the sweet, tasty chocolate coating. Time to get busy with something else.

"Dwayne, get in gear and unload lunch. I'm hungry," she yelled.

Will picked up his shirt and ran it over his chest. "Yeah, me too." He wasn't making this easy. He held her startled gaze until she flushed and looked away.

"Keep your shorts on. I'm getting it." Dwayne struggled with the oak picnic basket, banging it against the hard lip of the canoe.

"Be careful with that. You're going to break a strip." Patsy grabbed the basket and examined the side for damage.

"If it's that delicate, why'd you bring the thing?" Dwayne rubbed at a scuff mark with his thumb. "It's fine anyway."

If Patsy didn't know better, she'd have thought her brother was actually apologizing in his Neanderthal way. She adjusted her own tone. "I thought it would add a little class. Besides, Granny always packed picnics in a basket. It's tradition."

Dwayne didn't reply. Instead, he returned to his canoe where Jessica sat watching them.

"It's nice. I'm surprised you'd risk getting it wet on a float trip." Will stood close to Patsy, too close for her comfort. She could smell the sunscreen he'd rubbed on his shoulders earlier and that same musky odor she noticed last night. Patsy took a step back and almost lost her grip on their lunch. Will reached out and grasped the handle, his hand brushing hers. She jerked away from the distressing zap that accompanied the contact.

"This has real craftsmanship. Not like the stuff you buy today that's all made in China." He held the basket up to admire it.

"Thanks. I mean, it's no problem getting it wet. Water's good for baskets, keeps them fresh and clean." Warmed by his praise, Patsy felt herself flush. She reached out to stroke the basket with her index finger just as Will turned. Her finger drifted from the basket up his arm. Without thinking, she let the pad of her finger drift back down over the swell of his forearm. Will froze.

"We eating or what?" Dwayne grabbed the basket, and swung around toward a big flat rock. "Let's get the grub going."

What was happening to her? Thank heavens her lummox of a brother blundered up. She'd been a push-up bra away from channeling Jessica, for heaven's sake. She didn't think there was enough holy water in the Midwest for that exorcism. Doing her best to not look at Will, she followed her brother and her basket.

While Dwayne and Jessica unpacked the food and utensils, Patsy looked around for Ruthann. No sign of her. Giggling sounded from the brush about five feet away. Patsy's eyes narrowed as Ruthann and Randy emerged from behind some brambles. Randy carefully held a branch out like Cinderella's prince opening the door to her carriage. Ruthann giggled again and stepped through the space.

"Where you been?" Patsy asked. Her annoyance with her own close call with bimbohood colored her tone.

"Oh, Randy was just showing me the difference between poison ivy and Virginia creeper." Another giggle.

Ruthann lost all use of her brain when a man was around. A habit Patsy found hard to tolerate. She edged up next to her friend.

"You haven't confused poison ivy with Virginia creeper since we were seven and you made a wreath out of the wrong one," Patsy said in a low tone.

"That's true. I haven't, have I?" Ruthann arched one brow and strolled to where Dwayne was laying out the food.

They ate lunch sitting around the flat-topped boulder. Patsy had packed an old tablecloth embroidered with a daisy chain border, and a jug of Granny's sweet tea. Ruthann supplied Kentucky Fried Chicken. Randy had brought sugar cookies so weighed down with icing and sprinkles, Patsy was afraid to pick one up.

"Oh, look. They're dogs. Aren't they darling?" Ruthann gushed. "Did Luke decorate these?"

Randy beamed. "Yeah, we baked them yesterday. They're coonhounds. See, this here is a redbone, this is a black and tan, and this one's a bluetick." Randy shuffled through the multicolored cookies.

"Cute. He can learn his colors, his dogs, and how to bake all in one easy lesson." Patsy bit the head off a redbone hound.

"Don't mind her," Dwayne broke in. "She's just mad 'cause he left out Pug ugly."

"Pugnacious isn't a coon dog."

"Yeah, try telling her that," Dwayne responded.

Patsy ignored him. So Pugnacious had some kind of unexplainable attraction to anything and everything Dwayne's coonhounds did. She wasn't a coon dog. She was a purebred pug. Pugs were once owned by Chinese emperors. They did not run around in the dark woods baying and terrorizing raccoons.

"You have a dog?" Will asked as he watched Patsy shake the crumbs out of the tablecloth.

"A pug." Patsy gave Dwayne a keep-your-mouth-shut look.

"I've got a mutt. His name's Ralph. Looks like a big gray mop." Will grabbed the other end of the tablecloth and helped Patsy fold it. "I hated to leave him at home today, but I wasn't sure how he'd do in a canoe. With all that hair, he'd probably sink like Enron stock."

He took a step forward, holding the corners of the cloth out to her. Patsy grabbed them and jumped back.

"Wouldn't be a problem unless we tipped over." Smoothing the cloth with her hand, she watched him from the corner of her eyes.

He stiffened slightly, but before he could comment, Dwayne jumped into the conversation.

"You should bring him out to Mom and Dad's. Let him run. Damn leash laws. Can't let a dog get any exercise in town no more." He crushed his empty beer can in his fist and tossed it into the cooler. "Why don't you come by Saturday? We're having a barbecue. Then later, Randy and me are going to run our dogs. Coon season's not for a few months, but we like to take them out and see if they can pick up a trail. You're welcome to come along for that too."

Patsy thought Will looked less than enthusiastic at the mention of coon hunting. Not that she blamed him. Stumbling around in the dark while a bunch of noisy hounds chased down some defenseless critter was not her idea of fun either.

"What's back there?" Will pointed toward a footpath that led into the brambles.

"Some old ruins," Dwayne replied.

"Really? Of what?" Will asked.

"A hospital. There's a cave and a big spring too," Jessica shoved the picnic basket Patsy's direction and sidled toward Will. "You've never seen it? It's real pretty."

Patsy tightened a bungee around the picnic basket. Checking to see if it was secure, she pulled on the elastic.

It hit against the basket with a satisfying snap. "You can't get into the cave though. It's barred off to save the bats."

Jessica wrinkled her nose. "You would know that. Who cares about getting in a dirty cave, especially one with bats?"

"What's a hospital doing out here?" Will asked.

The group turned to Patsy. She sighed. Why was she the only one that seemed to know this stuff? "It was built back in like 1913 or so. The guy who owned it thought the cave would be good for people with asthma. Before that, there was a mill here."

"What happened to the hospital?" Will asked, his eyes alive with interest.

Patsy felt a stir of excitement. It had been a long time since anyone had shared her passion for local history. "I don't know, really, except the man who built it died and so did his business. In the late sixties the Park Service took the land over. There have just been ruins here since then."

She looked at Will, ready to describe more, but before he could ask another question, Dwayne jumped in.

"It's a little spooky. Makes a girl want to cuddle. Isn't that right, Jessica?" Dwayne draped his arm around her shoulders.

Jessica shook him off and grabbed Will. "You have to see it. I'll take you on a tour." Pulling her heart-shaped locket toward her breasts, she yanked him toward the trail.

Patsy stared after them. *And the breasts win again.*

Kicking a rock out of her way, Patsy followed Dwayne and the two couples down the uneven path. Patsy loved the ruins and cave, but she had no desire to see either with Jessica. She felt as welcome as an alley cat in a trout pond. And to make matters worse, she had Dwayne.

"Well, this is cozy, ain't it?" he complained.

For a tour guide, Jessica seemed to be having a hard time keeping her eyes on the sights. Maybe that was because her hands were so busy rubbing up and down Will's bicep. Patsy bristled. She wasn't tromping through these woods so she could watch Jessica grope Will.

"The hospital's this direction." Patsy pointed toward a rough path of rocks all but immersed in bubbling water. "You have to risk getting a little wet to get to it."

"Oh, we can see it just fine from here. Besides, I thought Will might like to walk down this path a little farther with me." Jessica pressed her palm against Will's bare chest.

"Suit yourself. But I'm not afraid of a little water." Patsy stared a challenge at Will and took off toward the rocks. She hopped from the bank to the first one, a big flat stone with plenty of space. "Anyone else coming?"

Patsy didn't wait to see if they followed. She continued jumping from rock to rock until she reached the middle of the stream. Here the water ran faster, covering her feet and grabbing at her ankles. She struggled a minute to keep her balance, then scissored her legs in a leap to the next stone. The closer she got to the ruins, the slipperier the rocks got. When she had made it off the last moss-covered rock onto the bank, she sighed in relief.

Will was only a few rocks behind her.

"Better watch out, city boy. You'll fall on your rich Internet behind," she yelled.

"You think so, do you?" Will stood with his feet firmly centered on a stone, three-quarters of the way across the ford.

"If the moss doesn't get you, the current will." Patsy crossed her arms over her chest and leaned against a tree.

"Patsalee, why didn't you warn us before we got out here? These rocks are slippery as grease on a slide." Dwayne teetered one rock behind Will.

"Give it up, Dwayne. You couldn't balance a ball in a bucket, much less make it across these rocks," Patsy yelled.

"Wait till you try and make it back. We'll see who

gets wet." Dwayne struggled to keep his footing on the moss-covered rock. He slid forward and inched his way back up. Patsy saw something floating down the stream toward him.

"Watch out, Dwayne. Snake."

"Where?" Dwayne twisted on one foot and slipped off his rock into the icy water.

Patsy doubled over in a fit of giggles. Will joined in. Unfortunately, he was still perched on his own slime-covered stone. His feet shot forward and his butt fell backward with a splash. Pow, two strikes for the bad boy.

Patsy took one look at his two-toned eyes, wide with surprise, and lost her battle with laughter. Tears were streaming down her cheeks. Seeing him swept under-water was a lot funnier when she was on dry land.

As Patsy wiped her eyes and got herself under control, Dwayne labored through the water back to shore. Jessica, who hadn't even made it to the halfway point, also scurried back to dry land. Randy and Ruthann were nowhere in sight.

"Sissies," she yelled.

"Who are you calling a sissy?" A deep voice vibrated just inches behind her.

She spun around to find herself staring into the well-developed and dripping wet chest of Will Barnes.

Chapter Four

"It's not polite to sneak up on people." Patsy's head came even with his chest. For a second Will thought she was going to retreat, he was definitely in her space, but she cocked her head to the side and looked up at him.

"Didn't your momma teach you any manners?" she asked. He could almost hear her heels digging into the soft dirt.

What was she thinking? Was she afraid of him? She, or at least his reaction to her, was beginning to scare him a little, and, aside from the sly remark after lunch, she hadn't mentioned their accident. Even when Dwayne asked why they were late, she'd covered for him. Why?

Remembering his resolve to play it cool, he replied, "Oh, but it is polite to taunt people into falling on their ass in ice-cold water?" Will shook his head, letting water drops fly like she had earlier on the log.

"Hey, watch it." Patsy jumped back a foot to escape the spray.

"Are you afraid of a little water?" Two could play at this game.

"If I am, I picked the wrong canoe partner today, didn't I?" She stared him in the eye.

Will flushed; here it came. He knew she wouldn't be able to resist for long. "About that . . . thanks."

"For what? Not like I jumped in and saved you."

No teasing, no taunts? "And you didn't tell the others either. You could have."

"And listen to Dwayne go on? Why would I put myself through that?" She rubbed her hands up and down her arms. The gesture forced her breasts together, making the small mounds visible above her bikini top. A bead of water rolled down tan skin into the crevice between her breasts. His gaze followed it, wishing he could trace its path with his lips.

"I like the other idea too." Longing for another drop of water to roll down her chest, he grasped a lock of her hair, twisting it around his finger.

"What idea?" Her gaze flitted to his chest, then up to his mouth.

"You saving me." Her hair was soft and strong. He could feel her breathing, the cool cloth of her bikini top brushing against his chest when she inhaled. He wanted to wrap her hair tighter around his finger, pull her closer until no space remained between them.

"Do you know mouth-to-mouth, Patsy Lee?" He grinned, hoping to give the question a light note.

"Patsy. It's Patsy now. I quit going by Patsy Lee when I was in the first grade." She looked annoyed and he could feel her withdraw.

Over the name?

He dropped his hand to his side. Fine. He wasn't going to make a fool of himself. "Is that so? Dwayne still calls you Patsy Lee."

"Yeah, well, I call him a donkey's patootie too, but I haven't noticed him sprouting a tail." She glanced around, the earlier moment broken.

It was the name. Only the name. Wanting to regain the intimacy, Will reached for her hair. He tucked a strand behind each of her ears, then traced the now visible skin with his thumbs.

"Okay, Patsy, do you know mouth-to-mouth?" This time, he didn't bother with the grin.

"I know a lot of things." She caught her lower lip between her teeth. Her eyes glimmered.

She did look afraid. Of him? He should be polite—back off. He should, but he couldn't. He wound the pale strand tighter around his finger and lightly ran his other hand up the back of her arm. She shivered and he wanted to pull her close, keep her warm, safe. He was sailing dangerous waters, without a life preserver or that elusive mast on which to secure himself.

"Anything you'd like to share?" he asked.

"I got the feeling last night you didn't want my help," she murmured.

He tugged slightly on her hair and she fell against him. "That was different." Will lowered his head, his lips grazing hers.

She shivered. Was she cold? Will wasn't. Even fresh from his second plunge into the river, he was hot. Another minute and steam would be rising from his damp shorts. That, and something else. *Get closer*, something deep in his brain urged.

Patsy's fingernails scratched against his chest, luring him, encouraging him. Focused on her parted lips, he bent forward. His lips caught hers.

She tasted sweet with a hint of spice, like the cookies they'd shared. He slipped his tongue into her mouth, urging her lips farther apart. She hesitated for a second, then met his tongue with her own. Her nails scraped up his chest as her hands made their way around his neck. As she tugged on his neck, he reached behind her, cupping her butt.

He paused for a minute, feeling the elastic of her bikini bottom through her shorts, remembering that white V of skin. He willed her to move upward. The smooth skin of one thigh edged up past his swim trunks toward his waist. Moving his fingers from the temptation of her buttocks, he ran his palm down her thigh, following the line of her hamstring. When his hand reached the underside of her knee, he prepared to pull her up, to wrap her legs around him.

"Patsalee, where the hell are you?" Dwayne bellowed from the other side of the rock path. "Beer's running low and the creek's running high. Time to get moving."

"Damn it," Patsy muttered. She attempted to jump away just as Dwayne clomped into view. Still in a haze, Will kept her firmly hidden in his arms.

"There you all are. What's going on?" Dwayne eyed the pair. His gaze lingered on Will's hands, which again cupped Patsy's backside.

"Nothing. We're doing nothing." Patsy shoved Will's arms down and stumbled toward the stones.

Will bit down a curse. He wanted to grab her and yank her back, but Dwayne still stood on the other side of the stone path, grinning like an idiot. "Hell." Ignoring the rocks, Will stalked toward him through the fast-flowing, frigid water.

Apparently unaffected by Will's glower, Dwayne greeted him, "Guess this means you don't mind if I give Jessica a little rub-a-dub-dub, huh?"

Patsy rolled her eyes, and Dwayne turned his attention back to her.

"You're just lucky Randy seems to have lit onto Ruthann, sis. Or I'd be on you like a fat kid on a Twinkie." Dwayne wiggled his index finger at Patsy. "As it is, with this opening the door for me with Jessica and all, I'm willing to let your indiscretion go on by."

Was there something between Patsy and Randy? That was an irritating thought. Will narrowed his eyes and evaluated her reaction.

"You're full of it. There was no 'indiscretion.' You're just inventing things in your minuscule mind." Patsy glared at her brother.

"Sure I am, and you must've taken a belly flop into the river when I wasn't looking too. 'Course, even then, I'd have thought the back of your shorts would've got just as wet as the front."

Will glanced at her recently dried shorts where the wet

imprints of his thighs were now obvious. He smiled. Nothing like proof positive. For some reason, he was annoyed she was denying their "indiscretion," and the fact that Dwayne had noticed the damp evidence of their encounter pleased him. He crossed his arms over his chest and watched Patsy. It would be interesting to see how she explained that. If Dwayne had been two minutes later, she would have had a lot more to explain. Or, if you were talking clothing, a lot less.

She turned as if to deliver an angry retort, but stopped short when Randy, Ruthann, and Jessica appeared, peering at them from behind a bush.

Patsy stomped past them, leaving an amused and frustrated Will behind.

"What are you thinking about?" Ruthann asked, after catching up with Patsy at the river. "Like I have to guess."

"Nothing." Patsy frowned at her friend. She wasn't ready to analyze what had happened between her and Will, much less discuss it. "Where'd you go this time?" she asked. The attempt to not dwell on what had happened by the ruins failed miserably. Busy reliving the feel of Will's solid thighs pressed against her, she almost missed her friend's answer.

"Randy and I decided to do some cave exploring." Ruthann reached up to smooth her hair.

A twig poked out of the back of Ruthann's moussed locks. Patsy yanked on it, ignoring her friend's squawk, and held it up. "The cave's barred up. You can't get in there."

"Oh, is that right? Guess we didn't notice." Grinning, she took the stick from Patsy, and flipped it into the river.

The next day, Will stared into the recesses of his harvest-gold refrigerator. It was bad when he bought the place, but going on forty-eight hours without electricity had converted it from a simple eyesore to a total health-code violation. That was disgusting. He slammed the door shut before Saturday's egg salad, or what it had morphed into, could reach out and suck him in.

This was getting desperate. Yesterday morning he'd managed to get the front window boarded up before leaving for the float trip, but that was it. He'd considered skipping the outing, but knew Patsy would realize he wasn't able to finish a few simple repairs. Of course, after tossing her out of the canoe, any attempt at looking self-sufficient was a moot point. He still flushed at the thought.

Other parts of him got a little flushed too. Memories of her pressed close, her fingers scratching against his chest, were accompanied by a tightening in his groin.

What if Dwayne hadn't shown up? Would things have continued in the direction they were going? Another image of Patsy, her back pressed against an oak, her thighs wrapped around his waist, nothing but her shorts and bikini separating them, filled his mind.

Friction. When he was around her, there was so much friction, but friction could be a good thing—and with Patsy, it was a very good thing.

Hell. He was getting distracted and he couldn't afford that. He needed to concentrate on the problem at hand, namely, no window and no electricity. Simple issues, compared to trying to figure out a woman, especially one as unpredictable as Patsy Clark.

He wouldn't think about her again. That shouldn't be difficult. He had plenty of other issues to focus on.

He flipped open the book on "Do-It-Yourself Wiring" he'd checked out of the library. His eyes drifted down the page to a section that detailed the joys of joining male and female connectors.

Like he needed a lesson on that. His personal connector jumped at the thought.

Sure, he could forget Patsy Clark, no problem at all.

***

Patsy dug into the back of the Bag & Basket's cooler and pulled out a bottle of Diet Pepsi. It was hot. Must be ninety-five degrees outside and, with the ancient air conditioner wheezing and clanking, the temperature inside was only a slightly more tolerable eighty-two. Her makeup had probably melted off hours ago. She checked her reflection in one of the polished metal doors that led to the storage area. Not pretty.

Her look matched her mood. Ever since her reckless behavior with Will by the river, she'd been in a funk. What had happened? How could she have let him get to her like that? She had been completely out of control, ready to strip off his shorts and roll around on the ground like, like—Jessica.

Then Dwayne walking up, bellowing at them. Patsy cringed at the memory. It had been so long since Patsy had slipped like that. Why now? Why with Will? She didn't even like him, certainly didn't like his past or the fact that his money opened doors for him that others, like Patsy, couldn't enter. Plus she was finally getting close to escaping Daisy Creek—she could feel it.

She couldn't mess up, not this time. Focused on the thought, she wiped a smear of eyeliner from under her eye and turned to leave. She almost bumped into Marcia Stephens, who was sneaking out the side door.

Not again. A knot formed in Patsy's stomach. Ruthann, strolling over with a Dreamsicle, spotted her too. She scurried to the door and stood up on her tiptoes to get a view through the round window.

"Get over here." Ruthann motioned to Patsy. "She's doing it again."

Patsy stood still.

"Come on." Ruthann waved at her. "Who does she think she's fooling? The whole town knows what she's up to. It's just a matter of time before Carl figures it out too."

Patsy gave up and trudged to the door.

"How long you think she'll wait out there? It must be a hundred and twenty in that car." Ruthann deserted the window long enough to take a lick on her ice cream bar.

"Who knows? Bruce is up front talking to Randy's momma about donating to the Daisy Daze fund. She may keep him tied up for hours," Patsy replied. The knot slowly moved up her throat.

"That's most likely what Marcia has planned for him too. A little lunchtime S & M. You think they role-play? She's the picky customer, and he's the burly butcher?"

"He probably just watches her squeeze her melons," Patsy replied, sounding lighter than she felt. How could Marcia do this to Carl, her daughter, herself?

"What does she see in him?" Ruthann asked. "He's bald, old, and has hairy knuckles."

"Maybe it's the size of his sausage," Patsy quipped, more from habit than humor.

Ruthann giggled.

Patsy sighed. "It's disgusting though, isn't it? She has Carl and her daughter, but every lunch hour she sneaks out to Bruce's car, waits for him to swagger out, then drives God-knows-where for a midday roll in the produce.

"And she's not even good at sneaking around. Does she really think we don't notice her hunkered down on the floorboard when they leave the lot?"

"At least they leave now." Ruthann took another peek out the window before continuing. "I heard Leroy popped in on them in the walk-in cooler one day. Marcia told him some tale about getting her hair stuck in the milk roller bar and Bruce helping her out. But even Leroy couldn't see how Bruce needed to have his pants unzipped at the time."

"Well, all I know is, if she dies of heatstroke out in his car, Bruce is going to have a hell of a time explaining it to her husband." Patsy turned on her heel and headed back to the front.

She gave Bruce a cold stare. He was no better than Marcia, in her opinion. Just because he was single didn't give him the right to mess up someone else's life. Carl deserved better, Marcia deserved better, Patsy deserved better. Yet another reason to keep away from Will Barnes and jump on the first job that got her away from Daisy Creek.

"What you thinking?" Ruthann followed her.

"Nothing important." Patsy banged her money tray into the drawer.

Ruthann watched her uneasily.

"What? Don't you need to get to work?" Patsy shoved the drawer closed.

"Bruce's busy and there's no customers." Ruthann chewed on her lip, then brightened. "Hey, did you drive by Will's this morning?"

"Why would I do that?" Did Ruthann think she was stalking him or something?

"He had a refrigerator on his porch."

"A what?"

"A big, old, ugly gold refrigerator."

Patsy peered at her friend. "How about his window? Was it fixed?" Not that Patsy cared what Will was doing. She was just making conversation.

"Guess that depends on what you call fixed. Looked like he had a road sign hung over it."

"A what?"

"A road sign. You know, 'detour ahead.'" Ruthann leaned over the conveyor belt, closer to Patsy. "I don't think his neighbors are gonna like that much."

Who would?

"You don't think he's gonna leave it there, do you?" Ruthann asked.

"The sign?"

"No, the refrigerator. You know, like people who have a couch on their front porch?"

An image of a polo-shirted Will entertaining Jessica and his snobby sister on his front porch, complete with velour sectional and harvest-gold refrigerator, popped into Patsy's mind. "It'd be worth seeing." She grinned.

"Somebody has to tell him he can't have a refrigerator and a road sign on his porch. Not on Oak Street. It's not like my street. Those people'll get out the torches."

Patsy wasn't sure if Ruthann meant to burn his house or to hunt him down, but the thought of angry townspeople chasing him through the streets made her grin again.

"I don't like that look."

"What look?"

"You got that 'I'm gonna do something bad' look."

"Don't be silly. That wouldn't be neighborly." Patsy looked around for Randy's mother. She'd left Bruce's side and was standing near the deli. "Watch my lane, will you? I need to talk to someone." With a parting grin at Ruthann, she trotted down the aisle.

Who could be at his door? Will brushed the cobwebs off his face and stumbled up the basement stairs. If you could call it a basement; it was really more of a cellar, dark, dank, and filled with scratchy noises Will tried not to dwell on.

Standing at his door with a chocolate cake and a cross look was a fifty-something matron—steel hair, stiff smile, poker up her back. Cindy in thirty years. Breathing a sigh of relief that he'd escaped the future on his porch, he pulled open the door.

Standing behind the older woman, out of view of his peephole, was Patsy Clark. She was wearing a hideous purple smock and a sly smile.

Will smelled trouble.

"Will Barnes, look at you all growed up." The matron sailed past him into his house. "I can't believe you've been living three doors down from me and I just heard tell of it." She held the cake out to him. "Just a little welcome to the neighborhood gift."

"Thanks, Mrs. . . . ." He grasped the cake in front of him like a shield.

Patsy sauntered past.

"You like German chocolate? I'm not too fond of it myself—the coconut, you know—but it was all they had fresh at the Bag & Basket and my boy Randy, he loves it."

"Randy Jensen?" Will looked a question at Patsy. She was busy studying her nails.

"That's right." The older woman patted his arm. "I can't believe he didn't tell me you were living here. Your momma was such a dear friend." She tsked.

He'd never actually heard anyone tsk before, and his mother was nobody's momma. He raised an eyebrow at Patsy.

Patsy, still looking down at her hand, grinned.

"God bless Patsy Lee here for telling me you were having problems. It's not right to leave a neighbor in need."

"Yes, bless Patsy." He gave Patsy a look relaying all the blessings he could muster. She practically glowed with angelic kindness.

Demoness.

"I mean, it's hard not to notice things are a bit—off, what with the sign and the refrigerator and all." Mrs. Jensen stepped between him and Patsy. Will angled his neck to keep a watch on the instigator of this torment while Randy's mother prattled on. "Truth be told, I was a bit concerned when I drove by this morning, but after Patsy Lee explained your situation, I just knew I had to stop by and help."

"What situation, exactly?" he asked, his gaze boring into Patsy. Seemingly unconcerned, she shoved her hands into her pockets and leaned against the wall.

Mrs. Jensen had wandered out of the foyer and into the front room where the floor sander still leaned near the broken window. Will stepped toward Patsy. She tilted her head up, her eyes dancing with humor.

Will took his most intimidating stance, using all of his height to tower over her. "Thought you'd help me out, did you?"

"It is only neighborly." Patsy pushed away from the wall and started after Mrs. Jensen. Will laid a restraining hand on her arm.

"There are a lot of ways to be neighborly," he whispered. "Perhaps you'd like to investigate a few others."

She paused for a moment, then looked into his eyes. "I think you've got the wrong neighborhood."

Something in Will's chest tightened at her challenge. "I spent a lot of time researching this one," he murmured.

"Too bad, 'cause it looks like you made the wrong choice."

Mrs. Jensen came back around the corner, and Will released Patsy's arm. This move might not have been everything he expected, but one thing was sure—he was liking his choice.

Patsy was in a good mood, downright skippy. She wasn't sure exactly what had possessed her to turn Randy's momma onto Will, or to follow her over there, but it had put a spring in Patsy's step.

Mr. I-don't-need-help-from-anybody had met his come-uppance. Plus, dealing with Randy's momma would keep him busy and out of Patsy's life, which she needed.

For some reason, she couldn't seem to stop thinking about the man, and now was not the time to be fixating on someone like Will Barnes. To make sure she didn't weaken and do something stupid like a repeat of the river scene, she decided to keep him busy and out of her path. Mrs. Jensen offered an easy means, and it had been fun to see him struggling against the small-town trap of hospitality.

So, she'd gone over there when she didn't really need to. Now he was tied up with every do-gooder in Daisy Creek, and he'd be so busy ordering bric-a-brac and eating casseroles, he'd have no time to cross Patsy's path. He might not even make the barbecue Dwayne invited him to. Patsy felt a stab of disappointment at the thought.

No, she didn't want to see him. She wanted him busy and tucked away in his Victorian mansion. Now she needed to concentrate on her goal to leave Daisy Creek.

The first step was breaking her dependency on Granny. Patsy picked up a pen and signed away two years of payments to AT&T. No more missing messages. After waving away the clerk's offer of a bag for her new cell phone, she jogged to her Jeep. There, she dialed Glenn's number. She had met him a month ago during a seminar at the University of Missouri–Rolla. This morning in the Rolla paper there was a notice that an engineering team was looking for someone to do web design and Glenn's name and number were listed. If she was lucky, this would be her big break. His voicemail answered, so she left a message with her new number.

Finally, she was making some progress. She clicked the daisy-decorated cover onto her phone and stashed it in her purse.

Now there was nothing Granny or Will could do that would get in her way.

Will could not believe the havoc Patsy Clark had wreaked with his life. Since the float trip, his nightly sleep had been disturbed by visions of Patsy parading in nothing but her bikini, water dripping from her hair, nipples erect from the cold. It was more than one man should have to bear. Then, in addition to haunting his dreams, the real living-breathing Patsy had unleashed a band of gray-haired matrons and coverall-wearing men into his home. He had no peace day or night.

But he was not going to admit defeat.

Okay, his house had been taken over by men in coveralls, and women bearing green-bean casseroles, but he was not beaten. No, far from it. Little did Patsy know, but this was the best thing that could have happened to him. He'd made a mistake buying a house so in need of work.

Starting over didn't mean strapping on a tool belt. It meant doing things his way. He was doing that.

He eyed the stack of paint cans and wallpaper samples. Anyway, home décor wasn't important. Starting a business of his own design was. Time to focus.

Hopping over the drop cloth Ralph was using as a bed, he picked up the phone. First he'd work on his business plan, then he'd deal with Patsy Clark and her green-bean brigade.

The doorbell rang while he was on hold for Richard Parks. He ignored it; no reason to aid the enemy.

Jessica Perry rapped lightly on the door before pushing it open. Wearing a sundress decorated with tiny red hearts, she swished her skirt back and forth while she waited.

Will turned his back on her as he strained to listen.

"Glad you called," Richard said.

Jessica's heels tapped across the bare floors. Will tried to block the sound and concentrate on what Richard was saying. "I just got wind of a great opportunity. It's got everything you could want—surefire moneymaker, build the community, all that. Couldn't ask for more."

Jessica leaned over to examine the floor sander, giving a more opportunistic man a full view of her cleavage. Ample, but he was more a perky man. Perky with a side of attitude. Will clenched his teeth as the dream Patsy and her green bikini popped into his head.

Great, she was haunting his daydreams too. The woman really needed to learn some consideration.

"You there?" Richard asked.

Will grunted.

"How about lunch tomorrow?"

After agreeing to meet at the newspaper office around noon, Will hung up.

"Making plans with anyone I know?" Jessica glanced down at her manicure, then snapped her gaze back up at him.

Will suddenly felt like the last nacho at a poker game.

"What a coincidence. I was stopping by to invite you to lunch." Her hand ran down the neckline of her dress, stopping somewhere a little north of impropriety.

Make that the last bratwurst at a tailgate party.

"I could show you some office space while we're out." She swished closer, breathing the words through a cloud of musky perfume.

The last Budweiser at the Super Bowl?

In search of fresh air, he took a step back. "I'm kind of fully stocked with casseroles right now."

Smoothing her skirt, she breathed, "I could help you out."

"Great idea." Zipping into the kitchen, he grabbed three casseroles—one tuna, two green-bean—and a bowl of something fluffy and pink. "Don't worry about washing them when you're done. I think a dishwasher is on the plan for Wednesday." Shoving the dishes into her hands, he hurried her to the door. "Just drop them by anytime."

"But . . . the office space."

"No rush. I'll call you." After shutting the door, he leaned against it and let out a sigh of relief. Another narrow escape. He already had one woman to deal with. She was more than enough.

"I applied at the BiggeeMart today." Ruthann pulled the curtain back, staring out into Granny's backyard. A bluebird poked his head out of a weathered birdhouse. "They said they had positions open in the pharmacy and jewelry—a lot classier than checking at the B & B."

"Yeah, I'd much rather be discussing foot fungus and hemorrhoids all day." Filling from a Hostess pie oozed onto Patsy's hand. She licked a bit of apple off her wrist. Three days since she'd left a message for Glenn, and *nada*. Why hadn't he called?

Two days since she saw Will. Why hadn't he called?

She chastised herself for the thought. She didn't want Will to call. Her plan was working. She should be happy.

"What about the jewelry? There's nothing wrong with that," Ruthann said.

Nothing right with it either. Patsy's mind drifted back to Will. Wonder if he got a new refrigerator yet. His window was fixed. She'd just happened to drive by his place yesterday. Couldn't help but notice. It wasn't like she was going out of her way to see him. He lived right on Oak Street.

"Momma's last boyfriend bought her a diamond tennis bracelet from the BiggeeMart. You should see how it sparkles," Ruthann continued.

"All that sparkles isn't gold," Patsy quoted, popping a corner of crust into her mouth. In Patsy's experience, most things that sparkled were just flashy lures.

Giving her a confused look, Ruthann replied, "'Course not, I told you it was diamonds."

It wasn't worth explaining. "Did you ask for jewelry?"

"No, I didn't want to be pushy. I told 'em I'd take whatever."

"If you want jewelry, why didn't you tell them that?" Sometimes Ruthann was as spineless as a jellyfish.

"I don't know. I'll just be glad to get out of the B & B. I ran into Leroy at the BiggeeMart too. If you wait too long, all their openings'll be gone."

Horror of horrors. "I'll risk it." Patsy touched her pocket to make sure her phone was still there. It was.

"I don't know why you're so set against working there." Ruthann slumped in her chair. "We've worked together since high school."

Patsy looked at her friend. "Don't you ever want more? See the world? Live someplace where everybody doesn't know everything about you—from when you started your period to your first kiss? Where people don't judge you based on your family or mistakes in your past? Where people aren't constantly scraping for a job to keep a roof over their heads? Don't you?"

Ruthann blinked. "I never thought of living anywhere else. I guess it doesn't bother me people know all about me. Saves me having to explain, but sure, I want more. Everybody does."

They sat in silence for a few minutes. Patsy's pie was almost gone. Should she open a second?

"You want a pie?" she asked.

Ruthann's look bordered on horrified. "I don't know how you eat those things. They're disgusting."

Patsy was unapologetic. "I like them. Besides, they have fruit in them. I just wish they still made the pudding ones. Then I could get my dairy too." To emphasize her point, she ripped into the second bag.

Shaking her head, Ruthann switched back to the earlier topic. "You really want to leave us? That's what you want more than anything?" A tear threatened to roll down her cheek.

Damn it all. Patsy didn't mean to upset her. She set the untouched pie to the side. "'Course not. I just want . . ." A chirping sounded from her pocket. It took a beat to recognize her cell's ring. Will. She yanked the phone out of her pocket, then realized he wouldn't have this number. Disappointment caused her to stare at the small screen blankly. The phone rang again, breaking the spell. Rolla number. Glenn.

She signaled Ruthann she'd be back, and popped out the back door onto the patio.

"Patsy, you interested in the web job?" Glenn's voice boomed at her. "It doesn't pay much, but it could lead to bigger things. You still interested?"

Nervous, Patsy's confirmation came out in a squeak.

"Great, meet me tomorrow for lunch? We can iron out the details then."

Clutching her phone to her chest, Patsy performed a little pirouette. This was it, her chance. She was leaving Daisy Creek.

The bluebird popped back out of his simple home, looked around and flew off over the neighboring house's roofline. Blowing him a kiss, Patsy skipped back into the kitchen.

Chapter Five

A pigeon stared down at Will as he pulled into the newspaper's parking lot. Probably looking for a good place to crap. The way his week was going, he was surprised Patsy Clark hadn't organized a whole flock to circle overhead and drop missiles like B-52 bombers on a raid. Giving his exquisitely clean Beamer a final look, he tromped toward the News building.

Only published Wednesdays and Saturdays, the *Daisy Creek News* was a small operation, not big enough for a separate building. Instead, they inhabited an old factory a block off the courthouse square. The front was occupied by a diner, the kind of place where coffee was served in thick china cups with a saucer, the tables were chrome with scarred Formica tops, and biscuits with white gravy was the special of the day.

Will wound his way up the metal staircase. A twenty-something with a gigantic coffee stain on her blouse gave him a tired smile when he stepped through the door.

Dabbing at her shirt with a shredded paper napkin, she said, "You Will Barnes? Richard told me to wait on you. Go on in."

With the unsettling feeling he should apologize for something, he quickly stepped past her and into the office.

Richard looked up from an oak desk yellowed with age. "So you planning on making your next million in Daisy Creek?"

Richard hadn't changed much over the years.

"You tell me. Is there a million to be made here?" Will settled into an office chair that matched Richard's desk.

Richard laughed, a startling sound in the little room. "There's always money to be made. The problem is you have to have some to make some, don't you?"

Will chose not to respond. He was smart enough to not volunteer financing until he'd heard the other man's proposal. Besides, he wasn't interested in backing something. He wanted to start something. Make something from nothing.

Richard leaned forward. "I'll be straight with you. I've got a line on what could be the best thing to hit Daisy Creek since the mines moved out and the factories closed up."

The chair's hard back cut into Will's shoulders, but he remained still.

"It's a real humdinger of an opportunity for the county—new jobs, and not flipping burgers either. Good paying work in construction to start and then driving and management."

Might as well let him talk.

"People around here need this. The problem is it's going to take some delicate handling. Now, I've talked to some of the guys on the town council and people like David Wood, and we're all in agreement, but there will surely be some folks as don't see it our way. We're going to need money to help convince them, especially if we want to put a road through somebody's hay field. Or, even better, with a little financial backing, we might be able to just step around them altogether."

Will didn't bother to hide his confusion. "What kind of project are you talking about?"

"A smelter." Richard beamed at Will like he'd just handed him a hundred million shares of Microsoft stock. "Sunrise Mines is working on starting a new mine south of here, and they're interested in building a second smelter closer to the excavation site. Daisy Creek is prime territory, right on the route north to St. Louis. We just need to help them smooth things over." He drew his hands out in a straight line. "You know, getting land for a new road and the smelter itself. Plus, there will probably be a few environmental types whining and stomping around. But if we can pull it off, it'll mean big money for everybody."

With his face devoid of emotion, Will asked, "I can see how this might bring jobs to the area, but how's it going to bring me personally a return on any money I invest?"

Richard grinned. "Simple. We'll all keep mum about the new smelter. No reason to get people riled up before we have to anyway. You go in and buy up cheap farm land for the smelter and as much of the roadway as possible. Then you get to turn it around for a quick profit to Sunrise."

Richard leaned forward, elbows on his desk. "Then there's the land around the new road. It'll be a major roadway. Taking it will cut off miles for folks coming down this way from St. Louis, with the benefit of still being scenic. By the time word gets out what's going on, you'll already own the best frontage. You turn over a few acres for the road itself. Wait a bit and sell that prime property for big money. In return, we're able to guarantee Sunrise no resistance from the locals who own the land right now, 'cause by then you'll be sitting on all the deeds."

Richard's grin indicated the Microsoft shares just split.

Will had doubts of how "scenic" a road past a smelter would be, but he let it pass. "And what's in it for you and the others?" he asked.

Richard pushed himself away from his desk an inch or two. "Well, mainly we're just looking out for the financial needs of Daisy Creek. That's the major motivator for all of us." He paused. "But since you'll be pocketing such a substantial chunk of change from the deal, we think it'd only be fair if we took a small cut. Say twenty-five percent of the profit once you sell to Sunrise."

Sounded like a fair cut for bilking farmers out of the profit on their land. Maybe they could talk some old ladies out of their wedding rings too. Or break into some preschoolers' piggy banks.

"That's certainly an interesting proposal," Will replied.

"I thought you might like it. Nothing like having a surefire moneymaker handed to you, is there?"

"Nothing like it." Will studied the man across the desk from him. Should he turn him down cold or let him simmer a few days?

"Sure wish I had the assets to let my money do my work for me." Richard chuckled. "It's a rough life, but one of us has to live it, right?"

"Right." Let him simmer.

Claiming problems with his home remodel, Will escaped without having to endure an hour over greasy biscuits with Richard. His Beamer sat where he left it, as did the pigeon. He quickly assessed his paint job—not a spot on it. Finally, his luck was turning.

Opening his door, he waved a thank-you at the bird. With a lift of his tail, the pigeon returned the gesture. Hell. Will slammed his door and drove for home.

Today Patsy would drive to Rolla to meet with Glenn. Her life was on track. Her latest tour past Will's revealed a convoy of panel trucks and a procession of welcome-to-Daisy-Creek casseroles. Hope he liked Campbell's mushroom mixed with everything. She grinned into the mirror.

Behind her reflection, Ruthann sulked on the bed.

"He didn't say what kind of job this was? Who it's for?" Ruthann roused herself to ask.

Patsy flung open her closet. Suit, too formal. Cargo pants, not formal enough. Patsy's hand touched the smooth material of an ocean-blue cotton skirt. Perfect. It stopped right below the knee, not too sassy, not stodgy.

Team it with a peasant blouse and she'd be set. She started changing.

Ruthann raised her voice. "Did he say who the job's for?"

Through the filmy material of her shirt, Patsy answered, "No, but it doesn't matter. I'd design a site auctioning souls for Satan if it got me out of here."

Ruthann crossed her arms and slumped against the pillows. "That's nothing to joke about."

After zipping up her skirt, Patsy climbed onto the bed to get a view of herself in the dresser mirror. "Damn. I need shoes. I wish I'd bought those sandals we saw at the Shoe Hut last week. All I have are satin pumps from my cousin's wedding. I'll look like a prom reject."

"You talked to Will lately?" Ruthann asked.

Busy analyzing her footwear choices, Patsy ignored her.

"Jessica said his house is looking real nice, guess he got that window fixed and now they're working on the kitchen."

Jessica had been at Will's?

"I guess he offered to take her to lunch, but she could see he was real busy. He insisted on sharing some of the dishes that people have been dropping off for him, though. She said it was real cute the way he pressed them on her."

Patsy would like to press something on her, or press her under something—like a semi.

Ruthann smoothed the wrinkles out of Patsy's bedspread. "He invited you over yet?"

Patsy was not playing Beat the Bimbo. Well, not unless there was actually some real beating involved. "What am I going to do about my shoes?" She thrust her bare foot into Ruthann's face.

With a sigh, Ruthann leaned over the side of the bed and yanked her backpack up beside her. Rooting inside it, she said, "I knew you'd do this. You never think about important things like clothes, at least not until it's too late. Here." She flung a package wrapped in rainbow paper across the bed. "They were supposed to be for your birthday, but since I don't even know if you'll remember me by then, I thought I should give it to you now. Think of it as a good-luck present." Her frown didn't exactly relay kisses and hugs.

"Are you sure?" Patsy lowered to her knees next to the gift. "My birthday isn't for . . ."

"Just open it." Ruthann shoved the box closer.

Patsy ripped aside a rainbow and peeled the lid off the box. "The sandals. But you can't afford . . ."

"I took the job at BiggeeMart. I start in two weeks."

Patsy blinked at her friend. "You took the job?"

"Yeah, now try on the shoes."

"Did you get jewelry?"

Ruthann reached into the box and removed a silver sandal, tiny shells hung from thin straps. "I don't know why you like this beach stuff. There's not an ocean for what, three states?"

Who thought in states?

"Here, try it on." Ruthann pushed the shoe into Patsy's hand.

Patsy pulled on the shoes and fastened the tiny buckles. "What do you think?" The shells clicked against each other as she twisted her foot.

"I think I'm losing my best friend," Ruthann replied.

Imagining Jessica spooning casserole into Will's open mouth, Patsy had to wonder if she might be losing something too.

Ruthann had walked Patsy to her Jeep, then sped off to her shift at the B & B. Patsy stuffed a notebook and some pens into a bag and headed to Rolla. She wasn't really worried about losing something to Jessica again. If Will started seeing Jessica, it would make him that much more off limits. Patsy wouldn't touch a man Jessica touched with rubber gloves and a face mask.

She hit the brake as she passed into Rolla's city limits. Glenn had let her pick the restaurant. She chose a childhood favorite, a pizza parlor with thin-crust pies cut into little squares and served on dented aluminum pans.

Glenn was waiting when she arrived.

Over six feet tall and what her mother would call bigboned, he was attractive in a kilt-wearing, caber-tossing kind of way. Not a bad thing in a man, if not exactly Patsy's taste. She shook her head to dislodge the thought. She was not thinking about Will. She was thinking about getting a job.

Glenn whipped a chair out for her to sit down. With butterflies performing a two-step in her stomach, Patsy plunked her bag into her lap and dug inside for a notebook. This was it. She had to act professional, put all other thoughts behind her. When she looked up, Glenn was watching her.

"You excited?" he asked with a huge smile.

The waitress wandered over, and they placed their order. Not surprisingly, Glenn was a meat eater.

"Top mine with pepperoni, sausage, hamburger, and ham."

"How about a little poodle? I think I saw one on my way into town," Patsy quipped.

"If you can round him up, roast him and toss him on. I haven't had good French food since I left Minneapolis." Glenn slapped the table and let out a belly laugh.

Patsy grinned back, but spoke to the waitress. "Onion for me."

"Guess I know where I stand."

Patsy couldn't tell if he was teasing or serious. She hadn't thought of today's lunch as anything other than an opportunity to get some web business. Did Glenn think it was more? Just what she didn't need, another man messing with her mind. Not that she thought the first one would leave too much room for a second. He seemed to fill every unguarded moment.

Glenn plowed on. "Well, let's get down to it. I'll fill you in on what Sunrise is up against and then you give me your thoughts."

Mention of the mines jerked Patsy back to the conversation. "Sunrise?"

"Yeah, didn't I say the site is for Sunrise Mines? They're starting a new operation south of Daisy Creek, near Sauk City."

Lead mines. The butterflies turned in their cowboy boots for clogs.

"Is something wrong? You got kind of pale all of a sudden."

The waitress arrived with their pizzas, giving Patsy a minute to consider her response.

"You have a problem with the mines? 'Cause that's the whole reason they want a special site. Some locals are putting up a stink and they want somewhere to present their side of things."

That sounded reasonable. "I wouldn't say I have a problem, really."

"But . . .?"

Patsy hesitated. Glancing at Glenn's earnest gaze, she continued, "When I was little, there was a creek near Blackhaw where we used to hunt sparkly rocks." Patsy paused. "All closed in by oaks and dogwoods, shallow water, perfect for wading in, but deep enough in spots for crawdaddies and minnows. We'd take off our shoes and splash around. My brother'd catch crawdads, and I'd hunt rocks."

Patsy picked an onion off her pizza with her nail. "Last time I was there, it was gone. The mines filled it with slag. The trees are dead. No stream, no crawdaddies, nothing but slag. It looks like a graveyard out of some old black-and-white movie."

Glenn set the slice of pizza he'd picked up back on his

plate. "If you don't want to do this, I can find someone else. There's no pressure."

Yeah, no pressure at all—just the only opportunity she'd ever have to get out of Daisy Creek. Patsy peeled another onion off the pizza. Face it, Sunrise wasn't Satan.

She picked up her new ballpoint, clicked the button on top, and replied, "No, I want to do it. Tell me what they need."

Glenn gave her a quick rundown on what Sunrise wanted, time frame, and pay. "So you think you've got a handle on it?" Glenn asked, a meat-laden square of pizza inches from his mouth.

"Yeah. Basically, they want to play up the pluses and downplay the minuses." Patsy twirled the aluminum plate around in a circle.

"I guess that's one way to put it, but I think of it more as showing there's two sides to every coin."

"Even a wooden nickel?" What made her say that? She smiled to take the edge off, but Glenn just chuckled.

"I don't think Sunrise is going to be buying land for beads. They aren't conning anybody, just reassuring more like." He took another chomp of pizza.

Yeah, just reassuring. She could do that.

The next day, Patsy wandered into work bleary-eyed and fuzzy-headed. She hadn't slept too well. Her dreams had been haunted by slag-covered beavers and hollow-eyed children, both in search of a stream free of mine waste. In her slumber she worked away the night, scraping gray gunk off the beaver and justifying her web job to the children.

It was like a bad episode of *The X-Files*.

Stopping her on the way to clock in, Ruthann asked, "How'd your interview go?"

"Fine."

"Who's it working for?" With a tissue she pulled out of her pocket, Ruthann rubbed her palm.

"It's really more of an internship than a job." Patsy squeezed by her friend to reach the time clock.

"Really? Not a job?" Ruthann tucked the tissue away. "You okay with that?"

She didn't have to sound so chipper.

"Yeah, I'm fine. If they like my work, Glenn says he thinks there's full-time potential."

"Oh." The tissue reappeared. "Who's the company?"

Patsy hesitated. "Sunrise."

"The mines?" The scrubbing stopped. "I hear they have good benefits."

Of course. If Patsy would auction souls to get out of Daisy Creek, Ruthann would dance naked down Oak St. for full coverage dental.

"Would it be here?"

"What?" The time clock buzzed as Patsy slid her card in the slot.

"The job. Would it be around here or somewhere else?"

"The internship is here. I have to drive down to Sauk City too, but the job would be in St. Louis."

Following her out of the break room, Ruthann said, "At least one of us is getting what we want, I guess."

Patsy stopped. "What do you mean?"

"Nothing."

Patsy let her eyebrow arch northward.

"It's Randy. He hasn't called me yet."

A man who didn't call, alert the news.

"You were expecting him to?"

"Well, yeah. He didn't say anything, but after Sunday I thought . . ."

"Thinking and men don't mix. Men don't think, and you shouldn't think about them." Patsy smiled at an elderly man stocking up on brown beans, hoped he had his hearing aid turned down.

Leaning in close, Ruthann stage-whispered, "Are you jealous?"

"What?"

"Jealous, of me and Randy. I didn't say anything about me and him before today, 'cause I know how everyone's always figured the two of you would someday . . ."

Good Lord. "I am not jealous." The octogenarian dropped his bag of beans. Patsy lowered her tone. "I'm not jealous."

"Good, I hoped with the way you and Will were carrying on . . ."

"We were not carrying on." The man gave them a disapproving look and pushed his cart toward canned goods.

"See, you're getting all prickly. I knew I shouldn't bring it up. Anybody brings up men or dating and you freak out."

"I don't freak out. You just read the situation wrong, and I'm correcting you."

Their boss, Bruce, appeared at the end of the aisle. "Can I help you two with something? Like directions to the front?"

Shooting him an annoyed glance, Patsy tugged on her smock and clomped to the front. Ten minutes into her shift and she already needed a break. The vending machine and its stash of pies were calling to her. Nothing like a healthy snack to take your mind off stress.

Five hours later, Bruce strutted up to Ruthann's lane. "Lock your drawer. I need somebody to do a clean-up on aisle three. A kid chucked his Cheerios all over the place and Leroy's at lunch."

Ruthann punched her code into the register and reached under the counter. She popped back up with a dustpan and hand broom.

"Where are you going with that?" Bruce asked.

"To sweep up the Cheerios, or do I need the push broom?"

Bruce laughed. "Honey, you need a bucket. The kid puked. It's all over the place. You might want to borrow a raincoat and some boots too." Chuckling, he walked off.

A horrified expression swept over Ruthann's face.

"You okay?" Patsy asked.

Her hands shaking, Ruthann replaced the broom and pan under the counter. "You know if Leroy has gloves somewhere?"

Damn Bruce. He knew Ruthann didn't handle things like this well—okay, at all.

"Unlock your drawer," Patsy ordered her friend.

"But Bruce said . . ."

"Screw Bruce, what's he going to do, fire you? I'll clean up the puke." Patsy locked her drawer and went in search of vomit gear.

She was up to her elbows in fluids she didn't want to analyze too thoroughly when two Dockers-clad feet stepped into her line of view.

"Lose a contact?" Will stared down at her, looking impossibly sexy in his dull khaki/polo uniform. Was it illegal to jump the mailman?

"Funny." Patsy looked back at the Dockers. She didn't realize anyone still wore those things. No socks either. Cute little hairs accented the lines formed by the bones of his feet. They were nice feet, sexy even. Damn, she was sick.

"Not to the contact, if it's in there," Will replied.

Wasn't he just the laugh riot? Why was he here, anyway? He was supposed to be busy pushing refrigerators off his front porch or scrubbing tuna casserole out of old ladies' dishes.

He crossed his arms over his chest, causing his pectoral muscles to flex. She didn't need this.

Eager to be safely away from him, Patsy rushed through her task. She slopped up what remained of the mess with paper towels, and after shoving them into a trash bag, peeled off her rubber gloves and threw them in too. Will leaned against the Heinz shelf, watching her. Why didn't he leave?

Picking up a bottle of disinfectant, she turned to him. "You need some help?"

"Well, now, that's your specialty, isn't it?" He arched a brow.

Still mad about her helping him out a little. The man had issues. He should talk to somebody about that.

"That's what they pay me for." She turned the nozzle to "squirt" and rapid-fired spray across the floor. Bending down to wipe it up, she inhaled a lungful of fumes.

"You okay?" Will grasped her elbow, stopping her from tumbling onto the cold tile.

His fingers were warm, strong. A tingle ran up her arm. Maybe she was having a stroke, or a heart attack. Should she sit down?

With a concerned light in his eyes, he grabbed her other bicep and held her upright like a rag doll. "You don't look so good. Are you okay?"

Maybe she could just rest her head for a minute. His chest was so close, so strong, so inviting. Patsy wobbled toward him, let her head drop.

"Patsy." He gave her a little shake. "Are you okay?"

She snapped out of the fog. "Oh, um, I'm fine. Just didn't get much sleep last night and then the spray . . ." With his hands still on her arms, she forgot what she was going to say.

"You should watch that stuff. Chemicals will kill you."

That's all he could think of? And besides, Mr. Internet Tycoon was an environmentalist? "I thought your dad worked for the mines?" she snapped out.

"He did. So?"

Wishing she'd kept her mouth shut, Patsy replied, "You just don't think of the mines as being environmentally friendly, is all."

"As far as I'm concerned, they're not." He dropped his hands from her arms.

"But your dad . . ."

"I'm not my dad." The warm concern in his eyes was replaced with something cold and distant.

Feeling uncomfortable, Patsy threw some paper towels onto the floor and used her foot to mop up the spray. Will watched her, arms again crossed over his chest.

"Hell, let me." He scooped up the towels and tossed them into the trash. "Don't say I never helped you."

"I won't. I don't mind a little help now and again." As soon as the comment was out, Patsy wished she could suck it back in, wished she could go back in time before her comment about the mines too. Bring that warmth back to his eyes.

"Come here, you need to wash your hands." Taking his hand, she pulled him into the break room. Her thumb brushed the sinews along the back of his hand. The contact felt strangely intimate. Suddenly on edge, she dropped his hand. "There." She pointed to the sink. "I'll be right back."

Without looking back, she jogged out the back door and dumped the bag. Something was wrong. The way Will had been so concerned, how he'd helped her, it made her feel all woozy. Shy. This wasn't good. It was one thing to admit the guy was good-looking, even mind-numbingly hot, but this soft stuff, this she didn't need. She had to snap out of it. Get back in there. Surely, he'd do something arrogant and ass-like.

Determined to see the underside of his personality, Patsy trotted back to the break room. Will stood with his back to her, facing the vending machine. When he heard her enter, he turned. Cradled in his hands were two Hostess pies and a Pepsi.

"I thought you could use some sugar, being light-headed, I mean."

Patsy stared at the green-and-white packages. Damn her luck.

Apparently misunderstanding her look, he explained, "I didn't know what you'd like. There's not a lot to choose from in there." He gestured to the machine. "But at least these have some redeeming qualities. They have fruit." The pie's paper wrapping crinkled as he held out the bags. "You want them?"

Too numb to answer, Patsy nodded. With a grin, he set them on the table.

"When I was a kid, I loved these things. The pudding pies were my favorite, though. Do you remember those?" His smile made Patsy's insides flip.

Averting her eyes, she tore into a pie.

"Remember the Ninja Turtle ones?" he asked.

Green glaze, gooey vanilla pudding inside—who could forget such ecstasy?

"I was a little old to watch the Turtles, but I loved those pies." The sparkle in his eyes added a flop to the earlier flip.

"Thanks." Patsy mumbled, around a mouthful of crust.

"No problem. Here, take the other one. I don't eat that junk anymore." With a reluctant shove, he pushed the second pie across the table. After popping the tab on the Pepsi, he sat it in front of her too. "All those preservatives will kill you, but every now and then, I guess it's okay."

"Yeah, every now and then." Patsy reached for the second bag.

"So, you feeling better?" The warmth was back.

Darn near perfect. Horrible. Where was the ass, the arrogant rich boy? "Much," she replied.

Taking another bite, she felt a piece of apple stick to the corner of her lips. That must be attractive. Discreetly, she slid her tongue out and slipped the bit into her mouth. Will's eyes seemed to zero in on her mouth.

Abruptly, he stood. "Well, I've got shopping to do."

He must think she was an ill-mannered pig. With regret, she dropped the remainder of the pie into the trash, leaving a streak of filling on her palm. Without thinking, she put her hand to her mouth and licked.

Following her movement, Will's eyes became as round as Oreos. "See you." He turned on his heel and strode from the room.

That was rude. So her table manners left a little something to be desired. That didn't mean he could just walk off and leave her standing here. That was ass-like, wasn't it? Patsy tried to work up a good head of steam, but failed miserably.

He bought her pie. What could be ass-like about that? Damn it all. She didn't need this.

He didn't need this. Standing in front of the dairy case, images of Patsy licking pie filling from her fingers, her tongue darting out of that full mouth, almost sent Will running back to the break room. And before that, when she'd swooned toward him, that was worse than the lust. Lust he could handle. But earlier, that was something more, something elemental, a need to protect her, to take care of her.

He had to get a grip. He wasn't looking for a relationship, not even a date.

No, he was looking for soy milk. Where the hell was the soy milk? How could you run a grocery store without soy milk? Grabbing a bottle of something with a cow on it, he stomped to the front.

Chapter Six

Sitting on her parents' front porch, Patsy examined a daisy she'd nabbed from her mother's garden. Still looked simple from a distance, still stunk up close. She pinched a petal between her finger and thumb. "Take the job." The white petal floated to the ground. "Don't take the job." Another drifted down to join it. "Take the . . ."

"What are you doing out here? Waiting on a guest?" Dwayne's grin pushed Patsy from melancholy to annoyed. He tapped the yellow center of the flower. "If you want someone to love you, you'd be better off spending more time being friendly and less killing daisies."

"And you'd be better off spending more time minding your own business and less bothering me." Patsy tucked the flower into the dirt under a geranium. She didn't want to talk about love. It was an overrated emotion.

"Hey, don't take it out on me because you can't get a man."

"I'm not worried about getting a man," she snapped, and she wasn't. There wasn't a man around she wanted "to get." Liar, liar, a little voice inside her chanted.

"Pretty cocky, aren't you?" Dwayne plopped down beside Patsy, stretching his legs out in front of him.

Exasperated, she rolled her eyes. "You don't understand."

She really needed to talk to someone, and Ruthann and Granny were out. Unlike them, Dwayne at least didn't care if she left Daisy Creek. She needed to figure out why she wasn't jumping for joy that Glenn had handed her a way out of her dead-end life. "I got a job offer," she blurted.

"At the BiggeeMart? I didn't even know you applied." Dwayne pulled a piece of wood and a knife out of his pocket.

"Not at the BiggeeMart. A web job." Why did everyone think the only thing she could do was scan peas?

"Oh." An oaken curl fell off the block of wood Dwayne held in his hand.

"The thing is, I'm not sure I should take it. It's just an internship, but it could lead to something bigger—a career, with a salary in St. Louis."

"That what you want?"

"Sure it is. I'm tired of punching a time clock, and I want to see things. Things outside of Daisy Creek County." She tried to keep her voice steady, confident, but she heard the hint of a shrill edge and wondered if Dwayne did too.

He ran the curved blade of his knife down the length of the wood and let another long curl drop onto the dirt before answering. "You sure you're not just running away?"

"Running away? Of course I'm not running away." Telling Dwayne was a mistake. He didn't understand her at all.

"Just checking. You haven't been the same since . . ."

Not wanting to hear what she knew was coming, Patsy cut him off. "I'm exactly the same—just stronger, more determined."

"Then take the job."

Patsy dug one finger into the dirt around the geranium, stroking the remains of the daisy. She voiced the only logical reason she could think of to turn the position down. "The thing is, the job, it's for the mines."

"So?"

"So, you know how they ruined Blackhaw."

"Yeah, but I never heard you fuss about it before."

"That doesn't mean I don't care. I just never had a reason to throw a fuss."

Running the knife along the surface of the wood, Dwayne chuckled.

"What?"

He looked at her. "Since when do you need a reason to throw a fuss? Besides, caring and fussing are the same thing to you."

"What's that supposed to mean?"

"It means you got some problem with this job besides working for the mines."

A problem besides the mines? No, she didn't. Nothing else made sense.

"Would you go to work for them?" she asked.

"Quicker than spit. But that doesn't mean nothing." He leaned forward, forearms on knees. "You're smart, Patsalee. Don't run and hide from something that happened years ago. Take the job if it's what you want, or turn it down. Either way you got options, be happy about that. Me, I don't have as much up here." He knocked on his Busch-cap-covered head a couple of times. "I gotta take what I can get."

"What are you talking about? Aren't you happy?"

"I'm always happy." His grin was as big and goofy as ever, but Patsy wasn't fooled.

"What's going on?"

Sighing, he laid his knife to the side. "The uniform factory's closing up soon. We don't know how much longer we got, but it ain't long. Cutting's the only thing I ever learned to do. That and carving, but that don't pay."

He caressed the square of oak with his thumb. "Unless I want to move back in here with Mom and Dad, I gotta find something else, quick like." Flashing a carefree but unconvincing smile, he continued. "Guess it's a good thing I'm not weighted down with all them morals like you, huh?"

Patsy left him sitting on the step. She'd given his Red Wing boot a little kick after she stood up, resisting the strange urge to pull him into a hug like a three-year-old with a boo-boo. That would have just made them both uncomfortable. Better to act like the serious side of their conversation never happened. They had a balance to maintain, and hugs would set everything off kilter. Better to act like neither one cared.

His words hung about her though, dragging her down. If her obnoxiously happy-go-lucky brother was being sucked down by the realities of life in Daisy Creek, how could she hope to survive here? Maybe he was right about her issues with the mines, maybe there was more to her reluctance, but their talk left her even more resolved to escape the trap of life in rural Missouri. And he was wrong about one thing. She didn't have any options either. Sunrise Mines offered her an opening, and if she let it close, she'd be stuck here just like Dwayne.

"Where's your brother?" Patsy's mother greeted her as she wandered down the hall to the kitchen.

Patsy took a moment to savor the smells of bacon, cornbread, and baked beans that filled the small room before replying. "He's sitting on the step out front whittling."

She picked at the fluted edge of an apple pie that rested on the glass-topped dining room table.

"Get your fingers out of there." Granny snapped at her hand with a tea towel.

Popping a bite of crust into her mouth, Patsy grinned at her grandmother. While her grandmother frowned, a knock sounded at the front door.

"That must be that Barnes boy Dwayne invited. Can't think of anybody else who'd bother to knock. Patsalee, go let him in," her mother ordered.

Wondering where Dwayne was, Patsy peered out the front window. Will Barnes stood facing the door, holding a bouquet of pink roses. Practically attached to his leg was a long-haired dog. Guess he managed to beg a break from Mrs. Jensen. Patsy hadn't asked Dwayne if Will was coming or not. Didn't want Dwayne crowing about her setting her sights for Daisy Creek's newest resident.

But there he was, as big and tempting as a case of Ding Dongs fresh from the freezer. And he was carrying flowers. Patsy gripped the curtains in her hands. She was strong. She could resist.

Besides, she was tired of the tug and push game. She'd tried to play nice at the B & B, but he'd walked away in a snit. And Patsy hadn't forgotten Ruthann's report that he'd been sharing casseroles with Jessica. Patsy was not going to be suckered in by good looks and fancy flowers. Enough was enough.

"What you doing, sis? Don't leave the boy out in the cold. Let him in," Granny bellowed.

Patsy didn't think there was much risk Will would suffer frostbite in the eighty-degree heat, but she whipped open the door anyway.

Will shifted uneasily from one foot to the other. He wasn't sure how to approach Patsy. Something had happened Thursday at the Bag & Basket. He wasn't sure what, but there was a definite shift. A shift toward something that could make him half of a couple again instead of all of a whole. A shift he wasn't ready for.

Escaping Cindy's plotting had been hard enough, and if he was being honest, he never really cared about her. She was just another example of following the track his family laid for him. Patsy was about as far off that track as you could get, but something warned him walking away from her wouldn't be easy. This was his chance to do things his way. Dating meant compromise and bending to accommodate the other person. Will had spent most of his life contorting to please someone else. He wasn't willing to jump back into that pattern again so soon.

He concentrated on that thought as the door swung open. Patsy stood in the doorway, an unconvincing smile on her lips. Denim shorts revealed a length of toned leg, and ribbons at the neck of her peasant blouse hung open, exposing the indentation at the base of her throat where a faint blue vein pulsed with each heartbeat. Will felt his own heart jump in response.

As he moved to step forward, a small, black body hurtled toward him.

"Pugnacious! What are you doing? Bad girl." Patsy bent down and grabbed for the small dog's collar. The pug slipped past her onto the front porch and bounced off Ralph, who sat pressed against Will's leg.

As Pugnacious rebounded onto her behind, Patsy gave Ralph an uneasy glance and scooped up her pet.

"Don't worry. Ralph won't hurt her," Will said. From the way the smaller animal bowled out the door, it was much more likely she'd do damage to Ralph.

"I'm sorry about Pugnacious too. I don't know what came over her. She's usually so good-natured and easy-going."

"Lazy and thick-skulled's more like it," a man's voice called from inside the house.

Patsy backed out of the doorway, still holding the wriggling pug in her arms.

"Put her down before she falls down. The boy said his dog wouldn't hurt her none." An elderly woman had come around the back hall and now spoke over Patsy's shoulder. "Well, well, he's a looker for a foreigner, isn't he?"

Foreigner? Should he be insulted? Will strived to look polite.

"Granny," Patsy muttered as her smile stiffened more. "Anybody not born in Daisy Creek County is a foreigner to Granny," she explained, then bent down and released her dog, who strutted up to her canine companion.

Ralph spared a short glance at the pug before dismissing her with a bored look down his broad nose.

Granny continued to eye Will like she was sizing him for a new suit, while Patsy introduced him to her parents. Her mother blushed and cooed when he handed her the flowers.

"I just love roses."

"I've never met a woman who didn't," Will replied.

"Well, not my Patsy. She's always loved daisies."

A frown creased Patsy's brow. "When I was five." Her tone held all the exasperation of a teenager being forced to mingle with annoying adults.

Her grandmother snorted and said, "Don't let her fool you like she's trying to fool herself. She's a daisy gal through and through."

Patsy crossed her arms over her chest, but refrained from answering.

Thinking of the fields of daisies that grew wild around Daisy Creek and the childhood days he spent lost in their midst, Will replied, "I've always loved them too."

A mixture of surprise and something warmer lightened Patsy's face. Will shook off the discomforting feeling they had just shared a moment. He carefully kept his face blank while Patsy completed the introductions.

"You planning on staying in Daisy Creek, son?" Her grandmother looked him in the eye.

She was a direct one. He wouldn't be surprised if she asked him to open his mouth so she could check his teeth, or maybe his checkbook so she could see his balance. Feeling like a double-dealing bookkeeper during an audit, he replied, "Yes, I bought the Barnett place. I've already started fixing it up."

"Hmm." Hazel eyes reminiscent of Patsy's green ones gave him another look up and down.

There had to be some escape. "Where's Dwayne?" he asked.

"He must not have heard you pull up. I'll go get him." Before he could stop her, Patsy scurried from the room, leaving Will behind to fend off her family.

With a sigh of relief, Patsy slid the back door shut in the middle of her father's tribute to oak woodwork. Will looked miserable, and he'd only seen half the show. Just wait till her Aunt Tilde made an appearance, then he'd get the full performance. Especially when Tilde learned he'd bought the Barnett place. Her antique-loving, flea-market maven of an aunt would make Randy's momma look as pushy as a Baptist in a beer line. Yeah, Mr. I-can-do-it-myself was about to meet his Armageddon.

Patsy briefly wondered if he was an everything-brand-spanking-new-and-modern kind of man or a they-don't-make-things-like-they-used-to kind. Things would go easier on him if he were the latter. Either way, Patsy'd bet her PC Will was going to be living in a house full of horsehair chairs and claw-footed tables in the very near future.

'Course, Patsy had problems of her own with her family. Granny'd been eyeing Will like he was a prize hog and she had a hankering for ham. And that talk about him staying. Granny could plot all she wanted. Will might be staying, but Patsy wasn't. She was just grateful Granny hadn't witnessed The Kiss, as Patsy thought of it. Then, it would be near impossible to convince Granny Patsy wasn't interested. Patsy was having a hard enough time convincing herself.

Despite her earlier resolve, seeing Will standing on her parents' doorstep holding those roses, surrounded by their sweet smell, had almost sent her leaping into his arms. Daisy gal, ha, she could be converted. If Pugnacious hadn't bounded out of nowhere, Patsy'd probably be dangling from his neck right now.

It was going to be a long night. Patsy picked up a stick and flung it into the woods. She had to rein in Granny before she did something embarrassing, like tying up little net bags of rice at the dinner table, or bonking Will with a frying pan and tossing him and Patsy in a sack.

Being stuffed in a sack with Will. That didn't sound so bad. Dark, warm, cozy. Patsy's pulse quickened at the thought. Forced to spoon, or maybe she'd lay with her face pressed against his chest. That would be nice. She'd tip her head up . . .

Snap out of it. Patsy slapped herself in the forehead. Will Barnes was nothing but heartache, with a capital ache.

Okay, first convince Granny she wasn't interested in Will.

Then work on herself.

Shaking aside the thought, Patsy rounded the corner of the house. Randy stood with a bowed head next to Dwayne. It was unusual to see the pair engaged in what appeared to be a serious conversation. She slowed her steps as she approached.

"Do what you like, but the creek ain't stocked like it used to be. Pickings are getting slim, and we can't be as picky." Dwayne rolled his knife into a piece of leather and tied the packet together with a strip of rawhide.

"I know, but you know how my mom is. She'll have a fit if I bring . . ." Randy stopped when he noticed Patsy. "Hey, Patsy. What's going on?" he stammered.

Patsy didn't like the guilty glint in his eye or the talk of slim pickings, but Dwayne just shrugged at her.

"Will's here," she replied, watching both of them for a clue as to what they were discussing.

"We better go save him before the folks send him running back to town." Dwayne slipped the leather packet under his arm and walked around the corner.

Patsy let him go. She knew to attack the weakest link. "What's going on, Randy?"

"Nothing." Randy rolled a rock around with the toe of his boot.

Patsy raised an eyebrow. "Sounded like something."

"Oh, it's nothing, Patsy. Just talking, you know?" Randy shrugged one shoulder and glanced at her before turning his attention back to the rock.

Patsy watched him for a moment, but decided not to pursue it. She'd get it out of Dwayne somehow. Right now, she needed to get back and watch Granny. She turned to follow her brother.

"Patsy," Randy called.

She turned back. The link was stretching.

"There any chance of us ever getting together?"

Randy looked vulnerable, standing with both hands shoved in his jeans' pockets, his eyes confused, but his body tense, like he wasn't sure he wanted to hear her response.

Patsy hesitated. She didn't want to hurt him, but it wasn't in her nature to lie. "No, Randy, there isn't."

Randy visibly relaxed, his shoulders slumping downward. He kicked the rock across the scraggly grass into the woods and strode past her, a slight spring in his step. "That's okay. I just needed to know. Nothing personal, right? It just wasn't meant to be."

"That's right. It just wasn't meant to be," Patsy mumbled. That wasn't the snap she'd been expecting. She was pretty sure she'd just been insulted.

Dwayne and Randy were standing near the now blazing grill when Patsy returned to the patio. Will was perched on the picnic table. His dog lay at his feet. Pugnacious was sniffing Ralph's behind in what was probably a very acceptable manner in dogdom, but still made Patsy flush.

"Pugnacious, leave him alone," she said.

"Don't be yelling at her. She's just being friendly."

Granny waddled out the patio door, a plate of pork steaks in her hands. "A gal's got to know how to let a man know she's interested. Isn't that right, son?"

Granny directed her question at Will, but Patsy jumped in. Time to set her straight. "She's not interested. She's just nosey. She should leave him alone."

"Oh, she's interested or she wouldn't be sniffing around like that." Granny nodded toward the dogs.

"Well, even if she is, he isn't. Sniffing around isn't going to change that," Patsy replied.

"Sometimes dogs need a little push to know when they're interested and when they're not. Besides, he's not putting up much fight." Granny set the platter on the table next to Will and faced Patsy.

Patsy picked up a fork and speared a steak. "Not putting up much fight? He's a guest. She should leave him alone. It's not polite to be pushy."

"You can't get nothing worth getting by leaving it alone. Pugnacious knows that." Granny turned to Dwayne. "You trying to burn the house down? We can't put them steaks on a fire like that. They'll burn to a crisp."

Patsy dropped the steak back on the plate and wiped her hand on her shorts. This was impossible.

Granny grabbed Patsy's hand and rubbed it with the tea towel she pulled from the waist of her apron. "The biggest problem most folks have is knowing what's worth having and what's not. You just be glad Pugnacious is smart enough to figure it out on her own. Not many in this family can lay claim to that." She dropped Patsy's hand and stomped back into the kitchen.

Taking a sip of the tea Patsy's grandmother poured for him, Will had to twist his head to the side to hide a grimace. Geez, that was sweet. He could feel a cavity forming with each swallow.

After meeting Granny, Will could see where Patsy got

her spunk. The woman had to be seventy-plus, carried an extra fifty pounds or so on her small frame, and according to Dwayne, survived at least one stroke, but seemed to rule the roost. Patsy's mother flitted around the kitchen like a butterfly victimized by a shifting wind, but her grandmother chose a course and shoved forward in a direct line of attack.

There was no doubt who was the object of Granny's current path. She looked at Will like he held the password to a lost file, an important file. The kind you spend months, if not years, trying to reconstruct after a crash.

Or maybe he should think of her in hunting terms. She was a hunter, a husband-hunter that is, and he was the prey. She looked at him with the same light in her eyes his dad had when he dragged home an elk from his annual hunting trip out west. If Granny had her way, he'd be gutted and hanging over Patsy's fireplace before dark. He scratched Ralph behind the ear.

He'd been down that path before, been a trophy of sorts to Cindy. Of course, that wasn't all he was to her. No, he'd also been a bank account with money for a 6,000-square-foot house, private schools and a gas-guzzling SUV. A freaking fairy-tale romance, except Cindyrella's prince had a platinum Visa instead of a missing slipper.

Was Patsy in on her grandmother's plans? Was she looking for a prince or a bank account? Or neither? Glancing at the house, he saw Patsy watching him through the sliding glass door, her figure cast in silhouette by the kitchen light. Will picked up his glass and slammed back another jolt of sugary tea. Swallowing hard, he thought, playing prince might not be all bad, at least for a while.

Patsy's shadow was replaced by a rounder, shorter one, followed by the door edging open.

"Well, it's about time. Where you been?" Granny stepped through the doorway, a middle-aged woman with foot-high, coal-black hair close behind. The woman's face was powdery white, her lips glossy red. Black eyebrows that looked like they'd been drawn on with a Flair pen arched above brown eyes.

Like an aged Betty Boop drawn by a cartoonist just off a two-week bender.

"Son, this here's Patsy's Aunt Tilde." Granny motioned from the newcomer to Will.

Trying not to stare, he stood. A firm grip quickly confined his hand. He tried to pull back, but the Betty wannabe gave it a squeeze while placing ruby-tipped fingers over the top of their clasped hands.

"Well, he's a looker, isn't he?" She grinned at Granny. Turning back to Will, she said, "What you do for a living, son, to get those muscles?"

Her personality was just as subtle as her make-up. Eager for some distance, Will tugged his hand free. "I owned an Internet business, but I sold it recently."

"I'm telling you what, I'd have never thought punching letters on a keyboard would build up a body like that." She squeezed his bicep.

Before he could stutter out a response, she moved on in a whirl of lime-green polyester and lemony perfume. "Randy Jensen, you just get better looking every day. When you going to settle back down with some pretty girl and get that poor mother of yours some more grandchildren? I swear all that lovin' is more than poor little Luke can handle all by hisself."

Happy he'd been dismissed, Will didn't listen to Randy's reply. His own encounter had left him drained. He fell back onto his seat. Wonder why Dwayne hasn't pulled out any beer yet. He was going to need it to make it through this gauntlet of a family.

"So, Tilde, what'd you find down in Henning this week?" Patsy's father had joined them on the patio.

"Not diddly. I liked to talk myself blue trying to worry an oak sideboard out of Billy Joe Blackwell. I'd have had better luck getting milk from a bull. That man wouldn't let the red-hot end of a poker go." Tilde shook her head.

"I did hear some gossip though." She grabbed a paper cup and poured herself some tea. "There's a rumor going 'round that someone's looking to buy up land down that way. Billy Joe said he heard people were talking two to three times the going price."

Will leaned forward. Could this be for the smelter? He hadn't gotten back to Richard yet. Had he found someone else to bankroll his land deal?

"What do they think they're going to do with the land?" Patsy's father asked.

"Oh, they don't know. It's the usual rumors. Some say it's a new airport, a couple claimed it was for a water park, and one old fool even swore he'd seen Merle Haggard tooling around in his limo. Said he was buying up land to start a game preserve."

She took a sip of tea. "None of it sounds too likely to me, but I know one thing. If I owned land down there, I'd be trying to find out who was handing out the cash and I'd dump my acres before they wised up."

Will swirled his tea glass around, watching the liquid flow around the ice. Did others feel this way? Would people sell off their land and ask questions later? And if they did, was it his problem? He wasn't the one ripping them off. He was going to turn Richard down. None of it was his business. So, why did he suddenly feel guilty?

There wasn't anything he could do to save people from their own stupidity. In business, it was survival of the fittest.

Will winced. That was his father's credo. Still, what could he do?

Chapter Seven

Patsy watched from the safety of the kitchen as Granny introduced Tilde to Will. He seemed to take her unique sense of style in stride, though he did turn pale when she caressed his arm. Just as well their conversation was blocked by the glass door. Patsy was better off not knowing what her aunt said. Tilde was well known around Daisy Creek for a lot of things, but tact and diplomacy weren't among them.

When it looked like everyone had settled into a civilized conversation, Patsy balanced the baked beans on top of a stack of paper plates and shoved the door open with her toe. Will looked up at her with a gaze so full of relief she felt herself flush.

There was no reason she should feel bad that he'd been left to fend for himself. He wasn't her responsibility. He was Dwayne's guest. Plus, she couldn't help it if he seemed to attract the women in her family like a trailer park did tornadoes. It was his own fault for being so tempting—clean-cut and fresh-smelling, but with an underlying masculinity that screamed a take-no-prisoners approach to life.

The short sleeve of his usual polo edged up over the bulge of his bicep as he reached down to pet his dog. Patsy felt a tightening in her stomach. Damn. He was a bad boy wrapped up in a take-home-to-momma package. No woman could resist that.

"Is the pork done?" She averted her gaze from the

enticement of Will, instead opting to watch Dwayne give himself an uncouth scratch. Rolling her eyes, she deposited her burden on the table.

"Looks it to me, and it's a good thing. I'm as hungry as a bear in the spring." Dwayne forked the steaks onto a platter and handed them to Patsy.

Looking around for a place to set the plate, Patsy bumped into Will. Their encounter left a red smear of sauce on his previously pristine shirt.

"Sorry," she mumbled, staring at the stain.

"No problem." He reached for the plate. They stood for a moment, both of them gripping opposite ends of the platter. "Let me take it," he said.

"No, I can do it." Her hands tightened on the dish.

"Let me help." He insisted, giving the plate a slight tug.

"I'm not the one who needs helping," she replied, yanking back.

"What makes you the proper person to judge who needs help and who doesn't?" Will asked. He held firm to his end.

She tilted her chin. "Upbringing. I know the difference between helping and interfering."

"So I've noticed," Will replied.

"You gonna serve that meat or just wrestle over it?" Granny eyed the platter poised between them. Patsy flushed. The party had gone quiet, everyone watching her and Will fight over a plate of pork steaks.

"Fine, you help." She dropped her end, just as Will dropped his. Both of them stood open-mouthed as the platter flipped from their hands, landing face down on the concrete. A horrified silence cloaked the area.

Dinner was beans and more beans. Will offered to drive to town to pick up something from a restaurant, but Granny wouldn't hear of it.

During the meal, Patsy had a hard time looking at

him. It was like she'd been caught writing dirty words on the bathroom wall—juvenile and embarrassing. She should have just let him take the platter. Practiced her own preaching. Now he knew how much he got to her, and so did everybody else.

"The boys are leaving. You going with them?" Granny elbowed Patsy in the side.

"Hunting? Why would I go hunting?" Patsy snorted. As far as Patsy was concerned, Will couldn't take off into the woods fast enough.

Granny nodded toward him. "Hmph. If you don't know, me telling you ain't going to help you none." After giving Patsy a disgusted look, she went inside.

Looking up, Patsy realized she was alone on the patio with Will. "Where'd everybody go?"

"Dwayne and Randy went to get their dogs, everybody else went inside. They walked right past you."

She really had to work on her concentration.

"About dinner, I should have let you handle it." He lowered himself onto the bench beside her.

Patsy moved over to leave space between them. "No, it was my fault. I was being . . ."

"Stubborn?" One eyebrow arched upward.

"Stubborn?" she objected.

"Stubborn," he stated.

Patsy's eyes narrowed. Try to be nice and take some of the heat for something that was obviously his fault and he had the audacity to call her stubborn.

"So, you ever been coon hunting?" he asked.

"Once or twice," she ground out.

He resettled himself on the bench, running his arm along the table behind her. "Did you like it?"

"What's not to like?" she replied. She could feel the heat from his arm along the back of her neck. Not quite touching, but almost. As she tensed, waiting for contact, her annoyance melted away.

He moved again, this time sending a wave of masculine

cologne over her. The need to curl in toward him, to nestle her nose against his chest and breathe the scent in, almost overwhelmed her.

She curled her fingers until her nails dug into the wooden bench. Life was so unfair. She didn't want this attraction. Wrong person, wrong place, wrong time.

Feeling vengeful, she looked him right in his two-toned eyes. "What's not to like?" she repeated. "You chase a cute little teddy bear of a creature up a tree with a pack of howling hounds, shine a bright light on it, and shoot it right between the eyes."

Will blinked.

Ha, she was getting to him. "And if you're real lucky, when he hits the ground there's still enough fight left in him to give the dogs some sport before they rip his furry little throat out."

Will's skin tone slipped from medium beige to somewhere in the ivory family. Patsy grinned. Teach him to walk around smelling better than Hostess pie a la mode.

Relief washed over Will's face. "You're kidding."

Patsy grinned wider. "No, I'm not. But don't worry. You'll have a blast." She motioned to Dwayne, who was strutting around the corner of the house, his dogs on his heels. "You got the crocodile hunter of the Midwest leading this expedition. Too bad it's not coon season. He could show you the classy way to skin and bleed out the poor little thing."

Will's color slipped another notch.

Standing up, she leaned close and whispered in his ear, "If I were less stubborn, I might be able to help you out of this jaunt, but then again I wouldn't want to offer help where it isn't wanted." With one last grin, she picked up some plates and sauntered into the house.

"What'd you tell that boy, sis? His face is longer than Uncle Sam's inseam." Granny peered over Patsy's shoulder at Will, who had stood up to follow Dwayne back toward the garage.

"Nothing. He just asked about coon hunting, is all."
Patsy ambled over to the trash and dumped in her load.

"And you made it sound like a cross between bashing puppies in the skull with a crowbar and eating your own young."

Patsy sniffed. He wanted a taste of southern Missouri life, and she'd obliged him. No reason for her to feel guilty. "I told him he'd have fun."

Granny nodded. "Sure you did, and he'll feel real good about it if he does." Her nod shifted to a shake. "Sis, you have a mean streak a mile wide."

Patsy dropped the paper plate she'd picked up. "I wasn't being mean. I was just telling him the truth."

"You know, some people really enjoy coon hunting. Fact is, I've seen you come back a time or two hauling a fat old coon behind you and a grin as big as sin plastered on your face."

"I was eight." Why did everybody assume she was still the same person she was as a child?

"And I've know plenty of folks who made ends meet selling coon skins. Times aren't as good for everybody as they are for you. Did you tell Will what Dwayne and Randy do with them coons when they do shoot 'em? Did you tell him about the Cuffe family? About those kids who probably get meat once a week? You tell him that?"

Patsy was silent. Granny had a talent for making her feel smaller than a dried pea.

"I didn't think so. Next time you start poking fun at something, you flip it over and look at the other side. There's no telling what you'll discover."

Patsy watched her grandmother stomp back out onto the patio. Why did things have to have two sides? Life was a lot simpler when there was only one, hers.

She tossed a scrap of dirty pork into Pugnacious' kennel. Patsy had shoved her in it after the steak-dropping incident. It also kept the pug from following the coonhounds when they took off through the woods.

The little dog was already looking suspicious. She knew when dark fell, the other dogs would get to hunt. She gulped down her pork and started scratching at the metal clasp of the cage.

"You just settle back down. You have no business tromping around in those woods, especially after a coon that would make two of you. And agree with me or not, I don't need anybody's help to control you."

Patsy shoved another scrap of meat through the bars and finished cleaning up the kitchen.

An hour later, Patsy decided it was safe to release Pugnacious. The sound of Dwayne's hounds baying hadn't echoed back at her for a good twenty minutes. They were either having a hard time catching a scent or they were too far away to hear their ruckus. Patsy bet on the latter.

"Okay, Pug Girl, come on out." She bent down to release her dog.

The cage was empty.

She grasped the metal bars and peered inside. "Pug Girl, where are you?" She whipped around and searched the kitchen. "Pug Girl, you come out right now."

"What you yelling about in here, sis?" Granny toddled into the room.

"Pugnacious isn't in her cage. Do you know where she's at?"

"How'm I supposed to know where that bug-eyed beagle got off to? I let her out to do her business a half hour or so ago. She should be sitting on the patio by now."

"You let her outside?" Patsy's voice quivered with outrage.

"Yeah, what'd you expect? You think I was going to hold her furry rump over the toilet? 'Course I let her outside."

Patsy's eyes narrowed as she watched her grandmother sway back into the living room. Who did she think she was

kidding? Patsy knew what was going on. Granny thought
she could force Patsy into going on the coon hunt with
Will. Just because Pugnacious was probably running as fast
as her stubby legs could carry her to where Dwayne and
his hounds were terrorizing a family of raccoons, didn't
mean Patsy would beat a trail behind her. The pug would
be fine. Dwayne was there. He'd watch out for her. Granny
wasn't manipulating her like that.

An image of Dwayne grumbling over his supper of
beans flitted through her mind. He hadn't been able to
have a beer while he was within sight of Mom and Granny.
It must have been killing him.

She checked the clock over the stove. They'd been gone
an hour. Dwayne had probably worked his way through a
brewery by now.

Patsy kicked the door of Pugnacious' cage. Damn it
all. She was going to have to find them.

There was only a sliver of a crescent moon tonight and
not much of its light would make it through the
branches of the skinny oaks surrounding her parents'
home. Patsy pushed the button on the lone flashlight
she could find, an old plastic lantern, probably from the
'80s. The light flickered on, illuminating a space about
five feet in front of her. It wasn't much, but it beat her
penlight. She searched the edge of the woods for a likely
path.

Off to the right, the brambles had been flattened. As
good a place as any to start. She strode into the woods.
A century of dry leaves crunched under her feet. Tree
frogs and whippoorwills sounded their calls. An orches-
tra of forest noises, but no baying hounds. Where were
they? She swung the lantern's beam around her, searching for direction.

Tufts of gray fur clung to a raspberry bush—Ralph.
Guess that's why hounds were all short-haired. Following
the trail of fur, she picked her way through the brambles
and down the hill.

***

"Not a scent yet. How long we been out here?" The glare from the light mounted on Dwayne's hat momentarily blinded Will.

"Going on an hour at least," Randy replied.

Thankful so far he'd been spared the sight that Patsy had so sweetly described, Will leaned against a tree and reached down to stroke Ralph on the head. If possible, the dog was sticking even closer to his side than normal. Will wondered if he was jealous of the other dogs or if he somehow knew what the guns Randy and Dwayne were carrying signified. Dwayne had explained the weapons were just in case something went wrong; there was no benefit to hunting out of season. The coon skin market was dependent on a nice thick pelt, and the heat of Indian summer precluded that.

Even so, Will had waved away Dwayne's offer to borrow a rifle. It was just a .22, but Will wasn't a hunter and he'd never handled a gun—yet another choice that drove his father crazy. After resisting his dad for almost thirty years, Will didn't see any reason to relent now, especially tromping around in the dark woods.

The sound of something pushing its way through the dead leaves that carpeted the ground startled him out of his thoughts. Heavy breathing signaled whatever the creature was, it wasn't far away. He lifted his hand from Ralph's head and pushed himself away from the tree.

"What in the blue moon is that?" Dwayne turned his spotlight toward the noise.

The breathing became more of a snort, but Will still couldn't make out what was creating the racket. The hairs on the back of his neck stood at attention.

Searching the darkness, he wished he'd taken Dwayne up on his offer. His hand dropped to Ralph's head. The dog seemed calm. That had to be a good sign.

More snorting and crackling of leaves. Sounded like

a Suburban charging through an ice storm. Dwayne's helmet light caught a flash of white. Will felt an accompanying flash of dread before recognizing the slobbering beast charging toward them.

"Pugnacious, how'd you get away from the sentry?" Dwayne dropped to one knee and rubbed the little dog on the white spot that decorated her chest.

The pug gave his hand a soggy kiss before swinging toward Ralph. She reared onto her back legs and pounced on top of the much larger dog. With Pugnacious attached to one ear, Ralph turned a woeful gaze to Will.

"Guess she's prince hunting." Will slipped his finger into Pugnacious' mouth and disengaged her from Ralph's ear. "That's what you get for being a heartbreaker, boy." A problem Will was not currently experiencing. The pug bounded off to the base of a tree where she continued sniffing and snorting.

"Patsy is going to have a fit when she figures out Pugnacious is out here. You think we should take her back before Patsy notices?" Dwayne asked.

"Might as well, we won't be missing anything here, that's for sure." Randy stepped toward the tree where Pugnacious now had her flat face smashed to the dirt. As he bent down to scoop her up, she lifted her chin to the sky and let out a howl.

Dwayne stiffened. "She's caught a scent. Beau, Piedmont, get over here, you worthless hounds. We're coon hunting."

Pugnacious took off at a run, her nose pushing a furrow through the leaves.

"Let's go, boys. We got a coon to tree." Dwayne jogged after her.

This sucked. Patsy had been stomping around these woods for twenty minutes and nothing, not a canine sound, not even a coyote. She'd gotten more tangled up in raspberry brambles than Brer Rabbit with his Tar Baby. She'd even tumbled over a rock and rolled into a sinkhole.

She hated sinkholes. The strange depressions in the ground gave her the creeps, like the world was being sucked back into itself. She clambered out of it as fast as she could, but dropped the flashlight on her way down, and it chose that moment to go out. She was stuck down there fishing through the leaves for what seemed like hours. Once she found it, a couple of good whacks got the light back on, but it flickered ominously. Her hair was littered with leaves, there were bloody streaks from the brambles on her legs, and she was pretty sure she'd become home for a colony of chiggers. She could not survive another tumble into a sinkhole. Damn that dog. Damn Granny. Damn it all.

A long howling bay rent through the air. Even though she had been praying for the sound, Patsy couldn't stop the shiver that flew up her spine. There was nothing as haunting as the noise of a hound on a hunt.

Well, they were out there. Now just to find them. She gave the lantern another shake, pulled some leaves from her hair, and strode toward the baying. As she got closer, it was impossible to miss the group of hunters. Lights bobbed across the trees, leaves crunched under running feet, and men and dogs barked out orders and replies. It was a wonder there was a coon left in Daisy Creek County, much less still in the path of this clan.

The beam of her lantern revealed a masculine profile, a very masculine profile. Will stood about fifteen feet from the cluster of men and dogs who bobbed and bayed around a rotted-out tree.

"It's a den tree," Dwayne yelled. "He's up there, but we can't see him."

Patsy crunched toward them. Only Ralph saw her approach. He stood in greeting, leaving Will's side long enough to sniff her leg. Will noticed Ralph's absence and turned.

"Oh, we were expecting you." His voice was warm as he stepped toward her.

Her heart did a little patter move. It was nice to be wanted, to have someone happy to see you. Nice, but not enough. Besides, she had a dog to rescue. Tamping down the warm fuzzy, she stomped forward.

"What do you mean, you were expecting me? Did you find Pugnacious?" Patsy suddenly realized she was tense. She had concentrated on her annoyance with the dog for escaping and Granny for breaking her out. Seeing Will broke through that barrier and the fear for Pugnacious poured out. "Is she okay? Why didn't you bring her home?"

Will pointed to the mass surging around the tree.

"You don't mean . . . She isn't in there?" Patsy swung her light to the base of the tree. Clawing her way upward was Pugnacious. Randy's and Dwayne's hounds slammed into her in their own attempts to get to whatever had holed up in the oak, but the pug held her ground.

Pugnacious couldn't take on a coon. She could be killed. In a panic, Patsy ran toward the tree. "Dwayne Clark, get my dog out of there. What were you thinking?"

Dwayne lowered his rifle to the ground. "Hell, Patsalee, she caught the scent. We'd been weaving through these woods for an hour and nothing. Then that pug of yours comes snorting out of nowhere and nails a trail. She led us right here." He swung the light on his helmet up the tree. "But damn if it isn't a den tree. It'd be a bad break if we was hunting for real."

Dwayne's light revealed a hole about fourteen feet off the ground rotted into the tree trunk. Sharp barking yells came from inside.

"Good for the coon." Patsy shoved Randy's dog out of her path and grabbed Pugnacious. The pug was not grateful for the rescue.

"You can't take her now. I told you this was her trail. Beau and Piedmont have been acting like they got corks stuck in their noses all night. Besides, look at her. She wants to stay."

Pugnacious wriggled in agreement.

"Too bad. I'm taking her home." Patsy wrapped both arms around the pug while struggling to maintain a grip on her flashlight. She stomped away from the ticked-off coon and past a grinning Will. She made it another twenty feet before her light went out. Great. Now what?

"Pugnacious, settle down. I'm going to drop you if you don't."

"I think that's her plan," Will spoke beside her.

Patsy jumped, barely maintaining her hold on the dog but losing her struggle with the flashlight. It fell into the leaves, where it immediately switched back on. "A lot of good it does me down there," Patsy grumbled.

"Do you want some help?" Will asked.

Patsy was not getting into another argument about who needed help. "Just hand me my light, please. I don't want to spoil your fun."

"Certainly." Will retrieved her lantern, which again flickered out. "I don't think you've got much hope of getting her back by yourself though." He flicked his Maglite on. "In case you haven't noticed, she doesn't want to leave."

"She doesn't know what's good for her. In case *you* haven't noticed, she's a pug, not a coonhound."

"Oh, I see."

Patsy didn't like his tone. She couldn't make out his expression in the dim light, but she suspected he was making fun of her. "What do you see?"

"Oh, just what you said. She's a pug, not a coonhound. It makes perfect sense. She was bred for what, sitting on a silk cushion? I guess that's all you can expect from her."

"First of all, that isn't what pugs were bred for." Patsy paused. Actually, he wasn't far from wrong. Pugs had been owned by royalty throughout their history, but the way he said it was insulting. "And second, she can certainly do anything a dumb coonhound can."

"Oh, so it's just that you don't want her to do what she enjoys."

This was exasperating and Patsy's nerves were stretched past their limit. She turned on him. "Of course, I want her to do what she enjoys, but she doesn't enjoy coon hunting."

Pugnacious took advantage of Patsy's lack of attention and broke free. She landed on the ground, legs fully extended. Without a backward glance, she bolted back to the den tree.

"See what you made me do?" Patsy started after her dog.

Will stopped her with a warm hand on her arm. She struggled to ignore the tingle that seemed to be the standard accompaniment to every contact between them.

"What are you afraid of? Do you really think she'll get hurt?" He asked with no hint of a taunt.

Patsy paused. "She could. Coons are bigger than she is and heaven knows Beau and Piedmont won't watch out for her." She could feel each of his fingers as they pressed into her arm. His hold was gentle, but she couldn't step away. There was that pull again, the need to lean against him, bury her face in his neck.

"You don't believe that. What's the real issue?" His voice was low, almost hoarse.

She wavered, getting so close his breath moved her hair. The clean smell of his soap mingled with the earthiness of the woods and the other scent she'd begun to accept as just—him. Patsy inhaled deeply. "Nothing. I just don't want . . ."

"What don't you want?"

There was that voice again, low and comforting. Saying trust me, confide in me. She fidgeted with the lantern.

"What don't you want, Patsy?"

She filled her lungs with air and unsettling masculine pheromones. She gave up. "A coon dog. Okay? I don't want a coon dog. I bought a pug because I wanted something different. Something no one here had, something not from around here, something no one here understands. Then what happens? They turn her into a coon hound. It isn't right. It isn't what I wanted."

Her lantern flickered back on, revealing an inscrutable glint in Will's eyes. He reached out and stroked her cheek. "Do you even know what you want, really?"

Chapter Eight

Patsy stared up at Will. What a question. Of course she knew what she wanted. She wanted a career, something she could be proud of, not just a paycheck from waving canned goods in front of a scanner. She wanted money, not win-the-lottery kind of money, just enough that she didn't have to use generic eyeliner and eat store-brand corn. She wanted a house or an apartment that was hers, a place that said "Welcome home, Patsy" when she walked in the door, instead of "Welcome to the WWE." She wanted relation-ships, not just with people who'd known her since she came squalling into this world, but with people who liked her and respected her for who she was, people who didn't know her daddy and judge her because she was "Irv Clark's girl."

And she wanted love, from someone who wouldn't run off to the nearest bar because it was Saturday night or cheat on her with the latest divorcée to file papers at the courthouse. Boiled down in one tidy little sack, she wanted out of Daisy Creek. And damn it all, she didn't want a coon dog.

Patsy jerked away from Will and turned to trudge back to the house. In two quick strides, he caught her.

"Where are you going?" There was an edge to his voice; annoyance? Fine, let him be annoyed. Patsy was darn near fed up.

"Wherever I please. Now let go of my arm." She pointed the beam of her lantern at the hand that gripped her upper arm. He loosened his hold, but didn't release her completely.

"You didn't answer my question."

She looked from his hand to his face. "And I don't intend to. I know what I want. I don't need to share any more with you."

Running both his hands up her arms, he replied, "Are you sure? Maybe you just think you know what you want. Maybe if you share a little with someone else, you'll discover you want something entirely different."

Exactly what she was afraid of.

His hands stopped their upward climb at her shoulders. He began massaging her there, his thumbs rubbing a spot that made her breath catch in her throat. She couldn't share with him. He wouldn't understand. He came from money, always had everything handed to him, never had someone he trusted in betray him. Never been made a fool of in front of the whole town, a town that never forgot.

"You wouldn't understand."

"Try me. Trust me."

Trust me. She'd heard that before, believed it before. Not again, not this time. She jerked away from his lulling touch. The motion caused her lantern to blink back out. Not waiting for her eyes to adjust to the sudden darkness, she strode noisily through the leaves back toward the house. This time, he let her go.

Back at her parents', Patsy pulled the picnic bench up against the house. The house was quiet. Her daddy'd already driven Granny home and her parents were in bed.

Patsy curled her legs under her and waited. Pugnacious better come back soon. If there was one hair on her flat face out of place, someone was going to pay. She just wasn't sure who she'd light into first. Dwayne for tempting her dog into something she had no business in, or Will for . . .

Who did he think he was anyway, questioning her like

that? Touching her like that? Okay, so she didn't exactly fight him off when he kissed her by the river, but that didn't give him the right to ask her personal questions and caress her cheek, rub her shoulders. She wasn't sure which was more disturbing.

Both were intimate. Something you shared with a good friend or a lover, and Will was neither of those— not to her. To her, he was nothing.

Okay, he was tempting, but that was just some kind of twisted joke God was playing on her, giving Will the power to stir up her hormones. She could overcome that.

She stared out into the darkness. She would overcome that.

Will listened to Patsy stomp off through the leaves. She was louder than her dog, even without the snorting. She was good and ticked. Probably had steam rolling out her nostrils. What was the big deal? So, her dog enjoyed coon hunting. A little irregular for a pug, maybe, but nothing to get in a snit over, and it wasn't like anything bad could happen. They weren't even hunting for real.

He couldn't figure her out. He'd felt the electricity between them, felt her leaning toward him. Just as he was getting geared up for some quality time under the oaks, she started ranting about wanting a dog no one else had or understood. What's to understand? It's a dog, not a calculus problem. You feed them and love them, and in return, they let you. Fair deal all around. He didn't know why he even tried to talk to her. It was obvious she was too stubborn to be reasonable.

Shaking his head, he returned to the hunt.

Three hours later, Will and Ralph were dragging. Pugnacious was as energetic as ever, bouncing from tree to tree. Dwayne had used a sailor's log of cuss words yelling at the coon dogs, who apparently couldn't smell a coon if its butt were stapled to their snouts. Dwayne did know how to turn a phrase. And Randy plodded along, acting neither tired nor happy, just thoughtful.

As they circled back close to the house, Dwayne announced he was calling it a night. Hidden in the darkness, Will sent a prayer of thanks to the gods of mosquito bites, ticks, and maybe even poison ivy. In fact, now that he was thinking about it, there wasn't a square inch of his body that didn't itch. He was contemplating if the strange tickling on the inside of his thigh might be a seed tick and how much higher it would climb, when Dwayne shoved the .22 into his hands and took off in a dash back through the woods.

"She's caught another scent. If I lose her, Patsy will have my hide on a board."

The itch in question crept higher. Not able to resist any longer, Will shoved his hand down his pants and promptly dropped the rifle. Already off balance, the explosion knocked him onto his ass. Lying in the dirt, he heard the sickening sound of the bullet making contact with metal, followed by a hiss.

Hell, that couldn't be good.

The sound of gunfire catapulted Patsy off the bench. What moron was shooting so close to the house? Dwayne knew better. She grabbed her lantern and jogged toward the front.

A sound like a balloon being relieved of its helium greeted her.

"I shot it." Will stood in the dark, a rifle pointing into the ground at his side.

"A little late in the season for hunting Fords, isn't it?" She nodded toward her father's Crown Victoria, which was hissing more than a mother cat guarding her brood from a stray pit bull.

"You think it's dead?"

Patsy flashed the lantern onto the car. A river of fluids

poured out the engine. "Don't know about dead, but it's seen better days."

"You think it might explode?"

"Have to ask Randy, but I'd say you made a quick kill, right through the headlights." She bobbed the light along the side until it illuminated a hole near the front. "Yep, looks like a clean shot, straight through and out the other side. Mighty fine shooting for a city boy."

"Thanks."

He looked miserable. Patsy grinned.

"Don't worry. Dad wasn't that fond of him anyway. He hasn't waxed Victor for at least two days."

"Victor?"

"The car."

"Oh."

"He always wanted a Crown Vic, but didn't have the money till last year. Got an entire estate dropped in his lap, made enough selling that off for the down payment, then with the trade-in, he can't have more than four years of payments left."

Will was silent.

"But don't worry about it. I mean, the new car smell's almost gone. He'd have been tired of ole Vic in a year or so anyway."

Granny was right. She did have a mean streak. Patsy grinned again.

He shot a car. What kind of moron shoots a car? Will stared in disbelief at the evidence of his ineptitude.

The flow of fluids had slowed to a steady drip, a welcome change from the river that poured out seconds earlier, but each plopping drip slammed into him like a two-by-four to the gut.

"I had an itch," he admitted for some insane reason.

"To shoot a Ford? Can't say I'm much of a fan myself,

but don't you think that's taking it a bit far?" Patsy replied.

"Not to shoot a Ford." God, she could be irritating.

"What then, a Crown Vic? They're kind of an old man's car, but still, taking a gun to them? Seems extreme."

How had she survived all these years without someone throttling her? "Not a Crown Vic. An itch, I had an itch." He imitated scratching his thigh.

"Hmmm." Patsy raised an eyebrow. "Ever think of getting a cream or something for that?"

"I thought I picked up a tick. It felt like he was crawling higher . . ." Embarrassed, he stopped.

"Hitting the high road?"

"Well, yeah. I guess you could put it that way."

"Heading for the hills?"

She was pushing it.

"Reaching for new heights?"

Whatever happened to not kicking a man when he's down?

"Cavorting in the . . ."

"Hey, what's going on?" Dwayne and Randy appeared, saving Patsy from certain death, or at least burning retort—if he could think of one.

"Will's been hunting." Patsy grabbed a wriggling Pugnacious from Dwayne's arms. "Why'd you give him a gun?"

"Hey," Will objected. That was uncalled for; it was an accident, after all. Could have happened to anyone.

While Dwayne flipped the hood, Randy strolled over to look at the damage. He used Dwayne's helmet light to illuminate the engine. "Don't think I've ever seen anything like this."

Great, an automotive repair first.

"Can you fix it?" Patsy asked.

While Randy and Dwayne poked every hose and belt to see what was intact, Will sunk deeper into depression. Two kills in one night; first a plate of pork steaks, now this. Not only couldn't he do anything on his own, he actually destroyed things other people then had to fix. There was no way he could fix the Crown Vic. He could barely check the oil in his BMW, never mind replacing hoses and God knows what else.

"The engine can be repaired, but these panels will have to be replaced." Randy thumped on the side of the car, next to the bullet hole. "I can recommend a good auto body shop for your dad."

"He won't need it," Will dug in his shorts' pocket.

"There's no good way to repair a hole like that . . ." Randy began.

"He won't need to." The keys to Will's BMW glinted silver in the lantern's light. "How do you think he'd like a BMW? Three months old."

Patsy stared at him, mouth open.

"Or if he wants a Crown Vic, I'll buy him a new one. He can drive the Beamer until he picks it out."

Patsy bent down to release Pugnacious. "Are you crazy? You just busted a few hoses." The hood slammed shut. "It's no big deal."

"Even if it's fixed, it won't be the same. He'll always know it isn't right." Will gripped the Beamer's keys in his closed fist, enjoying the pain of them cutting into his palm.

"Right enough. Buying a whole new car is crazy."

"I messed it up. I'll make it right."

"It's a car. He'll get it fixed and go on. You can pay for the repairs." She had her hands on her hips now and was shaking her head at him like his fourth-grade teacher when he drew naked pictures of her on the classroom wall.

"I'll make it right." He walked off, leaving Patsy behind. After securing a ride home with Dwayne, he snuck in the back and left a note with his car keys on the dining room table. He'd call the Clarks tomorrow.

When he returned to the front, an exasperated-looking

Patsy had stowed her dog in the Jeep and was arguing with Dwayne. She purposely ignored Will. Mumbling something about idiocy and Y chromosomes, she started up her car and charged down the drive. He watched her taillights disappear into the night.

"You need a beer," Dwayne said.

Will wasn't going to argue the obvious. He followed Dwayne, Randy and the dogs to the side of the garage.

"So, Patsy was annoyed about something," he said.

"Being mad comes as easy to Patsy as crowing does a rooster." Dwayne disappeared into the garage and returned with three lawn chairs, a leather packet, and some scrap lumber. "Mom says she didn't have first steps. She had stomps."

Randy chuckled. Dwayne unrolled the packet, revealing an assortment of knives and chisels. He selected one and returned to his seat with it and the wood.

"You whittle any?" he asked Will.

"No." After killing a car, Will was surprised Dwayne wanted to risk handing him a knife.

"It's easy. You should try it." Dwayne ran the blade down the wood.

Will watched, fascinated for a moment. Remembering their earlier topic of conversation, he asked, "What's she mad about all the time?"

"Who knows? She's what you might call a rebel in search of cause, or at least a good fight." Dwayne balanced the wood on his knee while he twisted the lid off a Budweiser. "If she wasn't my sister and I didn't know she'd been this way from birth, I might say she needed a good lay." He took a swig of beer. "'Course, it still might not hurt."

Dwayne looked at Will. "Of course, it goes without saying that anybody who hurt her would wind up a lot like a dead coon. Butt nailed to a board and wishing he'd never left his den."

Time to change the subject.

"So, Randy, what's up with you and Ruthann? You looked friendly Sunday."

Randy was apparently too engrossed in his beer bottle's label to answer. Will tried again. "So, have you seen Ruthann since?"

"No, not really." Randy gave Dwayne a sidelong glance. "You need to sharpen that knife?"

"It's fine. Not worth getting up for." Dwayne replied.

"You need something? I'll get it." Will stood.

"If you're up, sure. There's a stone on the shelf in the garage."

Inside the garage, Will called, "Which shelf?"

"The one with all that scrap wood on it, behind the door," Dwayne yelled.

Wedged between the door frame and the corner of the garage stood a metal shelf. Lumber of varying quality and color was piled on the two bottom shelves. At eye level rested an assortment of hand-carved items. They ranged from an oversized wooden chain with a ball that rolled back and forth carved inside one giant link, to miniature depictions of coonhounds, fishermen, and what looked suspiciously like Patsy as a child wading barefoot in a creek.

Will picked the last one up and ran his finger over the smooth surface. This took time and talent. He'd assumed Dwayne just played with whittling. He didn't realize he was actually capable of crafting something so delicate. Will envied people who could create something so beautiful with nothing but a few raw materials, some tools, and their own hands. He held the figure a moment longer before exchanging it for one of a raccoon perched in a tree. Seeing a whet stone, he grabbed it and stepped back outside.

"Here you go." He handed the stone to Dwayne. "This is more than just a little whittling." Will balanced the wooden figure on his open palm.

Dwayne glanced up. "Oh, it's nothing. Just me fooling

around. Did you see Dad's stuff?" He nodded back toward the garage.

Will walked back inside. On the other side of the space stood roughly carved raccoons, trout, and dogs. From the bark still apparent on their sides, Will guessed they were made from a single log.

"Dad uses a chainsaw for his. I like whittling better myself, more relaxing," Dwayne explained when Will returned from the garage.

"Do you ever sell them?"

"A few, but there's not much market. Mainly we just make 'em for fun."

"You getting a table at Daisy Daze this year?" Randy asked.

"Daisy Daze is part of the fall festival," Dwayne explained. "Some artsy types started it up about five years ago. People sell all kinds of things: homemade soap, Arkansas diamonds, baskets, that kind of stuff. A couple of times we've had a table." Dwayne smiled. "A real Clark family event."

"Is that the only place you've ever tried selling these?" Will stroked the small wooden figure he still held.

"Yeah, where would we sell 'em? A few people travel all summer to the different craft shows, but we don't have time for that. Besides, once you figure in the time to make one of them," Dwayne nodded to the figurine, "and add on the time and gas to cart the stuff all over creation, you'd be losing money. Still, we've got enough junk built up. It might be worth giving Daisy Daze a try again."

Will looked at the little coon. "Can I buy one?"

Dwayne raised a brow. "You want one?"

"Yeah." Even in the dim light, Will could see the detailed mask and tail on the tiny sculpture. "I wish I could create something like this."

"If you got a use for it, take it. It ain't no big deal to

make another." Dwayne lowered his head, back to his work. "Besides, I kind of like knowing people have 'em."

Will had to talk to Patsy. Maybe she could get through to her father. Will had called Irv Clark this morning to apologize again for blowing a hole through his Crown Vic. It had been the most exasperating five minutes of Will's life; well, aside from about every minute he'd spent with Patsy. The man refused to be reasonable. He'd agreed to the loan of Will's BMW, and to Will paying for repairs to the Ford, but that was it.

"There's no need to go off half-cocked. I could probably fix the ole fellow myself—few new hoses, some spackle and paint, he'd be fit to fiddle."

"But I shot your car . . ." Will began.

"Were you aiming for him?"

"Well, no."

"Didn't think so. You want to take a vehicle out, you're best off shooting for the gas tank. Probably get a nice big bang to boot." Mr. Clark paused. "No sense in buying a new car when you got a perfectly good one in the drive."

"But it has a hole in it." Will couldn't believe he had to point this out again.

"Two, actually, went clear through." Patsy's father chuckled.

"Won't you at least take my Beamer?"

This time her father laughed out loud. "Me driving some foreign make? No offense, but that ain't gonna happen."

He was turning down a practically new BMW, a product of the best German engineering, to drive a Ford with two bullet holes. Will considered banging the receiver against the wall.

As if sensing Will's mood, Mr. Clark continued, "Tell you what, we'll keep the Beamer till the Vic is fixed. Melba can drive it to the dress shop, and I'll take hers.

She'll get a kick out of tooling around in a hoity-toity foreign ride."

Apparently Randy and Dwayne had already replaced all the damaged hoses and driven the Crown Vic to an auto body shop for new side panels. It would be about a week before the Ford was road ready again. Will hung up, unsatisfied with the outcome.

He had shot the man's car. As if that wasn't humiliating enough, now the man wouldn't even take proper reparation gracefully.

Will picked the phone back up and dialed Patsy. The phone rang twenty times before he gave up. Who didn't have voice mail or at least an answering machine? Did she think it was 1979? Frustrated, he slammed the receiver down and went to throw on some shorts.

He needed a jog.

Chapter Nine

Patsy swung her Jeep into a slot at Sonic and studied the menu.

"I don't know what I've done wrong." As Ruthann cranked down her window, Pugnacious jumped into her lap and positioned herself with her front end dangling out the car.

"You haven't done anything wrong. Don't be goofy." Patsy leaned out the window to push the red call button. "What do you want?"

"I want him to call me. I saw his momma at church Sunday. She didn't even look at me. Do you think he told her something bad?" Ruthann scratched the pug at the base of her curly tail.

"I mean, what do you want to eat?" Patsy pointed to the menu.

"Maybe that's it. He probably thinks I'm fat. He saw you and Jessica in your swim suits and realized what a cow I am."

"You are not a cow."

"May I take your order?" a voice from the menu asked.

"Tell me what you want."

"Nothing." Ruthann slumped down in her seat. "Well, maybe a diet limeade."

After placing their order, Patsy said, "You're being ridiculous. What do you care what Randy Jensen thinks? You can do better than him."

"Easy for you to say."

Patsy twisted in her seat to face Ruthann. "What's that supposed to mean?"

"All you'd have to do is crook your pinkie and he'd be licking your boots. The only reason he gave me the time of day Sunday is 'cause everyone could see you were all wrapped up in Will."

"First of all, I think Randy's over me and my pinkie. Second, I was not 'wrapped up' in Will."

Pugnacious snorted and Ruthann threw her a skeptical look. "Whatever."

"I wasn't," Patsy insisted.

"Sure, if you say so. Anyway, all I asked for was a few leftovers and I can't even get that."

"When did you get such a low opinion of yourself? You don't need 'leftovers.' There are a ton of guys way better than Randy. He's divorced with a kid, for God's sake."

"I like Luke," Ruthann mumbled.

"He's cute, but you don't need insty family. And what about Randy's mother? You know she's part of the package. Nobody's ever going to be good enough for her. You could win the Nobel Prize and cure cancer and she'd still complain you wore too much blush or that your gravy had lumps."

"I don't make gravy."

Patsy couldn't stop an eye roll. "Then you're out for sure."

A girl dressed in black shorts and a Sonic shirt bounced up with a tray of food. Patsy shoved Pugnacious into the backseat before passing a limeade and a Coney dog to Ruthann.

"I said, I was dieting."

Patsy kept one hand on the pug, confining her to the backseat. "Just eat it."

Around a bite of hot dog, Ruthann asked, "Don't you understand, Patsy? I think I love him."

"You can't love him." Patsy refused to believe it. She

passed Ruthann a red plastic basket filled with onion rings.

The succulent smell of fried breading wafted through the car.

"Well, I do, Patsy. I've tried not to, but there's no hope for it, I love him."

Patsy stared at her friend. Nothing was going the way it was supposed to. Ruthann wasn't supposed to be with Randy. Pugnacious wasn't supposed to go coon hunting. And Patsy wasn't supposed to want Will. No one wanted to stay on the proper path. They were all shooting off on their own. Somewhere along the way Patsy had lost control of everyone, including herself.

Ruthann took a slurp of limeade. She even managed to make that sound forlorn.

Patsy sighed. Ruthann was her best friend. She might not understand her choice, but it didn't mean she wouldn't support her. "Don't worry about it. If you want him, we'll figure something out. Randy's slow, but he's not completely dimwitted. We'll get him to come around."

"Really? You think so?" Ruthann sat up in her seat.

"Sure, no problem. I'll talk to Dwayne or something. Now have an onion ring."

Ruthann grabbed a handful of rings and began munching away. "Thanks, Patsy. I knew you'd understand. Being in love is rough, isn't it?"

Rougher than sandpaper on a sunburn.

A red Volkswagen Bug pulled into the space across from them. Pugnacious broke free, nabbed an onion ring, and dove back onto the backseat.

"Look, Jessica got her new car. Ooo, and she got vanity plates too, SWTHRT. That's cute. Don't you think?"

"Yeah, cute. Must have taken her months to come up with that one. Just plain TART would've been more accurate." Patsy shook a ketchup package, slapping it against her palm.

"You are mean." Ruthann stuck her arm out her window and waved at the other vehicle. Jessica wiggled pink-tipped fingers back. "Why are you so prickly around her? She's never done anything to you."

Pugnacious reappeared, flat nose twitching. Patsy tore off a hunk of bun and handed it to her. She didn't feel like picking at old wounds.

"The question is, why do you ooze all over her? She's not any better than we are, you know."

"I never said she was." Ruthann grabbed another onion ring.

"You never said it, but you think it. You've thought it since the first grade. Remember, she brought that Cabbage Patch Kid to school. She was bragging and showing off and you lapped it all up. Ever since then you've acted like we should be grateful for any little scrap of attention she drops our way." Patsy clamped her teeth onto the corner of the ketchup package and ripped it open.

Ruthann blinked at her.

Patsy squished ketchup into the red basket and looked up. "What? Why are you staring at me?"

"You're jealous."

Jealous. How could Ruthann think such a thing? Maybe Patsy should tell her the truth. She glanced back at the gleaming bug and something tightened in her stomach—something still tender after five years.

"That is ridiculous. There is not one thing that . . ." Patsy jutted her head toward Jessica's new car, ". . . over-rated cheerleader has that I want. I can't believe you would say that."

"How about that?"

Patsy followed Ruthann's gaze. Jessica popped out of her bug to greet a sparsely dressed Will Barnes. His red running shorts covered more than a fig leaf, but didn't leave much more to the imagination. Rivulets of sweat ran down his chest. Another stream weaved its way through the coarse hair on his muscled legs while he bounced in place talking to the sweetheart of Daisy Creek.

Jessica preened as usual, running both hands down her hips. Her body language made an otherwise conservative business suit look as sexy as a peek-a-boo teddy. She flipped her fingers through her hair, tossing it back over her shoulder.

"They look pretty friendly, don't you think?" Ruthann asked.

"I'm just hoping she doesn't start humping his leg like a bitch in heat."

"Patsy." Ruthann's eyes were round in horror.

"What? I didn't call her a bitch. At least, not just then."

"Uh huh." Ruthann held two onion rings up to her eyes in imitation of glasses. "I wish I could read lips. I'd sure like to know what they're talking about."

Patsy had wondered the same thing, not that it was any of her business. Will could do what he wanted. That one little kiss by the river didn't mean anything, and neither did the subtle touches during the coon hunt, not to Will. From her experience, those things were only important to women, not men, and not to Patsy. She was too smart for that. She had lived and learned. She just wished Will would pick somebody besides Jessica.

A polo-shirted server bebopped up to the pair, carrying a tray with a round plastic bowl and a drink. Jessica reached in her car for her wallet, paid the girl, and snatched a paper napkin off the tray. Turning back to Will, she delicately blotted his face with the napkin. Will made some kind of reply that Patsy assumed was something along the lines of "Thanks, want to come over to my place and really work up a sweat?" and jogged off. Jessica folded the sweaty napkin lengthwise and used it to wave at Ruthann and Patsy.

Patsy looked down to see Pugnacious swallow the last bit of her chili dog. Damn. Her life sucked. On the bright side, maybe Jessica would choke on a lettuce leaf.

***

Geez, it was hot. Will placed his palms on the rough bricks of the Quick Trip building and extended his leg behind him. He was out of shape. It had been at least a month since he'd really worked out. Today's run was going to do him in. He should have asked Jessica for a ride home, but he couldn't. To be perfectly honest, she was a little scary.

He'd stopped at Sonic intending to get a cup of ice, but Jessica had popped out of her heart-on-wheels and blocked his path. In their five-minute conversation, she'd licked her lips more than a third-rate porn star in a sixty-minute flick. And the bit with the napkin. It was almost like she was performing for someone. He'd had just one thought—escape.

He dug into his pocket for the money he stashed there earlier. If he was going to have to jog back to his house, he definitely needed some water.

A few minutes later, he reluctantly left the air-conditioned comfort of the Quick Trip and walked back into the heat. It was like hitting a wall. As people kept saying, it wasn't the heat, it was the humidity. Like breathing underwater.

He really should have asked Jessica for a ride. He'd be leaning against that cool white upholstery right now, air conditioning blowing through his hair and Jessica sucking the soul from his body.

He could walk.

A familiar bark alerted him before twenty pounds of wriggling dog wove around his feet and sent him plunging to the pavement.

"Pugnacious, get back in the Jeep." A windblown Patsy jogged from the gas pump toward Will. "Are you okay?" She bent over him. The sun bled through her short hair like some kind of new-age aura, or a scene from an old painting of an angel.

Patsy the angel; that was an image he hadn't considered before.

He opened his mouth to assure her he was fine, but his words were blocked by a flat, snorting nose. He snapped his mouth shut. When Pugnacious continued her assault, he clamped both eyes closed too.

"Oh, Will. I didn't realize it was you." Was that concern in Patsy's voice?

He risked squeezing one eye open to peer up at her. Pugnacious promptly shoved her nose at the exposed iris.

"Pugnacious. Get off him." Patsy grabbed the pug's collar and tugged her off his face. "Are you okay? I don't know what comes over her sometimes. She has the manners of a . . ."

"Dog?" Will stood up.

"Yeah, I guess." Patsy's top was of some kind of filmy material, and cutoff jeans hitched up above her thighs. Not an angel, not unless she was sent to tempt him. Maybe a fairy, come to play a trick on him, to lure him away from his path and into trouble.

She bent over to pick up Pugnacious. The sun played the same trick through her shirt that it had with her hair, and her shorts lodged a little higher on her legs. Will's mouth went dry. He took a swig from the water bottle. Trickster fairy or rewarding angel, she was definitely temptation.

Tucked into Patsy's arms, the pug seemed content to just grin at him. "Anyway, I'm sorry. Are you sure you're okay?" Patsy asked.

Was he okay? He was feeling a little lightheaded and confused. Probably dehydrated, he slammed down the last of his water. It would be a long run home, and it was hot, not to mention humid. Plus, Patsy did look very contrite and he did need to talk to her.

"I'm sure I'll be fine. Let me just . . ." He took a step

and quickly hopped back in what, he hoped, appeared to be pain.

"Did you twist your ankle? Pugnacious, look what you did." Patsy gave the little dog a slight shake. The pug snorted at him with a complete lack of repentance.

"It's no big deal, really. I'll just walk it off." Will took another half step before hopping again. Yeah, there was a twinge.

"At least let me give you a ride home." Patsy gestured toward her Jeep, which sat at a gas pump. "I just have to pay for my fill-up. Here." She shoved the snorting, grinning pug into his arms.

Giving the obnoxious little devil a chuck under her chin, he sauntered over to Patsy's Jeep.

"Hurt yourself bad?" Ruthann leaned out the passenger door.

Shamefaced, he replied, "I told Patsy I'd be fine." He released Pugnacious, who squirmed into the backseat.

"I can see that." Ruthann grinned. "Don't worry about me. My lips are sealed. It's about time somebody was a step ahead of my best friend." Her gaze flitted to his shorts and back up to his face. "My guess is, you'll do just fine."

Will studied his shoe. Now Ruthann had the wrong idea. He hadn't faked an injury because he wanted time alone with Patsy—except to discuss her father, that is. Mainly, he just needed a ride home. He couldn't be jogging down the highway dehydrated and dizzy. It was just common sense, and it was easier to let Patsy believe Pugnacious hurt his leg than admit he was out of shape.

Not that there was any reason to be ashamed; in this heat, only a fool would try to keep running. Anyway, the point was, no matter how physically desirable he found her, Patsy just offered a convenient opportunity to get a ride home, nothing more. He didn't need complications right now and the more he saw of Patsy, the more complicated she got.

"Hop in. I'll ride in back. You won't even know I'm

here." Ruthann flipped the passenger seat up and crawled in next to Pugnacious.

"You don't mind if we drop Will off, do you?" Patsy asked Ruthann when she returned from paying.

"Actually, I was thinking I need to get home. Why don't you drop me off at my house first?"

Patsy attempted to catch Ruthann's gaze in the rearview mirror, but her friend was engrossed in something out the window.

"You didn't want to go by and see the new stuff Mom said they got in at the shop?" Patsy glanced at Will, who seemed to be ignoring their conversation. He twisted the lid off his water bottle and shook the few remaining drops onto his bare chest. Desperate, she turned a pleading glance to her friend.

Still staring out the window, Ruthann shook her head. "I need to lose a few pounds before I buy anything new. Besides, it's too hot to leave Pugnacious in the car while we shop, and you know that ole biddy Irene won't let us bring her in." Ruthann met Patsy's gaze briefly in the mirror. "We'll do it later. Just drop me off."

Patsy did not want to be alone with Will. She had no idea why she even offered to give him a ride home—the curse of being raised with good manners. He rubbed one of the water drops into his skin with the pad of his finger. Patsy swallowed hard. She knew she shouldn't get involved with him, but with his six-foot perspiration-soaked frame pressed into the seat next to her, it was difficult to remember why.

Even with the distance enforced by bucket seats, the heat of his body filled the space between them. It was like he had some kind of reverse force field that was sucking her toward him. Shifting gears, she leaned in his direction. Even sweaty, he smelled good. Better than good.

She glanced back at Ruthann, who steadfastly kept her

gaze focused out the window. You'd think she'd never seen the backstreets of Daisy Creek before.

They pulled in front of the small, white frame house Ruthann shared with her mother. Will hopped out and graciously helped Ruthann from the back. Patsy attempted to ignore the view of his very masculine back.

"Call me." Ruthann flashed them a grin before disappearing inside her house.

Patsy was alone with Will. She could handle it. Concentrate on all his shortcomings: spoiled, juvenile delinquent, stubborn, arrogant, eating casseroles with Jessica. She focused on the last one. If there was one thing Patsy wouldn't do, it was share with Jessica.

Stronger, she turned to face him. His chest glistened with sweat, making his muscles all the more obvious, like a bodybuilder oiled up to be judged.

"You should wear a shirt," she blurted out.

"Too hot. Besides, I always run without a shirt. I like the feel of the sun and wind on my skin." He smiled, creating the tiny crinkles she'd noticed that first time at Gordie's to form around his eyes. "It feels natural, more basic or something."

Yeah, basic. Nothing wrong with the basics. "You hot?" she asked. "You look hot."

He grinned. "Thanks."

She scowled at the steering wheel.

"You ever run?" he asked. "You look like you exercise."

Glad of the topic change, she answered, "Not unless something's chasing me."

"That happen often?"

"What?" This conversation was impossible to follow.

"Something chasing you. Does that happen often? You look like the type that might get chased."

What was that supposed to mean? She glanced at him; the heat in his eyes said more than his words. She flushed in response.

"Are you hot?" he asked. "You look hot."

Smart-ass. She was feeling a little hot and uncomfortable. Ignoring his question, she flipped the air conditioning on high. It chugged out warm air. Damn it, she'd meant to get that fixed. Frustrated, she twisted the knob to high; warm air had to be better than no air. Glancing at him, she could see the hundred-degree air flowing from the vents was doing nothing to dry off his chest.

"You should wear a shirt."

"You already mentioned that. Mind if I use this?" He picked a Mickey Mouse bandanna that sometimes adorned Pugnacious' neck off the floor.

"Help yourself."

"Thanks." He balled the blue cloth into his hand and rubbed the glisten of sweat off his chest in slow, mesmerizing circles.

Damn it all to Disney and back.

Chapter Ten

"So, how's the web work going?"

Web work? What web work? Patsy floundered, unable to mentally lock onto anything except the image of that blue cloth caressing that firm, solid chest. She pulled into the gravel drive that ran next to his house and gripped the steering wheel until her knuckles turned white. Deep breath. Oh yeah, web job, the mines.

"Fine." Back in control, she turned in her seat to face him. A swirl of chest hair drew her gaze. Fascinating, it was like one of those weird pictures by that Escher guy. The combination of sweat and the circular motion of the bandanna must have created it. Somebody should photograph it, a close-up of those coarse dark hairs twirled in a captivating design over that broad expanse of chest. They could sell it and make millions.

"Patsy?"

"Hmm?"

"You want to come in?" Will opened his car door and flung one leg out onto the drive.

"Oh, no." She fidgeted with her rabbit's-foot key ring that hung from the ignition. It was an ugly thing. Dwayne had given it to her for her sixteenth birthday. A gift from her brother was such an unlikely occurrence, she'd been sure it would bring her luck. She was still waiting. Looking back at Will, she replied, "Granny will be looking for me."

"Doesn't she think you're shopping with Ruthann?"

Damn, he was paying attention. If dishonesty doesn't work, try evasion. "Besides, you're probably still getting settled. I don't want to impose."

"No imposition. I'd like to talk to you about something." He stepped out of the Jeep and stood with the door open.

She raised an eyebrow.

Looking down at a patch of dirt that showed through the gravel, he continued, "Your aunt said you know a lot about local history—as much as the woman who runs the county museum. I want to restore things as much as I can." He peered up at her.

Et tu, Aunt Tilde? She knew Granny and Mom had been beating the Patsy-is-wonderful drum at the barbecue, but she hadn't realized Tilde had picked up the sticks too. Still, Will wanted her opinion? That didn't seem likely. She shot him another disbelieving look.

He took a deep breath. "Okay, I have a favor to ask."

Mr. I-can-do-it-myself wanted a favor? Now that was interesting. Patsy glanced from his sheepish expression to the backseat. Pugnacious was probably roasting back there. Except she wasn't.

The dog had escaped from the car and now sat on the deep wraparound porch of Will's house, her back pressed against the wooden screen door, tongue lolling.

Patsy was tired of fighting with the pug and losing. She had never much enjoyed losing and wasn't in the mood for it today. Better to give in gracefully, pretend it was her idea all along. She shoved the rabbit's foot into her pocket and followed Will up the steps. Pugnacious greeted them by raising her hind foot to scratch behind her ear.

"Let me get the key." Will bent down and stuck his finger in his shoe.

Patsy did her best not to notice how short his shorts were or how taut his hamstrings. She did her best, but when the slinky material of his shorts pulled tightly across his butt, she gave up. It wasn't her day for winning battles. Why fight? It was an awfully nice butt, probably his best feature, and the rest of him wasn't exactly hurting.

"After you." Will pushed open the heavy oak entrance door.

Pugnacious trotted in. With a sigh, Patsy followed.

The massive curved staircase greeted her. The carved oak newel post was topped by an ornate art glass lamp with blue and white stripes. She'd noticed it when she stopped by with Mrs. Jensen, but it hadn't seemed like the time to quiz Will on his home's decor.

"Is this original?" Patsy tapped the lamp with her fingernail.

"Yeah, see, it's actually set into the post." Will grasped the base and wiggled it, showing it was firmly affixed.

"It's beautiful." Patsy motioned to include the rest of the room. "I'd never been in here before you moved in." Will didn't comment so she continued, "I'd always wanted to see it. When I was little, I used to dream of living in a house like this. Seemed like in all the books I read, the girl lived in a grand old Victorian."

Will grinned. "It is pretty great, isn't it?"

He looked so happy, it made Patsy uncomfortable. It was too personal. Like she was trapped in an elevator with a stranger and didn't know where to look. She ran her hand down the newel post, tracing the daisies carved on its sides with her finger.

"I love old things," she said. The confession surprised her. She'd always thought of herself as neutral when her parents argued over their polar opposite design styles, but suddenly she realized it was true. She did love old things. They were comforting somehow.

"Me too." Will placed his hand on the other side of the post. "There's something about knowing something has history. It gives things a richness new things don't have. Like maybe whoever owned it before left a little piece of themselves—some kind of energy—behind."

Surprised, Patsy looked up at him.

He smiled like he was embarrassed. "You probably think that sounds strange."

Patsy shook her head. "No, I just never heard anyone say it like that before. Even Dad and Aunt Tilde, for all that they love antiques, I don't think they could tell you why." She walked toward a hall that opened off the foyer.

"That's the turret," he called after her.

"I thought so." Patsy spun in a small circle. A turret was magical. Anything was possible in such a space. She couldn't imagine why they went out of style.

Will followed behind her, filling the room. She pressed her hands against the wainscoting. "What's this? Leather?"

He skimmed the pads of his fingers over the tooled surface. "Strange, isn't it? Why all the trouble for such a small area?"

She leaned against the wall and stared upward at the beaded ceiling. "I don't know. If I had a turret, it's where I'd spend all my time."

He stepped toward her. "Like a princess waiting for her knight?"

"I gave up on fairy tales a long time ago."

"You're not old enough for it to have been that long ago." He placed a hand on each side of her head and looked down at her. "Maybe you just need a reminder."

A vein at the base of her neck began to pulse. "A reminder of what? Something that was never real to begin with?"

Will stroked her cheek with the back of his fingers. "How do you know if something is real or not, if you don't give it a chance?"

His gaze was intense. Patsy knew he was going to kiss her, knew she should stop him. She could feel him moving closer, slowly. His breath warmed her cheek. She inhaled. She loved his scent. His bare chest made contact with her breasts through the thin material of her shirt. He kept his eyes open, staring into hers until he slanted his face and pressed his lips against her mouth.

The kiss was slow, thorough, and torturous, too slow. He wasn't close enough. Patsy wanted more. She opened her mouth and his tongue swooped inside. Hers greeted him. As their tongues battled for dominance, she placed her hands on his sides, running them over smooth muscles, reveling in the strength she felt there. Then her thumbs hit the waistband of his shorts.

His hands were still pressed into the wall beside her head, his mouth still covering hers. His kiss was urgent, but controlled, like he was engaged in a calculated campaign to overwhelm her senses, as if expecting surrender. Patsy resisted. She lived for a good battle. This was no different.

She made small circles with her thumbs. Should she? The urge to slip her thumbs under the elastic band was becoming an obsession. Why not? She slipped her nails under the material, played with it for a second. The muscles in his back tensed, but he didn't take his mouth from hers.

The first skirmish was hers. With her thumbs moving downward, Patsy explored the smooth, soft skin hidden by his shorts. Will's stomach muscles twitched as she stroked. She edged lower until she encountered another barrier, the wide, flat elastic band of his underwear. Will stilled. She lightly flicked the band with her thumbnail. Again, should she?

Will moaned and moved his mouth from her lips to her earlobe. Taking the small bit of skin between his teeth, he tugged gently. Loving the sense of power, she caught the elastic on her nail and slowly slid her thumbs between his skin and the final waistband.

The ping of the ancient doorbell echoed through the house. Patsy jerked her thumbs out of Will's shorts and her hands away from his body. Will leaned into her further, resting his head on the top of hers. The sound of their breathing seemed to echo through the turret.

"Maybe they'll go away." His voice was thick, his words slow, murmured through heavy breaths. Patsy held hers. He didn't know this town like she did; whoever was on the other side of that door had already taken note of her car and probably how long she'd been inside. They would be all a-tingle with anticipation, hoping to catch her in the middle of something gossip-worthy, and just about anything was gossip-worthy in Daisy Creek.

"Patsalee? You in there?"

Patsy let out her breath. Aunt Tilde had come to call. At least this interloper was friendly, but her family sure had a talent for timing.

Groaning, Will pushed away from the wall. Patsy cowered in embarrassment. What was she doing? If Aunt Tilde had been a few minutes later, there was no telling in what state she would have found them. Second time in a week, she was almost caught with her pants down— literally. Patsy groaned. She was sure her aunt would read the guilt emblazoned across Patsy's face.

Will leaned in and whispered, "She's still on the porch. It's not too late to ignore her."

Patsy's only answer was to turn away and study the wainscoting. Cool air replaced his body, as Will strode from the room.

"Where's Patsalee? I saw her car in the drive. I was stopping by anyway." Patsy caught a flash of cerise and lime green as her aunt swirled into the house. "Irv said you were without locomotion, and I found something at a sale in Peabody I thought you'd want to see," Tilde continued.

"What's that you're wearing, son? That's not enough cloth to steep tea in."

Patsy knocked her head silently against the wall.

"I left my surprise out in the van. You scurry on out there and lug it in, but put a shirt on first. The neighbors'll think we're up to no good for sure, they see you in nothing but that scrap of cloth."

Footsteps sounded up the stairs and back down again, followed by the screen door creaking. Patsy peered out one of the windows that circled the turret. Will, dressed in jeans and a polo shirt, strode to Tilde's full-size van, slid open the side door, and began tugging on something in the back.

"He sure is a fine-looking boy."

Patsy jumped.

"Why you hiding out in here, kid?" Tilde arched one penciled-in eyebrow.

"I'm not hiding." Patsy pressed herself against the wainscoting. The feel of tooled leather brought memories of Will's lips on hers flying back. She flushed.

"You know a body might think you were up to no good, the way you're lurking in here." Tilde rubbed the side of her mouth with one finger. "And, 'course it doesn't help matters any that he wasn't wearing enough cloth to wad a rifle." She stepped farther into the room. "But now, I don't see any signs that you're missing any clothes. So I guess it's okay." She turned to leave.

Her aunt was leaving after just a few remarks. Patsy almost crumpled to the floor in relief.

Tilde turned back. "Don't get me wrong, kid. I've got no problem with a little afternoon delight. I just don't want to see you get yourself in a fix. You get me?" She raised both brows.

The birds and the bees from Tilde; could her day get any worse? Patsy swallowed hard and nodded. She should have known Tilde wouldn't leave that easily.

"I'm more modern than your mama. As long as everybody involved is in agreement and taken the proper preparations, I don't see any harm in it." She cackled. "And done right, it can be downright healthy."

Would this never end? Patsy willed the floor to open up.

"But don't you be forgetting those preparations, you hear?"

Staring at the shells on her silver sandals, Patsy gave her head a slight nod.

"Well, you have fun then, but if you need any help figuring out what's what and how it fits together, you give me a holler." Grinning, Tilde tromped out of the room.

If God was merciful, he would strike Patsy dead right now. Patsy waited, but as she suspected, she was still among the living and worse, Aunt Tilde and Will.

"Patsalee, get out here and see what I brought the boy."

Patsy trudged out of the turret in time to see Will, his face redder than Tilde's nails, wrestling a washstand in the front door.

With a groan, he set it down on the oak floor.

"So, what do you think?" Tilde beamed at them.

The thing was atrocious. Someone had covered it in at least four coats of pea-green paint. Stripes of chicken poop decorated the top and one door was missing. Maybe Patsy didn't love old things as much as she had thought.

"Now that door is out in the van and all the hardware is in the drawer." Tilde tugged a small drawer open, revealing hinges and a knob inside. "And this top." She knocked on the washstand. "Solid marble. I scratched off a bit of paint, and it's black underneath. I was always partial to black marble. White is so common, don't you think? Pink's nice too, but you just don't see much of that around here."

Someone had painted marble. Could you even paint marble?

"So, what do you think?" Tilde stepped back and beamed at Will. "The old man what sold it said it came from the sale here back in the seventies."

Will squatted down next to the dilapidated piece of furniture. "From here?"

"Yeah, this house. The last of the original family sold everything. If they could unscrew it or yank it out, it got a price tag slapped on it. I can probably help you find a lot of Barnett pieces, if you're interested."

"Like a picker?" Will looked up at Tilde.

"Sure, for say, twenty percent?"

Will hesitated for a minute, staring at the broken-down mess on his foyer floor. Looking back at Tilde, he said, "Sounds fair. What do I owe you for this? It's a great piece."

Good Lord, Aunt Tilde was going to work for Will. And he wanted the green-paint-covered, poop-encrusted washstand. How could he see anything worth keeping under all that?

Patsy sat on the bottom step, dumbfounded by the unlikely pair her aunt and Will made. She loved her aunt, but the woman was as tacky as a tube top at a wedding, and Will, he looked so cool and put together. Patsy guessed his shirt alone cost more than her aunt's entire outfit, hair dye and makeup included.

"So, kid, you hanging around here?" Tilde folded the bills Will had handed her and was shoving them into her leopard print handbag. Thank God she didn't shove them in her bra.

Ralph wandered into the room, Pugnacious on his tail. The pug trotted to the washstand and began sniffing the green base.

"I still haven't given you the grand tour." Will picked her dog up.

"Grand tour, hm?" Tilde's eyes sparkled. "That sounds like something that needs preparing for, don't you think, kid?"

Patsy leapt from the step and pulled Pugnacious from Will's arms. "I better get going. Maybe some other time."

"I'll be calling you, son. I got an idea where I can get that sideboard I told you about." Tilde stepped onto the front porch. Patsy followed.

Will stopped in the doorway. "Wait, Patsy, there was still the . . ."

Oh yeah, the favor. Patsy paused.

"Save something for another day, son. She saw your tower. That's probably as much as she can handle in one visit." Tilde cackled as she grabbed Patsy's arm and led her to the Jeep.

Hell. Will rested his forehead against the closed door. What happened in the turret?

Not enough, his libido yelled.

If Patsy's aunt hadn't rung the bell, what else might have happened?

Something dangerous. Something good.

He was walking in risky territory. He knew it, but couldn't stop himself. No matter how much Patsy did to complicate his life, he found himself drawn to her. He'd lied about his reason for inviting her inside—both to her and himself. He didn't seek her out for advice. He sought her out just to see her, be with her, touch her. And he couldn't get enough of the touching part, wished she was still there, pressed against the leather wainscoting, arms and legs wrapped around him.

He smacked his head against the wood. This was getting him nowhere. He should keep away from Patsy. She was a definite threat to his plans.

Come to think of it, her entire family was, and now he was entangled with Tilde too. He was either a masochist or a complete idiot. He couldn't decide which he preferred.

He walked to the washstand and flicked a piece of dried green paint off with his thumbnail. Maybe he was a bit of both.

Trying to forget Patsy, he focused on the project. It looked bad, but they made paint stripper. That should do the trick. Just pour it on and watch the green glop run off. Then he'd have a nice piece for his bedroom. He could do that.

A quick trip to BiggeeMart and he'd get to work, both on the washstand and on pushing thoughts of Patsy out of his brain. He walked to the kitchen to retrieve his keys. Seeing the empty peg by the back door, he remembered—no car.

Hell. He did need Patsy's help with her father.

There was no way around it. He'd have to search her out.

It had been two days since the embarrassing scene with Aunt Tilde and Will. Patsy had kept busy working on the web site for Sunrise. She enjoyed the process. It wasn't as relaxing as constructing a basket, but it still allowed her to be creative. She concentrated on the overall look and function of the site and tried to ignore the content. Glenn e-mailed her text files of what Patsy couldn't help but think of as propaganda. She read as little of them as possible, just inserting html code where needed.

Tomorrow she and Glenn were scheduled to travel to Sauk City. She wasn't looking forward to conning people into supplying her with pictures and quotes that supported the mines, so she blocked it from her mind as much as possible. She had other things to think about anyway, like her promise to Ruthann.

Patsy had pinned Dwayne down at lunch the day before, trying to pump him for information on what Randy's problem was, but Dwayne had been as close-mouthed as an atheist at communion. Not that it mattered. Patsy knew what the problem was. What she didn't know was how to get Randy to stand up to his mother. But, Dwayne had agreed to bring Randy to Gordie's tonight. It wasn't the best place to matchmake, but it was about all Daisy Creek had to offer, and if all else failed, at least they served beer. If she had to, she'd get Randy good and liquored up. At the very least, he'd be more willing to admit why he was avoiding Ruthann.

Patsy had been doing a little avoiding of her own. Will had called four times yesterday and three today. Granny shook her head and mumbled as she relayed each message, but hadn't offered her opinion—yet. Patsy was sure Tilde had filled Granny in on the scene at Will's house.

The whole thing was embarrassing enough without her entire family discussing her sex (or lack of) life. The worst of it was they thought she should jump Will's bones and worry about the consequences later. But Patsy couldn't do that. Sex wasn't something she took lightly, and after seeing him at his house, listening to him talk, Patsy had been forced to admit there was something special about Will. If she committed to him sexually, she was afraid she wouldn't be able to merrily walk away when the time came to leave Daisy Creek. Now, thanks to Glenn, she was closer to realizing that dream than ever before. She couldn't let a rampant sex drive get in her way.

A knock on the door signaled Ruthann's arrival. Granny looked up from the TV, where a wrestler dressed like a rapper yelled insults at the crowd. Patsy waved at her to stay seated, gave Pugnacious a kiss, and walked out into the thick night air.

"You ready?" Ruthann tugged on her denim miniskirt.

Patsy stopped for a minute, startled by Ruthann's hair. "What happened to you?"

"Momma helped me highlight my hair. You like it?"

Patsy wondered if Ruthann's mother was in league with Randy's to keep the two apart. She backed Ruthann up under the porch light. Ruthann's normally mousey hair had multiple wide stripes running through it. The overall effect wouldn't have been horrible if the stripes hadn't been as brassy as a new doorknob.

"Momma said I needed more style, something to make me stand out from the crowd."

"Well, it does that."

"She loaned me her shoes too." Ruthann twisted her foot, revealing four-inch mules with zebra-striped fur trim.

Good Lord, Ruthann was turning into Tilde.

"Can you even walk in those things?"

"Sure." Ruthann twirled on one foot and promptly fell off the porch into the wisteria bush.

Patsy hoped they were having a special on beer tonight. If Randy didn't need liquoring up, she would.

Chapter Eleven

Patsy got Ruthann into the roadhouse without either of them breaking a leg. She pushed her friend into a chair and ordered her to stay put. "I'll get us some drinks."

The line at the bar was short. Patsy paid for their drinks and turned to head back to the table. Ruthann was no longer alone. Will sat next to her, facing Patsy. Damn it all. Who'd have thought he'd be at the roadhouse on a Tuesday night? Patsy stopped twenty feet from them, condensation from the cold bottles chilling her hands. He and Ruthann seemed engrossed in conversation. He was dressed casually, in a Blues jersey and navy shorts. The hockey shirt emphasized the broadness of his shoulders and seemed to fit the clean-cut, bad-boy image he pulled off so well. Looking up, Ruthann flashed her a grin. Patsy took a long pull from her Bud Light and returned to the table.

"Here's your drink." She handed Ruthann her wine cooler and pretended she didn't notice the 190 pounds of enticement sitting next to her.

"Will said he gave you a tour of his house the other day," Ruthann commented. "But that your Aunt Tilde interrupted you."

Patsy studied the pattern of gouges and scars that adorned the wooden tabletop.

"He said you particularly enjoyed the turret." Ruthann continued.

Patsy flicked her gaze to Will. He was the picture

of innocence. Ruthann, oblivious to the undercurrents surging from her friend, kept talking.

"Something about the wainscoting. What did you say it was, leather?" She angled her head at Will. With a mild tilt to his lips, he nodded a reply. Ruthann glanced at Patsy before continuing, "He said you got really excited about the leather wainscoting."

Patsy slid her beer back and forth with short, quick movements. Will's innocent smile might fool Ruthann, but not Patsy. She knew a smirk when she saw one. It wasn't like he was Mister "in control" in that turret either.

Sure, Patsy got a little forward, what with the underwear thing, but she didn't remember him running away; quite the opposite, really. Now he sat there all smug, like he had a secret on her. Damn, he was annoying.

Ruthann glanced from Patsy's twitching bottle and narrowed eyes to Will's smart-aleck smile with alarm and placed her hand on Patsy's. "You need to pee? I think I need to pee."

Patsy stared at her, dumbfounded. Where did that come from? "Well, then pee. You don't need me helping you."

Ruthann glanced nervously at Patsy's beer and stood up. "As long as I'm up, let me get the next round." She grabbed the bottle and scurried away from the table.

"Hey, I wasn't finished with that," Patsy yelled after her.

Will slid into the seat next to Patsy. "What did you do to her?"

"Me? You're the one being all coy and smart-assy."

"Smart-assy?" He looked offended.

Let him pretend he didn't know what she was talking about. "Maybe she was protecting you." Someone fired up the jukebox. As the sultry strains of a slow song wafted over them, Patsy signaled the waitress for another beer.

"What game were you playing anyway?" Patsy asked,

resisting the urge to sway along with the music. Some silly song about feeling love in your toes; Ruthann probably picked it.

"No game. I don't play games, and I didn't realize I needed protecting." He edged his chair closer, pressing his bare knee against hers. Two square inches of contact had never felt so intimate. Patsy suppressed a shiver and the urge to run her hand up his thigh.

The voice from the jukebox advised she should let love show.

Let it show. There was an idea, she could just trail her fingers up that muscular thigh . . . Patsy shook her head. Where was Ruthann with her beer?

Let it show. How insane. There needed to be less showing around here, not more. For example, bare knees; men should wear jeans, not leave all that skin exposed, letting it press up against hers, all warm and rough and masculine.

It was lewd. That's what it was. Patsy needed to take a stand for decency. She attempted to pull her leg away, but her skin seemed to have formed some kind of bond with Will's. She should just stand up, or maybe shove Will off his chair onto the floor.

She should, but she didn't. She just sat there trapped by the heat surging between them and the seductive music wrapping them together.

Finally, the music faded into silence. Patsy exhaled loudly, releasing a breath she hadn't realized she was holding.

Thank God that song was over. Sweet and sentimental. Save it for the gullible.

Ready to set Will straight on a few boundaries, namely the one that kept his bare skin away from hers, Patsy opened her mouth.

"Howdy, Sis." Dwayne, Randy, and, to Patsy's further annoyance, Jessica pulled up chairs and sat down.

Just when she was getting ready to show Will he couldn't play cute with her.

"We're not interrupting nothing, are we?" Dwayne grinned.

"No," Patsy grumbled. She edged away from Will until a nice solid inch of air separated their knees. Not as good as lighting into him, but he got the message.

"Nothing at all." Will slid his chair over. Now, his entire leg, from knee to thigh, pressed against Patsy's. "That give you enough room?"

Patsy fumed. He might as well be sitting in her seat. She slid her hands under the edge of her chair to scoot it away from Will, and his hand dropped on her thigh.

Patsy froze.

"Oh, I don't need much room. I'll just squeeze in right here." Jessica turned sideways, pressing her chest Will's direction and pushed her way into the seat next to him. "You give any more thought to getting office space downtown? I'd just love to help you out." The bimbo ran her fingers down the neckline of her low-cut top, stopping at the swell of her breast.

She'd like to help him out all right, right out of his pants. Patsy snorted. Jessica had the gall to look annoyed.

"I'm working on something, but I don't need space right now. Maybe in the next month or so and for sure by spring." Will made little circles with the pads of his fingers on the inside of Patsy's thigh. "Did you have something special in mind?" Patsy clamped her legs together, trapping his hand. He responded by squeezing and massaging the soft flesh of her inner thigh.

Jessica wet her lips. "I'm sure I can come up with something very special. You just let me know when you're ready."

Distracted by the tramp's obvious invitation, Patsy relaxed her legs. She started to comment on what Jessica's specialty was, but Will's hand traveling farther up her thigh turned her thoughts elsewhere.

Dwayne raised his eyebrows at her from across the table. "You got something on your mind, Patsalee? You're wiggling like there's earthworms in your drawers."

"She's a little fidgety tonight, isn't she?" Will looked at Patsy with concern as his fingers inched higher.

Smart-ass. Correction, forward smart-ass. "I'm fine." Desperate to end the contact before she lost all control, she plucked Will's roaming hand off her leg and deposited it into his lap. "I was just hoping we could hear more about the special services Jessica has to offer." She turned a saccharine smile on her rival.

"We were talking about real estate," Jessica retorted. "Not that I couldn't be talked into a few special services on the side." She winked at Will.

Will, Patsy noticed, hadn't tried to put his hand back on Patsy's thigh, and now he was laughing with Jessica. Patsy fought the urge to shove her head under the table to see just what territory his hands were exploring now.

"What's everybody laughing at?" Ruthann wobbled up to the table. She'd applied a fresh coat of blinding pink lipstick.

At least it took attention away from her hair. "Where's my beer?" Patsy asked. Stuck at a table with Jessica and Will, and no drink.

"Oh, I forgot. Besides, beer's fattening. You should try something lighter." Ruthann held out a glass of clear liquid and ice cubes.

"What's that?" Patsy asked.

"Citron martini on the rocks. I read in *Cosmo* it's what all the stars of *Sex and the City* drink in real life."

"That show's not even on anymore," Patsy replied. Will picked up his drink with his left hand, and replaced his right on Patsy's thigh. Something inside her unclenched.

"I got the first three seasons on DVD." Ruthann fished the lemon out of her drink. "I thought I'd try something new."

Patsy was trying something new too, melting into the sensation of strong fingers caressing her bare skin. She barely noticed the conversation going on around her.

Ruthann squeezed in next to Randy. "Hey, Randy. I saw your momma and Luke at church on Sunday. Did she tell you I said hi?" Ruthann pulled a strand of hair through her fingers.

Randy studied the same pattern of scars and gouges Patsy had earlier. "No, she didn't mention it."

Will removed his hand to wave at the waitress for another beer and Patsy returned to her senses. She was losing it. She had to pay attention, both to what was going on with Ruthann and Randy and to what was happening with her. She picked up her purse and wedged it between herself and Will.

Ruthann was floundering. "Did you hear the BiggeeMart's having a coloring contest for Daisy Daze? First prize is a year's supply of Twinkies and juice boxes." She gave an attempt at eyelash fluttering. "I can get Luke a coloring page, if you like."

"That'd be nice," Randy mumbled.

This was painful. Patsy had to so something. Dancing was the ticket, but nothing slow. No more love songs. "Dwayne, put some money in the jukebox. Play something peppy," Patsy emphasized the last.

"Why should I . . ." Patsy's intense look cut her brother off short.

"Fine," he grumbled and meandered away.

Lynyrd Skynyrd began asking for "three steps, Mister." You could always count on Dwayne to avoid the sweet and sentimental.

"Ruthann, you love this song, don't you?" Patsy prompted. She felt her purse bump against her leg. Thank God she brought a big one. It'd be hard for Mr. Handsy to get past that subtly.

Ruthann studied her split ends.

"And this is a great song to dance to. It'd be a shame to waste it."

Ruthann just blinked back at her.

"I'd love to dance." Jessica grazed Will's arm with her fingertips.

Patsy frowned at Jessica while she kicked Ruthann under the table.

"Oh, me too." Ruthann exclaimed.

"So, Will, what do you say? How about a twirl around the dance floor? I'll show you some new moves." Jessica didn't even bother to hide the double entendre. She walked her fingers up his arm until her hand cupped his shoulder.

Patsy considered picking up her purse and flinging it across the table. She couldn't decide who was annoying her most: Jessica for being Jessica, Ruthann for doing nothing more enticing than chewing on a lemon rind, Randy for being stubborn and difficult, or Will for . . . well, she wasn't sure what was going on with Will, but she was damn sure annoyed.

"Come on, girl, let's dance." Dwayne solved one of her problems by grabbing Jessica's hand and dragging her away from the table. Patsy allowed herself a small victory grin before returning to her other concerns.

Her purse seemed to be slipping toward the floor. Time to give up on being subtle. "Randy, dance with Ruthann."

He started to object, but Patsy stared him down. "Now."

Her purse plopped onto the dirty floor.

"Things not going as planned?" Will asked as the rest of the table left.

His hand was back on her knee. How could he act so casual when he was turning her insides to pudding? "When do they lately?" she asked.

"Good question." The expression in his eyes was distant for a minute. "Maybe we should plan less." His fingers started the swirl thing again. Patsy really liked the swirl thing; 'course, that massage thing wasn't bad either.

Snap out of it. He was playing with her. She should act just like him, like this intimate contact had no effect on her.

She plastered a disinterested look on her face. "You won't get anywhere without planning, except right back where you started." Patsy set the *Sex and the City* drink on a Bevnap. "Ruthann asked me to help her with Randy. I sure wouldn't be matchmaking if she hadn't."

Will raised an eyebrow. "Hmmm, so you don't approve of her choice."

"I didn't say that."

"Some things don't have to be said." His hand went into massage mode.

Yeah, that was her favorite. Her head started to loll backward.

She jerked it upright and smacked the bottom of the glass against the table, burying the remains of the lemon under a pile of ice. "You never told me what the favor was you needed."

His hand stilled. "Your father won't let me replace his Crown Vic."

Patsy couldn't hide her confusion. "Dwayne said you were paying for the repairs."

"The repairs, yes, but I want to get him a new one."

She deserted the Citron. "A new one? As in a new Crown Victoria? Are you crazy? According to Randy, it was just some hoses and new side panels."

Will's face took on distinct shades of pout. "I shot his car."

Good Lord, talk about male ego. "It's not like he was in it."

"I shot his car."

Did he think she was slow on the uptake? "I was there, remember? So, you shot his car. Believe me, you aren't the first person around here to shoot something they weren't aiming at. If you'd hit the front door, would you have bought him a new house?"

The look on his face said he would.

An exasperated huff escaped her lips. "You are crazy. He doesn't need a new car. The one he has will be fine in about a week. Then you'll pay the bill, get your BMW back, and everything will be back to normal." A thought stopped her. "How are you getting around, anyway?"

"I want you to talk to him." Removing his hand, he folded his arms over his chest.

The man was frustrating. Did he really think he could boss her around? "I am not talking to him."

When he opened his mouth, to argue she guessed, she interrupted. "Money can't replace emotion. You screwed up. You apologize. That's it."

He stared off toward the dance floor.

She tapped him on the arm. "Did you hear me?"

"Money can't replace emotion?" His voice was soft.

"Yeah, you apologize and go on." Why did he look like that? "You never said, what are you using to get around?"

He blinked and turned back to her. "Your aunt's van. She dropped it off yesterday. I tried to talk her out of it, but she was . . . determined."

Patsy grinned. Will in Tilde's rust bucket of a van. She wondered what he liked most, the faux leopard fur on the dash or the pink poodle dangling from the rearview mirror. "I bet you look good in it."

His narrowed gaze warned her it was time for a subject change.

"Why didn't you dance with Jessica?" she asked.

"I'm wounded, remember." He rubbed his calf.

It was her turn to narrow her gaze. "I thought it was your ankle."

He moved his hand down. "It was. Sometimes these things spread."

Dwayne and Jessica returning to the table halted her retort.

"Woo, nothing like a little boot-scootin' boogie to get

Take A Trip Into A Timeless World
of Passion and Adventure with
Kensington Choice Historical Romances!
—Absolutely FREE!

Enjoy the passion and adventure of another time with Kensington Choice Historical Romances. They are the finest novels of their kind, written by today's best-selling romance authors. Each Kensington Choice Historical Romance transports you to distant lands in a bygone age. Experience the adventure and share the delight as proud men and spirited women discover the wonder and passion of true love.

Get 4 FREE Books!

We created our convenient Home Subscription Service so you'll be sure to have the hottest new romances delivered each month right to your doorstep—usually before they are available in book stores. Just to show you how convenient the Zebra Home Subscription Service is, we would like to send you 4 FREE Kensington Choice Historical Romances. The books are worth up to $24.96, but you only pay $1.99 for shipping and handling. There's no obligation to buy additional books—ever!

Save Up To 30% With Home Delivery!

Accept your FREE books and each month we'll deliver 4 brand new titles as soon as they are published. They'll be yours to examine FREE for 10 days. Then if you decide to keep the books, you'll pay the preferred subscriber's price (up to 30% off the cover price!), plus shipping and handling. Remember, you are under no obligation to buy any of these books at any time! If you are not delighted with them, simply return them and owe nothing. But if you enjoy Kensington Choice Historical Romances as much as we think you will, pay the special preferred subscriber rate and save over $8.00 off the cover price!

We have 4 **FREE BOOKS** for you as your introduction to
KENSINGTON CHOICE!
To get your FREE BOOKS, worth up to $24.96, mail the card below or call TOLL-FREE 1-800-770-1963.
Visit our website at www.kensingtonbooks.com.

Get 4 FREE Kensington Choice Historical Romances!

💙 **YES!** Please send me my 4 FREE KENSINGTON CHOICE HISTORICAL ROMANCES (without obligation to purchase other books). I only pay $1.99 for shipping and handling. Unless you hear from me after I receive my 4 FREE BOOKS, you may send me 4 new novels—as soon as they are published—to preview each month FREE for 10 days. If I am not satisfied, I may return them and owe nothing. Otherwise, I will pay the money-saving preferred subscriber's price (over $8.00 off the cover price), plus shipping and handling. I may return any shipment within 10 days and owe nothing, and I may cancel any time I wish. In any case the 4 FREE books will be mine to keep.

Name_____

Address_____ Apt._____

City_____ State_____ Zip_____

Telephone (____)_____

Signature_____

(If under 18, parent or guardian must sign)

KN0654

PLACE
STAMP
HERE

KENSINGTON CHOICE
Zebra Home Subscription Service, Inc.
P.O. Box 5214
Clifton NJ 07015-5214

your blood pumping. Ain't that right, Jessica?" Dwayne yanked out a chair and plopped down.

Patsy hadn't even noticed the music had changed and Brooks and Dunn now blared out of the jukebox.

"I'm more of a slow dance fan. How about you, Will?" Jessica slipped into the chair next to him.

Patsy's heart constricted.

"To tell the truth, I'm not much of a dancer. Certainly not good enough to keep up with that bunch." Will nodded toward the crowded dance floor where about ten couples twirled and two-stepped in a big circle.

"I could teach you." Jessica drew a little heart on his forearm with a pink-tipped finger.

Patsy wondered if it would be rude to shove Jessica's chair over with a well-placed kick.

"Not tonight. I suffered a little injury earlier this week. Vicious dog attack." He grinned at Patsy.

She rolled her eyes.

"Where's Ruthann and Randy?" Patsy asked.

"At the bar." Dwayne pointed to the front. Randy flipped a couple of bills onto the bar and handed a fresh glass of Citron to Ruthann. She reached for it, teetered on her heels, and fell forward onto Randy's chest. He pushed her back on her feet, but didn't remove his hand from her waist.

Well, at least something was working out. Patsy reached for the beer a waitress had just deposited in front of her. Maybe everything else would too. Sometimes people just needed a little nudge to get going in the right direction. She had probably been too subtle up to now. She wouldn't make that mistake again.

Now, to give Randy no way out, and to save herself by getting while the getting was good. "I think I'll head home."

Will stood up and grabbed Patsy's chair. "I can give you a lift."

Like that was going to happen. He was what she was

fleeing from. "No thanks, I'll take Ruthann's car. I just need to get her keys." Patsy turned on her heel and walked to the front to talk to her friend.

It didn't take a lot of convincing to get Ruthann to hand over her keys. She didn't even question Patsy's request, just dug the keys out of her bag and shoved them into Patsy's hand.

Patsy felt the need to make sure Ruthann understood what was happening. "You know you'll need to get a ride home now, right?"

Ruthann swished the tiny straw supplied with her drink and stared at Randy. "Uh huh."

Patsy snapped her fingers in front of Ruthann's face. "You won't have a car here."

Ruthann sucked the last remnants of alcohol out of the ice. "Whatever."

When Ruthann doddered back to Randy, Patsy followed. "Randy, can you give Ruthann a ride home later?" Maybe she should have said sooner. Patsy didn't like the glassy look in Ruthann's eyes.

Randy looked around like he was about to slip a twenty out of the collection plate and was afraid of getting caught. "Sure, if you need me to."

Ruthann wobbled into him and said, "Can you get me another drink, handsome?"

Oh, good Lord. She'd only had two drinks. Patsy and Ruthann had been known to down a bottle of Boone's Farm each on a good Saturday night in high school and still get up in time for Sunday school at eight. She shouldn't leave her here.

"I'll walk you out." Will stood behind Patsy. His hand pressed possessively against the small of her back. It was a primitive this-one's-with-me move that, despite her efforts to suppress it, sent a small thrill racing through her. She shouldn't let him keep touching her like this. People could see. They would get the wrong idea.

She turned to tell him so, just as the slow song from

earlier started playing again. Hadn't these people heard of variety? She could not bear another chorus of "love is all around," but she also knew walking into a dark parking lot with Will was like diving into fire. There was no way to escape without getting singed.

His hand firmly on Patsy's back, Will struggled to hide his impatience. She was driving him crazy. She avoided his calls, blew holes in his plan to undo the damage he did to her father's car, then, as things seemed to be progressing nicely, got up and announced she was leaving.

The "money isn't emotion" comment was unsettling, but still, he was not finished with their talk, and her evasion of him was more than irritating.

Not returning his calls was bad enough, but walking away as if he were inconsequential was beyond tolerable. She had to feel the attraction between them. He certainly did.

He'd come tonight saying he would only talk with her about her father, but when she stalked over to the table, the attraction hit him like a fast ball to the cranium. After that, he'd tried every trick he could think of to stay in contact with her, even resorting to blatant harassment. It wasn't his usual style, but something about Patsy made him want to toss aside his normal polite demeanor and get busy. Busy with her, on the beer-sticky floor of the roadhouse if necessary.

She had to feel that.

She turned to him, an unflinching look in her eyes. "I can make it. This isn't exactly a crime zone. It's even too early for a good bar fight."

"I'll walk you out." He pressed his fingers decisively against her back and guided her to the door. To his surprise, after one quick backward glance at Ruthann, she let him.

The night air was still humid. They walked down the

wooden ramp that led to the gravel parking lot in silence. When they reached Ruthann's Cavalier, Patsy said, "Thanks. I'll see you 'round."

I'll see you 'round? She wasn't getting away that easily. "I think we should talk."

"We just got done talking." She folded her arms over her chest and stared up at him.

"Have you been avoiding me?"

"I've been busy. It's nothing personal." Her green eyes snapped a challenge.

Whether she knew it or not, she was lying. "Oh, I think it's personal." He reached out and stroked her cheek with the backs of his fingers. Let her see how personal this was.

"You know, you really shouldn't go around touching people like that. Someone might get the wrong idea." Patsy gripped Ruthann's Care Bear key ring.

Prickly. He was getting to her—good. "What idea is that?"

Patsy wrapped her fingers around the pink animal's neck. "You know, that we're . . . involved."

"True, wouldn't want anyone to get the wrong idea." Pushing his hands into his pockets, he rolled back on his heels.

She twisted the head on the cheerful little bear until he was looking at his pink rear end instead of his rainbow-adorned belly. "Be serious."

"I am serious." Will extracted Ruthann's key ring from her grip. "Are you avoiding me for a reason?"

"No." As if unsure what to do with her suddenly empty hands, she tapped them against the side of the car.

"But you are avoiding me." He traced the line of her jaw with the bear's tiny pink ear.

"I . . ." Patsy glanced toward the roadhouse. Was she looking for salvation? If so, none came.

"And if you're avoiding me, there has to be some

reason." Will caressed the Care Bear's head in long, even strokes.

"Quit that." She motioned to the toy.

Ignoring her, he scratched the little creature's stomach.

A loud huff escaped Patsy's lips. "Listen, I don't know what happened the other day."

"You don't?"

She gave him a shut-up look. "But I'm busy. I have a lot going on."

"How about at the river? You know what happened there?" He edged closer to her, breathing in the now familiar floral scent.

"Nothing. Nothing happened." Her back was stiff, her gaze straight ahead.

"You have a funny definition of nothing. You trying to convince me, or yourself?" He stood there waiting for a response, but she refused to weaken.

"So, you're just going to pretend there's nothing here." He motioned between them.

She stared at a spot somewhere over his shoulder.

Fine. He shoved the bear into her hands. "When you're done lying to yourself, you let me know."

He turned away, back toward the bar. Let her avoid him. What did he care? She said she was busy. Well, he was busy too. This attraction was just a passing urge. He needed to keep away from her and concentrate on his own problems. He had plenty to occupy his time and thoughts. He didn't need Patsy Clark getting in his way.

"Will." Patsy took a step after him, placing her hand on his arm. "I . . ."

Dwayne barreled out of Gordie's. "Patsalee, you better get in here. Ruthann's passed out cold on the floor."

Chapter Twelve

Patsy pounded up the ramp toward Dwayne. She could hear Will right behind her.

"What do you mean, she passed out? Where is she?" Patsy asked.

Dwayne held open the door and pointed to where Ruthann lay crumpled on the floor.

"What are you idiots doing? Get her off that filthy floor. Why's she still lying there?" Patsy flew to her friend's side and placed Ruthann's head in her lap. "Where's Randy? I thought she was with him. Get me some ice or water or something."

Dwayne handed her the remains of Ruthann's martini. "Not that, you moron. Clean ice or just cold water."

Brenda pressed a glass of ice into Patsy's hand. "Calm down, honey. It just happened. She'd no more than hit the ground and Dwayne was out the door yelling for you. She'll be fine. Faintin's no big thing." Brenda squeezed Ruthann's limp hand. "You know what she's had to eat today? Sometimes that can be enough to drop a gal, especially after a couple of those." She motioned toward the empty glass Dwayne held. "You don't want to move her anyhow. Here, Dwayne, drag that chair over." She took the chair and placed Ruthann's bare feet on it. "Patsy, you just make sure she's a-breathing and watch out, sometimes a fainter will puke on you."

Patsy leaned down and pressed her ear against Ruthann's mouth. The sound of ragged breathing reassured her. She should never have left Ruthann alone. She knew something wasn't right, but she let herself get sidetracked by Will, by her damn hormones again. He touched her, and she lost all sense of responsibility. If something happened to Ruthann, it would be her fault for letting a man get between her and her good judgment. Well, that was it. It wouldn't happen again.

"What's going on? Why's Ruthann on the floor?" Randy wandered over from the direction of the bathrooms.

"Ruthann's gone and fainted," Dwayne replied. "There ain't nothing you want to tell us now, is there?"

Patsy threw an ice cube at her brother and hit him in the side of the head. "Shut up for once in your life."

"Is she okay? Do we need to call someone?" Randy squatted down next to Ruthann and took the hand Brenda had held earlier.

Ruthann's eyelids fluttered open. "Patsy, what's going on? What am I doing on this floor? If I get something on this skirt, Momma's gonna kill me." She attempted to push herself up.

"Be careful. You probably shouldn't try and get up too quick. Brenda said people who faint sometimes . . ."

Ruthann leaned over and vomited on Randy's Red Wing boots.

". . . puke," Patsy finished. She grabbed a napkin off a nearby table and wiped her friend's mouth.

"I'm sorry," Ruthann stuttered as tears welled up in her eyes.

"Don't worry about that. Randy's not afraid of a little vomit." Patsy helped Ruthann to her feet and gave her the water to sip. "Damn it all, Ruthann, what did you eat today?"

"Nothing, I swear. I told you I was dieting. I had a cup of yogurt for lunch, some diet pills Momma had, from last winter when she was trying to lose weight before her high school reunion, and then the martinis. Nothing bad, I swear."

Patsy rubbed Ruthann on the shoulder. If Ruthann wasn't already so pathetic, Patsy would have lit into her. Diet pills? Knowing Ruthann's momma, there was no telling what was in them or where she got them. And eating nothing but a carton of yogurt all day? Then downing at least two martinis? What was going on in that girl's head? Patsy ran her hand through her hair and said, "Come on. I'm taking you home."

"But what about Randy?"

"He and Dwayne can clean up the puke. Trust me. It won't be the first time." Hugging her friend, she led her to the door.

Will stood next to it, holding Ruthann's purse and shoes. "You need help?"

Patsy shook her head. The last thing she needed was help from Will. "We'll be fine, thanks." She slipped Ruthann's purse over her shoulder and wedged the hideous shoes under her arm. "Let's go."

"I puked on his shoes," Ruthann wailed. "For sure, he'll never want to see me again now."

"Just hope his momma doesn't get wind of it," Patsy muttered.

"Oh no, I didn't even think of that." Ruthann broke out in fresh sobs.

Patsy rolled her eyes. "Get a grip. If Randy Jensen can't stand up to his momma, you don't want any part of him anyway. Good Lord, he's pushing thirty. It's time to rip those apron strings off and shove 'em down the drain."

Patsy turned the car into Sonic.

"What are you pulling in here for?" Ruthann asked.

"For food. You're not starving yourself on my watch. And when we get to your house, you're showing me those pills, and we're dumping them in the toilet." Patsy pushed the call button on the menu.

"But they're not mine. They're Momma's. She had to get them from some doctor in St. Louis. It was a real hassle."

"Yeah, and your skinny-butted mother needs them like she needs another boob job."

Ruthann sniffed. "I don't think you should talk about Momma like that."

Patsy ordered two large fries and two limeades. "You know I love your mother. But let's face it; the woman shows some questionable judgment at times."

"You know she hasn't had it easy. It's rough being a single mother, especially in Daisy Creek."

It was rough being the daughter of a single mother too, Patsy thought. "No one said she had it easy. I just said some of her choices may not always be the wisest."

Ruthann crossed her arms over her chest and began to sulk.

Patsy paid the carhop and handed Ruthann her fries and drink. "Don't pout. You can't tell me you really think your mother always makes the smartest choice."

Ruthann sucked the salt off a fry. "Well, no, but it sounds worse coming from you."

"I hate to break it to you, but if you really want to get hooked up with Randy, you're going to have to get thicker skin. I'll bet Ding Dongs to dollars, his momma's issues with your momma are what's put a snag in your romance."

"But his momma is usually so nice to me."

"His momma has more faces than a deck of cards." Patsy chewed on her straw. "The point is, we have to get past her to Randy. He has to decide he cares more about you than his momma, or there'll be no living with him. If she's head hen, there won't be any room for you in the coop."

"So what should I do?"

"I'm not sure yet, but don't be skipping meals and popping diet pills. You are not the problem. It's Randy and his momma."

Patsy took Ruthann straight home after Sonic. The house was empty. The only sign of her mother was an empty cigarette pack crumpled on the counter and a smear of lipstick on the highball glass sitting next to it.

Patsy followed Ruthann into the pink ruffled bathroom and confiscated her mother's diet pills. She unscrewed the childproof cap and shook them into the blue swirling water of the toilet. The Ty-D-Bowl man would be happy tonight.

Head bowed, Ruthann watched as the last pill spun out of sight. "Momma's gonna kill me."

"No, she won't. She'd never think you'd dump her pills, and if worse comes to worst, you can always tell her I broke in and performed a sewer sacrifice. She won't blame you a bit."

Ruthann looked doubtful, but she didn't stop Patsy from taking the pill bottle too.

"I'll destroy the evidence. She'll just think she lost them somewhere." Plus, it would be harder to get a refill without the prescription number printed on the label.

"Is that Ruthann's car in the drive?" Granny looked up at Patsy from behind the white Formica-topped kitchen table.

"Yeah, she wasn't feeling too well last night." Patsy poured some coffee from the percolator warming on the stove and dug into the back of the refrigerator. "Do we have cream?"

Granny peered at her over the rim of an ugly green stoneware cup, part of a set she purchased in the eighties from the Bag & Basket. They were bad then, but gave Patsy indigestion every time she looked at them now.

Patsy dug around some more and located the carton

of cream. Pouring a dollop into her cup, she found her grandmother was still staring at her. "What?"

"I didn't say nothin'." Granny concentrated on spooning sugar onto her grits.

She thought they'd been drinking, which they had, but that wasn't the total reason Ruthann couldn't drive herself home. Patsy sighed. "Ruthann got the crazy notion she's fat. She didn't eat anything all day and then popped some diet pills her momma had. I had to drive her home." There was no reason to mention they were at Gordie's when she collapsed. Granny probably knew it anyway, but saying it would force her to comment.

"That mother of hers doesn't have the sense to close her eyes in a hailstorm." Granny plopped her fork down beside her plate. "I don't know what has gotten into girls these days, dieting until they're nothing but hair and teeth. Some of these gals you see on TV are just plumb scary. Is that what Ruthann wants?"

Granny didn't leave room for Patsy's answer.

"In my day, a man wanted something to hang on to."

The memory of Will's hand on her thigh danced through Patsy's mind. A man still wanted something to hang on to; wasn't a bad deal for the woman either. Patsy flushed.

Occupied with her lecture, Granny didn't notice. "A man tries to grab a gal around the waist today and he's liable to slide down and smack his head on the floor, no padding anywhere to slow him down." She picked her fork back up and pointed it at Patsy. "You ain't been taking those pills, have you?"

"Of course not. In fact, I took Ruthann to Sonic and got her some food and then went in her house and dumped the pills down the toilet."

"Should've dumped her momma in after them." Granny shook her head and popped up from the table. "You sit down and eat some grits. You want bacon too?"

Patsy wasn't hungry. The stress of going with Glenn

today, combined with her confusion over Will, left her feeling like she'd eaten a plate of lead biscuits. There would be no getting out of breakfast now, though. She pulled out a chair and prepared to eat a week's worth of calories.

"You ever going to call that Barnes boy back?" Granny pulled an iron skillet from the drawer under the stove and set it on a burner.

Patsy was not going to get caught telling Granny about seeing Will last night. Her grandmother could read her better than a hundred-foot-tall billboard. "I'll get the bacon." Patsy cut her grandmother off on her way to the refrigerator. "How about eggs? You feel like having eggs?"

"I done ate." Granny took the package of bacon and turned back to the stove. "Get 'em out if you want 'em."

Patsy didn't know how she was going to force down the grits and bacon, much less eggs. "No, that's all right. I'm going to Sauk City today with Glenn. We'll probably eat out. I don't want to be too full."

"Glenn, hmmm. He that boy from up north?" Granny forked some bacon into the pan.

"Minnesota. He found the web job for me." Patsy relaxed, Granny had already forgotten about Will.

"You think he's better'n Will?"

The woman was like a snapping turtle; she didn't let go until it thundered and Patsy didn't have the energy to stir up a storm. "I'm not dating Glenn . . . or Will either, for that matter."

"They know that?" Granny plunked a plate loaded with grits and bacon down in front of Patsy. "Eat up. Sounds like you'll need your strength."

Twenty pounds stronger, Patsy waddled back to her room to get dressed. Pugnacious was still burrowed under the quilt. "Get up, you lazy butt. I could have used your help in there." Patsy collapsed on the bed next to her. "I'm never going to fit into jeans now."

After rooting around in her closet, Patsy decided to go

with her interpretation of business casual: a slim-fitting skirt from the Gap, a short-sleeved burgundy top, and the silver sandals from Ruthann—no pantyhose. Her mother would kill her for wearing a skirt bare-legged, but since Patsy thought her mother's fashion sense was Laura Bush meets Martha Stewart (pre–prison stripes), she wasn't too concerned with being labeled a fashion don't.

Glenn pulled up in a red, sporty-looking car. Patsy was willing to bet it cost significantly more than her five-year-old Jeep. Not that she was impressed with a flashy ride. Will drove a Beamer, after all, and she wasn't drooling all over him—well, not much.

"Hey, can you do me a favor?" After explaining that she needed to drop Ruthann's car off before leaving town, she climbed into the Cavalier and drove to Ruthann's with Glenn roaring along behind her. She parked in the drive and left the keys tucked under the floor mat.

After trotting back down the drive, she slid into Glenn's roadster. The scent of leather greeted her. She had never sat on anything quite so decadent; her body seemed to glide onto the seat. She sighed as she relaxed against the upholstery.

"Did you bring your camera?" Glenn asked.

Patsy held it up in response.

"How about your laptop?"

"I only have a desktop." Patsy fiddled with the strap of her camera. The smell of the leather was starting to give her a headache. "Laptops cost too much."

"The convenience is nice though."

Sure it was, if you could afford it. Patsy couldn't.

As if reading her thoughts, Glenn continued, "You might be able to afford one soon. I've got some good news." He shifted the manual transmission as he picked up speed on the highway. "I showed the marketing manager at Sunrise the spec site you sent me." He glanced at her.

Patsy turned a little in her seat. She couldn't get

comfortable. She felt like she was going to slide onto the floor; only her safety belt stood between her and a broken tailbone.

"She loved it. I'm pretty sure she's going to be calling you about an interview for a full-time job." He grinned.

Patsy bit her lower lip. "That's great."

"I thought you'd be happy." He shifted again. "The job would be in St. Louis, and the pay would be decent. Plus, they have tuition reimbursement, so you could work toward your degree. That's something you want, isn't it?"

Did misery love company? Of course, Patsy wanted her degree, and she wanted out of Daisy Creek. This was exactly what she'd been hoping for. She sunk into the cushioned seat, preparing for the anticipation to flow over her. Nothing but a slight sense of nausea from the smell of cowhide and the view of trees whizzing by got anywhere near her. What was wrong? She should be bounding around the car like Pugnacious with a dirty sock.

It was just too much, too soon. When she actually got called for an interview, she'd celebrate.

They drove the rest of the way in silence. Patsy concentrated on keeping her legs stiff, pinning her body in the seat. Glenn seemed occupied with hugging the sharp curves of the road. Patsy was used to the ribbon-candy roads, but she still found herself hanging from the handle that hung from above the passenger door.

"Damn." Glenn pulled in behind a tractor that sputtered down the highway. "At least we're almost there. I can't stand being a passenger on these roads, but they're fun to drive—until you get behind somebody like this." He shifted down to match the putt-putt speed of the tractor, but edged the car out past the center stripe, looking for a place to pass.

"So, where are we going first?" Patsy asked, hoping to divert him from passing the farmer.

"We're meeting the mayor and some of the city councilmen first. They're all gung-ho to get Sunrise into the area, and they have names people will recognize."

With a surge of power, Glenn zoomed past the tractor and threw the car into fourth. Patsy gripped the door handle and gave the farmer an apologetic smile.

Sauk City was a lot like Daisy Creek, except smaller. Where Patsy's hometown could boast of being at the intersection of two state highways, Sauk City seemed to have grown up alongside just one, the definition of a wide spot in the road.

Glenn slowed to only ten miles an hour over the thirty-five-mile-an-hour speed limit as they entered town. A feed store surrounded by domestic model trucks was the first sign they were close, followed by a locally owned drive-thru restaurant with a giant soft-serve cone poking out its roof. Ahead, Patsy could see signs of Victorian houses, probably built in the same era as Will's home. She was curious to see the historic part of Sauk City, wondered if any of the houses rivaled Will's, but Glenn turned off the main drag before they reached them.

A few blocks later, they pulled in front of a bland-looking building of tan brick.

"What's this?" she asked.

"The courthouse."

"This is the courthouse?" Patsy was surprised. Most towns in southern Missouri had big, imposing Victorian structures that had served as their courthouses for the past hundred years or so.

"Yeah." Glenn didn't seem to see anything strange about it.

Patsy followed him up the walk and stood patiently as he talked to a receptionist in the darkly paneled waiting room. It reminded her of a dentist's office: old vinyl chairs and chrome tables with ten-year-old *Good Housekeeping* and *Agriculture Today* magazines stacked on them. The only things missing were the white coats and the oversized tooth, cut away to reveal the pulp and roots inside. She suppressed a shiver and smiled wanly at the receptionist, who was now motioning them down the hall.

Four men wearing cheap suits sat around a conference table. They introduced themselves, but Patsy could only think of them as suit one, two, three, and four. They seemed interchangeable: big smiles, big hair, and big rings. It was like being trapped in a room of TV evangelists.

After a few rounds of handshaking and backslapping, they settled in for their talk. Patsy set a mini-recorder on the table to catch the details of their conversation. She would need a few quotes for the web site. It was a good thing she did, because even though she and Glenn stayed for over an hour, Patsy couldn't have repeated back more than a couple of words the men had spoken. The answer to all her questions seemed to boil down to one basic theme.

"How are people here reacting to the news the mines are coming into the area?"

Suit number one replied, "Of course, a few people are bellyaching, but most of us are thrilled. Sauk City needs the money."

"What concerns exactly do these people have?"

Suit two handled this one. "Nothing major, nothing as important as the jobs the mines will deliver."

"What are you or the mines doing to address these concerns?"

Suit three jumped in. "It's obvious we need Sunrise here. The troublemakers will figure that out soon enough. Sunrise doesn't have to worry about that." He flashed her a wink.

Patsy fidgeted in her seat. She hoped the suits didn't think she was some kind of mine hit woman here to break kneecaps if the locals didn't go along easily. She gave up on trying to delve into the possible concerns of the citizenry of Sauk City and just went for total PR.

"So, tell me why you're excited about Sunrise starting the new mine here."

Suit four, apparently the mayor, blabbered on for twenty minutes about jobs, prestige, and money—mainly money. That was pretty much what their entire philosophy boiled down to: money good, Sunrise brings money, thus, Sunrise good. Patsy knew at least some of what they believed was true, but it seemed a simplistic approach to what should be a complicated issue. To her four suited friends though, it wasn't, complicated that was. They knew what they wanted, and they saw a quick way to get it, end of story.

As she and Glenn stood to leave, she asked one more question. "What happened to your courthouse?"

Glenn looked confused by the question, but suit four answered readily. "Tore it down. There was a fire back in the seventies. A few folks wanted to fix it up, but there wasn't much more than a shell left. Why waste good money on something already so outdated? We opted to take a more modern approach." He held his arms wide as if the darkly paneled space in any way epitomized current and contemporary.

Patsy gave a weak smile and followed Glenn to the door. In the name of progress, they had rejected rebuilding something that represented the history of their town and instead slapped up this graham-cracker box. It was probably outdated before the tar was dry on the roof. Patsy huffed out a breath.

"What?" Glenn asked as he opened the door to his car.

"Hmm?" Patsy shook her head. "Oh, nothing. Where to now?"

"It's almost noon. You want to grab a bite?"

They ate in a little diner a few doors down. Patsy had wanted to try the drive-thru they passed on the way into town. It reminded her of the Tastee Freeze she and her family frequented when she was growing up, but Glenn thought it looked seedy. Coming from Minneapolis,

Patsy suspected Glenn's idea of seedy didn't quite match her own. If a roach didn't greet her at the door, she figured it was safe enough.

The diner was nice though. Aproned waitresses bustled around refilling coffee cups for feed-capped farmers. The special was chicken-fried steak, and the apple pie was fresh. Patsy ordered a chef salad.

When their food arrived, Glenn raised an eyebrow at her lunch. "That's a chef salad?"

Patsy glanced down at the bowl. It was pretty much what she'd expected: iceberg lettuce, orange cheese food, some tiny dry-looking croutons, boiled egg halves, and a few strips of processed ham and turkey. She knew what he meant, though. It wasn't exactly gourmet. But she was happy with it; it was comfortable. There was nothing wrong with comfortable.

She shrugged off a reply and crossed her legs, bouncing her foot so the tiny shells on her shoes tinkled together.

"What's with the shells?"

Patsy stroked a pink-lined shell. "I like the ocean."

Glenn twirled a chunk of steak through a puddle of gravy. "Really? You go there much?"

Patsy bit her lower lip. "No, I've never actually seen it. I just like it."

"You should go. You're not that far from the Gulf."

Patsy arranged the shells into straight lines pointing down to her toes. "I guess, but what I'd really like to see is the Barrier Reef."

"You never know. Get this web job and maybe you can."

Patsy laughed. "I don't think even a full-time web job is going to pay enough for me to fly to Australia."

"You could work there. Sunrise has major operations in Australia. They ship people back and forth all the time. A buddy of mine just got back." He ran his fork over the surface of his plate, the metal scraping loudly against the china.

See, maybe even work and live in Australia? The possibility had never occurred to Patsy. Surely Glenn was wrong. She couldn't get a job there, could she?

After lunch they conducted a few "man on the street" interviews. Overall, the attitude to the mines was positive, but they did encounter a few with anti-mine sentiments.

Patsy chatted with one woman about her experience with the mines in Blackhaw and how they ruined the land surrounding her grandfather's farm. How they'd believed the mines would be their salvation when they came into the area in the forties, but how it hadn't changed anything except the land and that in a negative way. The woman was working with a group resisting Sunrise's move into the forest around Sauk City. Patsy took down her name and wished her luck.

"What did you mean, good luck?" Glenn questioned Patsy.

"Huh? Oh, it's just an expression. I didn't mean anything by it."

"We're here to get positive comments for the site, remember? I don't know what good talking to people who hate the mines is going to do."

"If you don't know what people object to, you can't address it." Patsy shoved her pen back into the wire ring that held her notebook together.

Glenn watched her with a confused expression. "Are you sure you want to do this?"

"What do you mean?" Patsy asked.

"I don't know, Patsy. I just get the feeling your heart isn't in this. I think you may agree with that woman more than you're admitting."

Okay, so maybe Patsy did agree with the woman. Maybe she did think the mines were bad, not pure evil like she did as a child, but still a payoff that wasn't worth the final price tag. That didn't mean she couldn't

do this job. The mines were moving into Sauk City with
or without Patsy's approval and that woman and her
group could fight all they wanted, but they wouldn't
stop them either.

   With that as the foregone conclusion, why shouldn't
Patsy at least benefit some? She might not like the
mines, but that didn't mean she couldn't use them for
her own needs, right?

Chapter Thirteen

Up to his elbows in green goo, Will heard the rusty 4 x 4 rattle up before he saw it. Tilde peered down at him through a dirty windshield.

Great. She probably had another project for him. Will stabbed at the washstand with a metal scraper. He'd poured four gallons of paint stripper on the thing, to no avail. Well, it might have removed the bird poop. Hard to tell in that mess. Peeling off his rubber gloves, he pasted a smile on his face and turned to greet Patsy's aunt.

"What you doing there, kid?" Tilde walked past him to survey the washstand. "You aren't using that, are you?" She gestured to an empty container of the "environmentally friendly" paint remover he'd found at BiggeeMart.

"You'd do better trying to charm the paint off that stand." Flashing him a wink, she added, "But then, you probably got a bit of experience charming things off, don't you?" She chuckled.

Will didn't join her.

"Now seriously, kid, you need to get yourself some of that heavy-duty stripper. That paint's been on there a good long time. It ain't letting loose easy."

Will looked at the green blob. He was tempted. "Aren't those chemicals dangerous?"

"I've been using them for years, and I'm fine and dandy."

Will looked from Tilde's proud grin to the eyesore in

his garage. Maybe it was worth killing a few brain cells. "I'll think about it."

"You do that. Now come on back here. I've got a couple things for you." She looped her arm through his and led him to the back of the truck.

Twenty minutes later, he'd unloaded an oak sideboard with the north wind carved into the top and a portrait of Joseph Barnett, the man who built Will's house. The picture was a little unsettling, but Tilde insisted, and Will hung it in the small formal parlor. He hadn't found a real use for that space yet. If he did, he'd have to find a new home for the portrait. There was no way he could live with Mr. Barnett peering down his long nose at him all day.

"It looks great, adds a real touch of authenticity to the place." Tilde tilted her head while she straightened the gilded frame. "I got a line on a horsehair loveseat too. I don't think it's got a connection to the Barnetts, but it would look fine pushed up against this wall here." She pointed to a space between two windows. "Be a cozy place for doing a little spooning." She cackled and elbowed him in the ribs.

Will wasn't one hundred percent sure what spooning was, but he doubted seriously he'd be doing it or anything else with Mr. Barnett standing guard. He did need to furnish the room somehow, though. "Sure, if you think it fits."

"Good enough." Tilde walked off the space between the windows. "Yeah, it should fit. I'll bring it by tomorrow. Well, I guess I'll be heading out. Need to stop by Mom's before I leave town."

She was going by Patsy's? "Any special occasion?" he asked casually.

"No, that niece of mine went out of town today for some reason." Tilde picked up her purse, a gruesome creation that looked like it was made out of an armadillo. "Mom's not expecting her back till late. I thought I'd check in on Mom, make sure everything's took care of."

"What was Patsy going out of town for? Something to do with her web job?"

Tilde gave him a sideways look. "I don't rightly know, but Mom said some big, good-lookin' feller in a snazzy red sports car picked her up after breakfast and then tore down the street like the four Horsemen of the Apocalypse were chasin' 'em." Tilde stopped in front of the hall tree and checked her lipstick in the mirror. "You know anybody fitting that description?"

Will didn't, but he didn't like the sound of Patsy riding around with some wild driver, especially on the crooked roads that surrounded Daisy Creek. He thought she was more responsible than that. Someone should probably discuss it with her.

"Well, I surely do appreciate your business, kid. You let me know if I can do anything else for you."

Anything else she could do for him? Glancing out his recently repaired window, Will recalled the disaster awaiting him in the garage. He hadn't been having too much luck doing things on his own. Maybe it was time to enlist some aid.

Picking up Dwayne's tiny wooden raccoon, he said, "Actually, Tilde, there is something you can do for me. Let's have some coffee and talk."

"Thanks for dropping off my car yesterday morning. When'd you come by? I didn't expect to see it out there when I got up. I don't think Momma even noticed it was missing."

With the portable phone in her hand, Patsy stepped out onto the back porch so she could hear Ruthann over the din of the TV.

"It was early. I went down to Sauk City with Glenn. Remember, for the web site?" Patsy brushed dew off the padded seat of a redwood chair and sat down. "He followed me over."

"Oh." Obviously, Ruthann wasn't interested in Patsy's day. Which was fine, because Patsy didn't feel much like discussing it either.

"So, what'd you do yesterday?" Patsy asked.

"Not much. To tell the truth, I wasn't feeling too hot. I didn't get up until noon."

Maybe that would teach her to not mix vodka with diet pills.

"Oh, but I got a surprise." Ruthann sounded perkier. "I got flowers and the cutest little teddy bear. That's what woke me up, the delivery van."

"From Randy?"

"I wish." Ruthann huffed. "He hasn't called me for nothing."

"So, who sent the flowers?" Patsy prompted.

"Will, and there was the sweetest little note saying how he hoped I felt better." Ruthann sighed. "I don't know why you aren't nicer to him. He's about as close to perfect as you're gonna get around here. Sure beats a certain coon-hunting four-wheeler I know."

"What kind of flowers were they?" Patsy didn't know why it mattered, but she wanted to know. "Were they daisies?"

"Hmm? No, pink carnations and like I said, a cute little teddy bear holding onto them."

The knot that had formed in Patsy's stomach relaxed. Carnations, that was good. Nice, but not too special. Not romantic like roses or personal like daisies. For some reason, Patsy couldn't stand the thought of Will sending Ruthann daisies.

She and Ruthann made plans to meet that night at Patsy's. Granny was getting her hair done, then going to dinner with Patsy's parents. Patsy had begged off, claiming she needed to check on Ruthann.

"I'll pick up a pizza from the Hut. See you around seven." Ruthann hung up.

As Patsy stood to return the phone to its cradle, it rang in her hand. Without thinking, she answered. The timbre of Will's voice echoing from the handset sent a reverberating tingle up her spine.

"Heard you took a trip out of town yesterday."

Yet another problem with living in a small town; you had less privacy than Brad Pitt at a public shower. "What, was it posted on the First National Bank's sign?"

Will chuckled. "No, at least not that I noticed. I had some business with your aunt yesterday. She mentioned it."

Will had been meeting with Tilde? That didn't sound good.

"So, where did you go?" he asked.

If Patsy didn't feel like sharing with Ruthann, she sure didn't feel like sharing with Will. "What business did you have with Tilde?" she countered.

"She said you left in a sports car. Anybody I know?"

Why was he snooping around after her? Well, he had to show his first. She wasn't giving in. "Tilde stopped by while I was gone, but Granny didn't mention her talking with you."

There was silence on the other end of the line, then a sigh and, "Actually, I was hoping I could talk to you about some things related to what Tilde's helping me with. Get your opinion. Could you stop by the house today?"

"You need my opinion?"

"How about lunch? I make a mean Gardenburger."

Mmm. Didn't that sound tempting? But Patsy was curious about what Will and Tilde could be working on. "How about I swing through Sonic? You like Coney dogs?"

***

Patsy pulled up to Will's and climbed out, holding a dripping bag filled with onion rings and a Coney dog for herself and a grilled chicken sandwich for Will. He had balked at her buying lunch, but she refused to eat a sprout patty. In her opinion, there were scarier things than hardened arteries and mad cow disease. A faux burger was one of them.

Will grabbed the bag at the door and ushered her inside. He was again dressed in shorts and a polo shirt, but his feet were bare. There was something strangely erotic about his meeting her with bare feet, almost more intimate than seeing him without his shirt. Maybe it was the casualness of it, like they were past pretenses. Whatever the reason, Patsy had a hard time not staring at his naked toes.

Feeling completely idiotic, Patsy glanced around the room. An ornate hall tree sat by the front entry and through an open door, she could see a marble-topped table and a picture of an austere gentleman. "You're furnishing this place fast." Skirting the marble, she walked toward the picture. "Relative of yours?"

"No, he's the venerable Joseph Barnett, builder of this fine establishment."

"For a rich guy, he doesn't look too chipper, does he?" Patsy spun around, facing Will.

"Someone told me money doesn't equal emotion."

"A wise woman, I'm sure." Patsy grinned.

"Wiser than me . . ." Will stared at the portrait, ". . . or my father."

Patsy wasn't sure how to respond. Will just stood there, staring, a hollow look in his eyes. She edged around him and retrieved her greasy bag. "You ready to eat?"

Snapping his gaze away from the picture, he followed her into the kitchen. Signs of recent renovation still cluttered the room.

She stepped over an empty microwave box. "Where do you want to eat?"

Will gestured to a small table shoved into a nook. His face had relaxed, but Patsy still got the feeling he was studying her. She pulled out their food.

"I got you chicken."

He didn't reply.

"What? Why are you staring at me?"

"I'm not." He took a bite of his sandwich.

Patsy knew when someone was staring at her, but she wasn't going to argue. Lately she'd felt a lot less like fighting, about anything.

"So, what's the project Tilde's working on?"

An enigmatic look passed over his face. "It's not important."

Patsy frowned at him over her Coney dog. Sure it was important. She wanted to know. "I thought that's why you asked me over here, for my opinion on something."

"It was."

Will no longer wanted to discuss his latest project. Before it had seemed natural; it involved her family, the Ozarks, and the web. Who better than Patsy to give him an opinion? But the reminder of her comment on money and emotion set him back. Sudden insight had flooded over him.

He was just like his father, trying to replace real feelings with money. It was a disturbing discovery, not leaving room for chitchat about web pages and Ozark crafts. As the shock of the realization wore off, a new, warmer emotion replaced it.

Patsy took another giant bite of hot dog; a dab of mustard clung to her pursed lips. A pampered lady she wasn't. Cindy would never eat anything so indelicate as a hot dog, and she certainly wouldn't wolf it down with such enthusiasm. Will smiled to himself.

Noticing his perusal, Patsy gave him an uneasy look. He took her lunch from her hands and set it on the table. With a paper napkin from the bag, he slowly rubbed the mustard off the sides of her mouth.

Turning her head, Patsy took a loud slurp of limeade.

"Well, then I might as well be going." She popped up from her chair and grabbed the trash, including her half-eaten hot dog. Shoving it into a garbage can, she said, "Looks like things are going good with the remodeling. Maybe I'll see you around."

"Wait." Will didn't want her to go. "We never finished the tour."

"Oh, that's okay. Maybe some other time." She edged toward the front door, stopping next to Ralph, who lay across the threshold between the kitchen and dining room.

"No, I insist." He patted his leg, bringing Ralph to a sit. "You said you wanted to see the house. Let me show you." Will tossed his dog a treat and watched him trot with it to the pantry. "Let's go."

Will strode into the dining room.

Patsy looked at the back door. She could sneak out. It would be incredibly rude, but there was something brewing in Will's eyes that she didn't trust. Or maybe it was the tightening of her stomach and the shaking of her hands she didn't trust. Either way it would be in her best interest to leave—fast.

"Are you coming?" Will called from the foyer.

With a sigh, Patsy followed his voice. She could handle this. So she found him attractive. She was a red-blooded woman of the new millennium. She was supposed to find well-toned, good-looking men attractive, but she wasn't ruled by her hormones. She wasn't. She could do this.

Will was standing on the landing halfway up the stairs when she arrived. Her gaze drifted to the tips of his bare toes.

"You've already seen the downstairs, so I thought I'd show you the second floor." He motioned toward the landing above them.

Sure, why not? She'd like to see the second floor.

"There's a library . . ."

See a library, how bad could that be?

". . . and four bedrooms."

Uh-oh.

"I took the master suite."

"What's in here?" Patsy flung open the door to a closet. "Great storage space. You don't expect that in a house this old, do you?" She ran her hand down the stacks of sheets and towels as she babbled.

"No, when the house was built most people used chests and chifforobes. Tilde found one for me a few days ago. Lucky for me, it's in great shape." He reached in past her, his arm brushing her back. Patsy shivered in response. "No need for any refinishing. Do you want to see it?" he continued.

"Sure." Why not? Looking at an antique cupboard couldn't be too dangerous, certainly safer than being tucked inside a closet with him. Bless Tilde.

"It's down here." Will led her in the direction he'd pointed earlier when mentioning the master suite.

"Oh, in your room?" Damn Tilde. "I don't want to intrude."

"I wouldn't show you if it was an intrusion." Gripping her elbow, he pushed open the door and steered her inside. With each step, an emotion dangerously close to panic crept over her.

The room was bare except for the big, boxy armoire Will stood in front of, a couple of night tables, and the bed. A bed that seemed to grow in size as she looked at it.

"I know it's not right, but I'm hoping to get something better."

Patsy jumped at Will's voice so close behind her. "What? What's not right?"

"The bed. It's too modern for the house, a leftover from Chicago. A lot of my old furniture I left behind, but you kind of need a bed. Don't you think?"

"Yeah, a bed is important," Patsy murmured. "I mean, you have to sleep somewhere." She took a step away from Will, a step closer to the bed. She turned around, putting her back to it.

Will followed her movement. He was within inches of touching her. The heat of their bodies was crushed between them, forming a tangible, but invisible bond. The force field again. Will exhaled. She felt his breath on her face, but he wasn't touching her. She drew in a shaky breath. How could something so innocent fill her with such anticipation?

His eyes darkened, the pupils dilated and glimmering. He was tempting, so tempting. She wanted to touch him, but held back. She shouldn't be here. She knew where this was leading. She couldn't let her guard down. If she did, what would happen to her dreams? Could she be with Will even just once and still move on? She couldn't risk repeating history. She tore her gaze from his to the door behind him. She had to escape. The attraction was too intense. The reality might melt her, destroy her, trap her in Daisy Creek.

"Patsy?" Will leaned in, but kept his hands at his sides. Starting at her ear, he blew a path of cool air down her neck, down to the indentation of her throat. She inhaled deeply and pressed her palms against his chest for support. It was too much. The pounding of her heart beat down the last of her control. She shoved her hands into his hair and pulled his mouth to hers.

Will groaned as their lips collided. They grappled to get closer. His hands swept down her back, cupped her buttocks and guided her pelvis until it nestled next to his. The hard ridge of his erection rubbed against her, almost painful, but exciting. The clothing between them added to the friction.

She reached down and yanked his shirt free from his pants, exposing his abdomen to her touch. She ran her fingers over the swell of muscles and slipped her arms around him to explore his back, to pull him closer.

Will leaned forward, tipping her backward. The backs

of her legs hit the bed and she fell onto the mattress, cradled in his arms. He rolled over with a frustrated groan and put Patsy astride him.

She pushed herself upright, her hands pressed against his chest, her arms straight. The intensity in his eyes gave her a sense of power. Looking down at him, she asked, "Is this where you ask me if I'm sure about this?"

He surged upward, attempting to capture her lips, but she kept her mouth out of reach.

"What?" he asked, falling back on the bed.

"You're supposed to ask me if I'm sure, right about now."

"Sure about what?" His voice was husky.

"About this." She wriggled her hips, reveling in the pressure of his hard arousal against her. She was in control. She had the power.

Will groaned and rolled over, flipping her beneath him. "To hell with that, you're sure. Trust me." He covered her lips with his, slipping his tongue past her teeth and into her mouth.

Patsy met the force of his tongue with her own. He was right. She was sure. Why had she even considered leaving? She could handle this. She was handling this. Her fingernails scraped along his back, then up his sides. She was in control, in every way. She chose to make love to Will, and she would deal with the consequences later.

She wanted to touch his bare skin, feel it against her own, but his shirt blocked her way. She struggled with the tight-fitting cloth. With a jerk on the knit, she bared a few inches of his warm skin. It wasn't enough.

Will pulled away, yanked the annoying shirt over his head and flung it against the wall. The cool air in place of his body was equally disturbing. Patsy grasped his shoulders, pulling him back. He skimmed the line of exposed skin between her shorts and shirt with the tips of his fingers. Patsy shivered at the light touch. She ran

her hand over his pectoral muscle, flicking her thumbnail against his nipple.

He jerked in response and let out a low laugh. "You
are dangerous, aren't you?"

"Only to myself," Patsy murmured. The control she
had felt only seconds before seemed to be slipping from
her grasp. Lost in a wave of sensation and emotion, she
pulled his mouth back down to hers.

Will's fingers brushed her shirt upward, exposing the
material of her lace-covered bra. Patsy squirmed under
him, impatient to feel his hand on her bare skin. Tracing the edge of the lace, he followed it to the front clasp.
One quick snap and her breasts were free. She pulled
her mouth from his and tugged her shirt and bra over
her head. In a fluid move, she fell back onto the bed.

Intense again, Will lowered his head to her neck. He
cupped her breast and nibbled his way down her neck,
over her collarbone to the swell of flesh in his hand. He
captured the other breast and as his thumb circled one
nipple, he lowered his mouth to the first. He flicked the
nipple with his tongue and then blew cool breaths on
her moist skin. Patsy arched against him, pulling on his
head in an attempt to return his mouth to hers. Will
smiled and gently pulled her nipple between his teeth,
tugging and sucking in a way that caused Patsy to clench
and quiver in response.

"Enough," she said.

"Enough?" Will turned his attention to the other
breast.

When Patsy thought she couldn't survive more, she felt
his hand leave her chest and slide down her side to the waist
of her shorts. She followed his lead, quickly unbuttoning his
shorts and tugging them down his hips. Grabbing the
elastic of his underwear, she pulled it down also, pausing
only briefly as it caught on his erection.

"Damn," Will whispered.

"Enough?" Patsy asked.

Will bit her earlobe in response and sent her shorts to join his on the floor. Patsy ran her leg up the side of his, relishing the feel of his rough hair against her smooth skin. The head of his penis pushed against the thin barrier of her cotton underwear. She pushed her pelvis upward, rotating her hips, increasing the pressure.

"Just a minute." Will leaned to the side, digging in a small bedside table. The sound of rustling paper and objects dropping onto the floor followed. After another muffled curse, he returned, foil packet gripped between his teeth. With a deft jerk, he ripped open the package and rolled the condom on.

Patsy sighed as his hands slid inside her underwear. He paused momentarily to caress her butt before pushing the fabric down her legs. Past this last obstacle, his penis rubbed against the entrance to her vagina. Patsy stroked his erection, guiding it into place.

"Now are you sure?" Will asked.

Patsy grabbed his shoulders and shoved her hips upward to meet his thrust. The pressure inside her built as he moved in and out, faster and faster. She grabbed his back and nibbled on the side of his neck. Will groaned and pulled her legs to his waist. She squeezed her thighs around him, capturing him, desperate to keep the rhythm going.

As the tempo increased, Patsy lost track of everything except the pressure building inside her. Higher and higher she seemed to go, as if flying from her body. Almost panicked with want, she tilted her hips toward him. His hands gripping her waist, Will surged upward until he was staring down at her, gazing into her eyes. With one last thrust, he shuddered and her world exploded into twinkling lights.

Panting, but still connected, they lay together on the bed.

"You're beautiful." He brushed the hair from her eyes and kissed her lightly on the forehead.

Patsy hugged him to her, loving the feel of his warmth, the musky smell they had created, and the sense of contentment that settled over her. It should always be like this.

He kissed her on the mouth, a simple sweet kiss with no pressure, no expectations, just acceptance. Slipping out of her, he rolled onto his side, then gathered her in his arms. With her held close, he pressed his lips to her temple and gently stroked her hair.

Patsy sighed. She was content, completely content. There was nothing in the world she wanted at this moment, everything was perfect. Curling up against him, she fell asleep.

Sometime later, she awoke. The room was dark, but Will's arms still encircled her. She moved to sit up, but his arm tightened around her. Warmth filled her, nice, simple, like she belonged—like they belonged, together. With his eyes still closed, he dragged his lips up her neck. Patsy sighed. This was how her life should be—straightforward, easy, and content.

Her hand reached up to caress his hair. Content. She couldn't be content. Contentment's what got her in trouble before. Got her stuck in Daisy Creek with a cheating husband and a dead-end job, at twenty, for God's sake. She stiffened at the thought. She could not make the same mistake twice.

It was great with Will right now, this minute, but when they rolled out of bed, things would change. They were still in Daisy Creek, and Patsy was still Patsy, and he was still Will Barnes. He still wanted to stay in Daisy Creek, and she still wanted to leave. Had to leave; it was the only way to get ahead. If she stayed here, even with Will, nothing would change. Sure, maybe things would be good for a while, maybe even longer than before.

He wasn't Johnny, but they had a lot in common—rabble-rousing in their youth and smooth manners that disguised a sexy danger. Sooner or later, history would repeat itself. He'd start leaving her alone while he visited the roadhouse. He'd dance with some woman, innocently at first, but eventually they'd be in bed together, maybe even this same bed, and Patsy'd be right back where she started—stuck in Daisy Creek with no career prospects and no future.

She couldn't get involved with Will. She had to be strong. She had to walk away. Better to do it now before she opened herself up for even more heartbreak and humiliation.

He was awake and staring down at her. As she looked up at him, she felt tears overflow her eyes and roll down her cheeks.

"What's wrong?" Will's eyes clouded with concern. "Are you okay? Are you hurt?"

"I'm fine." She brushed away the tears and looked away.

"Then, why the tears?" The sound of his voice upset her more.

"Nothing. I'm being silly."

"Tell me." He turned her face toward his.

"It's just. We shouldn't have done this." She gestured with her hand down toward their still-entwined bodies.

Will pulled his leg off of hers. "Why not? We're adults."

Patsy sat up and pulled the blanket over herself. "Yeah, but we can't get involved. I mean, I hadn't told you, but I'm leaving Daisy Creek. If I get a chance, that is."

"Oh, I see." Will stood up and retrieved his underwear and shorts from the floor. With his back to her, he said, "That's not a problem, at least not for me. It's not like I'm looking for a commitment. That's the last thing I want." He picked up Patsy's clothes and tossed them to her, his back still turned.

"I hope you're not worrying about hurting me." He jerked on his clothes and banged shut the bedside table drawer that held the condoms.

Patsy jumped at the noise.

"No, of course not. Like I said, I'm just being silly. Just post-sex emotions." She rubbed her eyes with the blanket and gathered up her clothes. She didn't look up until she heard the door slam behind him.

Chapter Fourteen

So, Patsy wanted to leave Daisy Creek. So, she didn't want a commitment. So what? Neither did Will. It was the perfect situation—a fun, no-ties relationship. No worry about Patsy trying to rope him into marriage. No house in suburbia, no country club membership, no 2.2 kids. What was there to complain about?

How about that she pushed him away? Barely gave him time to pull on his pants before his feet hit the floor and the door banged behind him. One quick roll in the sheets and she was done. How about that suddenly a no-ties relationship didn't have the same appeal it once did? No ties meant, well, no ties. Patsy was free to go as she pleased, and apparently that's exactly what she intended to do—go.

Will slammed the cabinet door shut, causing Ralph to leap to his feet and move next to his owner. Seeing his dog's alarm, Will sunk to his knees and pulled him onto his lap.

"Sorry, boy. It's okay. I'm not mad, not at you." It was a half truth. Will wasn't mad at Ralph, but he was mad, and insulted, and mainly—confused.

He thought he knew what he wanted or didn't want. Then Patsy sauntered into his life, and his bed, screwing everything up. He felt like she'd drop-kicked him across the county.

When she first started crying, he'd been worried. Who wouldn't have been? He wasn't a complete callous heel.

He didn't want to hurt her. He was prepared to reassure her. Tell her it wasn't a meaningless afternoon of sex, she meant something to him. He wasn't sure exactly what, but something. Then she'd told him she was leaving Daisy Creek and didn't want a relationship. It was the last thing he'd expected.

Rubbing Ralph a little harder on the head than he intended, Will stood up. Fine. She didn't want a relationship? Neither did he. It was just one afternoon of sex—nothing more, but if she thought she could pretend it never happened, she had a lesson to learn.

Patsy pulled into her driveway a little after seven to find Ruthann waiting. Her friend was going to want to know why Patsy was late, and Patsy couldn't think of a single excuse except the truth. Not much hope of hiding news like this from someone you'd known since diapers. Knowing Ruthann, she'd start chanting "Will and Patsy sitting in a tree, k-i-s-s-i-n-g."

Nothing wrong with that image, but the next passage wasn't a possibility. No space for love, marriage, or baby carriages in Patsy's plans.

"Where've you been? I been calling you on your cell phone for twenty minutes."

"Sorry, I left it in the car." Patsy staggered up the walk, smoothing wrinkles out of her shorts.

"What have you been doing? You look like you pulled your clothes out of the laundry hamper." Ruthann eyed Patsy while she unlocked the door and flipped on the lights.

Inside, Ruthann grabbed Patsy's chin. "What's this? Is that beard burn?"

"No." Patsy pulled her face away from her friend's gleeful gaze. "I better let Pugnacious out."

The dog blinked at her from the couch where she was sprawled belly up.

"She's fine. Tell me what's going on." Ruthann plopped onto the cushion next to the pug. "Where have you been?"

"Did you bring the pizza?"

Ruthann sighed. "I left it on the porch."

Patsy retrieved the cardboard box and carried it into the kitchen. "What do you want to drink?"

"Anything." Ruthann slid into a chair at the table. "Are you going to fess up or not? Was it Will?"

Patsy busied herself dropping ice into glasses.

Ruthann raised both eyebrows and said, "It was Will. Well, it's about time you decided to go for it. Everyone but you knew it was going to happen." She flipped open the pizza box and selected a slice. "I'm glad one of us has a love life, finally."

She was jumping to conclusions, just like Patsy was afraid she would. "It isn't like that. I don't have a love life. It was just, you know, one of those things." Patsy swirled Diet Pepsi around in her glass. "I told him we couldn't get involved."

Ruthann dropped her slice back into the box. "You what? Why would you do that?"

"You know. I may get a call for that job any day now, and I'm not letting a little lust sucker me into the same mistake I made before." Patsy tried to sound confident, but petulance snuck in toward the end.

"You're going to let someone like Will Barnes get away because seven years ago you made a mistake and married an idiot?" Ruthann might as well have been snapping a ruler against her palm, her displeasure was so pronounced.

"Johnny wasn't an idiot, at least not when I married him," Patsy objected. "It was this place, the marriage, everything. Nothing lasts in Daisy Creek."

"How about your parents?"

"They don't count. They got married years ago. Things have changed since then. Besides, even they've had problems." Patsy drew a heart in the condensation on the side of her glass, then drew an X through it. "The point is, I messed up once and I'm not doing it again. When I get a job offer that gets me out of Daisy Creek, I'm taking it, so there's no reason to waste time getting involved with anyone here."

"But . . ."

"No buts, it's the way it is. Hand me a slice of pizza. Did you get onions?"

Ruthann shook her head, but kept her mouth closed. It was a good thing. Patsy was in no mood to debate the issue. The smell of Will still clung to her and she could still feel the light touch of his hand brushing away her tears. Why had she cried? It made her look so weak, and she wasn't, she was strong. She was doing the right thing, the responsible thing.

She shoved the pizza into her mouth and asked around it, "How about you? Have you seen Randy?"

Patsy only half-listened as Ruthann bemoaned her lack of luck in securing Randy. Instead, Patsy let herself drift back to Will, his enthusiasm for his new house, the dedication of his dog, and his acceptance of her eccentric family. It was a shame things couldn't work out. But they couldn't. He was staying here and she was leaving, period.

"What should I do?"

"Hmm?" Patsy dropped the slice of pizza she was holding.

Ruthann watched her expectantly. "What should I do? About Randy."

It took Patsy a beat to change gears, but she was grateful Ruthann had gotten diverted by her own issues. For once, Patsy needed to follow her lead. "Well, like we talked about the other night, it's a two-prong problem. There's Randy and his complete lack of backbone."

Ruthann gave her a baleful look.

Patsy continued, "And there's his momma. Which one do you want to tackle first?"

"I don't see why we need to tackle either one. Why can't we just get him to notice me?"

"You already tried that. Besides, he's noticed you. Now we have to deal with the more basic problems. Here's what I think we need to do . . ." Patsy pushed the pizza box out of the way. "We start with his momma, this Sunday. I know I can get Granny to help us. Then we'll work on Randy. Growing him a spine is going to be the hard part." She ignored her friend's glare as she launched into her plan.

Sunday morning, Patsy dressed for church complete with pantyhose and heels. Her mother would be ecstatic. She'd filled Granny in on her plan to convert Randy's mother to Ruthann's charms and instructed Ruthann in her role. Granny had kicked some about lying, but Patsy had assured her she wouldn't have to out-and-out lie, just evade the truth a little.

"You just say, according to what I told you or what you heard. That won't be lying."

Granny tched and shook her head. "Never thought the day would come you'd have me lying in a house of worship."

"It's not lying, and you said yourself Randy's momma needs a boot in the hiney. She's never going to give Ruthann a chance as long as she thinks what she does about Ruthann's mother."

"You'd be doing Ruthann more of a favor by getting her momma to straighten up and act responsible. Wouldn't hurt her none to see the inside of the First Baptist."

"Those do-gooders wouldn't be waiting to see who picked up the first stone. They'd slice her open with their tongues and go home saying they'd served the Lord."

"You don't be sassing like that. There's a lot of good people that goes to that church." Granny picked up her Bible and hobbled to the door. "'Course, there's no need for Ellen Jensen to be taking the sins of the mother out on Ruthann. She's nothing but sweet. Kept your fanny out of the fires more than once, I'd guess." She waited for Patsy to lock the front door. "I'll help you, but you better watch what you say in the church. I don't want nobody saying we deceived the Lord."

Patsy and Granny arrived at church right as Sunday school was letting out. As they filed into line, Patsy searched the crowd for her quarry. Sighting a spit-shined Luke, she shimmied sideways, tugging Granny behind her.

"Hold up, sis. My body don't squeeze through the same spots yours does."

Patsy ignored her grandmother's complaints, not stopping until they were positioned right behind Randy's mother and his son.

Patsy tapped her on the shoulder. "Why, Mrs. Jensen, is that you? I didn't even recognize Luke, he's getting so big." She beamed down at the little boy.

"Well, Patsy Lee Clark, I declare, you 'bout scared twenty years off me. Mrs. Jackson, how you been feeling?" Randy's mother patted Granny's arm.

Granny shot Patsy a look, but hobbled forward a step. "Fair to middling. These old bones don't get around like they used to."

"Oh, let me help you."

Patsy stood back as Mrs. Jensen guided Granny into the church and toward a pew.

"Patsy Lee, will you bring Luke?"

Patsy held her hand out to the small child, who grasped hers in his smaller, grubbier one and grinned up at her. Maybe Ruthann was right. A ready-made family might not be all bad. Patsy ruffled the boy's hair and led him to their seats.

"So, Patsy Lee, I hear tell you been seeing that boy Will Barnes." Mrs. Jensen patted a space on the wooden pew next to her.

Granny raised her eyebrows at Patsy, but jumped into

the conversation. "I don't know where you heard that. From what Patsy's been telling me, he's got eyes for nobody but Ruthann Malone."

"The Malone girl?" Randy's mother didn't bother to hide her surprise.

"Yes, Patsy said he's done nothing but skulk around after her since he hit town. It's no wonder, her family being what it is and all."

"Her family? You don't mean her momma." Mrs. Jensen folded her hands over the top of her purse.

"No, her daddy's family. From what Patsy told me, he's from some big fancy family back east. I guess her momma never let on, wanted to make it on her own and not put on airs. As Patsy tells it, he got hisself killed when she was pregnant, leaving her widowed." Granny picked up a hymnal and thumbed through it. "What's the opening song today? I hope it's the 'Old Rugged Cross.' That's my favorite."

"Not to speak ill of folks in the Lord's house, but I thought her daddy was some trucker from down Licking way. Got her momma pregnant and took off."

Granny studied a page in the hymnal. "Is that the story they been passing around? Well, if that's what Ruthann's momma wants folks to believe, it's not my place to quarrel."

Ruthann entered the church, wearing a pink cotton dress complete with pearl buttons and Peter Pan collar. Perfect.

"Why, there's Ruthann now." Patsy waved her program toward her friend.

Ruthann waved back, but turned to grab the arm of a man who stood chatting with the mayor. His back was to the pews, but Patsy had no trouble recognizing the broad shoulders of Will Barnes. Even in a suit, the definition of his body was obvious. Patsy's heart constricted before she had time to remember her resolve.

What was he doing here? When she'd suggested using

him to make Ruthann more acceptable to Randy's momma, she hadn't meant to actually *use* him, just mention him. Patsy crumpled the program into a ball. The tight feeling around her heart quickly loosened to the point of pounding. Randy's mother said something to her, but she couldn't hear her over the sound of blood rushing through her body. She smiled vaguely and nodded her head.

They were coming over. She could handle this. She concentrated on smoothing the wrinkles out of her program.

"Good morning, Mrs. Jensen," Ruthann greeted them. "Mrs. Jackson, you've met Will Barnes, haven't you?"

Patsy could feel Will's gaze on the top of her head, but she refused to look up. She opened her program and studied the schedule for today's sermon.

"Patsalee," Granny called her. "Scoot down so these two can get in."

Patsy glanced up at Ruthann, who was busy complimenting Randy's mother on her dress. Will slid between the rows, pausing between Patsy and Mrs. Jensen.

"You don't mind, do you?" he asked Patsy. He was dressed in navy slacks and a crisp cotton dress shirt. At least he was covered today. She risked a peek at his feet. Shiny black shoes reflected up at her. Yep, he was covered.

"Patsy?" he asked, one brow raised, his expression revealing nothing of what had passed between them just hours earlier.

Forced to look at him, all Patsy could do was shake her head and slide down, giving him room to sit. Ruthann took the seat next to Randy's mother, leaving Patsy at the end between Luke and Will.

"You look nice today," he murmured, his lips brushing her ear.

The hairs on her neck unfurled.

"Thank you." She grabbed a hymnal and began searching for the first song.

"Here." Taking the book, he flipped it to the right page and handed it back to her.

"Thanks." She pretended to study the words, but they blurred and mingled until they were nothing more than black smudgy lines.

He leaned toward her. "You're very polite today too."

She could smell his cologne, or maybe it was soap. She couldn't decide, but it was woodsy and natural-smelling, and brought back memories of snuggling with him in his bed. She looked at him with wide eyes. He was staring back, his eyes dark and a little sad.

"You smell good." The words slipped out and she was embarrassed immediately, but he smiled and said, "You too."

The congregation stood up to sing. Patsy and Will stayed seated until Ruthann nudged Will with her elbow, propelling him upward. Patsy popped up after them.

When the song was done and they returned to their seats, he seemed to have moved closer. His leg was pressed against hers, just like the night at Gordie's when he caressed her thigh. She wanted him to touch her now, to run his arm along the back of her seat, to feel his fingers at the nape of her neck, something, anything, just a touch.

This was wrong. Here she was in church, and she hadn't heard a word of the sermon. She was too busy lusting after the man next to her. Every time the congregation stood, she tried to wiggle away from Will, but somehow once they sat, he was again attached to her side. She stared straight ahead, trying to ignore the electricity that sizzled between them and the images that rushed through her brain each time she caught a whiff of his scent.

After two hours, the reverend called for sinners to come forth and be saved. And Patsy sent up a special plea that they all keep their sins to themselves for another week. There was plenty of time for salvation, and she was already suffering through the fires of hell. She'd be seared for sure if she had to sit through anyone else's redemption.

When the service ended, and the preacher strode down the aisle to the front doors of the church, Patsy hopped from her seat, mumbling a small prayer of thanks.

Will followed her. "I didn't know you were so religious," he murmured. He exhaled softly, blowing warm air into her ear. She shivered.

"There's a lot about me you don't know." Patsy tilted her head to the side, away from his lips.

"Not so much anymore." Will grabbed her hand and made small circles with his thumb in her palm.

It was an innocent move that sent a bolt of awareness searing up Patsy's arm. She tugged her hand free. She couldn't let him touch her, not even slightly. Her body was playing traitor, giving her emotions away with every trembling breath.

Unaware of Patsy's sinful thoughts, Mrs. Jensen reached past Ruthann to grab Will's arm. With a guilty look at Will's back, Patsy squeezed past Luke to escape the pew from the opposite end. While some women gossiped about Merle Haggard and water parks, she waited for Will to be dragged out of the church by Randy's mother, Ruthann and Luke following close behind.

When she returned to her seat, Granny was waiting for her. "He's a looker, he is," Granny commented.

"I guess." Patsy picked up her purse and returned their hymnals to the shelf. "If you like that type." The books snapped against the pew in front of them.

Granny grinned at her. "Oh, you like that type. Don't be thinking you can fool me. Fool yourself all you like, but you won't be fooling me."

Patsy pushed past her. "You ready to go or what? We don't have all day."

"You got that right, sis. Time's a-wasting. You better get a move on, or someone else will."

Patsy left her grandmother to find her own way out. Granny didn't know what she was talking about. Patsy wasn't fooling herself. She knew all too well she liked Will's type, but that didn't change a thing. Some things were more important than sweaty palms and pounding hearts. Patsy had to stay focused and remember that. Frowning, she joined her parents near the back of the church.

"Where's your grandmother?" Patsy's father rolled back and forth on the balls of his feet. "If we don't leave now, we'll be sitting outside the Dogwood Inn for thirty minutes waiting on a table."

"I think she just went out the front," Patsy's mother replied.

Patsy tagged behind them, out the wide oak doors and down the concrete steps. Granny stood near the street talking with Will.

What was she up to now? As Patsy and her parents approached, Granny nodded their way and hobbled toward them.

"What were you talking to Will about?" Patsy's mother asked.

"Nothing important." Granny leaned on her cane and waved at Will. "Just a little business."

Patsy raised an eyebrow, but before she could question what kind of business Granny had with anyone, never mind Will Barnes, Patsy's father interrupted, "Let's get a move on. It's a quarter after already."

Patsy followed her family down the sidewalk. First Tilde and now Granny, what kind of business could they both have with Will?

Patsy tossed onto her side. The beaver was back. This time he had escaped his coating of goo, but wove between her ankles while she fought her way toward the Daisy Creek County courthouse. Something held her back, like the air was too thick to move through. Patsy stroked with her arms, crawling through a haze. She had to get to the courthouse to Will, who stood waiting with a giant bouquet of daisies.

In her path, Glenn munched on a chef salad, tossing bits of lettuce and boiled egg out of the bowl and yelling, "What's wrong with you? There isn't anything worth staying here for."

The beaver leaped onto her chest, pressing her down with his weight. His wet nose jamming into her eye startled her awake.

Pugnacious straddled Patsy's neck, her nose moved from Patsy's left eye to her right. "Get off me." Patsy picked the little dog up and set her on the mattress. "You about scared me to death."

Two marble eyes blinked back at her.

"Do you need something? You want to go out?"

Pugnacious grinned, hopped down from the bed, and sat by the door waiting. After pulling on her robe and stumbling to the back door to let her dog out, Patsy made coffee and returned to her room.

She had to get Will out of her brain. He was interfering with her sleep and her life. Avoiding him wasn't working. Daisy Creek was just too small. There was no help for it. She was going to have to address the problem head on. Seek him out.

She stared at her blank computer screen. She also had to finish this web site. The sooner she got done with it, the better she'd feel, and, the closer she'd be to leaving Daisy Creek. Then Will wouldn't be an issue.

She powered up her PC and grabbed her digital camera. Time to download photos.

A few hours later, Tilde's van pull up in front. The thing chugged like a diesel tractor. Patsy pushed aside her curtains to peer out. Her aunt popped out of the front and flung open the side door.

Guess Will had his Beamer back. There she went again,

thinking of Will. Furrowing her brow, she concentrated on her aunt's movements.

Tilde rummaged around inside her van, setting a strange assortment of old junk onto the sidewalk: a couple of washboards, a beat-up kitchen tabletop, and a couple of dirty cardboard boxes. Patsy shook her head. It was a wonder the woman could see to drive. Popping out of the vehicle, her aunt tugged a box of old picture frames out of her way, then clambered back inside.

As her aunt moved around, something teetered and fell onto the ground—one of Patsy's father's chainsaw coons. Now why did Tilde have that?

Tilde emerged laden with a stack of baskets. She shook her head when she saw the coon. Arms full, she stepped over the statue and walked to the front door.

Patsy saved her work and turned off the computer. Her aunt was up to something, and Patsy wanted to know what. Pulling on shorts and a University of Missouri T-shirt, she headed to the kitchen.

Tilde, Granny, and Pugnacious were gathered around the table. On the white Formica sat an assortment of baskets.

"I like the idea of this one, but the craftsmanship's wanting a bit." Tilde held up a basket designed to sit on a staircase.

"How about this one, it's wove nice and tight." Granny held out a round basket about the size of a dinner plate.

Tilde took it from her. "Yeah, but there's nothing special about it. What's gonna make someone pay good money for this thing?" She shook the basket by the handle.

"What are you two doing?" Patsy wandered up and selected a miniature basket that fit in the palm of her hand.

Granny looked down her nose at Patsy. "Nothing you'd be interested in, no fancy city stuff here."

"Don't be so rough on the girl. She might have an

idea." Tilde pushed a chair toward her niece. "Take a seat. I can use some help."

"What is all this?" Patsy sat down and pointed to the pile of baskets.

"It's my new job." Tilde held up an oak hamper. "What about this?"

Granny shook her head. "It'd never last. Look how they got those handles attached."

"Your new job? You're what, selling baskets?" Patsy asked.

"Not directly." Tilde dropped the hamper back on the floor. Pugnacious twisted over and shoved her small body inside.

"Those tiny things are awful sweet, but I don't rightly know what you'd use 'em for." Granny pointed to the petite basket Patsy still held.

Patsy glanced down at the basket. It was sweet. "Wedding favors? Maybe fill them with little bags of rice or flowers or something?" Patsy loved the idea of tiny baskets filled with daisies dotting reception tables, and these would be perfect. Realizing the direction her thoughts had taken, she dropped the basket on the table.

"See, I told you the girl'd have an idea." Tilde beamed at her. "And Dolly Hayes makes those lavender sachets and such. We could package them together."

"I reckon that might sell, but that still don't solve your basket problem. You can't very well say you're selling Ozark crafts and not have some decent baskets in the mix." Granny shook her head.

"Sure would be nice if we knew someone who could weave a nice bunch of baskets for our kickoff," Tilde replied. She and Granny both turned to stare at Patsy.

Patsy stared back at them. She was still hung up on having sweet, sentimental thoughts about daisies and little baskets. Next she'd be humming along with Ruthann about baby carriages. Besides, her aunt and grandmother hadn't explained what was going on yet.

"What you say, Patsalee? You think you could make a few? Maybe an egg or a picnic basket? People seem to like those. This here stair basket is nice too, and the hamper." Tilde motioned around the room.

"You want me to make baskets? To sell?" These women didn't pay attention to anything she said or did. Hello, she was designing a web site for a major company, major for Daisy Creek anyway.

"What else we gonna do with them? I'd make 'em myself, but I'm just too slow anymore. It'd take me a month to make one of those scrawny little things." Granny thumped the tiny basket with her cane.

"Is all this for Daisy Daze? You know it's a bunch of work for nothing. We never sell more than a couple baskets. Dwayne's carvings go a little better, but people around here just aren't willing to pay enough to make up for your time." Patsy got up to get a glass of tea and a Hostess pie. She needed sustenance to deal with these two. "Is that why you're hauling around one of Dad's chainsaw statues? You working on something for Daisy Daze?"

"As long as you're up, we could all use something wet." Tilde plopped down in a chair. "No, kid, we're not working on Daisy Daze. We got bigger plans. We're going online."

Tilde and Granny going online. Patsy didn't realize her aunt even knew what the term meant.

"That Will Barnes came up with an idea to sell Ozark crafts over the computer." Granny crossed her arms over her chest. "Tilde's helping him find things to sell."

"Got a name and everything. He wanted to call it the Daisy Gallery, but I convinced him to shorten it. Daisy Gal; catchy, don't you think?" Tilde took a drink of the tea Patsy had handed her.

"Will's starting a web site for Daisy Creek?" Patsy set her own glass on the counter.

"Not just Daisy Creek, that's just the name. I've found things from all over. Your daddy and brother are even

signed on. Will's letting people who have stuff ready for
the opening sell free for six months. He's covering the
lot. Got some kind of reporter coming down and inter-
viewing us for some magazine and everything. I'm
surprised he didn't say nothing to you about it. 'Course
he probably don't know about you weaving baskets."
Tilde took another slurp of tea. "So, you interested? Like
Mom said, we'd really like to have some nice baskets for
the opening."

Patsy was too surprised to ask all the questions that
were swirling around in her mind. Foremost being why
Will was doing this and why she didn't know about it.

"So, you gonna help?" Tilde prompted.

"When's the opening?" Patsy asked.

"Daisy Daze. The reporter's coming for the festival
and we're having a special booth for Daisy Gal mer-
chants. It'd be nice to have . . . What you think?" She
looked at Granny. "Twenty or so baskets?"

At Patsy's startled look, she backpedaled. "Well, maybe
five or six would do it, but give us some variety, and be
creative. We don't want a bunch of this." She brushed
the simple round basket away from her.

Patsy wasn't sure how it happened, but she thought she
might be working for her aunt. How was she going to do
that and still get the web site for Sunrise done? She knew
Will would be the end of her dream to leave Daisy Creek
and here he was getting in her way again without even
being present. She glanced at her grandmother, who
took a sip of tea and leaned back with a satisfied smile.

Chapter Fifteen

Will took another long drag of tea. Thanks to Tilde's efforts, he had more merchandise than he could house. Pretty soon he was going to have to get commercial space. He had never imagined so many handmade crafts existed—jewelry, kitchen collectibles, knives, and miniature antique tools. The list was interminable, but the best part was how enthusiastic everyone was. Not a single person he or Tilde had approached had turned them down. Everyone wanted their handiwork featured on Daisy Gal.

His dream was coming true. He had a business that mattered, that made people happy. That made him happy.

He picked up a tiny dining room set and wrapped it in tissue. Yes, he was happy. As happy as he could be, anyway. His mind drifted to Patsy, looking prim and proper in her good-girl dress at church. What made her so hard to forget?

When Ruthann asked for his help with what he knew instantly was Patsy's plan, he'd jumped at the chance. He'd been determined to take any opportunity to remind her of their attraction—even in church in front of her grandmother and a three-year-old boy. It was sick.

He had sunk beyond low.

He couldn't search her out again.

It was time to concentrate on Daisy Gal the business, and forget Daisy Gal the woman. A simple enough task,

except for one small problem—he was falling in love
with the daisy gal he should be forgetting.

Patsy twisted the bell next to Will's front door. It had
been three days since Tilde and Granny roped her into
making baskets. She'd stayed up till midnight every
night trying to fit everything in. And finally, the web site
for Sunrise was almost complete.

Glenn had called this morning, and he didn't sound
happy. "Sunrise is looking for the site, where is it?"

Patsy explained that some family issues had come up,
but she was almost done. Stretching the truth was becoming staggeringly easy. She assured him she would upload
the site later today. And she would, truly, after one final
run-through. She had to make sure all the code worked,
photos appeared where they were supposed to, things like
that. She wasn't procrastinating, not really.

Glenn sounded a little unsure, but not too annoyed.
He just reminded her that a job with Sunrise was riding
on this. "Get it right, but don't waste too much time. You
don't want them to think you can't follow a deadline."

Patsy would make a decision today. The site was nice.
It was time to move on.

Patsy slumped against Will's door. After Glenn's call,
she told Granny she might be getting a job offer. Granny's
enthusiasm was akin to getting socks for Christmas—socks
with holes. Her grandmother obviously hoped basket
weaving would divert Patsy from her plans to leave Daisy
Creek.

It was nice weaving again. She'd finished one basket
and was starting on a second, the picnic basket. Patsy
wouldn't admit it to her grandmother, but she was eager
to get started. First she wanted to talk to Will though,
and, if she was being honest with herself, not just to hear
about daisygal.com.

She missed him. There had to be some way they could

see each other without complicating her plans to leave. She'd expected to hear from him after operation Rescue Ruthann, what with the electricity that surged between them, but nothing. She'd even prepared an easy-letdown speech, let's be friends and all that jazz. Guess he didn't need it. Maybe he'd found someone else to share all that electricity with.

Leaning over, she peered in the front window. No clue as to what had been keeping him too busy to call. No half-finished projects, stacks of papers, or bras dangling from the chandelier. That was good, anyway.

"He ain't going to be home for another half-hour or so." Patsy jumped at her brother's voice. Dwayne struggled up the steps, weighed down with an oversized box. He propped it on the porch railing and took a deep breath. "What're you doing here, anyway?"

"Nothing." Patsy frowned at her brother. "What are you doing here?"

"Delivering." He nodded at the box. "Tilde told me to drop off my stuff so Will could start photographing it."

"You're putting carvings on the site?"

"Yeah, why not? They'll sell as well as anything else, I figure." He pulled a miniature coon dog out of the box. "'Sides, I got enough of them lying around. Might as well get rid of some. Here, take this." He shoved the box into her arms.

As Patsy teetered under the weight, he sprinted down the steps, back to his truck. She lowered the box onto the porch swing and walked to the railing to watch him. He strode back with two of their father's chainsaw carvings under his arms. He plopped one down.

"What do you think?"

It was Ralph with Pugnacious attached to his ear. "Dad made it for Will. As a thank you for . . ." He motioned to the box. "You know."

Patsy didn't know. Dwayne talked like Will and her family had been working together for weeks. Why hadn't

she known about this? She was the one who was into the
Internet, and she was as much into Ozark crafts as any of
them. How could Will talk with her family and leave her
out?

"You going to be here a while?" Dwayne asked.

"I guess." She didn't have anywhere else to be and
now, more than ever, she wanted to talk with Will.

Dwayne left after unloading five more chainsaw carvings. Patsy pushed the box of smaller pieces to the side
and sat down on the swing. Twenty minutes later, Will's
BMW pulled into the drive.

He hopped out of the car, a small plastic box tucked
under one arm. His steps slowed as he approached the
porch and saw her waiting.

"Patsy." He looked at the collection of carvings that
filled the space between the steps and the door. "You
dropping stuff off?"

"No, Dwayne did. I just told him I'd wait for you." A
water spot on the swing's arm grabbed her attention. After
licking her finger, she concentrated on rubbing it off.

"Oh . . ." He dug out his key and unlocked the door.
"Well, I can get it if you've got somewhere you need to
go."

He was awfully indifferent for someone who'd been
blowing in her ear during Sunday services. Annoyed, she
picked up a chainsaw beaver and staggered in the door.
"Where do you want this?"

"What? Geez, let me take that." He grabbed the statue
and walked into the turret. Patsy followed.

The round room was packed with boxes. An assortment of handmade crafts poked out of them. He set the
beaver down and turned back to the door. The expression on his face said he was less than happy to see she'd
followed.

What was up with him? To cover her confusion, she
said, "Wow. I had no idea." She walked to a box that
emitted a relaxing scent.

"Lavender soap. There are sachets too." Will kicked the box under it.

"What's that?" Patsy pointed to the plastic tote he still held.

"Flies." He flipped open the lid. "Hand-tied fishing flies." He stroked a yellow-and-black one with the pad of his finger. "Plenty of people will pay big bucks for these babies. Can you believe the man who makes them has been selling them for a couple of dollars each?"

Looking at the creations of snarled thread, Patsy believed it. "So, you're serious about this?" He couldn't really be this excited about carvings, sachets, and flies.

His eyes widened in surprise. "Of course, why wouldn't I be?"

"I don't know. I mean, what's in it for you? Maybe you can make a little on those flies, but the rest of this stuff?" She gestured to the boxes surrounding them. "You don't really think you're going to make a profit on it, do you? I mean, once you pay for space and advertising and everything else Tilde said you have planned, there won't be any money left."

Will chuckled. "I've done this before, you know."

"Not selling this kind of thing." Patsy picked up a hand-hooked rug. "How much money can there be in it?"

He took the rug, folded it, and laid it to the side. "You might be surprised. Have you ever shopped for quality handmade crafts?"

Patsy hadn't, but she thought Will was being incredibly naïve. "No, and there's a reason right there why it won't work. Why buy something handmade when you can get the same thing for a third the price at BiggeeMart?"

"Because it's not the same thing, it's better."

She looked at him, standing there all superior and confident, talking to her like she didn't understand. She'd lived here her whole life. He was the one who didn't understand.

"Yeah, and that's why there aren't any factory jobs

anymore. People don't care about quality as much as they do price. If that weren't true, Daisy Creek would still have the shoe factory and the uniform factory, and Dwayne wouldn't be about to lose his job cutting."

Will frowned. "It's not the same thing."

"Sure it's the same thing." She picked up a bar of the soap, took a sniff, and dropped it back in the box. "You're just getting everyone's hopes up that there's something else out there for them, something they can do here in Daisy Creek. It won't work out and they'll be right back where they started. It's not right."

"Giving people hope isn't right?" His voice was tense.

"Not if that's all it is. It's better to never have hope than to have it and get it crushed right in front of you. That's a pain that's hard to get rid of."

"I don't understand you." Tension was giving over to anger. "I'm offering people an opportunity to do something they love and make a little extra cash in the process. What's wrong with that?"

"You don't understand."

"You're right. I don't." He turned on his heel and strode out of the turret.

He didn't understand. He never had a dream squashed by reality. Patsy had. She didn't want to see it happen to somebody else. She ran her hand over the rug. The motion was soothing, the wool slightly coarse. She spread the rug out. A boxy cabin sat nestled against a rainbow. The design made her smile, a simple setting, but filled with hope.

Maybe he was right. He wasn't promising people anything more than a chance to make a little extra money. Maybe she was overreacting. Maybe there was room for some hope. After refolding the rug, she trudged back to the foyer.

"I'm making baskets."

Will paused in unpacking the box of figurines Dwayne had dropped off. "What?"

"Baskets. I make baskets, at least I used to. Tilde and Granny talked me into making some for the site."

"Really? I didn't know you did that. You've never talked about it." His annoyance faded into warmth. Patsy didn't want the mood to pass, wanted to stay immersed in this moment.

"There was never any reason. There isn't much use for it. I used to sell them at craft shows and to a few locals on special orders, but it didn't pay for more than my materials. Then I got busy learning web design." She picked up a figure of a trout jumping out of the water. "Besides, you've seen one at least . . . the picnic basket from the river."

"You made that?" He looked surprised, and impressed.

"Yeah." Suddenly Patsy felt shy. He'd admired it that day, but his approval was more important now.

"It was beautiful." Will touched her hand that held the trout.

Patsy tipped her head up, smiling at him. "Thanks."

"I mean it . . ." He ran his hand up her arm. "Patsy, about the other day . . ."

She wavered for a moment. The spell between them was so alluring. She didn't want to lose this closeness, but she had to. It wasn't fair to either of them to pretend.

"Let's just forget it, okay?" She stepped toward the box and laid the trout down. "What I said still holds. I'm leaving Daisy Creek, and you're staying. Getting involved will just complicate things." She said it softly, hoping to keep an ember of the intimacy going, but his face shuttered closed.

"We can be friends though," her voice quavered. "And I'd like to help you with the site. If you'd like the help, that is."

"I thought you didn't like the idea." His eyes were unreadable, his voice cold. It hurt, made her nervous.

"I was being hasty. You're not promising anybody

anything, just a chance at a little extra cash, like you said." Don't be angry. Don't block me out.

He weighed her words. "So what do you want to do?"

She picked up another figurine, this one of a dog sitting beside an outhouse. She twisted it in her hands. "I don't know. I could help take pictures or work on the design, whatever. Based on what Tilde said, you've got a lot to get done in the next month." She shrugged. "I just thought I'd offer."

He stared at her for a heartbeat. "Sure, you can never have too many friends or too much help, right?"

"Right." Patsy felt as pathetic as last year's prom dress.

Patsy spent the next few days finishing the Sunrise site, then dedicated herself to working on baskets, photographing crafts with Tilde, and scanning groceries. She was exhausted.

Her new picnic basket was turning out great though. She'd even talked to Dwayne about carving daisy handles onto the wood flaps she would attach to the top. She couldn't wait to show it to Will tonight.

He was coming to dinner. Granny invited him, and Patsy was looking forward to it. She told herself it was just nice to have someone her age who liked the things she liked, even admired her work. The sexual stuff might still be there, but now that Will understood her boundaries, she could keep things fraternal.

"You holding up the wall?" Bruce had exited the break room.

"My shift doesn't start for ten minutes. I was just thinking."

"Think in your own space. This is for paying customers." He flicked a limp lettuce leaf. "Leroy, get back here and hose down the produce."

Patsy suppressed the urge to stick her tongue out at him. He was a waste of space, air, and time. As she watched him walk away, Marcia Stephens stumbled out of the break room, tucking her shirt into her pants.

"How's it going, Marcia?"

Marcia jumped and flushed at the same time. "Oh, Patsy, I didn't see you standing there. You scared me."

"Uh huh." Patsy raised an eyebrow and let her eyes linger on Marcia's crumpled clothing. "Getting a shirt that'll stay in place is a real bitch, isn't it?"

Marcia placed her hand on her middle. "I was stocking."

"Yeah, I hear a lot of that's been going on in the break room."

Marcia flushed again and started to scurry away.

"Marcia—" Patsy waited for her to turn. "How's Carl? I haven't seen him around lately."

"He's fine." Marcia gave up on her shirt and pulled on her purple smock with a snap. "He's been working two jobs."

Patsy stared back at her.

Marcia straightened her spine and looked Patsy in the eye. "Things aren't always simple you know, Patsy."

"Some things are."

Marcia laughed, a low derisive sound. "No, Patsy, they aren't." Fastening her smock, she stalked to the front of the store.

The woman was cheating on her husband and didn't even have the good sense or manners to hide it. She could talk all she wanted about things being complicated, but what she was doing was plain and simple wrong. There was no other way to look at it.

Patsy was a little surprised at her own nerve. She was sure it was as close as anyone had ever come to out-and-out telling Marcia no one was fooled by her little act. Maybe if someone had done it earlier, she'd be spending more time thinking about her marriage and less arranging Bruce's stock.

Ruthann brushed past Marcia. "You're in early," she said.

"Not much, ten minutes or so." Patsy followed her into

the break room. It was a plain room decorated with cheap stackable plastic chairs and an old table that had been recycled from the KFC before their remodel eight years earlier. Not much of a romantic rendezvous spot. Although Patsy had to admit she'd had warm feelings about the place since Will stood in front of the snack machine with two Hostess pies cradled in his hands. Hard not to think of a place as romantic after that. She ran her hand over the top of the table.

"You think Bruce and Marcia use this for the horizontal hump?"

Ruthann looked at her with a horrified stare that gave way to a giggle. "You are terrible."

Patsy pulled out a chair and sat down, but kept her arms off the table. Her multiple jobs had kept her too busy. She hadn't seen Ruthann since church. "So, what happened with Randy's momma?"

Ruthann shoved her time card into the machine and slid into a chair across from Patsy. "Nothing. She was sweet as marmalade."

"She ask you about anything?"

"No, but she did pin Will in a corner for a while."

"Why?"

"I don't know. Something about some property her dad owns. I got the feeling Will was interested in buying it."

This was surprising. Will didn't exactly strike Patsy as the farmer type.

"What kind of land? Near the river or something?" she asked.

"I don't think so. It's near Henning. There's not much there but fields that I know of."

Henning. Tilde had been driving out to Henning a lot lately. Interesting, but not pertinent to the current problem.

"How about Randy, she say anything about him?"

Ruthann dug a compact out of her purse and checked her lipstick. "That's about all she talked about. She bragged on him nonstop. It was like she was trying to sell me on him or something. She's never done that before."

Patsy grinned. "Great. I think the first part of our plan is under way. Now we can start on the second. The only problem is, I haven't figured out the best way to handle it."

Ruthann snapped her compact shut. "If Randy's momma was the problem and now she isn't, why do we need to work on anything else? Why can't I just go after Randy?"

"Because sooner or later, his momma's going to realize some of what we fed her wasn't one hundred percent fat-free. When that happens, she's liable to turn on you faster than a barn cat on a field mouse, and you need to know Randy's going to stick by you."

Ruthann let out a deep sigh. "All right. You've been right so far, but I don't want to wait too long. If we don't have a plan by Daisy Daze, I may just jump him."

Patsy knew the feeling. If she wasn't out of Daisy Creek by that time, she'd probably lose all will power and launch herself at Will too.

Shaking her head at her own weakness, she replied, "Fair enough." She picked up her time card and punched in. "Let's go scan ourselves some peas."

Will looked over at Ralph, who rode with his head hanging out the passenger window, tongue lolling. In general, Ralph took life pretty seriously. It was nice to see him relaxed and almost dog-like. A cloud of dust signaled another car approaching. Will hugged the right side of the dirt road, giving the other vehicle plenty of leeway.

Tilde's van popped over the horizon. Will rolled down his window and waved his arm outside it. Crunching gravel signaled she had seen him.

She cranked down her window and poked her head out. "Where you headed, kid?"

"Going to see Randy Jensen's grandfather. I was talking

to Randy's mother and she said he was interested in selling."

"That so? I didn't really figure him to be interested. Things must be tough all over."

Ralph abandoned his window to investigate who Will was talking to. Will absently rubbed his head. "Certainly seems that way. I never dreamed so many people would be desperate to sell."

Tilde flipped down her visor and applied a coat of lipstick. "There'll be more. Word's just now getting out that the rumors are true, that someone's interested in buying up all this." She motioned with the gold tube. "If you aren't careful, you'll own half of Daisy Creek County."

"I don't think it will come to that."

"Maybe, maybe not. Folks can be pretty impatient when it comes to making cash."

That was certainly true. Richard Parks called Will daily about his plans. Pretty soon Will would have to call him back.

Will said, "I appreciate you helping me with all this."

"No need to thank me. I'm glad to have something to do besides haunt estate sales and farm auctions."

"Thanks for talking Patsy into making baskets too. I had no idea she was so talented."

"Runs in the family." Tilde laughed. "The good looks too." She snapped her visor up. "Mom's hoping it gets her mind off leaving Daisy Creek. I don't hold out much hope for that, but I figure it can't hurt none."

A truck pulling a trailer with two four-wheelers crested the hill.

"I better get moving. I'll stop by later this week with some more things for the site."

Will watched Tilde disappear in a cloud of red dust. So, Granny wanted Patsy to stay. Not surprising. From the way Patsy acted, though, it would take a lot more than a few baskets to keep her in Daisy Creek. Will just wished he knew what.

Chapter Sixteen

Patsy arranged rolls of oak strips, flat reed, and fabric into stacks on the back porch. It looked like she had everything: a pan for soaking, tape measure, scissors, pencil, and a beginner plan for Will to follow. She'd found a plan online for a miniature tobacco basket. She was going to show him some of the baskets she was working on, but thought he'd probably like to work on something of his own too. It was always more rewarding to do something yourself.

"Patsalee, get in here and start the pies frying. They'll need time to cool before we can eat 'em."

Granny was pulling out all the stops: fried catfish, hush puppies, green beans with bacon, and, Patsy's all-time favorite, fried apple pies. The way Granny'd fussed all afternoon, you'd have thought Billy Graham was coming to call.

Of course, Patsy had done her share of fussing too. She couldn't help it. She'd never known anyone like Will before, someone her age who really appreciated the things she did. It was hard not to be excited by that.

Patsy anchored the basket plans down with the scissors and headed inside. A knock on the door sent Pugnacious into a fit, barking and hopping on stiff legs.

"Look at her. She acts like she could take out 'Stone Cold' Steve Austin, Triple H, and the Undertaker all at once." Granny laughed. "Better let the boy in before she knocks down the door."

Patsy followed her genteel pet to the front.

On the other side, Will stood waiting, a bouquet of daisies in one hand, a WWE cookbook in the other. Ralph sat at his feet, one of the petite baskets from the site gripped in his mouth. Dog biscuits poked out the top.

Will shifted from one Dockers-clad foot to the other. "Your grandmother said Ralph was invited too. I hope you don't mind."

He looked awkward, out of place, and sexy as sin. Patsy bit her lower lip.

"Don't ask me. Ask Pugnacious," she replied as lightly as she could.

The pug surged forward, but stopped short when she saw the basket Ralph gently laid at her feet.

"You have got to be kidding me," Patsy said.

"What?" Will looked up from the flowers.

"Your dog. How did you get him to deliver those cookies without eating them?"

Will shrugged. "It's just who he is. He'd like to eat one just as much as the next dog, but he knows his job is to deliver them, so he does."

Patsy's less-mannered beast snuffled over and began chomping down the treats. For once, she was happy Pugnacious was being her usual pig-mannered self. It gave Patsy something to do besides stare at Will. "Pugnacious, leave some for Ralph." She tugged the pug's collar and grabbed a few of the dog biscuits.

Ralph watched, eyes alert, until Patsy tossed the treats in the air. He delicately snagged one and nosed the others into a manageable pile. Pugnacious whined and pulled, but Patsy maintained her grip on her collar.

"You have plenty. Eat those." Patsy pushed her dog toward the remaining treats and threw Ralph an apologetic look. "Sorry." Looking back at Will, she said, "I really admire how you've trained him. I wish I could teach Pugnacious half his manners." She sounded polite and distant. A passerby would never guess they'd been twisting naked in his sheets just days earlier. The company manners were getting on Patsy's nerves. She longed for a little less civility and a lot more heat.

"Don't admire me. It's just who he is." Will brushed his fingers along his dog's back. "There was a book that came out a few years ago. According to it, every dog has a song to sing. Taking care of things, doing the right thing is Ralph's."

Patsy looked down at Pugnacious. "I hate to think what Pugnacious is singing," she joked. She could barely concentrate on the conversation. Seeing Will up close and personal was proving harder than she'd imagined.

He knelt to scratch the pug on the top of her head. For the first time ever, Patsy was jealous of her dog.

"There's nothing wrong with her song," he said. "She's sure of herself and loves life. You don't see that kind of self-acceptance too often, in people or dogs. Right, girl?"

He made it sound so right, relaxing and rolling with what life threw at you, but Patsy couldn't believe that. Couldn't trust that being herself would be enough to secure her happiness.

After snarfing down the last cookie bit, the pug let out a belch.

Patsy grimaced. Obviously, self-acceptance wasn't such a great goal.

"Oh, here." Will held out the bouquet of daisies.

A lump formed in Patsy's throat.

"I'm sorry if you'd have preferred something else, but your mother said you liked daisies, and they just seemed right."

There was something vulnerable about his explanation and Patsy realized she'd been staring. She couldn't remember anyone buying her flowers before, except maybe a corsage for prom. Even though Will and she had agreed to simple friendship, something about him standing there holding out those daisies made her go all soft and mushy, a feeling past the physical attraction she was fighting.

He began to lower his arm.

"I love them," she blurted, reaching out to grab the bouquet. "Uh, thank you." She couldn't seem to think of anything else to say, just stood there staring at him.

He stared back for a second, then opened his mouth as if to speak.

"You inviting the boy in?" Granny hobbled to the doorway separating the dining and living rooms. "I need you to fry those pies."

Will and Patsy exchanged guilty glances.

After stepping inside, Will asked, "Fried pies?"

Happy the moment had passed, Patsy grinned. "I told Granny you were into eating healthy. She's not much on Gardenburgers either, but she planned a well-balanced meal: fish, vegetables, and fruit for dessert."

"It sounds delicious, Mrs. Jackson." He followed Patsy and Granny into the kitchen.

Patsy pulled out the biggest iron skillet and poured in a few inches of oil.

"Why don't you use the Crisco, sis?" Granny fussed at her from the kitchen table.

"I'm doing this." Patsy motioned to Will. "Hand me that platter of pies."

Will watched as Patsy carefully slid the pies into the bubbling oil.

"I didn't know you could fry a pie." His tone indicated he didn't know why you would either.

"Just like McDonald's," Patsy replied.

Granny snorted. "Them things are the sorriest excuse for a fried pie I ever ate." She gave Will a conspiratorial look. "The secret is in the crust. You gotta make it a little tougher than normal, so it won't get soggy."

Will nodded sagely.

"Tell him your secret," Patsy said.

"Ain't no secret. Folks just don't appreciate staples."
Granny leaned forward. "Lard."

Will's eyes widened.

"Nothing makes a piecrust like lard. It's good for you
too. I been eating lard for over seventy years and look
at me." Granny thumped her cane on the ground. "I'm
going strong."

Patsy hid her smile as she flipped the pies.

During dinner, Will was his usual charming self.
Granny preened at his compliments and bullied him
into eating seconds of everything. Patsy suspected he'd
never eaten this much fat at one sitting. He didn't complain though, and seemed to genuinely enjoy the pies.

He used a fork and knife to cut off a bite. "These are
great," he said after tasting it.

Patsy giggled. "Not like that. You have to use your
hands—see?" She picked up her pie and bit off a chunk.

"You leave the boy alone, sis. If he wants to eat it with
a fork, that's fine by me." Granny bit into her own pie.

Will dropped his fork and picked up the pastry. Holding it out, he examined it.

"What?" Patsy asked.

"I was just thinking, you made these from scratch?"

"Of course."

"Well, they look kind of like a Hostess pie, don't you
think?"

Patsy nodded.

"You ever try making one with pudding?"

Granny dropped her napkin over her plate. "A fried
pudding pie? Son, that sounds about as tasty as snails on
toast." She shook her head. "And people say folks from
the Ozarks eat strange."

When they were done with dessert, Will presented
Granny with the cookbook he had brought, and Patsy
sent her into the living room to watch TV.

"You worked all day. We can clean up."

"Don't you be making that boy clean up. He's our guest."

With Granny settled in her chair and with the WWE blaring, Patsy and Will cleaned off the table.

"Where's the dishwasher?" Will stood in the center of the floor, balancing a stack of dirty plates.

"You're looking at her, unless you want to volunteer. Scrape those dishes first." Patsy nodded to the trashcan.

"How do you live without a dishwasher?" Will slid his load onto the countertop and began dumping scraps into the trash.

Patsy laughed. "It's not like air, you know."

"Might as well be. If my mom or sister had to hand wash a dish, they'd be petitioning the president."

"For what, their God-given right to kitchen appliances?" Patsy slid a plate into the sudsy water. "You're exaggerating. Plenty of people don't have dishwashers."

"Nobody I know."

"Granny and I don't, and what about your house? It didn't have a dishwasher, did it?"

"There was some kind of ancient roll-around thing, but Mrs. Jensen had it replaced with a built-in."

"Here, dry." She shoved a dishtowel into his hand. "Well, I know plenty of people who don't have dishwashers, or microwaves, or, brace yourself, Internet connections."

Will staggered back in a fake heart attack. "Say it isn't true."

Patsy giggled. "Just dry." While he performed his assigned task, Patsy watched him out of the corner of her eye. This evening had been so perfect, cozy.

Will with Patsy's family was like peanut butter with jelly—from completely different beginnings, but perfection when blended.

After cleaning up, they joined the dogs on the back porch.

"What's all this?" Will picked up the roll of oak strips.

"You said you wanted to learn basket weaving."

"I do, but I didn't think—"

"You don't have to think, at least not this time. Just follow the plan, and do what I tell you. You *think* you can handle that?" Patsy shoved the metal pan into his hands. "Now get some water." She gave him a playful frown.

While Will wandered over to the spigot, Patsy fussed over the basket materials, smoothing out the plans and double-checking to make sure nothing had grown legs and wandered off—or been snarfed by a pug in search of a chew toy.

"What kind of basket are we making?" Will asked over the sound of running water.

"You mean, you're making. I'm just supervising."

"You have one bossy mistress, don't you, Pugnacious?" Will knelt down, letting the pug slurp from the pan.

"Don't let her do that." Patsy threw up her hands.

Will scratched the little dog behind her ear and pushed her toward Ralph. "Go tree something. Your mistress is going to teach me a thing or two."

"Put the pan down and grab that roll of reed." Patsy pointed to the other side of the wide, round table.

"This?" Will held up a bundle of sea grass.

Shaking her head, Patsy again motioned to the reed.

After he handed it to her, she said, "Now you have to measure and cut it into strips. The plan says thirteen-and-a-half inches long, but you can do whatever you like." She bent over the table, studying the tape measure.

Will leaned in close, sniffing her hair. "You still smell good."

Patsy pushed her hair behind her ears. "It's grease from dinner. You could fry a dishrag and it'd be appetizing."

"Are you saying you're appetizing?" His tone was light, but his words caused something to flutter in Patsy's stomach.

She wasn't going to play. The evening had been going so well. Sexual innuendo would just land them back at the same point—Patsy wanted out of Daisy Creek, Will didn't.

Flipping the reed over, she said, "See how one side is rougher than the other? You want the rough side to face up in the basket."

"Interesting." Will ran his finger down the length of reed and continued on, traveling up her arm. "You have a scar here." He traced a white patch of skin on her forearm. Again, his voice held only light curiosity, but his touch changed the flutter to a thump.

"Old hunting accident," she quipped.

"What were you hunting?" He ran his finger around the white skin.

And she'd always thought she had no feeling there. She pulled her arm out of his reach.

"Smart-aleck city boys." She pressed a wooden handle for the basket into his hand. "Fried, they're almost as good eating as a dishrag."

Will held the handle up to the light, inspecting it. "Who's the smart-aleck now?"

Patsy ignored him and continued with her instructions. "We're going to staple the reed to the handle, not one hundred percent authentic, but fancy enough for a beginner."

"What makes you think I'm a beginner? My technique not polished enough for you?"

Patsy flushed. If his technique was any more polished, she'd have him pinned to the table right now.

"Once we have five strips hanging down, we can start weaving, like this." She demonstrated moving a sixth piece of reed through the ones attached to the handle.

"I think I get it. In and out. In and out. In and—"

"What we're—" Patsy's voice was louder than she'd intended. She moderated it some and continued "—going for here are these square holes." She pointed to the picture of a finished basket, then moved on before he could add another comment she didn't want to deal with. "Now we staple again, so we have a diamond in the bottom of the basket."

Will stepped closer until he was looking at the basket over her shoulder.

"You could see better over there." Patsy gestured to the other side of the table.

"The view here suits me fine." He smiled at her, only inches from her face.

With her heart pounding in her chest, she raced through the last few steps. "One last staple and you're done. Now you can dye it or leave it natural. I like the aged look, but a walnut dye might be nice too." Her voice was shaky. He was so close. His breath was warm against the side of her neck and something deep in her stomach clenched with each exhalation.

Mouth close to her throat, he murmured, "I think I'll leave it as is. The best things in life don't need improving."

A shiver flew up her spine. She had to put distance between them. Using clean-up as an excuse, she slid from his reach. "I can't think of too many things that can't use improving."

"Maybe you just think they need improving. Once you try it, you may discover they don't." He stepped toward her again, letting his hand rest lightly on her arm.

"And I may discover they do." She jutted her chin up, looking him in the eyes. He was trying to confuse her, but she knew what she wanted.

"You may discover all kinds of things. I know I have." His eyes glimmered and his hand traveled farther up her arm, massaging her skin.

Patsy stepped backward. "Thanks for the flowers, and the cookbook for Granny, and the dog treats. Pugnacious loved them." It was abrupt, almost rude, but she was desperate. She'd resisted far more than any woman should have to.

Will let his hand fall from her arm, his gaze shuttered

closed. Looking at Ralph, he patted his leg and said, "Come on, boy. Looks like we're done here."

Patsy and Pugnacious followed them to the door. Patsy lasted until Will and Ralph were off the porch before allowing her knees to crumple and her body to land in a crouch. This friendship thing was way more complicated than she'd planned.

Will was in love with Patsy, and she wasn't interested. The discovery wasn't a pleasant one, but there it was. Spending time with Patsy at her house made it all clear.

Patsy laughing and teasing and relaxed. She brought out a side of him most people didn't see. He'd come close to pushing aside their agreement and his own earlier resolve, forcing her to admit she wanted more than friendship, but she'd made it more than obvious his feelings weren't returned.

He'd come close to humiliating himself, too close.

He had to put a stop to this. After Sunday, he'd thought he had it under control, knew his plan to toy with her, to prove she wasn't any more immune to the attraction between them than he was, was asinine, but alone with her he couldn't stop himself.

If Patsy wasn't interested, he had to move on. There were only a couple of ways to forget a woman—find another one, or lose yourself in work. Will picked up the phone and dialed Perry Realtors.

Another basket finished. Patsy placed the jack-o-lantern next to the hamper. It was great. A little quirky for her, but she loved it. She'd seen a basket like this in a fancy country decorating magazine and decided to make one. The magazine showed kids trick-or-treating, but Patsy suspected more people would buy them just to hold candy or for a centerpiece.

She picked up Will's daisies and set them inside. The colors weren't the best, but it was a good idea. Maybe she'd get some fall flowers, maybe even dried ones, for the web site photo. Even after the awkwardness at the end of last night, she couldn't wait to show Will. They got along so well together. They'd get past the other. They had to. She was removing his bouquet when the phone rang.

It was Glenn.

"Great news. Sunrise loved the site. The testimonials really sealed it."

Patsy dropped into a chair.

"Are you there? I said they loved it. The marketing manager is going to call you personally to compliment you."

"That's great. I don't know what to say."

"Well, think of something, because my guess is, she's going to be asking you to drive north for an interview. She asked me if you'd be interested and what kind of pay you'd need to make the move."

What kind of pay?

"I didn't know what you had in mind, but I told her you were already working on another project and she'd better get an offer in soon if she's interested." He paused. "Are you still working on the site for that friend of yours?"

Patsy looked at the daisies. "Yeah, but I'm not doing any real web work. Just helping with pictures and stuff."

"She doesn't have to know that. It's better if she thinks there might be some reason you want to stay in Daisy Creek, and another job is perfect. Don't let it slip that there's nothing keeping you there. I think you can negotiate a better package that way."

Nothing keeping her here. One daisy poked higher out of the basket than the others. Patsy tucked it back inside, breaking the stem in the process.

"Did you hear me?" Glenn interrupted her work.

"Yeah, don't let her know nothing's keeping me here."

She stared down at the broken bloom. "You're probably right."

"Damn straight. How about we get together for dinner to celebrate? Not tonight, I have a project to finish up, but tomorrow? Is there anyplace decent to eat there?"

Dazed, Patsy answered, "We could go to the Dogwood Inn. It's nice."

"Great, I'll pick you up at six. See ya then."

Long after he hung up, Patsy sat with the phone in her hand, the broken daisy resting on her leg, and the jack-o-lantern basket smirking at her.

"You're late."

Patsy pulled her smock off its hanger and ignored her boss. He got more and more charming by the second. She fed her time card into the machine and stomped into the store. Bruce started railing on Leroy about limp lettuce or dented cans or some other world catastrophe.

Patsy held her fingers an inch apart and mouthed to Leroy, "Tiny dick." At Leroy's chuckle, Bruce swirled around.

"Don't I pay you to scan groceries?"

If you could call minimum wage pay, he did.

"If you want to get another paycheck, I suggest you twist your behind up to that cash register and get to it."

After he turned back to Leroy, Patsy indulged herself in an adolescent eye roll and sashayed to the front.

"What tripped his trigger?" she asked Ruthann.

"I don't know for sure, but Marcia called in sick. Could be Carl's finally onto them."

Patsy's stomach coiled into a knot. For all that she'd lectured Marcia, she hadn't wanted this. She just wanted Marcia to wise up and stop cheating. Carl finding out about the affair would only cause hurt all around.

"So, I've got news." Ruthann sprayed her scanner with Windex and wiped it off.

"Really?" Patsy smiled at a twenty-year-old toting two kids and a cart full of Lay's and Mountain Dew.

"Randy asked me out." Ruthann beamed.

"That's nice." Patsy removed a half-eaten Hershey bar from the toddler's hand and passed it over the scanner.

Ruthann curled her lip at the chocolate stain left on Patsy's hand. After ripping off a paper towel, she handed it to Patsy. "Here."

She watched as Patsy counted out the young mother's change and bagged her purchases. "I thought you'd be happy for me."

Patsy looked at her friend's indignant face. "I am. I'm sorry. I just have a lot on my mind."

Ruthann dug stickers out of her smock pocket and handed them to the children. "Will?"

"No, I told you we're just friends. Actually, I have a date with Glenn."

"Hmm, where are you going?"

"The Dogwood Inn." Patsy paused. "I shouldn't have called it a date. It's more of a business meeting, a celebration."

"Really? What for?" Ruthann opened a pack of Juicy Fruit and folded a piece into her mouth.

Lining the quarters up end to end in her change drawer, Patsy replied, "I finished the web site for Sunrise. Glenn thinks they're going to offer me a job." She snuck a look at her friend.

"Hmm." Ruthann snapped her gum. "Can't wait to leave us all behind, I guess."

"You know that's not it." Another customer wheeled into Patsy's lane. Patsy flipped down the end of the cart and grabbed a box of Wheaties. "I just need something more."

"You mean more better."

Now was not the time to correct Ruthann's grammar. "Just more."

"Ruthann, I know I should be impressed you can chew

gum and jaw with Patsy at the same time, but since I'm not paying you to do either one, I suggest you get back to work." Bruce yelled from his elevated office.

Ruthann put her back to Patsy and motioned an approaching customer into her lane. For once, Patsy was glad her boss was such a giant pain. Her conversation with Ruthann was going nowhere fast. Why couldn't anyone understand that Patsy needed to leave Daisy Creek? Ruthann acted like it was a personal attack, and Granny'd been simmering like chicken soup in a crock pot for days.

Four hours later, Patsy was ready for a break. She locked her register and headed to the deli department to grab a bologna sandwich.

"I know what's been going on. I just want you to admit it." Carl Stephens stood next to a shaking Bruce.

"Really, Carl, I have no idea what you think you know, but trust me, you are way off track."

"My marriage may be off track, but *trust me*, I'm not." Carl leaned in, his face only inches from the other man's.

Bruce grimaced like he smelled something bad and twisted his head to the side. "There's no reason to get angry. If you'd calm down, I'm sure we could work this out."

"Where's my wife?" Carl took an unsteady step back, knocking a jar of deli mustard onto the tile. It hit with a loud crack, spilling yellow goop onto the floor.

Bruce didn't even glance at the stain on his otherwise pristine floor. "I already told you. Marcia called in sick today. If she isn't home, I have no idea where she is."

"She's not hiding out in your car? Don't think I haven't heard about your little lunch meetings. This town is too small. We're onto you." Carl slumped against the bread display, crushing the Roman Meal. "Everybody's onto you."

Bruce sidestepped out of Carl's reach. "If she calls in, I'll tell her you're looking for her."

Carl didn't notice as Bruce scurried away, leaving a trail of yellow spots in his wake. Carl looked deflated. Patsy hurt for him. She knew the pain of finding out someone you loved was cheating on you, making you into a fool in front of the whole town. She approached Carl. His head was bowed and his shoulders shook.

Placing her hand on his arm, she said, "Carl?"

He looked up, meeting her gaze with bloodshot eyes. "Yeah? Oh, hey, Patsy. I guess you heard. Not that it matters. You probably knew anyway. Everybody does."

The stench of stale beer enveloped her. She forced herself to stay put. "She's not here. Bruce didn't lie—about that."

"I know. She's left me. Can you believe that?" He ran his hand over his face. "She left me. She's been sneaking around with that bald-headed weasel, and I never said a thing. Then she up and leaves me."

There wasn't anything Patsy could say to make it better. "I'm sorry, Carl."

"Yeah, I guess you understand. It's rough, isn't it? Can't trust in anything anymore. Things used to be so simple. I had my life all planned out and now look at me, yelling at No-Balls Bruce in the deli section." He uttered a low laugh. "Pretty sad."

"You'll get past it."

"Will I? Did you?"

Patsy ignored the question and concentrated on steering him outside. "How are you getting home?"

"Does it matter?"

"You can't drive."

He leaned against a metal column.

"Don't be stupid, Carl. You still have a daughter and parents and a ton of people who love you. You'll get past this. You can't give up."

Slumping lower on the post, he said, "I can walk to Mom and Dad's. They just live over behind the KFC."

Patsy separated a Starlight mint from the stickers in

her pocket. "Eat this. It won't solve everything, but maybe it'll keep the complications down some."

He twisted it open and stumbled off toward his parents. He was a mess, but at least he didn't drive. And he was headed somewhere people would watch out for him, instead of airing his problems in front of every shopper at the Bag & Basket.

Damn Marcia for creating this mess.

What about this town caused people to cheat and drink? Patsy stopped. Carl smelled like the inside of Busch can, and Marcia'd said things weren't always simple. Was Patsy judging the wrong half?

She shook her head. Not that it mattered. They'd both screwed up, and they'd both pay the price, especially as long as they were in Daisy Creek. No one would let them forget this slipup. When you stepped in a mess in this town, you carried it around with you for the rest of your life.

She stamped on the automatic doormat and waited for the door to swing open. The loudspeaker greeted her.

"Leroy, clean up on aisle six."

Life should be so simple.

Chapter Seventeen

"Where you headed?" Granny set her chair to a gentle rock.

"The Dogwood Inn. Glenn's picking me up."

"That boy in the revved-up car?" Granny's chair thumped as it bumped against the wall.

"It's not revved up. That's the way it came." Patsy slumped on the couch, studying the pattern of granny squares that made up the afghan.

A squeak followed by another thump signaled Granny standing up. "You never did show me that basket you was so proud of, the one like a jack-o-lantern. Where'd you leave it?"

"It's in the kitchen." Patsy waved her hand in a vague motion, but pushed herself up to follow.

"Well, that's something. It is." Granny held the grinning basket at arm's length.

"You like it?"

"What'd you say it was for?"

"Trick-or-treating, or holding candy, or my favorite, a centerpiece. Look. I got some dried flowers today."

Patsy picked up a bag from the floor and pulled out the flowers. "See how nice that looks." She spread the stems out, filling the basket. "There wasn't much to pick from in town, so I just got gold and green, but you could use some other shades of green and maybe a darker orange." She held the arrangement out to her grandmother.

"Now that is right pretty. Let's set it right here in the

center of the table where folks can see it." Granny plopped the basket down.

"You have to put the face in front." Patsy twisted the basket so he grinned at the front door.

"Yeah, wouldn't do for him not to be facing the front."

The basket really was great. It would be perfect for Thanksgiving. Patsy could see it sitting on a table filled with turkey, cranberry sauce, and pies. She could even make little ones to match. Granny could fill them with her special spiced walnuts and people could take them home afterward. It would be a nice touch. Will would love it.

Will, she had to stop thinking of him. He'd probably be eating Thanksgiving in Chicago anyway. For that matter, come November, Patsy might not be in Daisy Creek either, not if she got the job with Sunrise. She'd be in St. Louis, her and Pugnacious eating frozen turkey TV dinners and Mrs. Smith's pumpkin pie. The cloud of disquiet that had surrounded Patsy all day settled back around her.

"What's wrong with you?" Granny's voice jarred Patsy out of her dreary holiday plans.

"Nothing." Patsy stuck another dried stem into the jack-o-lantern. "You think it needs more green?"

"I don't think there's much hope of getting it any prettier."

Patsy's gaze narrowed. "You don't like it."

"I like any basket you like making. You want some tea?" Granny tottered over to retrieve the pitcher.

Headlights flashed through the window. "There's Glenn. I'll see you later. Don't wait up."

Patsy grabbed her purse, and hurried to the door to keep Pugnacious from going into her normal "you're not welcome" routine. She turned to wave good-bye to her grandmother. Granny stood next to the table, sipping her tea. The pitcher sat in front of the basket, blocking his grin.

"I was going to knock on the door," Glenn greeted Patsy halfway up the walk.

"I didn't want to set my dog off." Patsy stomped to the passenger door and yanked it open.

He slid into the driver's seat. "Is something wrong?"

Her grandmother was a pushy, opinionated manipulator. "No, nothing's wrong. I was just hurrying."

Glenn gunned up the engine and roared out of town. The Dogwood Inn was about a thirty-minute drive. The roads were only marginally straighter than the ones Patsy and he had taken to Sauk City. She resumed her grip on the door loop.

"You hear from Sunrise yet?" Glenn swerved around a carload of kids, probably heading off somewhere to drink beer by the river.

"Not yet, but it's only Tuesday."

"True enough. I bet you hear from them soon though. The marketing manager sounded pretty pleased with the site." He twisted up the volume of his CD player, filling the car with Pink Floyd.

Patsy gripped the loop tighter. They made the rest of the trip in relative silence with Glenn nodding along to the music and Patsy struggling to not fling the CD out the passenger window.

"Not much of a parking lot, is it?" Glenn's little car bumped over a rut dried in the mud.

"There's a gravel area over there." Patsy pointed to a space near the Inn. "They haven't been open real long and before that, the place was deserted for about forty years. I guess they haven't gotten around to paving."

Glenn's head bobbed as his car hit another rut and Pink Floyd repeated their lack of need for an education. "Guess not." He flipped off the music—torture, whatever. At least it was off.

"Have you been here before?" Glenn held open the Inn's door.

"Just once." She replied, scanning the room. It was

dark, not a lot of need for windows in old flour mills. The walls were rough-hewn lumber covered with art of area landmarks and wildlife. Patsy stopped to admire a watercolor of a rainbow trout.

"You think that's the dinner special?" Glenn peered over her shoulder.

"They're selling them. See." Patsy pointed to a tag in the lower corner. "This was painted by a high school student from Sauk City. It's good." Will would love to have something like this for DaisyGal. Artwork would be a good addition to the site. Patsy fished a business card for the Inn out of a basket near the cash register. Maybe if she called the owner, she could get the student's phone number.

A waitress directed them to a booth in the back. Patsy was looking over the menu when she heard a familiar voice.

"I have been dying to come here." Jessica, looking annoyingly classic in a white halter and low-cut jeans, flicked a length of auburn hair over her shoulder. "It's so romantic, don't you think?"

Patsy leaned out to get a better view of Jessica's latest victim. Ruthann stood near the hostess station, searching the restaurant's interior.

Patsy's eyes narrowed. Traitor. What was she doing here with Jessica? She knew Patsy was coming with Glenn, and what about Randy? Why waste a romantic restaurant on trash like Jessica? Trampy trash.

Of course Patsy was here with Glenn, and that wasn't romantic, but it was business and a celebration. They had every reason to go somewhere nice. Ruthann and Jessica could have stuck to the Hut.

Male laughter caused Trash and Traitor to swing around. Randy and Will walked up behind them.

"Should we get a seat?" In khaki pants and a polo shirt, Will looked dressed up compared to the other diners. He held his arm out to Jessica, who smiled and grabbed onto it like he was the last lifeline on the Titanic.

Patsy's nails scraped the white tablecloth.

"I was just telling Ruthann how romantic this place is." Jessica pressed her already compressed breasts against his arm.

Patsy gripped the edge of the table till her fingers turned white.

"Are you ready to order?" A black-aproned woman with bleached hair and a crooked smile poured water into Glenn and Patsy's glasses.

"What's good?" Glenn asked.

Patsy wasn't hungry. She picked up her glass and stared at the two couples waiting at the front, focusing in particular on every treacherous movement of the front pair. Will was on a date with Jessica—a romantic date. Jessica laughed at something he said, and Patsy's fingers tightened around the stem of her water glass.

"Patsy," Glenn placed a cool hand on hers. "What do you want to eat?"

Patsy jerked her hand away, sending water flying across the table and onto Glenn's face. The back of his head collided with the back of the booth in a disturbing thud. Horrified, Patsy jumped from her seat. The glass whirled off the table, spinning, end over end, the last few drops of ice water splattering their server, Patsy, and the floor in its dizzying journey. All eyes focused on Patsy as it crashed in a jagged mess a foot from her deceitful friends.

"So, you not ready to order?" The waitress flipped a sliver of goblet off her toe.

Patsy shook her head and attempted to become one with the booth, but the foursome had already sighted her. A small smile flitted across Jessica's perfectly made-up face.

"Patsy, we didn't know you were going to be here." She sailed toward their table, towing a pale Will behind her. Ruthann and Randy were close behind.

"Hey, Patsy." Her traitorous best friend risked a weak smile.

Patsy flicked an ice cube off the table, and watched with satisfaction as it soared toward Will. Almost instinctively, his hand shot up and snatched it out of the air.

"Sorry," Patsy said with a complete lack of sincerity.

The ice cube melted in his fist. He held it, letting it melt and dribble through his fingers. What was Patsy doing here? And who was she with? Was she on a date? She couldn't be. Ruthann would have known if Patsy had a date and where they were going. She wouldn't have suggested the same place, would she?

But it certainly looked like a date.

Will shifted his gaze to the interloper with Patsy. What was he, a colossal Celt? Wrap him in furs, streak him with blue paint, and he'd pass as an extra from *Braveheart*. Big, burly, and blond. What was attractive about that? Will crunched the dwindling cube into splinters.

Jessica stroked his forearm, blathering on about something. "We should eat together. Wouldn't that be fun?"

Eat together? With Patsy and the Celt? Will shook the melted ice off his palm.

Sure, why not?

Will smiled a slow, deadly smile and grabbed a chair from a nearby table. "Sure, why not?"

Maybe flicking the ice cube wasn't Patsy's best impulse. She motioned to their small booth. "Too bad, there's no room."

"We could sit there." Ruthann, the traitor, piped up, pointing at a round table pushed back in one corner.

"Perfect." Will smiled the smile again and something in Patsy's stomach began to tremble. Why should she be nervous? She wasn't the one on a date. Besides, they were just friends. He had no right to be angry. She was the one who should be angry—at the lot of them.

Grabbing Glenn's hand, she tugged him out of the booth. "Come on. We're moving."

Glenn followed her to the table, a confused look on his face. "Are you going to introduce me?"

"Yes, Patsy, introduce us." Even on a date with Will, the tramp couldn't stop flirting with every Y chromosome in the room.

Patsy performed her duty. After they were all settled around the table, she hissed at Ruthann sitting next to her, "What's going on? I told you I was coming here with Glenn. Why'd you bring them?" She darted her gaze across the table to Will and Jessica.

"Oh, did you mention you were coming here? I must have missed that." Ruthann lined her knife and spoon up next to her plate.

Yeah, right. "What's with the double date, anyway? You didn't say anything about that."

"It was a last-minute thing. I ran into Jessica after work, and she mentioned wanting to come here, and since you and Will aren't dating, I didn't think you'd care if we invited him along."

Randy whispered in Ruthann's ear, keeping Patsy from screaming a response. Ruthann set Jessica and Will up? Sure, Patsy wasn't interested in him, but Jessica? And why would Ruthann consider going on a double date with her, anyway? Ruthann was Patsy's friend. She had no business going out to dinner with the tramp.

Traitor.

Patsy reached for her water glass.

"Don't you think you've had enough?" Will leaned across the table, removing her glass.

"Funny," she replied in a dry tone.

"How do you know Patsy, Glenn?" Will sipped out of Patsy's glass.

"We go way back. Right, Patsy?" Glenn's arm wound

along the back of her chair. "We met three years ago when she took some classes at UMR."

"Really? I met her when she was seven."

"Hell, I've known her since she wore diapers and drooled. You don't hear me bragging about it." Jessica wrapped her hands around Will's arm. "Would you order for me? I just don't know what I feel like tonight."

Spandex-wrapped silicone?

Glenn's hand cupped Patsy's shoulder. "We've been working on a project together."

"Really? So have we." Will's eyes glimmered.

Patsy elbowed Ruthann. "Give me your water."

"Hmm?" The traitor turned a love-fogged gaze toward Patsy.

"Water."

"Oh." Ruthann handed her the glass and edged back toward Randy.

Love was sickening.

"Are you the friend Patsy was helping? What was it, some kind of web site?" Glenn squeezed her shoulder.

What was he doing? When had he become so hands-on?

"She's helped me with a lot of things. How about you?" Will countered.

"Could we discuss something else, or order?" Jessica waved her menu in the air.

"I hooked Patsy up with Sunrise. Looks like she may get a full-time job out of it." Glenn flashed his teeth at Will.

Why did he say that? Patsy hadn't told everyone about Sunrise yet, and this wasn't how she'd wanted to do it. She shook off Glenn's arm and joined Jessica in signaling the waitress.

"The mines?" A stunned look passed over Will's face.

"The ones and onlys," Glenn replied.

"You're leaving?" Jessica dropped her menu. "How great."

She was awfully chipper. "I haven't had a job offer yet," Patsy replied.

"She will, probably by Monday. Sunrise was impressed with her work." Glenn held his water glass up in salute.

"This is good news. A toast to Patsy." Jessica's glass clinked against Glenn's.

The blonde waitress approached, struck a match to the votive candle on their table, and pulled out a pad. "The specials tonight are . . ."

As the sharp odor of the spent match mingled with the pine-scented candle, Patsy stared into the two-toned eyes across from her. She was leaving. Now he knew for sure.

"What are you up to?" Patsy turned on Ruthann the instant the bathroom door closed behind them.

"Up to? I'm not up to anything." Ruthann looked under the one stall in the room.

"You never go out with Jessica."

"I like Jessica. You're the only one with a problem with her." She pushed the door open and scurried inside.

"I've never known you to go out with her before." The reflection in the mirror revealed Patsy needed more than just a quick coat of lipstick. She dug out a compact to cover the flush on her cheeks.

"Well, times change, and with you leaving, I guess I'm going to have to find a new best friend." The door to the stall rattled angrily.

"Is that it? Are you punishing me because I'm leaving?"

"No."

"Then what?" Patsy snapped the compact shut and tossed it into her bag.

A mumble sounded from the other side of the door.

Patsy rapped on the stall. "What did you say?"

"I need toilet paper."

"Why did you bring Jessica and Will here?"

"Patsy—" Ruthann whined.

Flipping open the only cabinet in the room, Patsy

replied, "Sorry, fresh out. A good friend might sneak into the men's room and get you some."

Another mumble sounded from the stall.

"What's keeping you two?" The door to the restroom flew open and Jessica sashayed in. "Will ordered chocolate mousse, and I can't wait for him to feed it to me."

Patsy stomped out of the bathroom. A teenager in a dress shirt and tie paused with his hand on the knob to the men's room.

"Excuse me, T.P. emergency." Patsy pushed past him, yanked a roll of paper off the holder and trotted back to the women's restroom.

"Here." She flung the roll over the stall door and whirled out of the room.

Back at the table, things were quiet. Randy had formed a fascination with the gilt trim on his plate, while Glenn and Will seemed to be involved in a contest of who could look the most bored and disinterested—keeping their eyes on each other the entire time.

A cloud of tension, thick as mosquitoes at a riverside picnic, hung over the table. Patsy ignored it. She had her own problems. Men and their egos were such a pain. She didn't know what was going on between Glenn and Will, but as far as she was concerned, it was their problem. She'd never done anything to lead Glenn on, and she'd been as upfront with Will as a person could be—without being downright insulting, that is.

They needed to grow up and get over it.

Now she was the one with problems. She watched as two of them walked toward the table.

Jessica was prattling about French braids versus French fries or some such nonsense. Ruthann trudged beside her, her gaze glued to her toes.

"The mousse arrive yet?" Jessica slid into place next to Will, again draping her arm around his.

Patsy was not staying to watch this. She hopped up

from her seat. "Let's go," she ordered Glenn. With a raised brow at Will, he followed her.

The drive home was quiet. Glenn didn't even push in his CD. Patsy stared out into the darkness, trying to think of anything other than what happened tonight.

When they pulled into the drive, Patsy reached for the door. "Thanks for dinner." Her words were hollow.

"Patsy." Glenn placed his hand on her arm. She stared at it for a minute, like she didn't recognize the body part or the message. "Patsy," he started again.

She cut him off. "Listen, Glenn. I don't know what happened tonight, but I just want to forget it. You're a great guy, but I'm leaving and there's really no reason to pretend otherwise. Let's just try to leave this as a nice evening between friends." Nice evening; yeah, right.

He pulled his hand back. "Is it Will?"

Patsy shook her head. "No."

He was quiet for a moment. The porch light Granny'd left on didn't reach the car. In the darkness, she could only imagine his expression.

"I think you're lying to yourself," he said.

Why did people keep saying that? "Lucky for me then, I'm doing a damn good job." She gave him a quick buss on the cheek and headed inside.

Patsy couldn't believe Will showed up with Jessica Saturday night, and that Ruthann arranged it. Maybe Patsy had said she wasn't interested in Will, but still, they didn't have to flaunt their date in front of her. It was tacky.

Will shouldn't be dating yet. It hadn't even been a month since he and Patsy made love, and already he was replacing her. There had to be some kind of dating etiquette about that, like a waiting period. Six months seemed fair, maybe even twelve. Yeah, twelve; in a year, Will could do as he pleased, but any earlier was insulting.

Patsy slammed the kitchen junk drawer shut.

She needed pliers. The daisy basket was almost done. Dwayne had dropped off the flaps yesterday, but Patsy needed to attach them. She was on her way to the garage to find some when the phone rang.

The nasal accent on the other end of the line alerted her that this was the call she'd been anticipating. A knot leapt into her throat, making it difficult for her to answer. She croaked out her name and waited.

"This is Kelsey Masters, marketing manager for Sunrise Mines in St. Louis. We're very impressed with your design." There was a slight pause. "In fact, we're in the process of setting up our own web team and thought you might be interested in joining us."

Was she offering Patsy a job? What about an interview, references, a urine sample?

"I realize this may seem sudden, but you come highly recommended, and we have seen an example of your work."

Patsy's grip tightened on the flap.

"Of course, you may want to check us out before you decide. Should we set up a time for you to visit? You can meet the rest of the team, talk with Human Resources, that kind of thing." The woman paused as if expecting an answer.

"Yes, that sounds like a good idea," Patsy managed to stutter out.

"Fabulous. I'll tell the rest of the team to expect you Friday. Does that work for you?"

After setting a time and getting directions, Patsy hung up the phone. This was it. She had the offer. Any day now, she could be leaving Daisy Creek. Realizing she still gripped the basket flap, she relaxed her hand, leaving a perfect impression of a daisy pressed into her palm.

Chapter Eighteen

After months of sticky heat, it was getting cooler. Daisy Daze would be here soon, then Thanksgiving, then Christmas, and Patsy might not be here for any of it. She had never missed a Daisy Daze or a family holiday either, for that matter. She rubbed the smooth aluminum nose of the elephant. His clown hat was faded, but he still bobbed and twirled on his giant spring base, just like he did when she was six.

Pugnacious rooted along the banks of the drainage ditch that ran through Daisy Creek City Park. It was quiet today, no screaming middle-schoolers at the city pool. It had closed on Labor Day. No mothers chasing giggling toddlers when they escaped the family barbecue. Not even a lawn mower roaring past the jungle gym.

Patsy left the elephant and relaxed into one of the rubber-seated swings. Gripping the chain, she pumped her legs and soared skyward. A red VW bug turned into the park and buzzed toward her.

Just the person she didn't want to see. Not that there was anyone she did want to see right now. The people she normally confided in seemed to have deserted her. She couldn't talk to Granny. The job offer would send her into a fit of grumbling that would quickly escalate to lectures. There was something going on with Ruthann that Patsy wasn't quite ready to deal with. And Will had apparently chosen Jessica over Patsy. Not the first time in Patsy's life, but it hurt more now. Hard to believe that could be true, but it was. Maybe she was getting softer in her old age.

Patsy let the swing creak to a stop as she watched Jessica pop out of her bug and traipse across the grass. Even this late in the season, her legs retained a golden tan. Being jealous sucked. It would be nice if just once Patsy had something someone, anyone, envied.

"Didn't expect anyone to be here," Jessica greeted her.

"Yeah, me neither." Patsy leaned back in the swing and watched white, fluffy clouds roll by.

"I come here sometimes to read." Jessica held out a book.

"*Poems to Open Your Heart?*" Patsy asked.

"Yeah, why?" Jessica's eyes narrowed.

"No reason." Patsy sounded skeptical, even to her own ears.

"Tell me."

"I don't know. I guess I didn't see you as the poetry type, and then, love poems?"

"What's wrong with love poems? Poetry can help you see things in a new way, open your heart, just like the title says." Jessica's face took on a dreamy quality.

Geez, who knew Jessica was deep? Patsy tilted back again.

"It can." Jessica's eyes looked suspiciously moist.

Patsy leaned forward and looked at her in surprise. "I believe you."

Jessica clutched the book to her chest and leaned against the swing's metal frame. "Did you get the job offer?"

"Yeah." Patsy couldn't believe she was confiding in one of the people she most distrusted in the world. "They told me I could come up Friday and check the place out, but the job is mine if I want it."

"That's great. Why wait? Why don't you just take it? It's what you've wanted for a long time, isn't it?"

"I guess." Patsy curled her feet upward and let the

swing sway. Jessica wanted her to leave. Not a surprise, but a wasted effort. She already had Will and Ruthann. There wasn't much more of Patsy's to take.

Jessica studied one perfectly manicured thumb. "I have good news too."

The chattering of an angry squirrel drew Patsy's attention. Pugnacious had the poor critter trapped on top of a bird feeder.

"Pugnacious, leave him alone."

"Will's buying some land, and I'm representing him." Jessica beamed at Patsy.

"That's nice." Like Patsy cared about Jessica's next commission check.

"It's going to be a huge deal. He's buying about three hundred acres near Henning, and there's already another buyer lined up to buy it from Will. We should be able to triple the sales price in a week's time."

Land around Daisy Creek did not triple in value in a hundred years, much less a week. "What's it for?"

"Well, it's a secret, but I guess since you're going to work for the mines, it's okay to tell you." Jessica leaned forward. "It's for Sunrise. They want to put a smelter in near Henning. Richard Parks approached Will weeks ago. Will's bankrolling the deal, buying the land cheap, and then reselling it for a huge markup to Sunrise. Will makes a big profit, and Sunrise builds their smelter without the ruckus they're having down in Sauk City. Everybody wins."

Will was buying land from poor farmers for pennies, then reselling it to Sunrise for triple or more? "You're sure?"

Jessica looked confused. "Yeah, I talked to Richard about it months ago, but until Will moved back, there wasn't any one person with enough cash to pull it off. He met with Will to discuss it. Then last night, Will asked me about buying land near there. It has to be for the Sunrise deal."

Patsy jumped out of the swing, making it jump up and down on its chain. "Pugnacious, let's go. We have a call to make."

She stomped toward her Jeep, leaving an open-mouthed Jessica in her wake. Another thought stopped her. "Jessica," she yelled.

Jessica looked up from her book.

"Are you dating Will?"

"He took me to the Dogwood Inn, didn't he?"

Patsy waited.

She grinned. "And he asked me to lunch tomorrow."

Good enough. Patsy slammed the door of her car and peeled out.

Today was the day. Patsy had called Sunrise back and taken the job. Not having seen the place or met any of the people, she knew it was a risk, but really, what did she have to lose? There wasn't much left for her in Daisy Creek, even less than there was a month ago.

A scowling Dwayne was going to follow her in his truck. It was loaded with essentials that wouldn't fit in Patsy's tiny Jeep: Pugnacious' cage, her computer, pictures, and a few special baskets. Sunrise had found her temporary housing, a furnished apartment in south St. Louis. It was right off the Interstate, an easy twenty-minute drive to the east side and her new career.

Dwayne slammed the tailgate. "You ready yet? I don't want to be dragging back here late. Me and Randy got plans."

Of course they did. "What, an evening of opera and caviar?"

"You wanna find someone else to haul your junk?"

"Don't be so touchy. What's got your tail in a knot, anyway? I thought you'd be glad to see me go." Patsy grinned at him.

"Who said it had anything to do with you?" He pulled

a bungee tight across Patsy's computer box and hooked it to the other side of the truck bed. "Besides, there's nothing wrong with my mood."

Yeah, and Granny didn't put bacon grease in her green beans.

"What we waiting for?" he asked.

"Nothing, I just need to go in and say good-bye to everybody." Patsy knew she was dawdling. It wasn't that she wasn't eager to get to St. Louis and get started on her new life. It was just, well, it would have been nice if someone besides family had come to see her off. "I'll be right back." Patsy picked up Pugnacious and trudged into the house.

"Don't be scarce." Aunt Tilde gave her a hug.

"We expect you home next weekend," Dad said.

"Make sure you eat right and don't be going out at night. You don't know anything about getting around in that city. It isn't safe." Her mother's eyes glimmered with tears. You'd have thought Patsy was moving to the Gaza Strip, the way her mother had carried on about drive-by shootings and drug dealers for the past week.

Granny was last. She sat in her chair, her arms folded over her chest. "Guess you're doing what you think you need to do."

The lump that had been resting in Patsy's stomach all week surged up between her tonsils.

"You just remember, there's no shame in coming home. If'n it don't work out the way you thinks it will, pack up and come home. We'll be here and won't be a person say a word against you for coming back." A suspicious moisture showed in her grandmother's eyes too. "You hear me?"

Patsy gulped down the knot and turned for the door.

"Don't you forget where you come from," Granny called after her.

Without pausing to think, Patsy dropped onto her knees and rested her head on her grandmother's bosom. "I won't forget. Nothing could make me forget."

"I know you think there's something waiting for you up there." Granny stroked Patsy's hair. "But don't lose yourself searching for it."

Patsy sniffed and brushed the tears from her eyes. Leaving was hard, but it was for the best. Picking up Pugnacious, she headed toward her dream.

A blue Cavalier parked in the drive stopped her.

"I heard you were leaving today." Ruthann looked pale and unsure.

"I called you, but you weren't home." Patsy let Pugnacious jump to the ground.

"Momma must have deleted the message. She's been, you know . . ."

"I know."

They stared at each other, neither approaching the other.

Dwayne leaned out his truck window. "Hell, give each other a hug. I don't have all day to wait on you."

They both rushed forward, laughing and talking at the same time.

"I'm sorry."

"No, I'm sorry. I never should have invited Jessica along. I know how you feel about her."

"It's okay. I overreacted. You have the right to have other friends."

"But not Jessica."

"No, you can be friends with whoever you want."

"I wasn't trying to hurt you. I just thought if you saw her with Will, maybe you'd . . ."

"What?"

Ruthann's gaze dropped to her shoe. "Stay. Maybe you wouldn't leave."

"Oh, Ruthann, we'll always be friends. You know that. We've been friends forever, haven't we? A couple hours' drive won't change that. Besides, you have Randy now."

"It's not the same. I love Randy, but he's not you. I need you, Patsy. Who's going to tell me I'm doing something stupid or that I need to stand up for myself? Or that I made a bad fashion decision?" She pulled on the bottom of her halter.

"Like you ever listened to me anyway." Patsy laughed, blinking back tears.

"Did you talk to Will? Does he know you're leaving?"

"I don't know what he knows. There was no reason to call him. He has Jessica." Patsy couldn't voice her hurt over learning Will was cheating her neighbors. Word would get out about that soon enough. It wasn't her place to spread it; besides, she knew she'd look hypocritical criticizing him for selling to the mines when she was on her way to work for them herself.

"Are you sure? I know I brought them to the Dogwood Inn, but to be honest, he didn't act too interested. In fact, I thought he was pretty tense as soon as he spied you sitting there with Glenn. On the way home, he hardly said two words to any of us."

Ruthann was such a romantic. She couldn't see the truth when it was wrapped in spandex and attached to Will's arm.

"I'm sure. I saw Jessica. Besides, he's not important." Patsy swallowed the lump that accompanied her words.

Dwayne rapped on the outside of his truck door with his fist.

"Listen, I better get going, but I'll call you as soon as I'm settled, and you have to come up, and we'll go shopping. I'm not giving up on you yet." As she choked out the words, Patsy tugged on Ruthann's miniskirt.

"You better not." Ruthann grabbed Patsy in a bear hug, mascara streaming down her cheeks. "There's nobody like you Patsy, nobody. If it weren't for you, I'd probably still be wearing banana curls and ruffly underwear."

"You mean you don't?" Patsy yanked on Ruthann's skirt again.

"Stop it." Laughing, Ruthann pushed Patsy's hands down.

Patsy wiped runny mascara from underneath her eyes and walked toward her car. Dwayne shook his head as she approached. "You two act like you'll never see each other again. It's only a two-hour drive."

"You don't understand. It'll never be the same, never." Patsy climbed into her Jeep and waved good-bye.

Will maneuvered around the cardboard boxes that were taking over his house as he jogged to the phone. Breathless, he answered, and for one quick second he thought it was Patsy.

"You ready to look for that office space?" Hearing Jessica's perky voice sent his pulse plummeting.

"Office space?"

"At lunch you said to call today and we'd check out some office space. There's a great place near the BiggeeMart. You'd have road frontage."

"Is there nothing downtown? Maybe near the square."

Jessica hesitated. "Yeah, there's a ton of vacant spaces. Are you sure that's what you want? Some of them have been empty for years."

"I'm sure." Hopping over a stack of miniature log cabins, he added. "I need storage space too."

"That's easy enough."

"And character. I'd like something in an old building, maybe with a view."

"A view?"

"Yeah, a view, downtown or the courthouse, would be fine." He wondered which Patsy would choose. Too bad there was nothing near the river. Of course, if the business went well, he could always build something later.

"Oh, if that's all you want, it shouldn't be a problem . . ." Jessica replied, sounding about as sure as a two-dollar firewall.

"Fine, where and when should we meet?" He was eager to get the details sewn up and move on to straightening out more important things—like what was going on with Patsy.

"I'll make some calls and get back to you, or—"

"What?"

"Well, it's eleven. We could meet for lunch again. That should give me enough time to make the calls, and I could fill you in on the details before we visit the properties."

"I don't know. I need to call Patsy. She's working on some things for me." He needed them to be working on something.

"Haven't you heard?"

Will's heart thudded slowly. "Heard what?"

"Patsy's gone. She took that job with Sunrise and left today."

Patsy was gone? She couldn't be. He hadn't called or visited her since that night at the Dogwood Inn. Call it male pride, but he didn't think it was his place after she showed up there with that Celt. She should have called him. Maybe they didn't have any kind of commitment, but even friends let each other know when they were seeing someone. Patsy had acted like everything was perfectly normal, like there was no problem. Then the Celt dropped the Sunrise bomb. He'd never figured Patsy to be working for the mines.

He knew it was unfair to be angry about that, but at the time, he hadn't been thinking rationally. Patsy was everything he loved about the Ozarks: natural, spunky, unspoiled. To learn she was selling out for cash had rocked him.

A week had passed, though, and he needed Patsy in his life. He could afford to tell Richard to stick his plans to rip off every farmer between here and Henning. He could afford to lose money by paying the farmers who wouldn't wait to get a fair price for their land, just so

Richard and Sunrise couldn't rob them blind. He could afford a lot of things Patsy couldn't. What he couldn't afford was losing Patsy.

He'd decided to call her and tell her, if all they could be was friends, so be it. If she needed a job, she could work with him. If she had to date other people, he'd ... He hadn't thought that far ahead, but it wouldn't have mattered, because sooner or later, Patsy would have realized she belonged with Will.

"Will? You still there?" Jessica's voice knifed through his reverie.

"Yeah, what did you say?"

"I said Patsy is gone. She took the job with Sunrise and left today."

Will pulled back his foot and sent a tiny cabin hurtling into his front door.

Will pulled open the screen and knocked on the worn green wood. Nothing. No barking, snarling, or baying. Pugnacious wasn't here. Did that mean Jessica was right? Was Patsy gone too? As he leaned his forehead against the doorframe, the knob squeaked and the door jerked open.

Granny stood staring at him, a solemn look on her lined face. "She's gone, boy. She's gone and I want to know what you're going to do to bring her back."

Patsy was in awe. Staying in the far right-hand lane of the Interstate, she admired the cityscape in front of her. Downtown St. Louis was a mesmerizing mixture of old and new, buildings of all different heights and materials. Mirror and glass monuments to the millennium were tucked up next to turn-of-the-last-century brick structures. Murals decorated one. Another glimmered green in the early morning sun. She had seen St. Louis before, but this was different. Now it was home.

She passed the last Missouri exit and waved good-bye to the shimmering city in her rearview mirror. Sunrise's offices were on the eastern side of the Mississippi, in Illinois. A fact that sent her mother, who had apparently seen *National Lampoon's Vacation* one too many times, into perpetual spasms.

The Sunrise building did not reflect its name. The brown brick structure squatted next to factories that belched smoke and noxious odors. Hopping out of her Jeep, Patsy was submerged in the scent of rotten eggs. She hoped it didn't linger in her hair like smoke after a night out.

Entering the elevator, she realized she had no reason to worry. The smell of burning wires trapped inside the claustrophobic space would surely disguise the rotten eggs. After exiting the elevator, she walked to the security desk. The grizzled guard grunted out directions to Kelsey Masters' office. Patsy wound her way through the halls, the heels of her new, conservative pumps tapping against the ancient, yellowing linoleum.

When she came to the door the guard had indicated, she paused. This was it, the beginning of her new career. No more canned peas, no more punching a time clock. No more Will.

She pushed the thought aside. She had a career now and a salary to go with it. Will had Jessica and a wallet full of money from ripping off poor farmers. She pushed open the door and stepped inside.

In the center of the room sat a massive desk. Stacks of papers, magazines, and fast-food debris covered the top. Perched to the side, a tiny, birdlike woman pecked at a computer keyboard.

"Excuse me," Patsy's voice quavered. "Could you tell me where Ms. Masters is?"

"Patsy?" Rubbing her wrist, the woman looked up

from the screen. "We're casual around here. Call me Kelsey."

This was her boss? For some reason, Patsy had expected someone bigger, grander, neater.

"Have you looked around yet? Made yourself at home?" Kelsey popped off her perch and began rooting through the stack on her desk. "I have a packet for you somewhere here. H.R. sent it up." She continued to dig, shoving a half-eaten Whopper to the side and tossing a wadded napkin onto the floor. "Here you go." She shook the manila folder, sending a rain of crumbs onto the rug.

After gathering the paperwork, Kelsey escorted Patsy to her pod, cubby, whatever. It wasn't exactly what Patsy had envisioned.

"This is my desk?" She eyed the rickety black steel and pressed board monstrosity. It looked like a yard sale reject. Her dad wouldn't even take it on consignment at his shop.

"Yeah, I know it isn't ergonomic, but it's the best we could do on short notice. You should be fully stocked with office supplies." Kelsey yanked open a drawer, revealing pens, a stapler, and Wite-out.

Well, that was fine then. As long as she had a good supply of Wite-out, her world was okay. What did they expect her to do—use it to paint the screen? Patsy tapped her foot. Speaking of which, "Where's the computer?"

"Oh, and we don't have a computer for you yet, but there's one in the corner interns share. Until yours gets here, you can use it."

No computer. How was she supposed to design web sites? On the wall with a tube of Cover Girl Number 77? "When will mine be here?"

Kelsey, engrossed in straightening the stack of papers, ignored the question. "I hope you brought your social security card. H.R. will want a copy and there's information on health insurance here. Take your time filling it all out."

"When will my computer be here?"

Kelsey cut her eyes to the door of the cubicle. "Ah, well, it could be any time. I just can't say for sure. Budgets and all that." A nervous laugh escaped. "Take your time with the papers. I'll check on you in a half-hour." She scurried back to her office.

Patsy plopped down in her chair and glanced around at the padded fabric walls. It had to get better than this. She rolled forward, knocking against the papers and scattering them across the floor. Staring at the white sheets dotting the floor, she thought, it had to get better than this, or she had made a massive mistake.

Chapter Nineteen

Granny wanted to know how he was going to bring Patsy back. How was this his fault? Will slammed another stack of lavender soaps into a box. He didn't send her away. She'd been plotting this move long before he stepped back into her life. He'd offered her options, hadn't he? She could have stayed here in Daisy Creek and been with him. They could have worked on daisygal.com together, but no, she wanted something else—maybe even someone else. He frowned at the memory of the Celt.

What else could he offer her? Slapping a strip of tape onto the carton, Will shoved it toward the door. There was nothing for her in St. Louis. Why couldn't she see that? Even Pugnacious would be miserable.

Ralph nuzzled his palm. "You think Pugnacious is treeing pigeons, boy?"

Ralph leaned closer, forcing Will to run his hand down the dog's back.

"She's probably miserable. Patsy too, but she's so stubborn she won't admit it." He scratched his dog's ear. "I wish there was some way to make her see she doesn't belong there. That she belongs here. Once she's back in Daisy Creek, we can work out the rest, don't you think?" Will dropped down onto the step. "Why can't she be more like her dog?"

A box containing Dwayne's carvings sat by Will's foot. Flipping open the cardboard flap, he pulled out the tiny coon. He turned it over in his hand.

Coons. There weren't coon hunts in St. Louis, at least not where, according to Granny, Patsy was.

"That's it, boy. I may not have a pair of ruby slippers to bring her home, but maybe I can think of something just as good." Grinning, he ruffled Ralph's fur and headed to the computer. "C'mon. We have shopping to do."

It had been three days—three long, boring days since Patsy started at Sunrise. She was beginning to settle into a routine, but it was less than reassuring. Each morning she got up at six, walked Pugnacious, and got dressed. Breakfast was a cereal bar, no coffee until she got to work, which was two hours later. The drive from her apartment was not as simple as she had expected. Road construction, accidents, and pouring rain had banded together to extend her morning commute by at least forty-five minutes.

When she got home, she was too tired to do anything more than take Pugnacious for another quick jog around the block and collapse on the couch. It was amazing how sitting on your behind all day could wear a person out. Amazing and sick.

Patsy needed some excitement, something to take her mind off Daisy Creek, and who she left behind; something that offered a bigger challenge than fighting the pierced *Fear Factor* reject of an intern for computer time.

"Patsy, could you stop by my office around two?" Kelsey peered at her around the side of her cubby's wall. "I have a project I want to talk to you about."

Finally, a project. Something she could get excited about. Patsy popped out of her chair and went to do battle with the pointlessly perforated intern.

At two o'clock, she packed up her work and headed to Kelsey's office.

"Good, you're here." Kelsey motioned to a chair.

Patsy kicked an empty Chicken McNuggets box under the desk and sat down.

"I have the perfect project for you." Kelsey tipped back in her chair with an accompanying squeal.

Now we were talking. Patsy edged forward.

"As you know, you're one of the first members of our new web team." Kelsey paused. "And since we're starting out fresh, we want to get everything on the same page, so to speak. We have our corporate site. We hired out the design on that." She took a sip of Mountain Dew. "Then we have the site you did and a site Lex, the intern, has been working on."

Patsy waited.

"What we need is to get the code consistent on all of them."

Patsy sat up a little straighter.

"You know, make sure the code is all up-to-date, capitalizations consistent, things like that." She set the soda down, making a new wet circle on a file folder. "What I'd really like to see is a protocol, a list of how we do things here at Sunrise. After you've worked that up, you can put it to practice by getting the three sites to standards."

"You want me to write a manual?" Patsy would rather eat brussels-sprout pie.

"Not a manual, really, just a protocol, a set of procedures." Kelsey scribbled on a post-it note. "I got you set up with access this morning. Here's your password and where the files are located. If you need anything else, just let me know."

Patsy was frozen to her seat. Spend hours searching through someone else's code to see if they closed their paragraph tags or used comments? It was insane. Kelsey was insane.

"Is there something else?" Kelsey asked.

Groping for an excuse to weasel out of the job, Patsy said, "What about . . ." What was the pierced one's name? Oh, yeah. "Lex, is he still working . . ."

"Oh, yes, Lex. That's a great idea. You two have been working so well together. You should do this together. I'll tell him as soon as we're through." With a satisfied smile, Kelsey swigged down the Mountain Dew.

Patsy plodded back to her cell. She had just been given life with carpal tunnel syndrome and not with the benefit of solitary confinement. No, she was paired with a kid with more holes in his face than Spongebob Squarepants.

"Granny sent me over with this." Dwayne stood in Will's doorway a huge cardboard carton filling his arms.

"What is it?" Will was a little leery of accepting anything from Patsy's grandmother right now. When he'd stopped by her house after his conversation with Jessica, Granny had stared him down with an intensity that would have done Clint Eastwood proud. All that was missing was the "make my day." Will glanced from the box back to Dwayne.

"Basket stuff; she said you'd know what to do with it." Dwayne hesitated at Will's frown. "You know—reed, some baskets Patsy was working on, things like that."

What was he supposed to do with half-made baskets and materials? Granny's mind worked in an interesting way.

Dwayne bounced the box once.

Well, he couldn't send it back to her. "Bring it in." Will motioned toward the kitchen. After lowering the box to the floor, Dwayne watched, his hands shoved into his pockets, as Will searched through the contents.

Maybe he'd find some clue inside.

"Will . . ." Dwayne started.

Will pulled half a jack-o-lantern grin out and set it on the floor. What was that thing?

"Will . . ." Dwayne studied the toe of his worn boot.

Realizing Dwayne expected a response, Will said, "Sorry, didn't mean to be rude. I just don't know why your grandmother thinks I should have this . . ." Will held up the partial pumpkin. At Dwayne's shrug, he dropped it back in the box. "Can I get you something? It's a little early for a beer, but I have pop or tea."

Dwayne was already shaking his head. "I was wanting to talk to you about somethin'."

Dwayne seemed uncharacteristically serious.

"See, things ain't so good for me right now. The factory I work at . . . I'm a cutter there." He pushed his feed cap back on his head. "The way things is looking, it's gonna be shutting down real soon and, to be one hundred percent honest, I don't have another job to fall back on. Now, I mean, I got the carving, thanks to you." He nodded. "But I don't likely think that's going to pay the bills." He sighed. "I was hoping maybe there was something else I could do for you. I'm not the quickest hound in the pack, but I'm honest and a hard worker."

Dwayne's earnest gaze held Will's. Dwayne work for him? Doing what? Will searched his brain for an idea.

"Dwayne, I wish I had something, but I really don't. I could maybe use some help managing the site, but . . ."

Dwayne didn't let him finish. "No, I know I can't do that. Patsy's the smart one. I couldn't figure all that computer stuff out."

"Aside from that, I don't know what I'd have for you to do."

Dwayne pushed his cap back. "I got an idea, if you don't mind listening to it. I'm not asking for a handout. If you don't think this'll work, just tell me, and I'll be on my way." He grinned. "And I'll take that Coke you offered too."

Will pulled open the Sub-Zero's door. What kind of idea could Dwayne have for him? This should be interesting. If nothing else, working with Dwayne would keep him one step closer to Patsy, it was better than nothing—not much, but better.

***

Saturday Patsy lounged in bed until eleven, something she would never have done at home. Of course, this was home now, and if she wanted to trot around the apartment all day in her Daisy Daze T-shirt and little else, she could.

Wasn't quite the thrill she was hoping for.

She fell onto the couch and stared at her pug-faced slippers. She should be abuzz with delight. No one telling her when to get up, what to eat, or that Hulk Hogan was on the news. She sighed, clicked on the television and searched for the WWE. It wasn't on, but an ad for one of St. Louis' mega malls inspired her. She would go shopping. She didn't have a lot of spare cash, but she could look.

Three hours later, she had walked twenty miles, eaten three chocolate-chip pretzels, and drank a pickle barrel's worth of hand-squeezed lemonade. She was tired, fat, and sticky. And she hadn't seen a single thing worth seeing. All the shops seemed to have the same interchangeable fashions, and the girls that worked in them made Ruthann and Jessica look like nuns. Not that Ruthann, at least, was trampy, but she did flash more belly than a toddler at daycare.

Wonder what was going on in Daisy Creek? Probably not much. Ruthann should be working. She'd started her new job at the BiggeeMart two weeks ago. No more arguing with Bruce for her. That was always Patsy's job anyway.

Granny was probably watching the WWE or jawing with Aunt Tilde. And Will? Patsy slumped onto a bench. He was probably stripping some old piece of junk Tilde hauled in, or sorting potpourri from dried thyme, or draping Jessica with pearls and roses.

Patsy shoved another bite of pretzel into her mouth. He could do what he liked. Patsy didn't need him. She had everything she needed and wanted right here in her new hometown of St. Louis.

The pretzel collided with the other three already

bunched up in her stomach. Whoever thought putting chocolate chips in a pretzel was a good idea?

Groaning, she levered herself up. She needed something to take her mind off Daisy Creek and Will Barnes. She was afraid she might be getting just the teeniest bit homesick, nothing she couldn't handle, but a diversion would be nice. It was natural, being in a new place. Even Pugnacious had seemed down lately.

That was the ticket. She'd buy something for Pug Girl, a new toy or treat. Patsy set off down the marbled halls of mercantile in search of deliverance. An hour later, she'd turned up nothing more exciting than a chew stick and catnip-stuffed ball.

Depressed she hadn't found something more appropriate, Patsy trudged to her Jeep. She knew it was silly, but she'd wanted something special, something to make her dog and her forget about home.

Slash that, Daisy Creek. This was home now, but, a little voice whispered, it wasn't where her heart was.

Will whistled as he boxed up the half-finished pumpkin. The Clarks were an interesting clan. They came off country and simple, watching the WWE and hunting coons, but they were a shrewd bunch. He'd thought Granny had cracked when she sent him Patsy's basket weaving materials, and he'd assumed Dwayne was incapable of coming up with a sound business idea.

He was wrong on both counts.

Will unwound a small coil of reed before placing the remainder in the box. He weighed the coil in his hand. That should be enough; the box wouldn't hold much more anyway.

Now to get this little piece of Daisy Creek to the post office and start luring his daisy gal home.

***

Monday arrived more quickly than Patsy would have liked. Back at Sunrise, she plodded her way through miles of code. To capitalize or not to capitalize, that was the question. To bash her head against her desk or to not bash her head against her desk, that was a better question. Lex poked his metal-speckled face into her space.

"You decide on alt tags yet?"

What, like they were optional? What a moron. "Anyone ever tell you body metal attracts lightning?" Probably worked as a brain drain too.

"Huh?"

"I saw it on TV. Makes you into a human lightning rod."

He gave her a "you are so out of it" grunt and left. She returned to work. To bash Lex in the head or to not bash Lex in the head, that was the ultimate question.

"Patsy?" A chipper Kelsey stood in her doorway. "I want you to meet someone."

Glad for the break, but quickly learning a call from Kelsey was not reason to celebrate, Patsy trudged over. A sleek-haired blonde in flowing pants and a waist-nipping silk jacket stood at Kelsey's side.

"This is Lisa Barnes. She used to live in that little town you're from."

What a treat.

"Patsy Lee Clark?"

"Lisa Barnes." Will's sister looked cool and polished. She made Patsy feel like a pound puppy standing beside a pedigreed champion.

Kelsey expressed the normal niceties and excused herself. Patsy stared at the flesh-and-blood reminder of what she had left in Daisy Creek. There was a definite family resemblance. Their coloring was different, but they shared the same sculpted features.

"How long have you been in St. Louis? You know Will's in Daisy Creek."

Patsy winced. So, Will hadn't mentioned her to his sister? So what? "I've only been here about a week."

Lisa looked surprised. "Oh, then did you know about Will?"

"I ran into him a time or two."

"How was he?"

"Fine." Okay, mind-numbingly hot was a better assessment.

"I don't understand him." Lisa shook her head. "Why he wants to live in Hicksville is beyond me—no offense."

Patsy take offense? Now why would she do that, self-centered . . .

"I mean, really, it was bad enough living in every two-horse town in the country when we were kids, but now he could live anywhere."

"I think he likes it."

"What's to like? There's nowhere to eat but a greasy drive-thru, and the best you can hope for in shopping is some overpriced 'boutique' with old-lady clothes." Lisa flicked imaginary lint off the arm of her jacket. "But you understand. You left, didn't you?"

Her teeth clenched in a smile, Patsy asked, "What are you doing in St. Louis? I thought your family was in Chicago."

"Oh, um, I recently had some life changes."

"Life changes? Little early for menopause, isn't it?" Annoyance lent an edge to Patsy's tone.

"Funny." Will's sister didn't seem to be laughing.

Patsy gave her a minute smile in return.

Lisa pulled a blond lock out of its chignon. "I'm getting divorced. My father suggested I contact Sunrise about a potential career move."

In other words, hubby dumped her, and daddy was pulling her fat from the fire. "How nice. The career part, I mean."

"Of course." She pushed back a silk sleeve to glance at her watch. "I'd better get going. Perhaps I'll see you again. Either here or even in Daisy Creek. I really must visit Will sometime. Just need to make sure my shots are up-to-date first."

Ha ha.

Lisa twirled off.

It was reassuring to know people didn't change that much from childhood. Lisa was a snotty little girl, and she'd developed into an equally snotty woman. How could brother and sister be so different? And Will was different.

Patsy hadn't admitted it before, but Will wasn't like his sister. He loved Daisy Creek, maybe even as much as Patsy did. Patsy paused. She loved Daisy Creek. The realization stopped her. She hadn't thought about it in a long time. In her focus to leave home, she'd forgotten how much she loved the place.

Not that it mattered. Daisy Creek was where she failed, where her heart led her astray, where she was stupid. She let Johnny cheat on her. People thought she was smart, but she wasn't. It was all an act. No one with brains would have married Johnny to start with, or maybe it was more than that. Maybe if she'd loved him more, he'd have been happy with just her. Maybe he needed more than she could give. Either way, it was her fault, and she couldn't face it anymore. Love it or not, she couldn't go back to Daisy Creek.

Not even to be with Will.

Patsy tromped back to the computer to sift through a few more thousand lines of code. Lex slumped in the chair, dragging a virtual ace of hearts across the computer screen. She tapped on his shoulder and prayed for lightning.

Finally, it was here. Will cut open the carton and poured Styrofoam peanuts onto the floor. The figure nestled inside was perfect. He couldn't suppress a chuckle as he held it up.

"What do you think?" he asked Ralph.

His companion sniffed the object and sat back on his haunches, one eyebrow tilted.

"It's for Pugnacious. You think she's going to like it?" Ralph nudged it with his nose.

"I think so too." Will dropped the figure back in the box, along with the note, and sealed it up. The doorbell rang while he was wiping excess ink off Ralph's foot. Jessica stood on the front porch, a high school annual in her hand.

"Hey." Her Daisy Creek High T-shirt was stained with paint and her sweats had holes in the knees.

"Jessica." He tried not to stare. "Is something wrong?"

"No, yes, maybe . . ." She turned a bare face upward. "We need to talk."

What? Was there a sign on his door?

"It's about Patsy and . . . us."

There was an us? Will led her to the horsehair loveseat.

"I was Daisy Darling freshman through senior year in high school."

Okay.

Jessica clutched the high school yearbook. "I was also Sweetheart Dance princess." She flipped open the book. "Here's the picture."

It was the typical high school "court" picture: girls with stiff hair in slinky dresses, escorted by gawky boys in football uniforms.

"This is Patsy's ex." Jessica pointed to the boy seated next to her in the picture.

"Patsy's ex?"

"Her ex-husband. They got married right out of high school."

Will was silent. Patsy was married?

"What happened?" he asked.

"I'll get to that." Jessica wiped a tear away from her eye with her index finger. The tiny hearts on her charm bracelet tinkled like an out-of-tune piano. "The point is, I wasn't supposed to be Sweetheart that year. I cheated."

Still stunned by the earlier revelation, Will remained quiet.

"The football team picked the court, and the cheerleaders gathered and counted the votes. I didn't win. Patsy did."

"But she isn't in the photo," Will said.

A tear ran down Jessica's cheek and plopped onto the red velvet upholstery. "I know. Like I said, I cheated. When I saw Patsy won, I trashed the ballots." Her voice quavered. "I had to win, to know everybody liked me."

"But you didn't win." The woman's logic eluded him.

"I know." Jessica wiped her cheek with the back of her hand. "It didn't matter. Everyone thought I did. That's what was important, at least that's what I thought then."

"I can understand you feel guilty, but that was a long time ago. I doubt Patsy cares." Who was he kidding? Of course Patsy cared.

"It gets worse." She sniffed loudly. "After high school, after Patsy and Johnny got married, I—"

Will pulled back. This didn't sound good.

"I, there's no right way to say this. I flirted with him. People always liked Patsy better than me, but the titles were mine." She pointed at her chest. "Then, Patsy got that too. I couldn't handle it. I knew she loved Johnny, and I was jealous. I wanted to love somebody like that, be loved like that. So I ruined it."

"How does flirting ruin love?"

"It's complicated."

"Explain it." It wasn't often Will could resist a crying female, but this time he could.

"Johnny cheated on her." At Will's shocked expression, Jessica explained, "Not with me, with some girl from Boss. Patsy's always been independent. I think Johnny wanted to get her attention."

"That was one way to do it." The idiot, he didn't deserve to wipe Patsy's shoes.

"He hooked up with this girl. I'm not sure how. Anyway, Patsy found out." Jessica shivered. "It was ugly."

Will could imagine.

"She ran his truck into the Current River, ruined the interior—he was always real proud of that truck." She looked at him like she expected a response. Will nodded.

With a sigh, she continued, "Once she cooled down, they tried to work things out. That's when I stepped in." Jessica bit her lower lip. "He was still hanging out at the roadhouse a lot, and I just started flirting with him. I couldn't stop myself. I didn't love him. I wanted to prove I could get him. Patsy came in one night when we were dancing. That was it. She just left. It was cold, like she wrote him off. She filed for divorce the next day."

"What happened to him?" Like Will cared. As long as he was out of Patsy's life, that was.

"He went back to the girl from Boss. She wound up pregnant, and they got married. They don't come around here anymore. I think they're scared of Patsy, though truthfully, I don't think she'd waste spit on them. The rest of her family's who they should worry about."

And Will.

"Why are you telling me this?"

Jessica's eyebrows lifted in surprise. "Because of us." She picked up his hand, squeezed it. "I don't love you, Will. I was doing it again. Taking what Patsy has."

After reassuring Jessica he would survive the heartbreak, he escorted her to the foyer. She managed one last tearful hug before he closed the door on her.

Well, that explained the tension between Patsy and Jessica. Knowing Patsy, he was surprised she tolerated Jessica at all. To be honest, he was surprised anybody involved in this little drama survived Patsy's temper longer than it took her to rev up her Jeep. Jessica said she just walked away. That didn't seem like Patsy. The experience must have hurt her more than anyone knew.

If nothing else, this had been an interesting week. Wonder who would show up next?

Chapter Twenty

Patsy fought her way down 44. The stop-and-go traffic was giving her a splitting headache. When she got home, she was going to watch whatever mind-numbing selection the networks had to offer and fall into bed.

A giant cardboard carton blocked her path. She unlocked the door and jostled the box inside.

"Look, a package," she announced to Pugnacious.

The pug scampered over, apparently sharing in Patsy's delight.

"And it's a big one." Enveloped by the same thrill as discovering the biggest box under the Christmas tree was hers, Patsy ripped at the tape. Nestled at the top of the carton was her half-finished jack-o-lantern basket.

"Who would send this?" She set it to the side and dug deeper. The rest of her basket materials were carefully wrapped and packed below it. Digging more, she found a note.

> *A deal's a deal. Less than two weeks to Daisy Daze and you owe me three baskets.*
> *Will*

Of all the nerve. Did he think she had nothing else to do? What made him think he could boss her around? Patsy picked up the orange basket and tossed it back into the box.

"Come on, Pug Girl. Let's go for a walk." She snagged the leash and headed down the street.

Ten pigeons, two golden retrievers, and a thousand stop-and-sniffs later, Patsy and Pugnacious trudged home. Pugnacious, after being released from her lead, trotted over to the box and attempted to climb inside.

"No, girl." Patsy was going to have to find somewhere to keep this stuff. She grabbed one cardboard flap and, with Pugnacious bouncing around her ankles, tugged the box toward the closet. Three feet from her destination, the flap tore, sending Patsy and the contents of the carton spilling to the floor.

"Damn it all."

Pugnacious bounded over, nuzzling and snorting. Clawing her way to the top coil of oak strips, she looked down at Patsy.

"Get off there." Patsy shooed her dog away and hooked her arm through the coil. The heavy weight of it surprised her. Not that she hadn't lugged around plenty of coils of wood strips, she'd just forgotten. Already.

It hadn't even been two weeks since she left Daisy Creek. It seemed like months. Running her hand over the wood, she squatted next to the mess and began sorting through it. Everything she needed was here. Wasn't like she had a hot date or even a cold friend to occupy her time.

Pugnacious scampered back, sending the pumpkin basket rolling toward Patsy. She picked it up and studied the half-finished grin. She hated to leave things incomplete. Pushing herself up, she went to the kitchen to find a pan for water.

No word from Patsy. The basket materials should have arrived yesterday and nothing. The note had to have ticked her off. Will'd hoped enough that she would call and yell at him. He missed being yelled at by Patsy.

He looked down at his project. It was ugly, really ugly. Not a redeeming quality to it. He swallowed. He hated to fail, and the atrocity in his hands was proof he wasn't perfect, he wasn't good at everything. Lately, he wasn't good at much.

He couldn't go through with it. Sweeping bits of reed into the garbage, Will considered his options. Maybe he should give up on the covert lures and be more direct. Approach Patsy head on and tell her she didn't belong in St. Louis. It couldn't be worse than this. He thumped his creation with his finger. He couldn't let anyone see that. No, its destiny was at the bottom of the city dump.

He was disposing of the evidence when the bell rang. Not again. Resigned, he trudged to the door.

Ruthann leaned against the porch swing, a stuffed lion in her hands.

Sighing, Will swung open the door.

"I don't know what to do." Ruthann confided as she stroked the lion's mane.

Will wandered outside and collapsed on the swing. Patting the seat beside him, he said, "Join me."

"Patsy always tells me what to do and when to do it. With her not here, I'm lost." Ruthann perched on the edge of the seat.

"What's wrong?" Will heaved out.

"Randy." Ruthann drew the name out into three syllables.

Great, just what Will wanted to do—discuss someone else's love life, someone who had a love life.

"I thought you were getting along now," he said.

"We were, but his momma . . ."

"His momma?" Who cared about Randy's momma?

"Patsy says she's an old biddy."

Will smiled. That was his Patsy.

Ruthann yanked the lion's mane into a makeshift bun. "Patsy gave me this, when we were twelve. Some older girls were making fun of me. Calling me names, saying my clothes were Goodwill rejects, and . . ." Her voice tapered off to a whisper. ". . . that my momma was a . . ." Will leaned forward to catch the last word. ". . . whore."

Will wondered briefly if his sister had been part of the gang. Sounded like her loving nature.

Ruthann continued, "Patsy brought me this and told me I had to learn to stand up for myself. Every time somebody hurt me I was to think of this little lion and roar right back." She shook her head. "I can't do it though. Patsy can. She's the strongest, bravest person I know, but I can't."

Will shifted his weight, making the swing sway back and forth. "What happened?"

"Nothing yet, but it's going to. Randy's momma isn't stupid. She's going to figure out all that stuff we told her at church isn't true, and then what am I going to do? She'll hate me even more, and I'll lose Randy."

"You think Randy's that weak?" And if so, why did she want him anyway?

"He loves his momma," Ruthann mumbled.

"More than you? You think he'd dump you just because his mother doesn't approve?" Will could not track the way these women thought. First Jessica, now Ruthann; how did he become the keeper of Patsy's problems?

Ruthann pulled the lion's mane so hard Will thought the king of the jungle was going to need transplants.

"If he'd do that, you don't want him anyway," he said.

She looked up at him. "That's what Patsy said. But then I talked her into helping me, and we came up with that big act at the church. It was just supposed to buy me some time—to get closer to Randy. Then Patsy was going to work on him, convince him he should stand up to his momma . . ." Her voice quavered. ". . . but Patsy's gone, and I don't know when she's coming back."

No tears. Not twice in one week. Keeping his voice firm, Will replied, "Patsy can't solve this for you."

"She can't?" Ruthann blinked close-to-overflowing eyes. "She always has before."

Geez, Will had no idea how dependent these people were on Patsy. "Take a risk." Get some balls. "Don't you think it's time you confronted something on your own?"

Will walked a bewildered Ruthann to her Cavalier. Leaning through her car window, he tucked the tiny lion onto the dash.

"Time to roar, Ruthann."

Lex lounged in Patsy's cubicle, painting his fingernails with her Wite-out.

"Lexter, any new holes in your head?" Patsy glided in, plopped down on her desk and shoved her chair back with her foot. Working on the baskets had made her a strange mixture of happy and depressed. While she was weaving, she was at peace. When she stopped, she thought of nothing but the man who sent them back to her.

Lex quit blowing on his nails. "You talking to me?"

"Not that sharp first thing in the morning, are you? Might want to cut back on the habit." Patsy nodded to the bottle in his hand. "Can't afford killing good brain cells; need to leave a few for the drugs and alcohol."

"Do you know who I am?" With one eye squeezed shut, Lex blew on his fingernails. "I have connections you may need."

"You think?" In her current mood, ticking off the grim reaper himself wouldn't intimidate Patsy. He couldn't put her through anything worse than the self-doubt she'd been stewing in.

"I know." He tossed her Wite-out into the lap drawer and sauntered off.

"Stop in again anytime. On Friday we have a special on French tips," she called after him.

Pulling her "protocol manual" out of her bottom drawer, Patsy flipped it open. Time to tackle the delicate issue of code comments. Didn't want to step on any toes. It was a matter of such earth-shattering importance. One person's comment might be another person's insult. Had to be diplomatic about the whole issue.

Let's see, how about "when using comments, take utmost care in constructing them in a manner least likely to be effective in any way." Yes, that would cover it.

Now to review Lex's work from yesterday. She flipped to the section on closing tags. "*Closing tags, good. Not closing tags, bad.*" Patsy smiled; had to love a smart-aleck.

After jotting down changes for both sections on pink post-it notes, she stuck them on the pages and shut the manual.

"Patsy, could I see you in my office for a moment?"

Uh-oh, Kelsey sounded more tense than normal, not that she was ever what you could call tranquil. Inside her office, Patsy moved a stack of files off a chair and sat down.

"You and Lex getting along?"

"Why?" Had the little rat ratted her out?

"No reason."

Kelsey reached into a McDonald's bag sitting on her desk and pulled out a cherry pie.

"Apple's better," Patsy announced.

Kelsey looked at her in surprise.

"There's not enough cherries in those, it's mainly juice," she explained.

"Oh, I bought an apple too, but I felt like the cherry." Kelsey nipped the end off the pastry with her teeth.

Patsy nodded her head. "Are we done?"

Pie juice dribbled between Kelsey's fingers. "I know he's worthless."

Patsy shrugged.

"His father's a vice president. If you want to keep your job, you have to get along with him." Kelsey's tone became apologetic. "It's just how it is."

Patsy shrugged again. Lex was growing on her, and it didn't sound like he snitched. "I understand. That it?"

Waving the pie, Kelsey indicated she could leave. "Patsy?" she called. "You want the apple?"

Fried pastry in hand, Patsy strolled back to her desk. Had Lex ratted her out? No, not his style. Kelsey must be keeping a closer watch on her than she'd realized. But why?

Trash day. Will pulled out a twist-tie and yanked open the built-in garbage drawer in his kitchen. Grasping the sides of the plastic bag, he tugged it out. Something inside poked through the plastic, tearing the sack and spilling garbage onto the plank floor.

Ralph wandered over to investigate.

"Careful, boy, don't step in it." Using a whisk broom, Will brushed coffee grounds into a pile. When he looked up, Ralph was sitting in the mess, holding Will's creation from the day before in his mouth.

"Pretty awful, huh?" Will asked. He pulled the item from Ralph's gentle hold. A few coffee grounds were wedged between the reeds, but overall it was clean.

Will shook his head. He hated failure. Why couldn't he make something with his hands? Why did he think he could make something for Patsy? He'd tried, but he botched it. Holding open a new bag, he started to drop the embarrassing mess inside.

Patsy helping him measure reed and weave it into a basket flashed through his mind. She didn't care that what he made that night was lopsided and unattractive. She loved the process. He set his creation on the counter and spun it in a circle. Ugly, but he made it; maybe Patsy would appreciate that.

A cardboard box he had sat aside to haul off sat near the back door. Before he could change his mind, he placed his gift inside and went to look for packing peanuts.

Patsy knew why basket weaving was thought of as therapy for neurotic old women. There were only three things that even came close to calming her like this—Granny's chamomile tea, Hostess pies, and sex. None of which she had access to at the moment.

She attached the bail handle to her jack-o-lantern and set him on the floor. One down, two to go. With the time crunch, she was going to have to switch plans for the last two. The hamper and picnic basket were both too involved. An egg basket would work; classic, but simple. Selecting some reed, she headed to the kitchen to soak it in Ritz dye. Up to her elbows in robin's-egg blue, she heard the doorbell ring. Pugnacious began her alarm. Patsy ripped off her rubber gloves and rushed to the door.

Another cardboard carton sat outside her apartment. She picked it up and kicked the door shut behind her.

"Presents," she announced to Pugnacious.

With the box hugged to her body, she dropped to the floor. She shook the package. "What do you think it is? No return address, but it's postmarked Daisy Creek." She waited for Pugnacious to complete her inspection. "You think it's from Granny? No, she won't even talk to me on the phone. I don't think she'd be sending me presents. Will again?" Patsy's heart skipped a beat at the thought.

Her pug gave a loud snort.

"I know, I know. Just open it, but it's fun to guess too. Don't you think?"

Another snort.

"Fine." Using the scissors she'd been cutting reed with, Patsy sliced open the packing tape.

"Look, a card and there's a dog print on it, a real dog print."

> *Pugnacious,*
> *I miss you.*
> *Ralph*

"Aren't you the lucky girl? It's for you." With a trembling hand, Patsy set the card to the side and removed the tissue-wrapped object. Tearing off the paper, she sat it on the floor between her and Pugnacious.

"Oh, my God, Pug Girl. It's a raccoon, with a daisy."

The small hard rubber figure stood six inches tall. Its tiny masked face was tilted to sniff the daisy that was grasped in its paws. Patsy cradled it in her arms like a newborn baby. She'd never seen anything so . . . perfect.

"I can't believe he did this. How did he . . . ?" A tear crept into the corner of Patsy's eye. She wiped it away with a jerk of her hand.

"I am not crying over a rubber raccoon." She wasn't sure who she was trying to convince, but saying the words aloud made her a little stronger.

Pugnacious sniffed the little figure, tilted her chin to the ceiling and began to bay. Laughing, Patsy wiped new tears off her cheeks and rolled the toy to her dog.

"Have fun, girl. It's nice to be loved."

Fog rolled in the next morning, forcing Patsy to drive with her lights on to avoid being lunchmeat in a semi-sandwich. As she pulled into her parking place, big, fat drops of rain littered the parking lot.

A day like this made the prospect of being trapped in her gray cell almost cheerful. She grabbed a copy of the *Daisy Creek News* she'd received in the mail the day before and jogged to the building with it held over her head like a halo.

Lex loitered near the coffee machine, snitching sugar cubes. "Nice day."

"If you're a slug."

He popped a cube in his mouth and crunched down. "You calling me a slug?"

"You feel like a slug?"

"Not today."

"Well, then?"

He shrugged. "Okay, just checking."

Patsy shook the rain off her paper.

"What's that?" Lex stacked two cubes together and slowly demolished them with his molars.

Amazing—disgusting, but amazing. "Can you do three?"

"Sure." Three perfectly aligned cubes went into his mouth. Within seconds they were dust.

"Impressive."

He shrugged off the compliment. "What's that?" He pointed to the paper.

"Oh, an old paper from home." Patsy held it out.

"Can I see it?"

"Sure." Patsy tossed it to him, grabbed a sugar cube, and wandered to her cubby.

Around one, he sauntered over to her desk with the paper tucked under his arm.

"You know this Will Barnes?" he asked.

Patsy started at the name. "Will? Yeah, why?"

"No reason, he sounds righteous though."

Confused, Patsy asked, "What do you mean?"

Lex pushed some papers to the side and sat on the corner of her desk. "In your paper, it talks about him buying a bunch of land near where the company wants to put in a smelter."

"Yeah?" Patsy didn't realize the *Daisy Creek News* had printed the story of Will's greed.

"Brilliant, the dude is brilliant."

Patsy blinked. That wasn't exactly how she'd been thinking of it.

Lex sighed. "It doesn't say it in your little rag there, but this Will, he's negotiating for the whole area. See, he bought a key piece of property, and he won't let go of it until they agree to a price he 'deems fair' for all the land owners."

Patsy frowned. Lex had this all wrong. "Where'd you hear that?"

"I got ears. Half the people 'round here don't think I use them, but I do. The powers are all twitchy about your pal Will, but he's got them by the jewels. This land is the best spot for the smelter, and he knows it." Lex crossed his arms and leaned against the padded wall of Patsy's cubby.

"He also claims he doesn't care whether they build it there or not and won't even consider selling it until they meet his price. Even then, the sale might not go through. He's hired some hotshot attorney to work up the contract. It's got all kinds of stuff about testing along the drive route, clean-up, that kind of thing." Lex chuckled.

Patsy felt sick. She had jumped to the worst conclusion as soon as the smallest piece of evidence was given to her, and that evidence hadn't even been presented by a reliable source. She believed Will was greedy and selling out Daisy Creek because of what Jessica, of all people, said. She'd judged Will, betrayed him in thought if not deed, just like she'd been betrayed five years ago.

He trusted her, and she walked away without even a phone call. And he'd been sending packages. Why was he doing that? He should hate her. After the confusion wore off, before the apathy set in, there was hatred. Why wasn't Will there?

The fog never lifted. It seemed to roll off the river continuously like cold out of an icebox. It was early for the weather to turn so ugly, but Patsy didn't question it. It fit her mood.

After staying late to avoid the traffic she knew would be the result of hours of foul weather, she spun through White Castle for a bag of burgers, and drove home. A yard from her door, the fog gave way to rain, which almost instantly converted to hail. The hard pellets beating against her, she ran up the walk. Another box greeted her.

She stood staring at it, icy BBs bruising her back and face. Shoving the key into the lock, she opened the door and rammed the box inside.

Seated in one of the obnoxious brocade wing chairs that came with the apartment, Pugnacious peered down her snub nose at Patsy.

"Another box." Patsy attempted to put a light tone in her voice. The pug continued to sit in judgment. "Come on, we don't know it's from him."

Pugnacious hopped down, sat next to the box, and snorted.

"I guess we should open it." Patsy looked at Pugnacious for confirmation.

"That's what I thought." Patsy trudged to the kitchen and got the scissors. "I guess I'll do the honors." Repeating the ritual, she ripped open the tape and flipped back the flap.

Inside was the ugliest, most lopsided egg basket she had ever seen. "Look at the bottom." She held it up to her dog. "An egg would fall right through there. Why would he send me this?" She poked her fingers through reed. "It's horrible." Pugnacious blinked at her. "You don't think—"

Patsy stared at her fingers where they stuck out the bottom. "He didn't—"

Glancing down, she saw a note mixed in with the Styrofoam peanuts. After a deep breath, she flipped it open.

I need you.

Will

Patsy stared at the words. Need was tricky. It could get you into a lot of messes, thinking you needed something, almost as bad as wanting or loving.

Patsy needed to follow her dream, but she wanted to be with Will. That left one issue: love.

"What's up with you?" Lex rolled up to the computer where Patsy sat.

"Nothing, just checking code." The black lines of print blurred and swayed.

"They called you in yet?"

"For what?" Rubbing her eyes, Patsy blinked at him. Another sleepless night. She hadn't had a good slumber since spring—before Will came back.

"The Sunrise family found out you're from Daisy Creek. Probably been watching you. They're going to ask for your help with this Will."

"They're what?"

"Yep, they had the sister in a few days ago, but she made no headway with him. Since you're from the area, they're hoping you'll be able to pull some kind of local need angle—you know the smelter will benefit the whole county, he's being selfish only thinking of the few who own the land, that kind of thing."

Lex tipped back and threw a handful of candy corn in his mouth. "Word at the water cooler is, they're gonna make you an offer you can't refuse." He spoke around the candy.

Great, just what she needed, a mob reference to make a bad choice worse.

"Patsy?" Kelsey chewed on the end of a mangled ballpoint.

Grinning, Lex formed a gun with his hand. "Ba-daBING." As Patsy followed Kelsey, he shoveled another fistful of candy into his mouth.

"Have a seat." Kelsey pushed the door shut.

Picking her normal spot, Patsy balanced on the edge of the cushion.

"I have great news for you, a great offer."

"An offer I can't refuse?" Patsy asked.

"What?" Kelsey paused in unwrapping an Egg McMuffin. "Never mind."

"One of the vice presidents called down this morning." The smell of toasted bread and fried egg wafted over to Patsy, reminding her she'd skipped her cereal bar this morning.

"There's a job opening up we think you'd be perfect for." Kelsey spread grape jelly inside the sandwich. Patsy preferred blackberry, but grape was good.

"It's kind of a liaison job," Kelsey continued.

A rumble echoed from Patsy's stomach.

"You did such a good job getting the testimonials. This is along those lines. You'd work with local people answering their questions, smoothing out any bumps." A smear of jelly stained Kelsey's finger.

Patsy licked her lips. "Don't you have people that do that now?"

"Yeah," Kelsey sounded unsure. "You'd work with them, but you have more of a local tie. The V.P.s think you might connect better.

"And there'd be perks," Kelsey continued. "If you did a good job here in Missouri, you'd have a shot at traveling to our operations in Australia."

Patsy's gaze snapped from the Egg McMuffin to Kelsey's face. "Australia?"

"Yeah, we have a huge operation in Australia. It's one of the biggest producers of lead and zinc in the world. Of course, it would be more money too." Wiping the jelly off her finger, Kelsey took a giant bite of sandwich. Patsy waited for her to swallow. "Probably ten grand more to start."

Ten grand more? And Australia?

"Think about it. H.R. is working on a formal offer now. It should be ready by the end of the week." The sandwich returned to Kelsey's mouth.

Patsy stood to leave. "Oh, Patsy?" Kelsey reached into the paper bag and pulled out an apple pie. "You hungry?"

Pie in hand, Patsy wandered back to her desk. Australia. If Granny found out, there'd be more than a horse head in her bed.

Chapter Twenty-one

Will replaced the phone in its cradle. Disconnected. What did that mean? Tired of waiting for Patsy, he'd given in and called, using the number Granny gave him two weeks ago. But now this. What did it mean? Was she coming home? Or just moved to a new place? Would she have moved so soon?

Maybe Dwayne would know something. Will grabbed his laptop from the black marble top of the newly refinished washstand and shoved it into a case. The two were driving to Branson today to scope out sites for Dwayne's addition to DaisyGal.

The ding of his front door bell interrupted his task.

After hurdling a warehouse worth of boxes, he yanked open the oak door. His sister smoothed her hair back before pressing her cheek to his. He should have used the peephole.

"What are you doing here, Lisa? I told you on the phone, I'm not lowering my price. If Sunrise wants that property, they're going to have to pay fair market value."

"Spoken like a true Barnes. At least you haven't lost all your senses." Will's father folded his sunglasses and slid them into his pocket.

Will glanced at his sister. Her smug smile told him he wasn't hallucinating. "Dad, what are you doing back?"

"Not just me. Don't be rude, Will. Help your mother and . . ."

Glancing at the Mercedes parked in his drive, Will saw her before his father could finish.

". . . your fiancée."

The next morning, Patsy pressed her hand against the bumpy rock, embracing the pain as it cut into her palm. She was home, in Daisy Creek. Had she made the right decision? Taking a deep breath, she pushed open the door and walked into her grandmother's living room.

Granny sat in front of the TV. An announcer screamed as The Undertaker took center ring. With her eyes still on the screen, she asked, "So, you back, are you?"

"Yeah."

Pugnacious bounded forward into Granny's lap. Scratching the pug behind her ear, she said, "There's tea in the kitchen and fresh sheets on the bed."

Patsy rolled her suitcase toward her room. Granny's voice stopped her. "I'm glad you're back, sis, you and the hound."

Smiling, Patsy went to unpack.

An hour later, Patsy wandered into the kitchen. She'd called her parents and Ruthann just to check in. Both knew she was coming home. She'd called them after she talked to Kelsey. It hadn't taken long to shut down her life in St. Louis. She'd worked out a deal with her boss, allowing her to move back to Daisy Creek before her two weeks' notice was complete. Her lease wasn't up for a while, but she'd disconnected her phone and cable. Now here, she was unemployed, unfettered by commitments, and unsure what to do next.

There was one person she hadn't talked to yet, that she had to. The person most responsible for her coming home. Will. There was too much to say to do it over the phone. She needed to see him in person, make sure she wasn't repeating history, make sure his boxes and notes meant what she thought, what she hoped.

Rummaging around in the cupboard, she found a Hostess pie. After pouring herself a glass of tea, she sat down to enjoy the pastry and contemplate the rest of her life. She bit into the pie, letting the filling melt in her mouth. Delicious. For some reason, she hadn't had a Hostess pie since she left. A chunk of glistening apple fell onto the table. Will liked Hostess pies too—pudding ones. She never would have guessed him to be a Ninja Turtle pie fan.

The image of him sitting at this table less than a month earlier flashed through her head. Could you make a fried pudding pie? Suddenly, it was very important she find out.

The clattering of pots and pans, not to mention the smoke, cussing, and aroma of burnt pudding lured Granny into the kitchen a little before lunch.

"Sis, what kind of mess you concocting in here?"

A pudding-coated Patsy waved her arms in disgust. "Pudding pies."

"Uh huh." Granny flicked a misshapen mass with her finger. "Any reason in particular?"

"No."

"That Barnes boy, he was asking about puddin' pies, wasn't he?"

"Maybe. I don't remember."

"Uh huh." Granny pulled her apron off the hook where it hung near the refrigerator. Tying it around her waist, she said, "Nothing wrong with going after what you want. I think I told you that once before. Now throw that mess out. You know the secret is in the crust. You want to keep pudding inside, you're gonna need a nice tough crust."

Patsy adjusted the cloth covering the pies in her basket. They weren't perfect, but they were close. Granny'd been a huge help. She'd fussed when Patsy mixed up the glaze, but she'd given in.

Twisting the bell of the Barnett house, she waited for Will to answer.

The trip had been a success. Who'd have thought Dwayne would have such a good idea? Will flipped on his blinker, leaving Branson behind, and glanced at his passenger. Dwayne leaned back in the seat, his cap covering his eyes. On the trip down, Will had been too preoccupied with thoughts of his uninvited guests for much conversation. Once there, all talk had centered on DaisyGal, but he needed to know about Patsy. How could he work up to it without being obvious?

"That went well, don't you think?" he asked.

Dwayne replied, "Yeah."

"What's wrong? I'd think you'd be pleased. The shop idea was a good one and starting in Branson is perfect."

"I don't know." Dwayne stared out the window. "I guess I never thought of myself as running some little shop. Kind of girly, don't you think?"

Will laughed under his breath. "No, I don't think. Lots of men run shops. You should be proud. It was your baby, down to finding the location and figuring out how to keep the inventory stocked. People spend a lot of money getting degrees in marketing to learn how to do that."

Dwayne sat up. "You think?"

This time Will laughed out loud. "Yeah, I do think."

Dwayne removed his cap and studied the Busch emblem. "Maybe you can give Patsy a job too."

Will's head snapped to the side. "I thought she had a job."

"Not anymore. I talked to Mom last night. Hadn't talked to her in a while, been busy working on logistics and all."

Even intent on what Dwayne had learned about Patsy, Will had to smile at his use of "logistics."

"Patsy quit. Mom didn't have details, but she's coming back today. Probably already there." Dwayne bent the bill of his cap and tugged it back into place.

Patsy was in Daisy Creek? A warmth filled Will's chest. Patsy was back in Daisy Creek. He couldn't wait to see her. They'd get this all straightened out. They could work together on DaisyGal.com. They could be friends—or more. He wouldn't push her either way. It would be enough to just see her again. He pressed the accelerator, nudging the Beamer's speed from seventy to seventy-five.

Dwayne interrupted his thoughts. "You never told me what was going on at your house. That Mercedes. It belong to your folks?"

The Mercedes. Patsy was back in town, but so were his family and . . . Cindy.

Patsy gaped at the perky brunette staring at her from inside Will's house.

"May I help you?" The woman's gaze slid to Patsy's basket. "Are you selling something?" Unnaturally bright green eyes looked at her quizzically. The woman brushed an auburn lock away from her face and smoothed the skirt of her sixties-style sundress.

Staring at the psychedelic swirls, Patsy felt sick.

"Who is it, Cindy?" Will's sister popped into view. "Hello, Patsy. What are you doing here?"

Still holding the basket in front of her, Patsy stuttered out a reply. "I brought something by for Will."

"Hmm, what is it?" Lisa reached for the basket.

"Pies." Without thinking, Patsy released her grip on the handle.

"How nice. We'll be sure to give them to him." The brunette smiled as she flipped off the napkin.

"Oh, I'm sorry. Patsy, did I introduce you to Cindy?" Lisa looked from Patsy to the brunette, who still stared into the basket. "Cindy is Will's fiancée."

The porch shifted under Patsy's feet. Fiancée?

"We'll be sure to give Will your little gift." Lisa gestured to the pies, stopping when her gaze fixed on the pastries. "Oh, my. They're green."

Wishing for a quick exit, like a tornado to swoosh her away, Patsy turned on her heel and concentrated on walking in a dignified manner to her car. With no job, no place of her own, and no Will, she'd have plenty of time for falling apart later, why treat Will's family to the sight?

The Mercedes was still in his drive, meaning his family and Cindy were still camped out in his house. A morose-looking Ralph greeted Will as he snuck in the back door.

"What's wrong, boy? Dad lecturing you on the proper way to manage your life? Don't want to bury your bones all in one hole, you know."

"Your dog would probably do a better job than you have lately." Lisa leaned against the granite countertop.

Assuming she meant at life management and not bone storage, Will retorted, "Doesn't sound like your life's exactly on the fast track." He yanked open the refrigerator and pulled out a beer. At Lisa's elevated brow, he popped it open.

"Better not let Dad see you drinking beer in the middle of the afternoon."

"Like he doesn't have a three-Scotch lunch a few times a week."

"That's different. That's business. This—" She gestured to the can in his hand. "—is just tacky, and with your history . . ."

Will flicked her a look meant to singe. "I've paid for my mistakes. How about you?"

"Speaking of tacky," she continued. "You had a visitor earlier."

On his way back out the door, Will paused.

"Patsy Lee Clark. She brought you a gift."

Will ignored Lisa's snicker. "Patsy stopped by?" Had she seen Cindy? Did his father say anything to her?

"Shore 'nuff did," Lisa mimicked.

Will ignored her immature act.

"It's over there." She pointed to the kitchen island. "I thought we should throw them out. There's obviously something wrong with them, but Cindy insisted we keep them for you."

Already at the island, Will flipped back the yellow-checked cloth. Pies. And not just any pies. Green pies. Not pausing to think, he picked one up and bit into it. Sweet vanilla pudding flooded his mouth. Oh, my God. She'd made him Ninja Turtle pies.

"I guess Cindy was right." Lisa eyed the pudding oozing from his mouth with disgust.

Lost in heaven, Will almost missed her comment. "What about Cindy?"

"The pies. I thought we should throw them out, but Cindy insisted we keep them."

"Cindy met Patsy?" Please say no.

His sister sauntered over to the island and peered inside the basket. "She did. I have to say Patsy seemed a bit, shall we say, disturbed."

Will's world swerved from heaven to hell. "What did you tell her?"

Handing him a paper napkin, she replied, "This town seems to have a questionable affect on your judgment. What exactly have you been up to, big brother?"

"What did you tell her?"

"Tell her? Tell who? Cindy saw as much as I did. There wasn't anything for me to tell her."

Had Lisa always been this dense? "No, Patsy. What did you tell Patsy?"

"Oh, her." Lisa folded the dirty napkin and tossed it into the trash. "Not much. She didn't stay long. As soon as I introduced Cindy, she turned and stomped off." The eyebrow rose again. "Are you going to tell me what you've been up to?"

Pudding ran down Will's fingers. He didn't bother to wipe it off. "How did you introduce her?"

Her arms crossed over her chest, Lisa answered, "As your fiancée, of course."

What was he going to do now? Looking at the basket of pies, he knew. He was going after her. This had gone on long enough. It was time they had a talk.

He was halfway to the door when his father's voice stopped him. "I think it's time we had a talk. Don't you?"

Patsy had run away—again. She thought she was stronger now, but she wasn't. It hurt just as much the second time; more, really. She'd had a chance at everything—career, new beginning, Australia even, and she'd given it all up for Will. Only to be betrayed again. Why had he led her on? Sent her those gifts? Had she misread everything?

She had to talk to someone, but couldn't believe she was making the choice she was. Still, she needed to face old demons before she could battle the new ones. Turning the brass knob on Jessica's office door, she stepped inside.

Her nemesis sat behind a sleek glass-and-chrome desk, writing in a journal. "Patsy, I didn't know you were back." Her voice trembled as she glanced from Patsy to the door.

Patsy wasn't in the mood for niceties. "Why'd you do it? Why'd you go after Johnny?"

Jessica wet her lips, but for once there was nothing sexy in the gesture, just nerves and maybe a touch of fear.

Let her be afraid.

Patsy continued, "I know we weren't friends before that, but I never did anything to hurt you. You lived your life winning crowns and breaking hearts, and I lived mine. Why go after the one man I loved?" Patsy took a step closer.

Jessica dropped her pen. Her nail polish was chipped and her cuticles ragged. "I . . . I know."

"Then Will. You were doing it again, weren't you? Do you even care about Will, care about anything?" Patsy leaned over the desk. "Well, the joke's on you this time. He doesn't want either one of us. Turns out he's got a fiancée."

Patsy whacked the pen Jessica had dropped off the desk, sending it spinning into the wall. "Yeah, the joke's on you." She wasn't going to cry. She didn't cry the last time. She wouldn't cry now. Pushing away from the desk, she turned to leave.

"Patsy," Jessica's voice shook. "I know it doesn't mean much now, but . . ."

Patsy paused.

"I . . . I'm sorry. I was wrong. You're right. I didn't want Johnny, not really. I wanted what you had. Everyone respected you, not me. Everyone liked you."

Patsy felt herself softening.

"I just won crowns. That didn't mean much, just that I'm prettier."

Patsy rolled her eyes. So much for warm fuzzies.

"Then . . ." Jessica took a deep breath and stared at the journal open in front of her. "You won Sweetheart Princess."

"What are you talking about? I never won anything. You won every piddly prize handed out from here to Wisconsin, from Sweetheart Princess to Dairy Queen."

"Dairy Duchess." A spark of the old Jessica appeared.

"Whatever, you won them all."

Jessica tugged on her heart-shaped locket. "Not really. You won Sweetheart Princess. I . . ." She paused, then continued in a rush. "I cheated. I trashed all the ballots and made sure I won."

Well, hot damn, Patsy was royalty. She laughed. "Where's my crown?"

Jessica, eyes filled with distrust, answered, "At home, in a box. I couldn't stand to look at it so I put it under my bed, not in the showcase. Every time I vacuum I see it, but I've never opened that box. Not once in all these years."

Patsy grinned. Jessica had her own personal "Tell-tale Heart."

"You want it?" Jessica sounded eager to be rid of the thing.

"No, you keep it, put it with the others. It'd just be lonely at my house." Lonely, like Patsy. "So, that's why you went after Johnny, because of a stupid crown?"

"It wasn't stupid. The Sweetheart Princess is almost as big as Prom Queen. Everybody knows the most popular girl wins."

Now she was pouting? "But you didn't?"

Jessica shook her head, her gaze on her desk.

She was pathetic. Patsy couldn't even be mad anymore. What felt like a lifetime of hard feelings drained out of her. "It's okay. I forgive you."

"Really? For everything? I mean the crown and . . ."

Patsy nodded. "And Johnny, everything."

"How about Will? I went after him too."

Didn't the woman know when to shut up? "He doesn't count. There was nothing between us."

Jessica retrieved her pen from the floor and tapped it against her desk. "I'm not Ruthann, you know."

"What's that supposed to mean?"

"You're not fooling me. I may not be an expert in a lot of things, but I know when something is going on between a man and a woman, and you, Patsy Clark, had something going on with that man." She returned to her journal and made a note. Looking up, she said, "Something hot."

Patsy felt her cheeks flush. Was she that obvious?

"Of course, that doesn't mean I couldn't have taken him." Glancing at Patsy's face, Jessica backpedaled. "But I didn't. I told him a week ago I couldn't see him. Right after I realized I had to make a change."

"That so?" Man, this woman was arrogant.

"He took it real well. I was proud of him."

Patsy wasn't sure whether to gag or scream.

"You see, I met someone. Someone special." Jessica clasped the journal to her chest. "Finally, really loving someone and having them love you, it makes you look at everything differently."

"Glad to hear you're happy."

Jessica beamed. "Oh, I am. I've never been so happy."

Patsy escaped twenty minutes later. She preferred Jessica bitter and unloved.

Chapter Twenty-two

Will faced his father. Perfectly groomed as always, he looked as if he'd just left the golf club. His lemon-yellow pants and tangerine shirt reminded Will of expensive sorbet. Except the image wasn't cleansing, it just left a bad taste in Will's mouth.

"Yeah, Dad, I do."

After Lisa scooted out of the room, Will and his father slid into the breakfast nook. The same nook he'd shared with Patsy just before they . . .

"Are you listening to me?" His father frowned.

Would the polite thing be to say no, he was thinking about having sex with a woman his father wouldn't let sort his golf tees?

"Will." The stern expression on his father's face said he was losing patience, fast. Nothing new there.

"I appreciate that you've made what sound like some promising investments here, but I don't understand why it was necessary to sell your business and purchase this." He gestured at the room. "You have to know this house is not going to be easy to resell, and if you manage to unload it at all, you definitely won't get back the money you've poured into it."

"I don't plan to resell."

His father paused, his mouth open in surprise. "Not resell? Why on earth would you want to own a house in this hellhole of a town when you and your wife will be living in Chicago? This isn't exactly the best place for a vacation home. Have you discussed this with Cindy?"

So, his father still thought he was marrying Cindy. "As a matter of fact, I did discuss it with Cindy, right before I broke our engagement."

"You what?" His father's face took on a distinct reddish hue.

"I'm not marrying Cindy. I'm not going back to Chicago. I live here now. And, so you know, I have no intention of making money on the property I may be selling to Sunrise. It's more of a brokerage deal on my part. I'm simply negotiating the best price for the local landowners."

His father, always one to concentrate more on business than love, said, "But you bought the land. It's yours. Any profit is yours."

"Not if I give it back."

"Give it back? Have you lost your mind?"

"No, in fact, I think I've just begun to discover it." And his heart.

Will walked to an open box of Dwayne's carvings. Pulling out a figure of two coon dogs baying at the moon, he said, "I haven't completely given up on business though. This is the basis of my newest company—DaisyGal.com." He set the figurine on the table in front of his father.

"This? This is your idea of a good investment?" His father poked the wooden statue with his finger.

Digging in another box, Will ignored him.

"You cannot be serious. Selling these . . ." His dad was dangerously close to sputtering. Will'd never heard his dad sputter before—it was kind of amusing. ". . . trinkets is going to suck every bit of capital you have right down the toilet."

Will lined up a miniature basket, a bar of lavender soap, and a cornhusk doll on the island. "It's my money, Dad, and my life."

"You cannot stay in this town. How can you even think

of it after what this place did to you last time?" The sputtering was transforming into blustering.

Taking a deep breath, Will looked at his father. For the first time in years, he saw emotion in his eyes—pain touched with desperation. "This place didn't do anything to me. At least, not what you think it did."

"You were young. I realize that, but this place is no good. The people are no good." He glanced at Will's beer can. "It's starting again, isn't it? You're hanging around the same losers you did in high school. That's why we left here last time, and it still wasn't enough. Have you forgotten the time you spent in jail?"

Will sighed. "Juvie, Dad. It was juvenile hall, not quite the state penitentiary."

"Might as well have been. It was that humiliating, but it did seem to straighten you out. Good thing too. Even my connections wouldn't have got you where you are now, not if you'd kept heading the direction you were going." He thumped his fist on the table. "You know how many favors I called in to get your consulting business off the ground? And now you say you're throwing it all away? For what? To live in a town of drunks and druggies?"

Struggling to stay calm, Will took a deep breath. "Daisy Creek is not a town of drunks and druggies." Will paused. "It is a town of hard-working people I care about. I'm not leaving."

"Then I'm not helping you."

Will smiled. "Good."

His father stared at him blankly.

Will took mercy on him. "Listen, I don't need your help. I'm doing what I want. I like it here. I belong here."

"You don't."

"No, *you* don't, but I'm not you. I belong here." His father looked like he was going to argue some more, so Will kept talking. "Yes, I screwed up when I was sixteen, but it wasn't because of Daisy Creek. It was because I didn't know what was important. Didn't know how to please you and be me at the same time. Now I know that being me will have to be enough. If that doesn't please you, nothing ever will."

Will left his father to recover from meeting his son for the first time. Will had one more piece of his past to say good-bye to before he could move forward. He didn't know why Cindy had made the trip south with his family, but she deserved one last explanation.

She was outside, sitting on an old metal bench near the carriage house.

"You're going to have to get rid of that, you know." She pointed to his Beamer. "No one here drives a BMW; besides, you need something with room to haul all those boxes."

He settled onto the seat next to her. The sun glinted off her hair, reminding him why he found her attractive in the first place. "You know I'm staying?"

"I know." She reached down and plucked a daisy from the ground. "It's nice here. Not settle down and raise a family nice, but nice."

"Yeah, it is." A bluebird landed on the birdbath which sat a few feet away. It dipped its beak in the water and looked up at them, as if listening.

They sat for minute in silence.

Cindy dragged the daisy down her lap, brushing the petals against her skirt. "You going to marry her?"

He didn't answer.

"She loves you, you know. She didn't say anything, but I could tell. And the pies. They were a message, weren't they?" Cindy looked at him.

Cindy thought Patsy loved him; was she right? Not wanting to let his ex-fiancée know what he was thinking, he shrugged.

"They are. I could tell. You don't bake green pies without a reason. I saw that basket of pies, and I knew. She knows you better than I ever could. I'm not the pie-baking type." Cindy laughed. "If mine were green, it wouldn't be on purpose."

Reaching up, she tucked the daisy behind his ear. "You belong here, Will. Take care of yourself and your pie baker." With a quick kiss on his cheek, she wandered inside. The bluebird pushed off the birdbath and disappeared over the roofline.

Will retrieved the daisy from behind his ear and twirled it between two fingers. His life in Chicago was over.

Time to really settle into Daisy Creek. Time to talk to Patsy.

"I ain't lying for you." Granny tossed a dirty dish towel into the hamper. "That boy stops by here again and you're gonna have to deal with him."

Tucking a piece of reed around the oak frame, Patsy ignored her grandmother.

"You hear me, sis? I ain't lying for you. You can't hide from that boy forever." Granny yanked a clean towel out of the drawer and attacked the dishes in the drain board with such fervor, Patsy thought she might rub the glaze right off them.

Whipping around to face Patsy, she added, "Can't hide from yourself neither. Not and be happy anyhow." She snapped the towel like a lion tamer with a whip. "You listening to me? You been hiding too long. That's what sent you to St. Louis to start with. You got a problem with the boy, you need to face it. Hiding here ain't gonna solve nothing." Tossing the clean towel in the hamper with the dirty one, she stomped out of the room.

Why couldn't Granny mind her own business? Patsy was back in Daisy Creek, wasn't she? She'd given up her dream of leaving, hadn't she? Why wouldn't her grandmother back off? There was no reason to face Will, not now, not ever. He and his fiancée wouldn't be hanging around too long. Daisy Daze was tomorrow. Patsy couldn't imagine they'd stay past that. She could hide that long.

Patsy hurried to unload the baskets and leave. Somehow Granny and Tilde had conned her into helping them set up the DaisyGal booth. It was seven a.m. The only people around right now were vendors and festival coordinators, and not many of them. No way Miss Perky Fiancée would be stirring around yet, and Will was probably still snuggled in next to her. Patsy threw a handful of soaps into a basket and kicked it under the table.

A bleary-eyed Ruthann, loaded down with boxes filled with wreaths and arrangements, wandered up to the table. "Where do you want these?"

Patsy motioned to an empty space on the table. "Where's Randy and Dwayne?"

"How should I know?"

Patsy paused, a wreath of dried roses in her hands. "Trouble?"

Ruthann shook her head quickly, but Patsy could see the glimmer of tears in her eyes. "What happened?"

"Momma's got a new boyfriend."

Like that was a surprise. "So?"

"He's married."

Another shocker.

Ruthann sniffed loudly. "To . . . to Randy's momma's best friend."

Now that was a problem. "Guess she knows about it?"

"Uh huh. She quit talking to me two days ago, and Randy hasn't called either."

Patsy had been so caught up in her own issues, hiding from Will, she'd completely neglected her friend. Feeling lower than a snake's slither, she asked, "You seen her yet today?"

Ruthann nodded. "She's setting up the First Baptist

booth. They're selling hot dogs. I was supposed to help, but now . . ."

"But now you're going to haul your behind over there and steam some dogs. You've as much right to work that booth as anybody. Stand up for yourself. You aren't going to get anywhere by hiding over here with me."

"You think?"

Ignoring the nagging feeling that she'd heard that speech before, Patsy said, "I know. Go on."

Ruthann glanced toward the area reserved for food vendors, but didn't move.

"Come on. I'll go with you." Looping her arm through her friend's, Patsy led her toward the First Baptist booth.

Randy stood near a truck, unloading boxes of buns and hot dogs. His mother was directing Dwayne, who had an orange extension cord wrapped around his arm.

"You know where to plug that in?" Mrs. Jensen fussed.

"Think I can figure it out," he drawled.

"Get over there." Patsy nudged Ruthann.

"I don't know. What am I going to say to her?"

"You don't have to say anything. You aren't dating her best friend's husband."

"Yeah, but . . ."

"Is there a problem?" Will stood behind them, a cardboard box in his arms.

"No." Patsy turned her back on him and tried to slow her heart, which was suddenly beating like she'd downed a pot of espresso, then ran to Rolla and back.

"I'm glad to hear that. I thought there might have been some kind of misunderstanding. That happens, you know. People are told one thing, when something completely different is true." He repositioned himself so he was again in her line of view.

As much as she wanted to, Patsy couldn't run away. Ruthann needed her. She had no choice but to ignore him. Patsy nudged Ruthann toward the booth. "Get over there."

Ruthann didn't budge.

"I just hate misunderstandings," Will said. His gaze drilled into Patsy. She again turned her back on him.

"Yes, misunderstandings, they can be a bad, bad thing." His voice was closer. Where was he? Patsy refused to look, but it was clear he wasn't leaving.

Over her pounding heart, Patsy muttered, "That a fact?"

"Fact." The box hit the ground with a thump, and Will glided up next to them.

"How're you doing, Ruthann?" He actually sounded interested.

"Okay." Ruthann's gaze was riveted on Randy's mother, who ignored all of them.

"That didn't sound okay. Is there a problem?" Will glanced at Randy, who was also pretending not to watch them.

"Not really." Ruthann's voice cracked.

"Remember our talk?"

What talk? What had Patsy missed?

Ruthann nodded. Intrigued by their interplay, Patsy forgot to run away.

Placing a hand on her shoulder, Will murmured in Ruthann's ear. "Time to roar."

When had Will started giving Ruthann advice? Patsy opened her mouth to object, but Will stopped her. "She has to do this herself."

Patsy wanted to argue with him, but he was right. Ruthann had leaned on her long enough. This was a battle she had to win on her own.

Ruthann walked toward the booth like she was wearing iron-ore sandals. Randy's mother made a point of snubbing her, turning to face the opposite direction as Ruthann approached. Randy paused, a box of buns in his arms.

Ruthann trailed a finger along the length of the table, looking about as comfortable as six-inch heels.

Randy's momma brushed past her. "Randy, you're

done. You might as well head home. There's nothing here for you."

Randy hesitated, looking from his mother to Ruthann.

"I said to get going. You got a son to get." His mother pushed him toward the truck.

Ruthann glanced back at Patsy and Will. Seeing the moisture in her eyes, Patsy made a step toward her. Someone needed to straighten that old battleaxe out. Will's hand on her arm stopped her.

He shook his head slightly at Patsy and mouthed to Ruthann, "Roar."

Ruthann bit her lip, but turned to Randy. "How've you been, Randy? Good day for Daisy Daze, don't you think? It's warmed up nice after last week's storm."

Randy shuffled his feet. "Yeah."

"You bringing Luke up later?" she asked.

Mrs. Jensen stepped between them. "Randy, you get going. There's nothing left here for you."

"I'm here," Ruthann said.

"I said to get." Randy's mother looked a little desperate.

"I'm here, and I love him."

"What?" Mrs. Jensen turned on her. "You what?"

"I love him." Ruthann looked scared, but stood steady. "I know you don't think I'm good enough for him. I know you don't like my momma, but I love him and nothing's more important than love."

Mrs. Jensen pulled herself up to her full height and placed her hands on her hips. "Well, he don't love you. He's got a son to look after, to set an example for—that's more important."

"That true, Randy? You don't love me?" Ruthann seemed stronger.

His mother jumped in. "No, he don't. Now you just get on home before I say something unchristian I'll regret later."

Ruthann ignored her. "You gonna answer me?" she

asked Randy. He maintained his place by the truck, his
face three shades paler than normal.

"You don't love me, I'll leave, but you have to say it."
Ruthann bit her lip so hard, Patsy was afraid it might
bleed.

"He don't love you. Now get." Mrs. Jensen grabbed
Ruthann by the arm.

Randy stepped forward. "Let her go."

"What?" Confusion clouded his mother's face. "You
can't be choosing the daughter of that piece of . . ." she
gritted her teeth, ". . . over me."

"I'm not choosing anybody's daughter. I'm choosing Ruthann, and I'm not choosing her over you. I love
her and I love you. I reckon you're the one with a
choice to make." He stepped past his mother and
grabbed Ruthann's hands. "I love you, Ruthann."

As Ruthann slipped into his arms, Patsy relaxed
against the warm chest behind her. She'd never seen her
friend happier. It made Patsy happy too, and sad.
Ruthann had something Patsy never would. Remembering whose chest she leaned against, she jumped away.

"Where are you going?" Will asked.

"Home." Patsy stomped across the grass that made up
the courthouse square. Will strode after her. "You've
been avoiding me again."

Patsy tried to remember where she'd parked the Jeep.

"Are you hiding from me?"

Where was that Jeep?

"You planning to run away?"

There it was. Patsy started toward her car just as the
vehicle pulled away from the curb, her aunt Tilde at the
wheel. Tilde was stealing her Jeep. Damn her finagling
family.

"Again?" Will added.

The word stopped her, hit her hard—again? What did
he mean again? She wasn't running away from anything
or anyone, especially a lying, no-good man.

Spinning on her heel, she attacked. "Just who do you think you are, playing all coy and cute, buying me pies, sucking up to my dog, sending me packages, making . . ." she couldn't spit out the word, ". . . to me, and all along you've had a fiancée pining away, waiting for you in Chicago."

Will stood still, letting her rant.

"Do you know what I gave up for you? I could have gone to Australia, but no, I turned it all down. Came home—to what? Nothing. I came home to nothing." She swallowed hard. She would not cry.

Will grasped her by the upper arms, gave her a little shake. "I wasn't playing, and I don't have a fiancée."

There had to be another escape. Patsy turned to head back to where Dwayne still stood near the truck.

Will grabbed her again. "Listen to me."

Patsy stared at him through tears she wouldn't let fall.

"Cindy and I used to be engaged, but that was over before I came back to Daisy Creek. Before I bought you pies," he smiled, "sucked up to your dog, sent you packages, or," he paused, softening his grip on her arms, "made love to you." His touch changed to a caress. "I love you, Patsy Lee Clark, and I'm not going away—no matter what you say or do."

She blinked, a tear rolled down her cheek. He loved her?

"I wanted to tell you before you went to St. Louis, but when I saw you with the Celt, I thought . . ."

The Celt? "You mean Glenn?" she asked.

He made a dismissive motion with his hands.

He was jealous of Glenn? A tiny speck of joy began to break through. "Glenn's just a friend. I don't care about him. I don't love him like I . . ." She stopped. Could she say it? Would she regret it if she did?

"Like you what?" Will gripped her arms again, giving her another little shake.

Glancing over to where Randy stood with his arm

around Ruthann, his mother looking pale, but resolved, Patsy swallowed. You didn't get anything worth having without taking a risk. Tilting her face to Will's, she said, "Like I love you."

Will's breath left his body in a pent-up whoosh. Tightening his hands on her arms, he jerked her against his chest. With his lips pressed to hers, he plunged his tongue into her mouth. As she grappled to get her hands behind his neck to pull him closer, the brief realization that they were giving a good portion of the town quite a show darted through her head.

Her brother's uncouth whoop confirmed it.

Holding tight to Will's neck, she hopped up and locked her legs around his waist. If she was going to give Daisy Creek something to talk about . . . might as well be something good.